PHOENIX

THE PHOENIX SERIES BOOK 1

KIMBERLY PACKARD

Staci,
Welcome to Phoenix!
I hope you enjoy
Amanda's journey.
Best,
Kim

abalos
publishing

Abalos Publishing
P.O. Box 333
Colleyville, TX 76034

Book cover designed by okay creations.
The text in this book is set in Baskerville.
Library of Congress Cataloging-in-Publication Data
Available Upon Request

ISBN-13 Print: 978-0-9992015-0-3
ISBN-13 Ebook: 978-0-9992015-1-0

 Created with Vellum

ALSO BY KIMBERLY PACKARD

Pardon Falls | Phoenix Book 2

Prospera Pass | Phoenix Book 3

The Crazy Yates | A Christmas Novella

For Zelma Dodson and Sutton Helvey-Chandler
Two women whose belief in me never wavered,
even from above.

1

Amanda Martin didn't believe in casual Fridays.

Sloppy dress, sloppy work, she thought as matching golf-shirt-clad tellers ignored the growing line.

Amanda paused at the door as she weighed her options. How long would it take her to deposit eighty hundred dollar bills into the ATM? Why didn't Josh have HR cut her a check? Should she just wait it out for a teller? Why did Josh clean out his office? What is in El Paso? Or, who? And, what's her bra size? The thumping headache from polishing off a bottle of wine alone jumbled her usually decisive thoughts.

"Dammit, Josh," she murmured.

The line curved back on itself twice and each of the three tellers had four customers before it would be her turn at the window. The envelope of money poked at her collarbone from its haven in the interior pocket of her coat. No matter how she tried to maneuver it to a more comfortable position, the corner of the envelope continued to jab her.

She sighed, *it's probably a sign*. Quarterly bonuses were standard for her at the mid-sized investment firm where she worked. But, this was different. It felt like a payoff.

After days of being avoided by Josh in every sense of the word—text messages unanswered, emails neglected, voicemails unreturned and his assistant running interference for him—Amanda strode into his office the previous evening ready to end their relationship. As CFO, Josh kept their office relationship professional, but Amanda found it difficult keeping his behavior at the office from bleeding into the bedroom.

"Who is she?" Amanda didn't bother knocking; she wanted the element of surprise to catch him with his pants down, literally or figuratively. Instead of finding Josh, either with or without a junior trader, Amanda found his office devoid of the stacks of files that reminded her of a childhood fort. She often teased that he used the piling system, with his desk stacked with an endless amount of paper. It looked naked now. The top of the heavy wood desk sat empty except for a single manila folder that looked out of place without its brethren, like a lost sheep left for the wolves.

Amanda was just able to read that the top sheet was a boarding pass for a flight to El Paso before she heard Josh's voice outside his door. She snapped the folder shut and marched to the door just as he hurried into his office. No matter how mad she felt, the first sight of his wavy blond hair and light green eyes made her feet go cold.

"Eh, Amanda, what are you doing here? How long have you been waiting?" He pushed past her to his desk and put the folder in his briefcase.

"I just got here. So, what's in—" Her question about El Paso was smothered by a sudden kiss.

"I owe you an apology," he said. Amanda glanced behind her shoulder to check his open door for snooping colleagues, but he gently turned her face back to him. "Don't you think everyone here already knows about us? Anyway, I've been distracted with a problem client and haven't been attentive. Why don't you pick up some wine and take-out? I'll be over in a couple of hours."

Amanda nodded. *I'm just being paranoid. He wasn't avoiding me, he was just dealing with work.*

"One more thing," Josh said, going back to his briefcase. "I almost forgot to give you this. Go buy some shoes and lose the receipts." He handed her a bulky envelope. She knew without looking that it was filled with cash, lots of it.

"What?" She couldn't get her question out before his phone rang.

"I'll explain later. Oh Amanda, please close the door behind you. Thanks, babe."

After midnight and a bottle of wine, Amanda went to bed with no word from Josh despite the numerous calls to his cell and office. She woke up hung-over and ready to give him her iciest treatment.

Amanda stepped towards the ATM, the line for the tellers having grown in her moment of indecision. Her BlackBerry buzzed as she reached into her purse for her debit card. With her throat cleared, she put on her best professional voice.

"Amanda Martin," she answered.

"Hello, love, Roland Burrows here with *Financial News*."

The smooth British accent of her favorite reporter put her at ease. Her shoulders drooped as she dropped her act. The envelope jabbed into her collarbone.

"How are you darling?" Her animated voice echoed in the cavernous bank lobby. "We need to meet up for martinis soon."

"Listen, Amanda," he started, but she was distracted. She loved the way he pronounced her name ending in an 'er' rather than an 'a' and launched into a catnap of a daydream imagining herself with a British boyfriend after Josh. Her trance soon ended, catching only his last sentence. "So that's why I was calling, to see if you had any comment."

Her heart thumped against the envelope when she realized this was a serious business call and not their usual banter.

"I'm sorry Roland, can you say that again? I'm getting horrible reception in here."

"Right. I just got a tip from someone inside the SEC that they're pursuing indictments against several executives at Jefferson Williams Investments: chief legal counsel Keith Cooper, CFO Josh Williams and you, Amanda." He paused. "I'm breaking this story in a few minutes and wanted to see if I could get a comment."

Amanda tried to breathe, but her throat closed as tight as her French twisted hair. "Roland, I'm going to have to call you back."

Amanda didn't wait for a response. She ended the call and dashed out the front door.

The late March freeze accosted her with a burst of cold air as she pushed through the door. BlackBerry still in hand she dialed Josh's number while navigating the busy sidewalk. The line didn't ring—it went straight to voicemail. She tried it again. Same result. Third time was no different. Amanda didn't leave a message. *I'm not giving him any opportunity to come up with excuses. I want to hear his reaction.* She dialed her office number.

"Diane, it's Amanda. Transfer me to Josh," Amanda said, cutting off the receptionist during her greeting.

As soon as the receptionist transferred the call, Josh's voicemail picked up. Amanda looked at her watch. It was past nine in the morning; Josh was always in early to get a start on the day.

"Dammit," Amanda screamed at her phone, punching the end button with such force it lodged in the down position for a few seconds before popping back into place.

She moved out of the flowing traffic of pedestrians and leaned against the side of an office building. The smooth granite chilled her through her cashmere coat, the cold reassuring and frightening.

"Think, think," she whispered. "Ten … nine … eight …" she counted backwards, a trick her anesthesiologist father taught her as a child when thunderstorms scared her in the middle of the night. The raw power from above and the inability to control her surroundings terrified her as a young girl, and even now as an adult, a particularly booming shock of thunder caused a pulse of fear down her spine.

When Amanda got to one, she still faced a catastrophic news story and indictment, but she could breathe. Her BlackBerry buzzed with her office number flashing on the display.

"Josh?"

"No, it's Liz. What is going on? Roland Burrows just called me, something about indictments. Where are you?"

Liz was going to be her next call, but it would also be her toughest. Friends since college, Amanda recommended Liz for a job in the legal department. "I'm on my way in. Can we talk? I'm going to need some help."

"*You're* going to need some help? What the hell is going on Mandy?" Amanda winced at her nickname. "I'm sorry. You're on your own with this one. I have to comply with investigators. I can't risk going to jail, especially now that I have Jackson to think about." Amanda couldn't fault Liz; the woman threw herself into motherhood the same way Amanda did her career. "I'll give you the names of good attorneys. I can do that for you, but nothing more. I can't risk getting dragged into this," Liz added, softening her voice as if sensing her friend's defeat through the phone. Amanda heard someone speak rapidly to Liz in the background. "Crap. The story posted."

"Dammit," Amanda said, letting her body fall back against the side of the building once again. She wished the building wasn't there, that instead it was just a gaping abyss that allowed her to fall into nothingness. "What is it I'm being accused of?"

"You manipulated the market through media announcements with false information. A lighter offense than Keith and Josh, but nonetheless, you're in trouble." Amanda heard the phone shuffle in Liz's hand. Her voice was a whisper when she spoke again. "I shouldn't ask you this, but I need to know. Did you know what you were doing?"

If bad judgment was a crime, I would be guilty as charged. Amanda knew better than to get involved with her boss, but they were a classic power couple; attractive, blond, wealthy and successful. Three years earlier, when her former boss abruptly quit and Josh asked her to dinner to offer the vice president job, she thought her life was on the fast-track she longed for. There she was, at the tender age of twenty-four, given the responsibility heading communications for the company. Initially, she thought Josh's dinner request was simply a professional courtesy, but after his second invitation she realized it was much more.

Only recently did Amanda suspect something was amiss with the investment firm's business practices. She remembered innocently asking, "How is it the firm and our clients continue to turn a profit when our competitors are losing money?" She shuddered at the memory of his enraged reaction, "You should never question me, as my girlfriend or my employee. You got that?" he yelled. By the end of his outburst, she feared he would fire her or break up with her, or both.

"I trusted Josh."

For the remaining ten minutes of her walk, Amanda tried to reach Josh on his cell phone, but each call went straight to voicemail. She left no message, but composed one in her head. *What the hell did you drag me into? Is it true? Why did you do it? Where the hell are you? When I find you, I am going to kill you.*

Rather than board the elevator to her office, she sank into one of the fashionably uncomfortable, contemporary armchairs in the building's spacious lobby and stared out the soaring glass wall. The weather outside was clear and bright, completely wrong for the way she felt.

Her ringing cell phone alternated between displaying her office number and various media outlets. After sending the twelfth call to voicemail, she shut her phone off. *What did I do?* Amanda went over her press releases and statements in her head. All the information came from Josh. Keith had the final approval before she sent out anything over the wire. The long hours she put in to get everything right, the dinners with friends and family she canceled to answer to the media's beck and call, and the lies she inadvertently told—they only lined the pockets of Josh and Keith. *And, mine. That's the reason for the bonuses, to keep me happy.* No amount of blinking could stop the fresh tears from springing.

Unable to sit there any longer, she boarded the elevator for her solitary ride to the forty-second floor. When the door opened, she saw a flurry of activity, but Amanda couldn't become part of that. Her colleagues were accustomed to the unflappable Amanda Martin, the one who could handle the toughest question from the harshest reporter. Not the woman standing outside the office with mascara running down her face.

Inside the ladies room, Amanda stared at her reflection. Her normally porcelain skin was gray, her hazel eyes were bloodshot and her carefully applied makeup was gone. Before Roland's call, she was an average ambitious businesswoman who was dating, or maybe just sleeping with, her CFO. She felt untouchable as one of the highest-ranked executives at the firm. Now, she just saw a haggard-looking criminal. Her eyes fell to the brown roots fading into her straight blond hair flawlessly twisted back. No need to keep her hair appointment for that afternoon. Chances were there would be no salon services in the federal penitentiary.

Leaning against the bathroom wall, she heard the elevators on the other side whooshing past her. The mechanical whir of the motors and the hum of the cables put her in a trance only interrupted when a ding sounded on her floor. "Josh. Finally," she whispered as she hurried to catch him.

Amanda stepped through the heavy glass door of her office lobby just as she heard a man ask for her. Instead of Josh, she saw the back of an older gentleman, clad in khaki pants and a windbreaker standing in front of the receptionist. With a backpack slung over one shoulder and a baseball cap covering his white hair, he looked as though he should be heading to college instead of a retirement home. The woman motioned to Amanda's office as she tried to answer the constantly ringing phones.

He thanked the receptionist, pulled a pistol from inside his backpack and shot her in the head. The phones continued ringing as though nothing happened. Some of the traders in the cubicle area stood up at the sound of the gunshot, and he emptied his magazine on them as though they were ducks in a video game.

Amanda's office door swung open and Liz froze in the threshold. "Amanda Martin?" the man asked, casually reloading his gun.

Amanda could see the fear in Liz's eyes ten feet away. Liz shook her head, "I have a son." Her voice was soft and weak.

The man was unflinching. "I have a wife who is very sick. My retirement fund was going to make her better, until some greedy bastards stole it all. She's going to die and so are you."

"I'm Amanda Martin," Amanda shouted at the man's back, but her voice vanished in the thunder of his gunshot. She watched Liz crumple to the floor. Amanda felt her own body go numb as she released the death grip on her purse and phone. She covered her mouth to stifle her scream.

The man reached into his backpack and pulled out a grenade.

"A few weeks ago, I called Williams about cashing out my retirement fund to pay for my wife's cancer treatment. He gave me the runaround: forms, taxes, bullshit. I knew something was fishy, and I was on my way down here to have a little chat with Mr. Williams when, guess what, my wife called to tell me he's been indicted for stealing people's money," his commanding voice presided over the screams. "I'm not here to hurt everyone. I want Josh Williams and Keith Cooper. If you can point me in their direction, I'll finish what I came to do and leave." While he said this, he tossed the grenade up and down in his hand, toying with it like a tennis ball.

Liz's outstretched hand beckoned Amanda, but she would be shot if she moved in plain sight. She edged over to the receptionist desk and sought cover under the heavy brown wood.

The man quizzed her colleagues as to the whereabouts of her co-conspirators, but she couldn't register what he said. With each blast from his gun, her ears rang louder, muffling his voice. She didn't see him pace the office; instead she focused solely on the body of her friend.

Please be alive, please be alive ... Amanda mouthed silently.

"It's clear you are all in this together and therefore, all guilty. You have until the count of five to tell me where they are, or we're all going up together. I've got a bag full of grenades, and I'm not afraid to use them all. Got that?" the man bellowed over the startled silence of the office.

Amanda got up on her haunches to make her way to Liz, but a rush of blood to her head made her dizzy. No matter how much Amanda commanded her body to take deeper, slower breaths, it wouldn't comply. She steadied herself.

"Ten...nine...eight...," her quivering lips barely moved.

The man began his count much louder. "One," he boomed, the pin of the grenade clicked out of place. "Two... three..."

They reached "five" at the same time. When the grenade went

off, it knocked her backwards against the swinging glass door. A second blast forced her against the door again and this time pushed her all the way through. When she opened her eyes, fire blazed through what used to be her office, and a heavy breeze blew through the blown-out windows of the forty-second floor. Papers floated like soft snowflakes. The piercing screech of the fire alarm joined the ringing in her ears. Her hand automatically felt her body, acting purely on instinct to make sure she was still in one piece. When her right hand moved over the breast of her coat, the envelope inside gave a little jab signaling it was okay. Amanda decided to move.

2

Alex Kostas didn't particularly care if his whistling was off-key or that his ear-piercing tune annoyed the people on the packed elevator. This was going to be the best day of his life and he couldn't be happier. He fought the urge to announce that he detected fraud and launched the investigation against one of the strongest investment firms in Chicago. Of course, no one knew anything about it yet, but his fellow passengers would soon as the SEC delivered the indictments.

I should ask for an office with my promotion, he thought, assuming his reward would be in the form of a much-anticipated career boost.

It took only a few strides of his long legs before he settled into his cube. It was moments like this he wished he were just a little shorter so it would take more time to cover ground. So people could notice him.

"It's going to be a good day, Dennis," Alex said to his cube-mate as his computer chimed to signal its awakening. Alex didn't wait for a response, or even expect one for that matter. The antiquated system slogged to life, and Alex salivated at the thought of a laptop with a fancy docking station in his new office. His phone rang just as the screen prompted for his password.

"Kostas, we've got a problem," his boss Harrison skipped morning pleasantries. "I need you down in the north conference room pronto."

Alex glanced over his shoulder at Dennis, who seemed oblivious to the conversation, with his nose just inches away from his computer screen. Alex grabbed his portfolio and used his long stride to make it to the conference room in record time

The door was cracked open. Harrison paced the length of the conference room table with several members of the SEC's legal team scattered throughout, their open laptops stationed like tombstones. Harrison's gray hair stood straight up, a tell-tale sign he employed as one of his many nervous tics.

"Alex, close the door behind you. Have a seat," Harrison ordered.

"Is everything all right?" He had to say something; the air in the conference room buzzed with tension.

"It has come to our attention that Williams and Cooper began cashing out their stock options four days ago," the man paused and locked his laser-focused eyes on Alex's face. "Please tell me this isn't the first you're hearing of this."

Alex's Adam's apple bobbed. It was the first he had heard of that. When he turned everything over to the attorneys, his job was done; there was no reason for him to continue monitoring the three suspects' financial statements.

"Alex?" Harrison continued to pace, a new habit that took the place of a severe nicotine addiction a few years back. The lawyers all kept their heads focused on their laptops, not appearing to notice Alex's presence in the room nor the pendulum-like motion of Harrison's body.

The only response he was capable of at that moment was clearing his throat, but it said everything he didn't want to.

"That's what I thought," Harrison said. "Did you think your job was over? Your job is not over until I say it's over. And, if you weren't my best damn analyst, I'd say it's over."

Alex's stomach dropped. The same feeling that exhilarated him as a child on his favorite roller coaster only nauseated him now. *This was not supposed to happen. The indictments should be in motion, and Harrison and I should be talking about my promotion, mapping out my future. Those attorneys dragged their feet on the indictments, I can't help that.* Sitting in the conference room with his boss's face turning red and an army of attorneys looking at him was not on his agenda for the day.

"Mr. Harrison, there has been another development," said one of the attorneys. She turned her laptop towards Harrison, his lips moved as he read the words on her screen.

"What's going on?" Alex couldn't control his bouncing legs. He directed the question to Harrison, but a member of the legal team answered him.

"Do you know Roland Burrows of the *Financial News?*"

Alex shook his head. "Not personally, but I've read some of his articles. Why?" He asked this question of the attorney that answered him, but another spoke next, forcing him to swivel his head the other direction.

"He just released a story about our indictments, citing an anonymous source. Martin is tipped off now. He called her for comment."

"Get someone to pick her up ASAP," Harrison said. Another attorney sprang to life and punched numbers into her cell phone. Alex wondered if these attorneys shared some sort of collective consciousness.

"I got confirmation that both Cooper and Williams are not at their homes or in their offices. They may have fled, sir," another spoke.

"Fled? Fled?! What the hell is going on here people?" The Harrison pendulum halted with his back to Alex. The air in the room froze when he stopped moving. *Please forget I'm here. Please forget I'm here. Please forget I'm here.* "You," he said, revealing a red face as he turned to Alex. "If you had been doing your job instead of jacking around, we could have sped things up, and everyone would be in custody now. You don't stop monitoring the suspects until they are locked away in jail. You got that?" Alex swallowed again. "Now, go see if Martin has cashed out any of her stock options, and see if Cooper and Williams are using their credit cards."

Alex raced to his desk, hoping that no one would notice him on his way back to his three-walled haven. *Harrison was right*, he rubbed his hands over his eyes. "I stopped paying attention, I screwed this up," he muttered to his shoes. Instead of noticing that two of the suspects moved money, he set up news alerts for when the story would hit the press, daydreamed of his promotion and perused websites for motivational wall art. He regretted his order of the "Achievement" poster.

Alex slid into his desk chair, the squeak louder than ever. Dennis asked him repeatedly to sit down gently, the sound broke his concentration, but Alex didn't care today. He tapped into Keith Cooper's credit card account. The man hid his criminal activities well; he carried a mortgage on his modest townhome, drove an ordinary sedan and carried very little credit card debt. It was only when Alex stumbled upon Cooper's secret bank account that he'd had any clue the firm's attorney was part of the fraud. Just as Alex suspected, there was no recent activity on any of the man's accounts.

Josh Williams wasn't so careful. The firm founder's son was the polar opposite of his cohort in crime. An unabashed playboy, Williams spent money lavishly on his swanky condo, drove an enviable sports car and rang up a four-digit credit card bill on most weekends. Despite his history of reckless spending, Alex guessed it took every bit of self-restraint for Josh to cease using his credit cards more than a week earlier, according to the statement he read. His notepad flew across his desk. "Damn, another dead end," he whispered.

He pulled up Amanda's account on his screen. "Gotcha," he said to his computer when he saw she got a pedicure and a bottle of wine the evening before, and her employee stock options sat untouched. "Ahh ... just what I needed to fix the case," he whispered. *And, save my career.* He banged his kneecap into the keyboard tray as he sprang from his desk. The excitement he felt muted the radiating pain.

The army of attorneys was still stationed in the conference room when Alex returned, but their stony faces displayed worry instead of calm indifference. Harrison leaned over a telephone; the green light indicated the line was live. Before Alex announced that he'd saved the case, a voice floated out of the speaker.

"Sir, the reports are unconfirmed, but it appears there is a gunman on the forty-second floor, possibly in the same office as your suspect, Amanda Martin."

"A gunman?" Alex couldn't help himself, he was completely unprepared, but no one seemed to notice he spoke.

"What do you mean there's a gunman there?" Harrison's face turned red again, and he paced the length of the room. "Who the hell is it?"

"9-1-1 started receiving calls just as we pulled up to the building. There are several reports of shots coming from an office on the forty-second floor. What's that?"

The officer's voice was muffled amidst what sounded like an alarm system shrieking in the background. Harrison stopped pacing and stared down at the telephone. Everyone collectively leaned forward, closer to the speaker, trying to hear what was being said behind the screams of people and the alarm.

"Sir, it appears there was an explosion on the forty-second floor. I repeat there was an explosion on the forty-second floor."

The officer paused, and Alex heard more shouting.

"Sir, I'm going to have to call in for back up, this situation turned critical."

The line died. Everyone in the conference room stared at the phone. No one moved except Harrison. He paced up and down the length of the room. On the fourth pass, the man stopped to pour himself another cup of coffee.

"Alex, if you're standing there, you better have some news for me," Harrison said to his coffee. "Otherwise, I want *your* butt in *your* seat cleaning up *your* mess."

Alex's voice was slow coming. "Well, sir, I have good news," he paused to ensure everyone focused their full attention on him. "Martin seemed unaware of what was coming. Her employee stock is untouched, and she used her credit card last night," his voice gained strength with each word.

"That tells me nothing. You said yourself her charge is a lesser crime, that by all accounts Williams and Cooper are the master-minds. Anyway, it's likely she's dead now, so move on from her and find Williams and Cooper." Harrison turned his back on Alex and addressed the attorneys. "Okay people, we've clearly got a situation unlike anything we've seen before. Go back to your desks. Monitor Williams' and Cooper's credit cards for movement. I'll let you know if there's news from the police. Let's go ahead and plan on working a full weekend to watch for these two."

Several seconds passed before everyone moved towards the door. Harrison turned his back on the room and looked out the office window. Alex stared at his boss's reflection in the glass. He didn't know where to direct his frustration, with himself for missing a crucial turn in his case, the unknown gunman in an office building on the other side of downtown or Harrison for giving up so easily. Alex waited until they were alone to speak.

"Sir, are you sure that is the best? What if this is a distraction to get Martin out of the building? Or, what if she can lead us to Williams?"

"This is a police matter now. Not something for us accountants."

Alex's neck flushed in anger. His admiration for Harrison was more than what an employee would feel for his supervisor. Harrison had been a father figure for Alex, filling in a hole that his own father left when he was killed fifteen years earlier. He worked hard to avoid letting Harrison down, but the heart-wrenching feeling of defeat coursed through his veins. Harrison never turned around, never looked Alex in the eye.

"Mr. Harrison, let me go down there. Shouldn't we have someone on the scene to make sure Martin doesn't get away?"

"The police will take care of it."

"But they don't know the case. They don't know Martin. What if she slips away?"

"Go back to your desk, Alex. I'll let you know if there's more."

"Sir, please." Always the dutiful employee, he did as he was told without question. Asking something of his supervisor was long over-due. "I can do this."

"She's dead, Alex. Go back to your desk." The man slammed

down the coffee pot, the sound of the glass carafe cracking shattered the air.

Rather than return to his desk, Alex hurried into the men's room and checked the stalls to make sure he was alone.

"Dammit, dammit, dammit." The final punch to the metal door broke open the skin on his knuckle. He looked up at the tile ceiling and took several deep breaths. His hand tingled with pain, and he washed the blood off at the sink to examine the damage. Luckily, it appeared to be a pretty shallow cut, and he wrapped his hand in paper towels while waiting for the bleeding to stop.

"Son-of-a-bitch," he said to his knuckle. "Forget the promotion. I'm going to sleep on a flat futon and eat takeout for the rest of my life."

When he got back to his desk, the office was quiet without the whir of the computers and tapping of keyboards in the analyst area. Harrison was nowhere in sight; his boss must have broken his vow of nicotine chastity. Unable to do any work, he logged on to a local news website to see if they had any reports of the shooting at Jefferson Williams Investments. All he was able to find was a brief breaking news story.

A gunman is believed to be on the premise of a downtown Chicago office building, according to 911 calls. Emergency personnel are on the scene and the building is being evacuated. No word yet on the motive behind the attack, but it could be linked to a report posted by a financial news magazine regarding indictments of three members of an investment firm in the building. Reporters are heading to the scene.

Alex felt the urge to ignore his boss's orders, to walk out of the office to apprehend Amanda, or at least to confirm she was dead as Harrison suspected. He imagined himself storming up to Harrison as the man dangled a cigarette from his lips, shouting that he worked out, he was in good shape. He could fight against the current of people evacuating the building to swim upstream to the forty-second floor. If Harrison couldn't appreciate him, maybe the FBI would be so impressed by his bravery and physical prowess they would hire him on the spot. *The boys at the Bureau would feel like asses when they realized that I was the fat kid who failed my physical years earlier, only to emerge a decade later as a super-agent.*

But none of that happened. Alex spent the remainder of his day glued to his desk searching for any financial signs of life from the three suspects while the news alerts of his failure taunted him.

3

The red glow of the exit sign lured Amanda with promise of escape. She hesitated, staring back at the open glass waiting to see if anyone emerged. The only movement was the current of fiery papers pushed out by the wind gusts from the missing windows. The stillness in the midst of the bedlam felt unnatural to Amanda. It would have felt more appropriate for people to dash out of the office, for screams to form an off-pitch melody with the screech of the siren. Chaos seemed to skip a beat. Amanda trained her eye inside the smoky office towards where Liz fell, but only a spreading fire stared back at her. With a final glance behind her, she pushed through the exit door.

The dark stairwell bustled with a stream of people scampering to safety. No one seemed to notice her as she stood with her back to the door. Women clutching their purses flowed by her. Some took the time to slip on their tennis shoes before the descent, while others made their way down in heels. Men were on their cell phones, carrying on conversations over the incessant ringing of the fire alarms.

Amanda found an opening and slid into the school of people.

She looked over the spiral staircase, a small pinprick of light shined below them. With each landing, the ringing fire alarm grew louder, and her ears reverberated from the sound.

At the landing for the thirtieth floor, the surge of people behind her pushed, and the floor below them shook. Amanda heard someone scream over the ringing that there were more explosions. She grasped the handrail with white knuckles as the stairwell shook under her feet.

The flow slowed as people from the lower floors filed into the stairwell. When she finally emerged, Amanda squinted at the bright sun. It took her a few minutes to get her bearings between the intensity of the noonday sun and the disorientation of a forty-two-floor spiral descent.

The door dumped her at a loading dock in the back of her office building. She moved as far away from the exit as she could and positioned herself in the shadow of the tall building. Firemen and police officers swirled around her as they tried to help the ever-flowing stream of people exiting the building, but it seemed to Amanda there were more victims than first responders. People shouted and pointed up at the gaping hole in the side of the building, but Amanda didn't look. She knew what it looked like from the inside.

Amanda's head swam in dizziness, and she inhaled deeply, hoping to convince her body to breathe again. Her eyes remained focused on the exit door, hoping to see someone from her office. She feared she would see the assailant instead. *God, what would I do if he came out that door? Point him out to the police, or tell him to take his best shot? Or, break down crying and beg for forgiveness.*

More ambulances arrived to tend to the wounded outside. She took a few more steps back to lean against the bank of dumpsters. Smells of rot mingled with the fresh odor of sulfur stuck in the back of her throat. She wretched behind one of the dumpsters. Her stomach was empty, but it didn't stop her body's reaction. The heaving stopped, but her head began spinning again. Amanda leaned against the side of the dumpster, using a small ridge as a seat. Doubled over with her head in her hands, she began her first countdown from ten. *One*. Still nauseous. She started again. *One*. A pain throbbed through her temple in rhythm with her heart. She started again. This time, she reached seven and blacked out.

A warm light flooded her field of vision. *Heaven after all this?* Distant words asked if she could hear. She blinked and saw the face of a man behind the penlight.

"Can you hear me? What's your name?" he asked.

Amanda wanted to answer him, but the gag reflex in her throat muted her words. The man called for help. Four hands lifted Amanda to her feet and walked her over to the back of a waiting ambulance. Perched on the bumper of the vehicle, Amanda watched him pull on latex gloves and dab a cut along her temple.

"Good news, I don't think it's going to leave a scar," he said, smiling at her. "And, I don't feel any bumps so no broken crown for you."

Just a shattered tiara.

He finished his examination and pulled off his gloves. "An emergency checkpoint is setting up over in that building's lobby. You may want to get crackers and ginger ale. It'll settle your stomach." He gestured his head towards one of her building's neighbors in the business district.

She wrapped the coat tighter around her and felt the now familiar prick at her collarbone. The envelope was the root of her trouble. She fingered the tip through her coat and toyed with the idea of leaving it for the paramedic to thank him for his help.

The office building across the street beckoned. She watched for a moment as mobilized volunteers brought box after box of drinks, packaged food and clothing into the lobby. Another scan of the crowd yielded none of her office mates. She pushed off the bumper and followed the magnetic pull across the street.

The volunteers worked like an efficient colony of ants. There were no words spoken, yet everyone seemed to know exactly what to do. Two volunteers silently stacked packaged pastries on a fold-out table to the right of where she stood, and just past that table another two volunteers quietly provided coffee and bottled water.

The need to wash her hands and face won out over the paramedic's advice to eat. She passed the tables of food towards a sign acknowledging restrooms around the corner. Her pump's broken heel caused her calf to ache as she walked on her toes to prevent awkward hobbling.

Hidden away in the far corner of the lobby, she spotted several boxes of clothes. The volunteers must have set these aside for those in extreme disarray. Amanda looked down at herself and saw her black pantsuit covered in lint. She smelled the overpowering smoke odor, and the broken heel of her pump hung on like a stubborn loose tooth. She fell into the "disarrayed" category.

From a box marked "women's jeans," Amanda found a pair of well broken-in jeans one size too big. The best she could find in the "women's shirts" box was a thin t-shirt from someone's summer softball league, cheering on Mervyn's Marlins. A smaller box labeled "women's shoes" had few options. Amanda pulled out a pair of laceless sneakers two sizes too big.

In the lobby bathroom, Amanda studied her reflection. The paramedic covered the cut with two small bandages, but there was some dried blood on her temple. Her formerly perfect hair clumped together in a stringy mess, the strands around her face held together by blood.

Someone had left a brush in the bathroom.

"I hope you don't have lice," Amanda said to the brush.

Her scalp stung as she brushed her hair, but it only made her pull through the knots in more forceful tugs. When her hair finally de-matted, it flared out full of static electricity and the smell of smoke. Amanda ducked as much of her head under the faucet as possible to wash out the smell, the blood and the static. She towel-dried the water out of her hair with the coarse paper towels and began disrobing in the middle of the bathroom.

Her body ached as she tried to pull off her coat for the first time since she left for work that morning. The envelope scratched at the base of her neck, as if clinging to her. She kicked off her ruined designer heels and tossed them in the trash, not blinking an eye at the shoes she once coveted. Her button-up shirt and black pants fell away effortlessly and followed the pumps into the trash. She studied herself for a moment, not only looking for physical bruises and cuts, but to see if the emotional ones were visible as well. She turned to examine her back. The ghost of a gray bruise took shape on her left shoulder blade. The diamond earrings that Josh bought for her birthday joined the rest of her clothes in the trash. The Tiffany bracelet she bought herself to celebrate her promotion followed, as did the ruby birthstone ring. She stopped at her watch.

The silver-banded Rolex was a gift from her father on the night of her college graduation. She remembered his words perfectly. "Your time here is limited; don't waste it living someone else's life." Standing half-naked in the lobby bathroom, she could smell the freshly cut grass and bug repellent and feel the wood planks of the dock at her parents' lake house beneath her bare feet. Amanda couldn't part with her watch. *I didn't take his advice*, she thought, shuddering both from the chill of the air in the bathroom and the realization that she disappointed her father, *but I still have time.*

She dressed quickly and carefully, soreness setting in now that the adrenalin wore off. Before she threw her coat in the trash, Amanda pulled the envelope from the interior pocket and held it in her hands. Part of her wanted to throw it away with the coat, but there was a reason Josh gave it to her. *To find him.* Without another place to hide it, Amanda lifted up the t-shirt and placed the envelope in the waistband of her jeans. Amanda took a step towards the bathroom door and nearly stepped out of the laceless tennis shoes.

Moving with a shuffle, Amanda slowly entered the lobby's tucked away little corner. A cacophony of voices filled the space, some low and murmuring, others wailing in high tones. She peeked around the corner and saw several police officers trying to calm a large crowd of people. She recognized Liz's husband Ben in the crowd. He held their infant son Jackson, demanding to know where his wife was. The baby turned his head and locked eyes with Amanda peering around the corner. Liz's eyes. *Young eyes that will never look into his mother's eyes again because of me. How can I explain that*

I'm responsible for Liz's death? And Jackson, he will never know his mother because of me.

Her chest pumped in and out faster and faster as the walls closed in. Her legs grew restless and she paced. At the end of the corridor, just past the row of boxes, she saw a small door marked "garage exit." Without a second thought, she made her escape.

4

The garage spit her out on a street parallel to her office building. Grayness settled over downtown Chicago as the sun set behind the skyscrapers. The sidewalks were surprisingly empty for a Friday afternoon. She guessed people left work early and were home glued to the TV news.

Amanda walked with no particular destination in mind. She ambled up one street, turned a corner and walked back down the next. This zigzag pattern continued for several hours as darkness settled over the city. At first, the chill penetrating her thin t-shirt was welcome relief, but she began to shiver as an unforgiving wind blew off the lake. The sound of the emergency vehicles grew faint as she continued to put more distance between herself and her now tattered office building.

The city felt like a catacomb. Only a few other brave souls were out on an evening when the bars and restaurants were normally filled. Part of her wanted to absorb the innocence of those she passed on the street. Did they look at her and see a criminal, a murderer? Walking along Lakeshore Drive, she flagged the first taxicab she saw.

"Where to?" the driver said. Amanda's nostrils filled with the mixture of curry and cigar smoke that scented his cab, reigniting the queasy feeling. Usually, Amanda would feel claustrophobic when cab drivers kept their heat on high, but tonight she welcomed the blast of warmth.

"Can you take me to the closest bus station?"

"Dan Ryan and 95th. Is that good?" He eyed Amanda through his rearview mirror. She nodded.

Numbness cascaded down her body as she realized the radio was tuned to an all-news station speculating on the day's events.

"The President elevated the terror alert in the event this was something more than a random office shooting; however, all signs point to an armed gunman who opened fire on an investment firm named in an indictment," said a weary, warm voice on the radio. Amanda held her breath waiting to hear her or Josh's name on the newscast, but the story cut to a police officer saying the death toll could be as many as seventy and some members of the investment firm were still unaccounted for.

Amanda suffered the rest of the ride listening to the unnamed voice of a family member frustrated over the lack of information. The man said that his daughter was a receptionist at the company and calls to her cell phone continued to go unanswered. He broke down weeping just as the interview ended and Amanda's cab pulled to the front of the bus station. She tried to feel concern, or remorse knowing the man's daughter was the first casualty, but she only felt numb. "Is it because I'm freezing?" Amanda said, watching her words turn to frost in the frigid night air. "Because, I can't be that cold of a person. Can I?"

Only two windows were open at the bank of ticket counters; at one a pockmarked college student with his head close to a textbook, at the other a woman with long red talons engaged in a heated phone conversation. Amanda looked up at the giant, ornate clock on the wall; unsure what bus would leave at this time of night or if she even wanted to be on it. A map of the country lured her over. She examined the faded areas covered with smudges that blotted several cities out of existence.

Amanda went to the woman's window, but she continued her

phone conversation, studying the lacquer on her nails and avoiding Amanda's stare.

"I know the world is going crazy, but I've got to work. He's just fine with his cousin and should stay put. Hang on," she pulled the mouthpiece of her hands-free earphone away from her face. "Can I help you?"

"I'd like a ticket to El Paso. One way, please."

After a dramatic sigh and eye roll, the woman struck the keyboard and continued her conversation.

"I know we need to move out of the city, but do you think I work two jobs to afford a country home?"

Amanda looked around the empty terminal. The only people there were those with no one to go home to. She imagined the elderly gentleman buffing the floors lost his wife years ago, the only woman he ever loved. The man asleep on the plastic chairs was kicked out of his house by an angry spouse, only to find shelter among the transient. The college student spent too much time working and studying to have friends. The woman at the ticket counter had a string of lovers, each one leaving behind a child to keep her forever bound to thankless jobs. This was where she belonged.

"You can get a seat on a bus leaving tonight, connecting tomorrow in Memphis. You want that one?"

"Yes."

Amanda tried to casually pull the envelope out of her waist-band; she realized if seen with this amount of cash, she wouldn't make it out of the state.

The woman handed Amanda a ticket without another glance or word, continuing her phone conversation. As she walked towards the bus departures, her laceless tennis shoes made her feel like a patient in an asylum. Piercing squeaks echoed over the sound of the man buffing the floors as she shuffled her feet to keep from losing the clunky, oversized shoes. Every few seconds she caught the powerful smell of citrus from the disinfectant, the only smell that could cover the dissonance of colognes, sweat and bus exhaust that mingled daily in the lobby.

The one newsstand still open late at night sold a limited array of tabloids, stale coffee, cigarettes and Bears sweatshirts. She vowed to get rid of the sweatshirt as soon as she was able to buy more clothes, but in the meantime, she needed warmth. Her damp hair hung heavily down her back, as if frozen from the hours spent on the frigid streets.

She sipped her coffee and grimaced at the bitter taste, yet grateful for feeling something other than cold and emptiness. Her eyes burned with exhaustion, but every time she tried to close them, she could only see Liz's limp hand on the office floor with blood soaking her shirt and an accusing, unblinking stare.

A voice over the intercom called for pre-boarding. She got a seat near the middle of the bus, recalling that only the kids who did drugs and made out rode in the back. With her head resting against the window, she allowed the wave of uneasy exhaustion to wash over her.

5

Happy hour would have been the perfect opportunity for Alex to commiserate with colleagues over the unfortunate turn with his case. That is, if he had colleagues that he wanted to socialize with. His usual Friday evenings at the gym didn't appeal to him tonight. Instead, he walked the streets of downtown Chicago.

With his legs on autopilot, he found himself standing in front of a bar. Inside, people smiled, talked, laughed. Regular people who expected their government to protect them from white-collar criminals who defrauded innocent individuals of their savings. If he told these people what was going on, surely they would be outraged to the point of demanding he find Cooper, Williams and Martin and bring them to justice. He promised himself he would just duck in for a quick beer and brief, yet rallying, conversation, but three hours later, he sat atop a barstool with an empty basket of what was once cheese fries in front of him. The greasy food kept him from feeling all the dizzying affects of four pints of beer.

"It just pisses me off," he slurred. "I mean, here I am, the best damn analyst—his words, not mine—and the son-of-bitch won't give me a chance to bring in the bad guys. I'm one of the good guys. They," Alex pointed to imaginary villains at the door. "They are the bad guys."

The elderly bartender, his only audience, allowed a well-practiced head shake to encourage Alex.

"I mean, I can do it. I've been one of the good guys my entire career, my entire life actually. I go to church. I don't smoke. I don't drink too much," he paused to drain the last of his pint, nodding when the bartender pointed at the empty glass to ask if he wanted another. "And I'm respectable," saying the last word with one too many syllables. "I'm respectable because I've only been with one girl. I'm a good guy because I'm working hard so when I meet a good girl, I can be a good husband."

Alex hoped the bartender understood the injustices being inflicted upon him and the potential for life-altering consequences.

"Mate, I hate to tell you this, but not sure if being with just one girl necessarily makes you respectable in a bar like this."

Alex turned to the British voice beside him. With an eye closed to give him a better view, he studied his neighbor. The man wasn't much older than Alex, but his hairline receded severely, which he hid by buzzing his hair to a stubble matching the short beard covering the pock marks on his cheeks. He was dressed casually, in a leather motorcycle jacket, jeans and boots and sipped what appeared to be Scotch with no rocks.

"What is that supposed to mean?" Alex puffed up his chest, but nearly lost his balance on the stool.

The man took a sip of his Scotch and gave Alex a sideways glance. "Oh I don't mean to offend, mate. I was just warning you that saying something like that in a bar like this isn't going to win you any points."

"Oh," Alex said, his voice rose with his bravado. "Really so, *old chap*?" Alex mocked the man's British accent. "How many girls have you been with?"

The man laughed into his Scotch. "Actually, the same as you, but for much different reasons."

The old bartender let out a loud laugh and the Brit joined in. Alex wasn't sure what the joke was, but he hoped he wasn't the butt of it. He watched a handful of bubbles fizz from the bottom of his glass. The motion of the bubbles made him feel seasick, and he swayed on his stool.

"Steady there, mate." His companion said, putting a hand on Alex's shoulder. "Mickey, you got any coffee brewing? Think Superman here is going to need it soon."

"Yeah, you're right, I am Superman. Did Clark Kent's boss tell him he couldn't fly around the world and stop moving bullets with a single bound?"

"Well, actually."

"The world would have been destroyed if his boss would have told him that he couldn't do that. So see, I'm just like Superman."

"Right, just without the tights."

Alex laughed and flung a heavy arm around the man's shoulders. "Exactly! You see where I'm coming from. Hey bartender, another drink for my friend here."

The old man brought another drink over, and Alex toasted his half empty beer to the man's double Scotch.

"So tell me, what type of good guy are you exactly?" the man asked.

"Man, I find cheaters, people who steal other people's money." Alex repeated his story of personal injustice, exaggerating how he singlehandedly discovered the fraud taking place at Jefferson Williams Investments, how he led a team to indict those defrauding innocent people and how someone, he left out exactly who, didn't realize that the two masterminds were privy to their indictments and were now gone. When he finished, both he and the man ordered another drink, Alex switching to double Scotch to mirror his new friend.

"Let me get this straight," the man said after their next round of drinks were delivered. "These men got a heads up that this was coming, and they're gone?"

"Horrible, I know. Would the British Empire have made the same mistake?"

Both men took a drink, staring straight ahead into the mirrored wall behind the bar. Alex's stomach rumbled, signaling that it was ready for another round of cheese fries. But, sitting there with his suave new British friend, he fought the urge to look less than classy by downing something so greasy and…American.

"So what are you doing to find them?"

Alex took a long drink of his Scotch. His lips lost their grasp on the glass and some of his drink dribbled down his chin.

"Right now? Nothing. When that bastard shot up the office it became a criminal investigation. My boss pulled us out of it, citing lack of resources, other cases that need the team's attention, blah blah blah."

The man took another sip.

"Why can't you keep working on it?"

"I could, but it's more work than one man can handle. I need support staff, people going through data, research, you know, feet on the street."

"What about one man?" the Brit asked. "How much could you accomplish if you had a partner?"

"Oh I could find them easily," Alex said. He hoped the conversation was purely theoretical but didn't want to lose face with his new friend by appearing unsure. "Who do you have in mind?"

"Me."

"You? What do you know about investigations?"

"Actually, quite a bit. You had the good fortune, mate, of striking up a conversation with a seasoned journalist." The man drained the rest of his Scotch in one swallow. "Call me tomorrow when you come out of your hangover, mate," he said, pulling his wallet from his pocket, tossing a couple of twenties on the bar and handing Alex a business card.

With a pat on the back the man departed, leaving Alex with half a double Scotch to go. He motioned for the tab while trying to read the card under the dim lights, but the fine black letters blurred together. When the check came, he closed one eye hoping he misread the total, but all the numbers were present.

As he stood outside under a streetlight waiting for a cab to pass by, he pulled the card out of his pocket to try to read it again. With the white square held close, he finally made out the words.

Roland Burrows. Senior Reporter. *Financial News*.

6

"Who'd you kill, sweetheart?"

A disembodied voice spoke in the pre-dawn darkness. *They took less time finding me than I thought*, as her heart sped up and warmth filled her cheeks.

Amanda looked around at the motley crew that made up her traveling companions. At the front of the bus she spied the back of a nun's habit and felt reassured that at least someone prayed for their safe arrival. She turned and saw a disheveled man sitting behind her. His sandy blond hair flopped over a shiny forehead that made him look half his age, but the gray stubble on his cheeks added the years back on.

"That is the worst pick-up line I've ever heard," Amanda mumbled, shifting in her seat. "Go bother someone else. I'm trying to sleep."

The man laughed, moving to the seat directly across the aisle. "Good looking girls don't get on buses like this unless they're running from something. So, what's the story? You catch your man cheating?"

This bus jockey Casanova had no clue how right he was. Yes, Amanda caught her man cheating, but not in the arms of another woman, although it wouldn't surprise her if infidelity was part of his crimes.

"You could say that."

A passing car lit up his self-satisfied smile. She avoided staring at him, afraid he would recognize her face in the future in wanted posters.

"I knew it. So what method of murder do you prefer?" He pulled a cigarette out of his shirt pocket. He didn't light it, but let it sit idly on his lips. She studied the cupid's bow of his mouth, willing her cheeks not to flush. His greasy hair clumped together, in need of a good shampoo. The faded jean jacket was soft from overuse and the collar of his t-shirt was ripped. If it were the eighties, he would drive a black Trans-Am and listen to Iron Maiden. *Actually*, she thought, *he probably still has that Trans-Am and Iron Maiden cassette.* This was not the type of guy she usually found attractive, but the dirty, sexy confidence lured her in.

"Let's see," he said. His eyes studied her as if she were a painting in a museum. "Now I wouldn't peg you as the type of woman to knife someone. That's too messy. However, I could see you drawn to the power of a firearm, so maybe you shot him. But you wouldn't shoot him too close, because again, you wouldn't want to ruin your manicure with blood splatter. No, you're definitely not the type to get messy."

Amanda rolled her eyes and turned her back to the man. She started to regret encouraging him to guess her preferred method to kill her boyfriend. Then again, his ideas sounded attractive for when she finally did get her hands on Josh.

It was too dark to see the landscape outside the bus windows, but she was able to make out interstate truck stop signs towering above the road. These beacons for the road-weary made Amanda feel less lonely. She could now find solace in those who were true individuals, those without a family or home to call their own, those without the social network or colleagues to make them part of something larger. She relished the idea of spending the rest of her life as a member of true outsiders, not those who isolate themselves merely to commune with other so-called outsiders. Truly alone. The way Josh left her.

The hypnotizing effect of the road began to lull Amanda back to sleep. Just as the luscious floating sensation before succumbing to sleep washed over her, she felt his breath in her ear.

"Sweetheart, I didn't mean to offend. Really, I swear."

His hot and musky breath smelled of tobacco and cinnamon gum. She turned to face him, no longer concerned that he would get a good look at her face.

"Why are you still here?"

"Hey, hey, no reason to get bitchy on me," he exaggerated a pout. She began to lift herself out of her seat. "Wait, don't get up, I'm sorry, I'm sorry. Look, I can't sleep and just thought we could talk. You know, share the journey or shit like that."

Amanda settled back in her seat and examined him through narrowed eyes.

"Okay, fine. What do you want to talk about?"

"Let's go back to how you offed your boyfriend. Poison, now I can see you doing that."

"I didn't kill my boyfriend." *Yet.*

"That's too bad. But you did catch him cheating," he said as he leaned forward, his face just inches from hers. For a split second, Amanda thought he was going to kiss her; and for a millisecond of that split second she wished he would. "You ask me, love ain't worth it. All monogamy does is set you up for the greatest disappointment ever."

He leaned back, placing the unlit cigarette back in his shirt pocket. Amanda wondered if his addiction were so strong that just the feel of the little stick of nicotine between his lips satisfied the craving.

"Love isn't that bad."

"Tell me one good thing about it."

Mentally rewinding her relationship with Josh, she tried to find something profound to share.

"Intimacy."

"Sweetheart, you can be more intimate with someone you meet

on a bus than a man you've known for years. Love has nothing to do with that. Love simply makes you a burden."

He was right. Loving Josh meant he became her burden. Unknowingly, she helped Josh steal money. They didn't talk; they never shared secrets. It wasn't that type of relationship. It was superficial, convenient. Amanda recalled a recent dinner conversation with their group of friends, and when someone asked Josh what Amanda wanted from life, he replied with a pretentious laugh, "Manolo Blahniks." Amanda was the only person at the table who didn't laugh.

"I'm Tom," he said, reaching a hand over the back of the seat. The heat from his hand burned her cold fingers.

Amanda took a deep breath. "Mandy."

Even in the darkness of the bus she could tell that his probing eyes searched for cracks in her foundation; a place he could permeate like liquid looking for a crevice in which to freeze.

"Fire," he said in a low voice, his lopsided smile pulling up the right side of his lips. "I can smell smoke in your hair. You set the son-of-a-bitch on fire, didn't you?"

"Go to hell." Her voice was low and acerbic. "You have no idea." No idea of what? She couldn't finish that thought. She wouldn't play the victim and rehash how Josh had used her for years. She couldn't tell him that she was responsible for the death of her colleagues. Nor could she tell him that if she had cared enough to know Josh, to really know him, she would have uncovered his crimes and none of this would have happened. Then she wouldn't be sitting on a bus in the middle of the night talking with a mysteriously seductive stranger.

Tom leaned back, his hands raised in apology.

Amanda went back to observing the world outside her window. Somewhere on the bus she could hear soft sobbing, another one of the poor souls sharing the journey with them. The nun in front of the bus was either still awake or sleeping with her head straight and focused in front of her. Amanda figured that either way, the nun practiced the strict self-restraint to which she'd religiously adhered. Someone else snored loudly and consistently enough that Amanda could set the metronome her childhood piano teacher used to it. There couldn't have been more than fifteen people on the bus, their faces briefly illuminated by ghostly shadows of oncoming cars or passing truck stops.

"So, Mandy," he said in a low voice. "I'm going back to the head to take a leak. I've got a couple of jimmies on me, and you look like you could use some intimacy. Come back in a minute if you're interested. If not, no harm, no foul."

He headed to the rear of the bus. Amanda studied the back of the nun's head, silently begging forgiveness for so many things, asking for guidance. For the first time she could remember, she felt the urge to pray. She used the band of her wristwatch to say the rosary; sure this was sacrilegious in some way, but she hoped God would understand.

The nun's head began to droop, as if she dozed off. Amanda looked around the bus again; a passing car illuminated the sleeping faces of her fellow passengers. She reached the bathroom door just as she heard the toilet flush.

"He used me. To help him steal money," she said when he opened the bathroom door. "He stole a lot of money, and then he left me to take the blame."

Tom didn't seem surprised to find her. "Think you'll ever see him again?" He stood aside to let Amanda join him.

"I don't know, but that's where I'm headed," she said, her face moving towards his. "And, when I do, I'll kill him," the words rolled off her tongue like a caress.

His mouth tasted exactly as she suspected, sweet yet nauseating. The cramped lavatory made the sex awkward. But Amanda didn't care. She didn't want to kiss Tom, look in his eyes, or even feel his hands on her body. She didn't want any intimacy between them. She simply wanted to close her eyes and be somewhere else. Be someone else.

7

T om took a bus transfer in Missouri. He didn't ask her to
join him, she didn't ask him to stay on the bus. Tom simply
grabbed his bag and with one last lopsided smile, departed
the bus. Amanda didn't bother looking out the window to see if he
stood on the platform, staring after the bus as it drove off in the
early morning hours. Much like the nights she spent with Josh, she
felt unfulfilled, and a final glance at Tom would only reinforce one
fact: that her boyfriend of three years shared no more intimacy with
her than sex with a complete stranger in a bus bathroom.

As the bus pulled away, Amanda stared so hard at the back of
the nun's habit she was afraid the woman would turn around. *I am
so sorry Sister*, she apologized to the nun, *I promise to make up for
my mess.*

Liz's question ran through her mind as she stared at the blurring
landscape outside the window. *What happened to me? Okay, I admit, I
wasn't really a good person, but I wasn't that bad, was I? I was vulnerable,
perched somewhere in the middle between good and bad.* "And all it took was
a good-looking guy and some money to topple me to the bad side,"
she said to her faint reflection.

As the bus neared its stop in Memphis, Amanda paid close

attention to the street signs in order to backtrack to two stores that caught her eye. The door chime of the pawnshop announced her arrival. Metal shelves greeted her, displaying banged-up toasters, twenty-year-old electric keyboards and tools in varying stages of rust. Her heels lifted out of her laceless shoes as she stood up on her toes to find a clerk in the quiet shop. With as much grace and confidence as she could display, she shuffled down the first aisle.

"Can I help you?" The greeting finally came from a hunched man perusing a newspaper sprawled across a display case. Amanda moved closer to the display case and casually scanned the costume jewelry, rusty pocketknives and small electronics.

"I need to get a fake ID.

"I don't make those," he said, his eyes never left his paper.

"I have cash. I'll pay you double."

"You don't look like you need a fake ID to buy beer," he finally looked up at her, eyeing her over his bifocals. Crumbs from his breakfast took shelter in his mustache. His t-shirt barely covered his protruding belly. "How do I know you're not a cop anyway?

"Do I look like a cop?

The man studied her for a moment and then spoke. "Does a cop ever look like a cop? Follow me." He got off his stool; he was shorter than she realized.

Amanda followed him through a curtain into a back room. It was small and dark, filled to the top with goods waiting to be sold. In one corner sat a camera with a digital printer and an oversized machine

"Do you have a preference on state? I wouldn't recommend Tennessee. Cops here see those all the time and can pick out a fake."

"I don't care. Surprise me."

He instructed her to sit in a metal folding chair against a white wall. Just like a trip to the DMV, she barely had time to smile before he snapped the picture. *Score one for authenticity*.

"What name would you like to use?" He settled in front of a computer that showed her picture in the corner of a driver's license.

"Mandy Jackson," she said, settling on a way to always

remember the infant boy who would grow up motherless. *Saying the name of Liz's son every time I introduce myself will be as punishing as a daily flogging*, she thought, *but necessary*.

He pressed the print button, bringing to life a large grumbling machine. As the printer warmed up, he started another machine. After printing and laminating her license, he studied his handiwork.

"Pretty damn good job if I say so myself. That will be two hundred dollars," he said, his eyes trailing down to her wrist. "Is that a real Rolex?"

Amanda tugged her sweatshirt sleeve over the watch. "I'll give you four hundred dollars cash."

"Nah, I'd get more money selling that watch. It'll be two hundred dollars cash and your watch. Or, I call the cops."

For a moment, Amanda considered letting him call the police. It would be so much easier. She would tell the police she panicked, had some sort of mental breakdown to explain how she traveled from Chicago to Memphis only to be captured buying a fake ID in a pawn shop and that the real criminal could be in El Paso. But she wasn't ready to do that.

"Fine," she said, scraping her arm as she pulled the Rolex off. She took one more look at the watch, her thumb caressed its face as she recalled her father's suggestion to live her own life. *I'll make this up to you, Dad*. With her eyes closed, she offered the watch to the man. She felt the emptiness of its relinquished weight, only to be replaced with the flimsy plastic of her new identification.

Without the benefit of her wristwatch, she had to steal a glance at the wall clock on her way out of the back room. Thirty minutes before her bus left.

She scurried in her awkward shoes and stopped when she saw the Salvation Army logo beckoning her. Without sparing time to peruse the store, she grabbed a cardigan sweater with a hole in one elbow, and spied a pair of running shoes that had good tread and shoelaces, a bonus. On her way to pay for her new wardrobe, she found a backpack that had been broken in several times over.

With twenty minutes left, she ran to a dollar store for toiletries. After a dead sprint back to the bus station, she hurriedly brushed her teeth and used the coarse paper towels in the bathroom to give herself a sponge bath. The loudspeaker announced the final boarding call.

She once again found a seat in the middle of the bus and looked around. None of her fellow passengers from the first leg of the trip joined her. She felt rejuvenated from the sponge bath and ran her tongue across her teeth, feeling the smoothness of a recent brushing. Washing down a couple of over-the-counter sleeping pills, it wouldn't be long before the bus rocked her back into oblivion.

THEIR ARRIVAL in Dallas woke her from her drug-induced sleep, and she had no choice but to leave the bus and stretch her legs. With the bus station in the heart of downtown, Amanda hoped it would give her several options for distractions, especially on a Saturday night. Girls in short dresses and tall heels wiggled out of sports cars and clambered into restaurants along the entertainment district.

Amanda watched one couple wait at a club door as the bouncer checked their IDs. The man reminded her of Josh, blond and self-confident, but she noticed the nervous girl on his arm clutched her expensive purse. Amanda thought about shouting out to the young woman that she should leave the guy before it's too late, but when she opened her mouth, the bouncer at the door approached her.

"You need to move on before I call the cops," he bellowed.

Amanda looked up to argue with the man, but he cupped her elbow and pulled her away from the door. "Look, I'm sorry if you're hungry or need a place to sleep, really I am. You just need to go somewhere else. I can't have you standing in front of my club scaring off my guests."

"What are you talking about?" she asked, but when she caught a glimpse of her reflection she understood perfectly. Two days ago, she was one of those girls, but in secondhand clothes carrying all of her possessions in a broken-in backpack, she had more in common with the homeless than these young professionals. Unable to explore the city further, she went back to the bus station to sip stale coffee.

When the final leg of her journey resumed, Amanda didn't notice the bus roll away from the station, leaving the city behind her. She slept deeply, so deep in fact that when she did wake up to reposition herself, she had no recollection of any dreams. No drugs were necessary for this slumber.

When she finally woke, the bus was empty and the rising sun lit the parking lot of a gas station alive with activity. Cars and trucks pulled in; people came out with coffee and donuts.

"Why did we stop?" she asked a woman who juggled a fussy toddler on her hip.

"Engine trouble. We're stuck here until a mechanic shows up. Shouldn't be much longer, an hour maybe."

"Where's here?" Amanda asked, but the child entered meltdown mode and the woman ignored her.

It was a calm, crisp morning. The sun was hidden by a slight haze in the east, but the sky above her was a pretty shade of baby blue. She looked down the road and saw that it was a two-lane highway with little traffic. Squat, mesquite trees lined the barbed wire fence across from the gas station and a few content cows munched on grass. Cacti jutted out of the rocky earth. She walked over to a smaller road that ran perpendicular to the highway. The road was lined with oak trees that were just showing the first signs of new leaves.

Intrigued by the quietude of the road and reinvigorated after a full day of sleep, Amanda stretched her legs with a short walk. The narrow road had no shoulder, and she glanced nervously behind her. After a few minutes, she became less worried about traffic and began to admire her surroundings. To her left, rolling hills were home to cattle grazing on scrubby brush. A house and a barn sat just on the eastern horizon. On her right, the trees grew thicker, and she thought she could hear the sound of rushing water just out of view.

She was so enthralled with her surroundings that she didn't realize she stood in front of a city limits sign until she nearly walked into it. Amanda took a few steps back to look up at the giant sign, proclaiming that she was about to enter Phoenix, population six hundred.

The road curved towards the sound of the running water, and she was hit by the delectable smell of bacon. To her left, was the cause of her sudden hunger. A small house that had been converted to a restaurant beckoned. It was painted a deep red, and the front yard was transformed into a parking lot, already full of work trucks and American-made sedans. A sheriff's car stood sentinel near the road, a warning to anyone who had sinister thoughts toward the little restaurant.

With her stomach leading the way, Amanda drifted over to the house. A few men in plaid work shirts looked up from their breakfast, but returned to shoveling their grits and eggs. A hurried waitress directed her to a seat at a small counter.

The waitress returned with a menu, the lamination peeling at the corners and with what looked like ketchup permanently splattered across the top. Amanda ordered the biggest thing on the menu: two eggs over easy, hash browns, sausage, bacon, a biscuit, coffee and orange juice.

She sipped her coffee and studied the restaurant. The wood-paneled walls were adorned with a variety of knickknacks. Above the cash register at the end of the counter was a calendar for the Phoenix High School Booster Club. The wall behind her held framed copies of the *Phoenix Talon*, the local paper sporting some kind of big news. Amanda craned her neck to see the year on the calendar, with Olivia Newton-John in her workout gear, next to the swinging door into the kitchen. She would never find a place like this in Chicago, but it seemed well suited for a town as small as Phoenix.

The bell above the door chimed, and she swung around on her stool. After greeting several people, an elderly gentleman in a white, three-piece suit and a white fedora made his way to the counter.

The waitress brought Amanda's plate, and the busy little restaurant melted away as she tasted her first bite of food in days, savoring the warmth and texture of her hash browns.

"Good morning, Dugan. You want the usual?" the waitress asked with a cup of coffee already placed in front of him.

"Thank you, my dear, but I think I would like to have what our guest is having. That smells delightful." A soft lilt floated to Amanda's ears, something that didn't sound Texan to her.

Amanda was unaware he was talking about her until she looked up from her plate for her glass of juice, mouth full of bacon. She looked over and saw him smiling serenely at her.

"Pardon me for the interruption. My name is Dugan McWilliams. I would offer my hand, but I see that yours is otherwise engaged." He nodded toward the biscuit she held in her left hand and the fork in her right.

"Mandy Jackson, sir. It's nice to meet you." She could have gulped her food to answer him, but his patient peacefulness made her take the time to chew first. Amanda noticed she took deeper, slower breaths. She even somehow managed to slow the thoughts in her head of how much time she needed to make it back to the bus. She had never lived in a small town, but maybe the slower pace was infectious.

"Ah, a good name, Mandy. Short for Amanda, I'm sure, which means she who must be loved," as he took a sip of his coffee. His perfectly groomed white beard matched a full head of white, pristinely styled hair. "So, Mandy, what brings you to our fair town of Phoenix?"

"A bus," Amanda said taking another bite of bacon, her hunger winning over the desire to eat slowly. She felt her face flush after her curt answer. "I'm sorry, I'm on a bus to El Paso, and it broke down on the highway. I went for a walk to stretch my legs and here I am," she finished after swallowing.

Dugan chuckled. His plate arrived, and Amanda watched him as he deeply inhaled the steam rising off the food, eyes closed.

"Well, Mandy from the bus, are you going to El Paso looking for love or money?"

"Excuse me?"

"Are you going to meet a loved one or for work?"

"Both. Neither," she said. She needed to steer the conversation away from her. "Mr. McWilliams."

"Please, call me Dugan," he interrupted her.

"Dugan, I can't help but notice your accent. Where are you from?"

His blue eyes lit up as she asked about his accent. "Ah, I was afraid I had lost that by now. You see, I left Ireland as a teenager to travel the world on a merchant ship. I was a bit of a hothead in my youth and a bar brawl in New York resulted in the ship sailing on without me." By the time he finished his history, Amanda wasn't sure how much was fact or fiction. He was a masterful storyteller, and if what he said was true, this man was a living piece of twentieth century America.

The waitress cleared their plates and warmed up their coffee. Amanda was determined to stay in control of the conversation and keep the questions away from her. "Is Phoenix named after the city in Arizona?"

"That is a fascinating story. A century ago, this town was called Rio Pueblo. One night, the town drunk tried to get into bed at the boarding house on the square when he knocked over his lantern and passed out rather than go for help. The whole town square went up in flames, but the grand old courthouse was saved. At first light the next morning, all the town's residents came out to inspect the damage. It was quite a scene as you can imagine; clouds of smoke and dust filled the air. As the people mourned the loss of their city, a little boy, no older than six, pointed out that a single beam of light shone down on the courthouse, and that it resembled a phoenix rising out of the ashes," he took another sip of his coffee while Amanda clung to every word, even though it sounded like the lore behind the big fire of her native city.

"From that point, many of the residents vowed to stay and rebuild the town, but only if they named it Phoenix," Amanda noticed that Dugan eyed her steadily, as if he were trying to read her mind. "You know what that's like, right Mandy, to rise out of the ashes?"

Amanda hoped the shock that coursed through her veins didn't show on her face. *Can he smell the smoke on me like Tom,* she wondered, *or can he see something else, like the truth?* Her eyes flitted to the wall clock while sipping her coffee.

"Oh no," Amanda said as soon as she could swallow the hot liquid. She dug in her backpack for a small bill to leave for her breakfast and tip. "Crap, crap, crap."

"What's the worry, dear Mandy?" Dugan said.

"I think I missed my bus. I should have been back half an hour ago. I'm sorry to run. It was nice speaking with you." Amanda continued to dig through her backpack for something smaller than a one hundred dollar bill.

"I could inquire about finding a willing soul to speed you to your bus," Dugan said, motioning to Amanda that he would pick up their tab. "However, if you don't have any firm plans for El Paso, I'm sure we can find you a place to stay here. Of course, if you have luggage on the bus that you need, I would be happy to make the effort."

"No, this is all I have," Amanda said. She looked back around the restaurant. A few families had come in, dressed in their Sunday finest. An older police officer laughed with a table of men in plaid work shirts and dusty jeans, their skin weather-worn but jovial nonetheless. Even though she was a stranger, nobody gave her any curious glances. *Those who said that it was about the journey and not the destination never traveled by bus. Josh can wait, I need a break.*

"You know, I think I wouldn't mind staying here for a bit," Amanda said turning back to Dugan. The wide smile on his face revealed perfect teeth, and she imagined how handsome he must have been when he was younger.

"Good, good. Well, if you will lend me an arm, we will walk over to your new home," it was then that Amanda noticed a cane perched on the counter on the other side of him.

She led him outside and helped him down the steps of the porch. "You already have a home for me?"

Dugan laughed again, "My dear friend Myrna has a garage apartment available." Dugan pointed his cane to the road ahead of them. "Her home is just a little further up the road, and if we hurry, we can catch her before she leaves for church."

8

_____

Curing a hangover was much harder than Alex remembered. He rarely drank that much, even in college. The moment his eyes opened they fell to the small two-by-three-inch white business card perched between the key rows of his open laptop. He wondered if the card stared at him all night. Waiting. It was a reminder as bitter as the taste in his mouth that the previous day really did happen. He really did screw up his case. His two prime suspects really did skip town. His third suspect was probably charred beyond recognition and lying in the morgue. And, he really did meet the reporter who broke the story—the first domino to fall in the horrible Rube Goldberg machine known as his life. With all these thoughts rushing back to him, no wonder he drank as much as he did.

Rather than hurry into the shower and race down to his office to show his dedication to the case and his fellow Americans, Alex crawled across his small apartment and carefully picked up the business card, testing it first before actually gripping it between his two fingers, afraid it was wired to shock him. *What the hell happened last night?*

"Bartender," he said aloud as the image of the white-haired

man flashed through his sore brain. "Nice guy, I hope I tipped him. Okay, British dude. Shit, that had to be Roland." Alex swayed as a wave of nausea washed over him. *Did I say anything disastrous about the case? Was I being recorded?* Alex could see the headlines now: *Drunk SEC Agent Spills All Over Beer.* Alex belched. *And Cheese Fries.*

He didn't realize he held his breath until a quick search of the *Financial News* website resulted in no such headlines. "Thank God, I'm safe," he exhaled.

His stomach wasn't ready for coffee, but he needed something to wake him up. He knew it would be all hands on deck at the office that weekend. Coming in late the day after a major catastrophe was not an option. Lucky for Alex, working on Saturdays was second nature to him, so hangover notwithstanding, he figured he would be on his way to the office before any of his colleagues finished their bagels.

A quick scan of the newspaper during his train ride to work revealed nothing he didn't already know. "The gunman was a veteran whose wife had been battling cancer for years," he read. Their insurance wouldn't cover an experimental treatment, her last hope, and the man became apprehensive earlier in the week when he tried to cash out his investments, only to have his suspicions confirmed when he saw the *Financial News* story. The gunman died in the shooting and subsequent explosions, the death toll continued to rise, and his widow was stunned and heartbroken.

As Alex walked the last few blocks from the train stop to his office, he wondered if any of the responsibility of the dead JWI employees rested on his shoulders. Sure, there was no way he could have known someone would react so violently, but what if his suspects were locked away? Would the gunman have felt the need to exact his revenge if the SEC moved faster in its investigation?

The security guard waved at Alex when he entered the empty lobby. Murmured voices filled the air as the elevator door opened onto his floor. The overhead fluorescent lights were still off, but the sunny Chicago sky lit up the office. After dropping off his briefcase and starting his computer, he quietly strolled through the office for the source of the voices. He found half of his team already at work in the conference room, the lights out there as well, with their faces eerily illuminated by their laptops. From the empty coffee cups and bagel wrappers, they had been there for some time. Alex cursed himself for his overindulgence the evening before.

"Mr. Harrison, what can I do, sir?" Alex said when his boss walked into the room.

"I think we've got it all under control, Alex. Why don't you take this weekend off? You always put long hours in anyway. It'll do you some good to relax, get refreshed and come back on Monday refocused and ready for work."

"Sir, with all due respect, is this really the best time for me to take off?" Alex said, hoping he sounded more self-assured than whiney. "I am dedicated to this case. Tell me what I can do."

"If you were so dedicated to this case, why did you fail to notice that Williams and Cooper cashed out their employee stock?"

All of the eyes in the conference room shifted to Alex's face. Self-hatred churned in his stomach with the leftover Scotch and coffee. His brain told his face to not betray him, to not show the hurt he felt when those words flew across the room. But, his shoulders didn't get the memo and slumped in defeat. Harrison seemed to realize the potency of his words and motioned for Alex to follow him.

"I didn't mean to be so hard on you back there, but I spent the better part of last night and this morning saving your job." Harrison closed his office door behind Alex and took his seat in his office chair, motioning for Alex to sit in one of the guest chairs.

"Well, sir, what about the case? What's the next step, shouldn't I be here helping you with the strategy?"

Harrison sighed as he leaned all the way back in his office chair. The two men stared at each other for a moment. Alex studied the lines on the man's face and noticed that his gray hair looked a little thinner than he remembered. The collar of his shirt pressed against his neck, a new feature since he quit smoking.

"Look, I'll level with you. I don't know if there is a case anymore."

Alex felt his jaw drop. "What do you mean?"

"I mean that there are a lot of crooks out there, a lot of bad people, but in the grand scheme of things, Williams and Cooper committed a smaller crime than others. They only stole a few million over the life of the fraud. And, as of yesterday, their actions were nothing compared to the man who decided to kill nearly the whole damn office."

Alex felt like he was dunked in murky water and the words floated by him, following a current to some far-off place rather than sinking in.

"You mean—you mean we're closing out the case?"

Harrison sighed, locked his fingers behind his head and began rocking forward in his chair. "Alex, we're short staffed, and we've got bigger fish to fry than these guys. It turned into a criminal investigation on Friday, no longer a white-collar crime. We're not closing the books permanently, but for the time being, we're just going to put it aside and wait for Williams and Cooper to turn up."

"Wait for them to turn up?" Alex stood up as his voice went up an octave. Disbelief and anger exploded through his body.

"Sit down Alex. And, keep your voice down."

Alex obeyed, collapsing back into the chair. "Mr. Harrison, shouldn't we at least try to figure out where they are, look into if they purchased plane tickets somewhere? And, what about Amanda Martin, shouldn't we confirm she was killed or if she took off as well?"

"We're going to keep a check on their credit cards and known bank accounts, so we'll get dinged if they use any of them," Harrison said. "And, Martin is probably dead. A female fitting her age and description was found outside her office door. It'll be a few days before the tests come back, but we are working under the assumption that she's deceased."

Without leaving Alex's gaze, Harrison's left hand instinctively moved to the top drawer of his desk and pulled out a piece of nicotine gum and popped it in his mouth.

"Anyway," the man continued, chomping on his gum. "I need you to keep your head down. I don't like my best analyst screwing up. On Monday, when you come back in, I need your help with some other cases, some real interesting ones."

The man rambled for a few minutes about mundane cases that lacked lovers on the run, a vengeful gunman and corporate playboys. Alex didn't want to work on these cases; he wanted to salvage his own. Barely twenty-four hours later, and his boss and the agency swept this one under the rug. *What about the gunman? He sacrificed his life for his wife. I can't let this case die. I'll keep searching. Even if it means doing so without Harrison's support or the SEC's or even the U.S. government's. I may have to put myself in harm's way, but I would gladly do it for that poor lady dying of cancer. Whatever her name is.*

Alex got so carried away with the patriotism running through his body that he stood at attention and repressed the desire to salute an imaginary general. Lucky for him, Harrison was finishing his spiel about the boring projects Alex had to look forward to.

"Great, Mr. Harrison," Alex said, turning his back to hurry out of the office. "That sounds fine, sir. I'll see you on Monday."

In several long strides, he was out of the office building and back on the sidewalk as the sun lazily heaved itself over the lake.

9

Dugan chatted as he led Amanda further down the road towards her future home. She was in awe of the greenery around her and never thought that Texas could yield an area so lush and green. They turned down an adjacent road just before a narrow, concrete bridge, and her eyes instantly fell upon a white Victorian house with dark green shutters. Even though the house was large, it was anything but pretentious, and warmth radiated from its open windows.

As they walked toward the wrap-around porch, an elderly woman emerged from the side of the house in a wide brim hat and overalls spotted with dirt around the knees.

"Good morning, Dugan. I was just about to get cleaned up for church." She walked towards them on the gravel driveway, pulling off her gardening gloves.

"Well then, just another example of fortuitous timing," he said, tipping his fedora and planting a quick kiss on Myrna's cheek. "I wanted to introduce you to Mandy Jackson. She just arrived in Phoenix and may be interested in boarding in your garage apartment. Mandy, please meet Mrs. Myrna Morris."

"Ma'am, I'm so sorry to barge in on you," Amanda said, stepping forward offering her hand to Myrna. "I'd love to take a look."

The woman waved off her apology with a warm smile and clasped Amanda's outstretched hands with both of hers. "Not a bother, let's go see that apartment." Myrna smiled at Amanda, and her face quickly lit up. If it weren't for the few wrinkles around her eyes and her white hair pulled into a bun, Amanda would have thought Myrna was decades younger than her actual age.

"Wonderful. Well, Mandy, I must be off. I look forward to our next encounter," Dugan winked at Amanda and tipped his hat once more to Myrna before he slowly set off down the road. Amanda could make out the tune of an Irish jig whistled over the sound of the river.

"Mrs. Morris, you have such a beautiful home." Amanda admired how the blue hydrangeas popped against the white backdrop of the house.

"Oh child, call me Myrna, and thank you for your kind words. My Edward and I built this home a lifetime ago. Follow me."

Myrna pointed to the side of the house, and they walked to the backyard. At the end of the driveway stood a two-story garage-style structure, a miniature of the gorgeous house, with Myrna's late 80s Buick parked inside and stairs leading up to a second-floor landing.

"Edward planned for the second floor of the garage to be a playhouse for our children and grandchildren, but the good Lord never blessed us with our own, so we decided to make this a place for other people's children," she said as they walked towards the garage. "You go on ahead, I'll be right behind you. My knees aren't like they used to be."

Amanda climbed the white wooden steps. At the landing, she looked out past a live oak that sat beside the garage and finally discovered her river. It wasn't large, but appeared to be a shallow, swift moving current.

"So you found the Tejas, the lifeblood of Phoenix," Myrna joined her. "That's what attracted Edward to this piece of land; that and this big old live oak here," Myrna took a moment to look out over the grassy green banks of the river. "Well, it's open, let's go on inside."

What appeared to be a small apartment on the outside was deceptively spacious inside. The one room was open with windows on three sides, and directly in front of the door was a small kitchenette with a dorm-sized refrigerator and a small range. Next to that was a bathroom with a shower stall instead of a bathtub, and a closet completed the wall. A full-size bed sat beneath a window that looked out over the river. The apartment was spartan, but it exuded that warm feeling associated with coming home.

"I know it's not much, but it's comfortable. It's got air and heat. You can cook your meals up here if you would like, but I always make plenty for breakfast, lunch and dinner and won't charge you extra if you take your meals with me. I have a set of dishes up here in the kitchen, sheets are in the closet and towels in the bathroom. I would appreciate if you left them here." Myrna was opening the aluminum blinds to the windows and dusting off the top of a small card table that served as the dining table. "The water heater is pretty small, so I'd be careful about washing dishes and then taking a shower. I'd hate for you to run out of hot water halfway through your shower."

Amanda stopped listening to Myrna prattle and looked out the windows of her new home. She closed her eyes and took a deep breath. Amanda's nose tickled at a slight musty smell covered by a rich, spicy potpourri candle. Even over Myrna's chattering, Amanda could hear the consistent trickling of the river. The live oak next to the garage offered an added layer of shelter, and the leaves rustled in the soft breeze. She loved her apartment in Chicago, the expansive views of the lake, the deep hardwood floors and designer furniture, but this place with its linoleum floor and small windows was comfortable in a way her former residence could never be.

"Rent is two hundred dollars a month and due on the first. I just ask that you give me that plus one month's rent as a deposit before you move in. Now I don't mind a boyfriend coming over from time to time, but I am a Christian woman and if too many men starting hanging around I will give you a piece of my mind and ask you to find another place to live," Myrna laid down the ground rules. Amanda guessed this was a sign that the woman intended to rent the apartment to her. "I go to church on Wednesday evenings and Sunday mornings, and you are more than welcome to join me," Myrna took a deep breath, as though about to make a serious proposal. "So, Mandy, it's yours if you're interested."

Amanda turned back from the window facing Myrna's house and smiled at her, looking deep in the woman's dark brown eyes. "I'll take it."

"Oh good," Myrna clapped her hands. "So when do you want to move in?"

Amanda reached into her backpack for her money. "I can move in right now if you would like." She handed Myrna four one hundred dollar bills.

"Child, is that all you have? Where are your clothes and your things?"

Amanda shrugged her shoulders. "I travel light I guess." She felt her lower lip tremble, and she was unable to make eye contact. For the first time in days she thought about some of her favorite possessions that she would never see again. She thought of books she loved to read, the new set of dishes she bought just a few weeks ago with the vintage bird pattern, and she thought of jeans that actually fit. They were possessions, things, insignificant items that could be forgotten and replaced. But, for better or worse, they defined her. "I probably do need to get a few things though, some clothes and stuff."

"After church, I need to run to K-Mart. How about you come along, and we'll get anything you need," Myrna waved off her earlier question to Amanda. "I'll be back from church just after noon, and we'll grab lunch and then head to the store," Myrna had her hand on the door and turned back to Amanda, her face beaming. "And, Mandy, welcome home."

Amanda smiled back at the woman and watched her as she descended the wooden stairs and strode across the green lawn. As soon as she was out of sight, Amanda ran into her tiny bathroom and threw up her breakfast. Her body had become so accustomed to movement on the bus that sitting still made her nauseated; a sort of reverse car sickness. She sat on the cool floor, her legs wrapped around the toilet with her cheek resting on the toilet seat. "I hope Myrna cleaned the bathroom," Amanda said into the refilling toilet bowl. After a few minutes, she felt strong enough to stand; even with the only nourishment she had in the last two days swirling away.

The small shower stall beckoned. Without a fresh change of clothes, Amanda tried to resist, but was soon overcome with the desire to stand under a jet of steaming hot water, washing away all of the dirt and grime that covered her body. *Baptism by shower. I need to start chipping away at my sins*, she thought as Tom's scent flooded her nostrils. *Starting with Tom.*

She stripped her clothes and tossed them to the floor. If she had a choice she would have chucked them in the trash, but that would come soon enough. A small bottle of body wash and hotel-sized bottles of shampoo and conditioner waited for her in the shower. The water heated up fast and Amanda stood under the piercing jet of water, letting it sting her skin. When she couldn't stand it anymore, she turned on the cold water faucet, finding the right balance that kept the water warm but not scalding. She washed her hair three times. Each time she saw more dirt and grime at the bottom of the shower basin. She scrubbed her body four times, washing away layer after layer of sin. Tom. Then Liz. And, then her crimes against the people she didn't know, those represented by the man in the sneakers and baseball cap. She tried to wash away Josh, but that was going to take more work. She squirted more soap on the washcloth, hoping that body scrub number five would finally suffice.

With the bottle of body wash exhausted and the hot water cooling, Amanda finished her shower feeling better than she had in days.

The standard-issue clock radio read 11:45. She scurried back to the bathroom and worked on detangling her hair with the brush she picked up from the dollar store. With her long hair finally combed out, she glanced around the small bathroom and sighed, adding another item to her shopping list. Hair dryer.

"Starting your life over from scratch is really hard," Amanda said to her reflection. "It's all the small things that bite you in the ass, no hair dryer, no deodorant, nothing." She pulled her hair into a bun and grabbed the dirty, worn clothes for the last time. She closed the door to her new home, locked it carefully and went to Myrna's back door to commence one of the most anticipated shopping sprees of her life.

10

The K-Mart lingerie department was no Victoria's Secret. Standing among the throng of white nylon panties that covered more than necessary, Amanda wondered if Myrna had a computer and Internet connection so she could just order what she needed. But, that would require a credit card, which she left on the forty-second floor of her now burned-out office building; or her social security number for a new one, which was surely being monitored for any activity. Amanda shook her head to rattle those thoughts out of her brain and went back to her hunt for decent underwear.

"Ah-ha, gotcha. You're mine," she said when a pair of thongs emerged from their hiding place behind a pair of control top hose.

After marking off the foundations of her new wardrobe from her shopping list, Amanda moved over to the clothing section. She applauded the marketing person behind the idea that a somewhat famous designer should partner with the discount retailer. This line of clothing was suitable with simple skirts and pants, light sweaters and knit tops. The search for a good pair of jeans, however, was as frustrating as the search for underwear. With one pair of jeans in her size left from the somewhat famous designer's line, she clung to them like a security blanket, fearing that someone would steal them from her shopping cart if she turned her back. The other options available used words like "tummy tuck" and "behind lifter" on the tags. It didn't matter that no one here knew her; her vanity followed her across state lines.

It had been a long time since Amanda last saw her natural hair color. This was something she could do; something she had to do. Using a mirror to examine her roots, she tried to determine if she was a natural light brown, or was she natural light neutral brown. Under the fluorescent lights of the retailer, they all looked the same to her. What about natural medium neutral brown? Or, maybe some of the more exotic-sounding colors, like tawny breeze, or bronze sunset? Why not take it to the extreme and just go for fire-house red? Frustrated at too many options, Amanda went back to the basic browns, closed her eyes and tossed one in the overflowing shopping cart.

She approached the checkout line at the same time as Myrna. The wheels on her shopping cart locked up, forcing Amanda to scoot the cart across the linoleum floors with a screech.

"Oh my, Mandy," Myrna said, digging through her full shopping cart. "You sure do know how to shop."

Myrna checked out first so she could pull the car up and more easily her load her loot curbside. The overly chatty checker made a comment about everything she scanned.

"Did a tornado get you?" the clerk asked.

"Airline lost my luggage," Amanda quipped.

After paying the bill with the cash stashed in her jeans pocket, Amanda scooted the non-rolling shopping cart out the automatic doors to Myrna's waiting Buick. She packed the trunk and backseat with her bags, and realized that Myrna made the trip for only a gallon of milk.

"Mandy, can I help you get all this upstairs?"

"That's okay, I could use the exercise," Amanda answered. She craved a bit of privacy after spending so many days in the company of strangers on the bus, but didn't want to hurt her new landlady's feelings.

Carefully removing the tags from her clothes and hanging them on the plastic hangers reminded her of back-to-school shopping. The excitement that she felt as a child with the fresh start of a new year of school was nothing compared to the feeling for a fresh start to a new life. Even though the clothes were nothing like those from her previous life, she stroked the simple tweed of a black skirt with love as she coordinated it with a light chiffon shirt and a pair of faux crocodile pumps.

Myrna invited her to have an early supper that evening, but Amanda politely declined, citing her exhaustion from the trip and an eagerness to get to bed early; which was partially true, but she really wanted to complete her make-under before she lost her nerve. After reading the instructions three times, she finally felt confident enough that she could color her hair without disastrous results.

She studied the back of her hair through the reflection of a small hand mirror.

"Boring, could use some highlights," Amanda critiqued her work. "But it looks natural."

When she turned to examine the hairs framing her face, she marveled at how the years reversed. The soft brown hair warmed her skin tone, and her light hazel eyes seemed more at home. She was no longer staring at the reflection of Amanda Martin, business-woman extraordinaire, but Mandy Martin. No, Mandy Jackson. All that determination, self-assurance and ruthless ambition was concealed by the natural medium neutral brown hair color. *Maybe there was something behind blond ambition.*

The cut on her temple stood out like a gaping wound. With a deep breath to steady her hands, Amanda lifted a section of her hair and carefully cut a layer of bangs. The fringe fell against her fore-head, covering the scab and further masking the woman staring back at her.

When she climbed into bed at an hour she'd normally sit down to dinner with Josh, her body succumbed to sleep faster than she anticipated. When her eyes opened twelve hours later, Amanda marveled at the softness in her muscles, and her face felt loose and refreshed. The reflection in her bathroom mirror displayed no dark circles under her eyes and skin that glowed as if freshly scrubbed. Amazing what sleep could accomplish.

"Child, I could swear you were a blond when you showed up on my front lawn," Myrna said after eyeing Amanda over breakfast. Slipping back into brown hair was like putting on her favorite coat for the first cold spell of the season; it was warm and enveloping and felt like time never lapsed.

"Tell me about Phoenix. What is there to do around here?" she asked, pouring a second cup of coffee and refreshing Myrna's.

"We're a sleepy little town here, mostly farming and ranching out in these parts," Myrna said. "There's not much in the form of entertainment either. But there is Riley's, a bar just south of the square on the banks of the river. Anytime something happens, everyone gathers there."

After a very brief geography lesson, Amanda decided to fill her day with getting acquainted with her new town.

It took her only a few minutes to make her way to the town square. The mix of store fronts gave a better explanation of the town than Myrna ever could. A law office snuggled between a hardware store and a feed store. A video store advertised a special tanning package, indicating that one could get a deep tan and rent the latest Tom Cruise movie simultaneously. The menu of the Tex-Mex restaurant was brief, but the crowd inside suggested the chef perfected those few items.

A "Help Wanted" sign on the door of one store front caught her attention. Amanda took a step back to get a better view of the faded letters on the dirty windows. The *Phoenix Talon*. *Guess if I'm going to stick around, I should get a job. This would be better than working as a cashier.*

A chime sang when she pushed the warped wood door. The front room was dingy with an old metal desk covered with plastic wood that flaked from one corner. The desk chair behind it looked older than she was, and a big rip across the seat exposed the beige padding. The office smelled musty and piles of newspaper sat as high as the ceiling. The old clock on the wall revealed it was forever three thirty. Directly behind the reception area was a workroom in an equal state of disarray. To the right sat an office. Amanda peeked in and saw the nameplate on the desk claiming that it belonged to Frank Diamond. But there was no Frank.

"Hello? Anyone here?" she called out, hoping the newspaper was still in print. "Or, did I add breaking and entering to my list of crimes?" she added under her breath.

A toilet flushed and a door to the left opened. A tall man with a large belly and stick skinny legs came out with a newspaper under his arm. His disproportionate frame reminded her of a horse. He stopped just outside the bathroom door to tuck the shirttails into his too tight black pants. Once he got his shirt tucked in, he acknowledged Amanda's presence.

"I'm here about the job," Amanda said, motioning to the help wanted sign.

"What job?"

"The help wanted sign on the door? Do you still need any help?"

The man swayed slightly. Amanda worried he would topple over.

"Who said I needed help?"

Amanda explained one more time about the sign on the door. If he was going to argue with her again, she was prepared to just walk out and find some other way to make money.

"Look, I have a journalism degree, you have a newspaper. I thought I could be of some assistance."

"Oh," he said, her words finally making sense. "That sign. Frank Diamond," he offered a thick paw and Amanda softly took it, hoping he washed his hands.

"Mandy Jackson, nice to meet you."

"Have a seat," he pointed to a beat-up Naugahyde chair across from his desk. "Anything to drink?" He pulled the top off a whiskey bottle and a snifter out of a desk drawer.

Amanda shook her head at the offer. *I know it's five o'clock somewhere, but still ...* "So tell me, what kind of help are you looking for?"

"I've had that sign up so long I damn near forgot," Frank took a long draw of whiskey. "Well, first and foremost I need an office manager, and I need someone to help put the paper together. You said you're a reporter?"

He poured another drink, nearly running the alcohol over the edge of the snifter.

"Yeah," Amanda said, guessing that someone who downed two snifters, at least, of whiskey at work wouldn't do a background check.

"I'm afraid you won't have much opportunity for any serious reporting because not a damn thing goes on around here. Most of the paper is made up of wire reports anyway, stuff any of the idiots around here could find on that Internet if they were smart enough to use it. You'd also do the police blotter and write obits. Probably the most exciting thing that happens is when someone dies."

"Okay, I can do that," Amanda answered, relieved this seemed to be a pretty low-profile job.

His cheeks expanded with a burp. "Although," he said. He leaned his chair back, lacing his fingers behind his head to reveal yellow sweat rings under his arms. Rocking back and forth for a minute, Amanda saw that far off look of contemplation. "I bet I could charge more for advertising if I have an honest-to-God reporter working for me." He poured himself a third drink and seemed to forget Amanda sat in front of him. "Some of these assholes have been paying the same thing for a decade," he said more to himself than to Amanda.

"I can do reporting, too," Amanda said, hoping to remind the man that she was still sitting there.

"Well, in that case, the pay is two hundred-fifty dollars a week." Frank started sweating, and Amanda stopped herself from wrinkling her nose at the smell of whiskey coming out of his pores.

"Understood, and I want to be paid in cash."

"Suit yourself. That works for me; I can keep Uncle Sam out of it if you know what I mean. But, you better not go blabbing to any accountant, you hear? I got enough trouble with three ex-wives all with their hands out."

"Deal," she agreed. "So, when do I start?"

"How's tomorrow morning? Hours are nine to five, nine to six if you want to take an hour to leave for lunch."

"Fine. So, who else works here?" Amanda asked as she stood to leave.

"Just me and you, sweetheart," Frank said with a smile. Like his legs, his bridge of teeth was better suited for a horse than a man.

She was disappointed when she arrived home eager to share the news of her employment only to find Myrna's car gone. Instead of locking herself away in the apartment, she opted to lie on her stomach on the riverbank and enjoy the beautiful day.

Everything around her was still and quiet. She closed her eyes and just listened. She heard the laughter of children playing after school. The occasional car passed over the bridge. Dogs barked playfully somewhere nearby. The leaves of the tree rustled above her as a cool, gentle breeze blew her hair off her cheek. She never heard a car horn, an airplane overhead, people shouting or a cell phone ring. The loss of these sounds that were so much a part of her life in Chicago frightened her a little. Could she be still long enough to enjoy living here? For the first time in days, she yearned for her lost BlackBerry. The device tethered her to Josh and to her career. Its loss cut the umbilical cord to her old life, and her emergence from that bus outside of Phoenix made her feel like a newborn eager to take in a whole new world. The desire for her BlackBerry was just one of the many growing pains she would have to conquer.

11

Alex spent the remainder of his weekend working up the nerve to touch the white business card guarding his computer. By the time he made it back to his apartment, his patriotism and resolve had waned, and his self-loathing and doubt grew. Every time Alex reached for Roland's business card, he recoiled. A force field seemed to plant itself around the rectangular square.

He skulked into the office Monday morning; his head looking down registered only the shoes of his colleagues instead of their faces. Alex lumbered into his cube, and Dennis offered a curt greeting. Alex nodded his response. With his computer fired up, he checked email and launched into his tasks for the day.

"I'm going to lunch," Dennis said. *No invitation for me*, Alex noted.

Alex grudgingly pulled out the peanut butter sandwich he brought. The rest of his team still worked on the case. He could hear their voices in the conference room and picked up snippets of conversation from the other side of his cube. He was never invited to join them.

Alex ate his sandwich alone at his desk, spending the time checking baseball scores. The office was quiet; no phones rang, printers remained silent and conversations were strangely muted. Alex didn't feel like completing any of the tasks on his to-do list. He drummed his fingers on his keyboard, not striking hard enough to create any words, just to create the illusion that he was hard at work. He felt dejected, uninspired and bored.

Mid-afternoon an email came in from Harrison.

Alex,

Why don't you make sure all of your information is up to date in the JW1 case file. We're going to move that one to suspended status by the end of the month and need to make sure that all information is current. Thanks.

Alex stood up and walked towards the men's room craning his neck to see if Harrison's door was open. It wasn't. The men's room was empty; he leaned his back against the wall and closed his eyes. Indictments against the three people were just going to sit there like a cup of ignored coffee, growing cold and eventually moldy while his agency did nothing about it.

"This is it," he whispered. "I'm never going to be promoted to investigator. I'm never going to get married. I'll never get to coach my future son's Little League team. That's it. My life is over."

Alex hadn't felt this despondent since his father died. The same light-headed feeling combined with an overwhelming desire to be sick - the familiar and distinct feeling of the end. Standing on a cliff, he could step in either direction and guarantee a change in his life forever. He could choose to move forward, and face whatever hit him as he fell towards it. Or, he could step back to the world he knew and just be satisfied.

He stood there alone in the bathroom, on the edge, unsure of what else to do with his life. All he knew was wrapped around this dying career at the SEC. What would he do now? He thought about applying to the police academy. He thought about starting his own business. He thought about just going home and never leaving his tiny apartment again. One of his father's favorite sayings ran through his mind, "Life doesn't just happen, you make it happen." But ultimately, the step he made was back to his cube, back to the life he knew, back to what was safe.

He thought about his response to Harrison's email. *Sure, sir, what-*

ever it takes, sir. I would be happy to do the best job I can, sir. You can count on me, sir. I am your loyal whipping boy, you may kick me in the gut, but just like that mangy mutt that follows you around, I'll come back wagging my tail, sir. He opted for brevity instead.

Sure thing, Mr. Harrison. Whatever you need. Please let me know what else I can do.

Alex

Thanks. That was the response he got. Nothing more. *Thanks.* Harrison didn't even have the courtesy to give Alex the more formal "thank you." It was just "thanks."

Rather than go home each night that week, he went back to the same bar he visited on that fateful night. Each night, he sat at the same stool, ordered the same beer and cheese fries from the same bartender in hopes of recreating whatever voodoo it was that made Roland Burrows appear by his side. No such luck.

The old bartender knew his name, drink and routine well enough to have his order of cheese fries placed before he walked in. Unlike the first night, he managed to stop at two beers. If it worked and Roland Burrows showed up again, he wanted to remain sober so he could have his wits about him.

Each night when he got home, he sat on the edge of his futon and stared at the white card, still lodged between the Q and A rows on his open laptop. He never woke his computer from its hibernation. He never touched the card. Instead, he watched it and wondered if it was real, waiting for a sign.

"Why don't you just call him?" the elderly bartender asked on Alex's seventh night of vigil.

Alex raised his eyebrows. "What do you mean?"

"I mean that it's obvious you are looking for that British guy. He gave you his card, just call him."

Alex didn't respond. Instead, he stopped at one beer and left his money on the bar now that he'd memorized the cost of his tab.

When he got home, he reassumed his position on the edge of his futon, staring at the card. If he called Roland, he wouldn't be able to undo it. He wouldn't be able to change his mind. He knew that once he opened this door, he would essentially slam the door on his career. That was evident from the countless times he played the possible scenario in his head. Calling Roland for help would mean that he would breach confidentiality at the agency. He tried to determine if his actions would be deemed illegal, but as far as he could tell, they would just be unethical and grounds for dismissal. But it didn't matter to him. In his mind, he had already been dismissed.

Alex looked at his alarm clock. It was after eight. He crossed his small apartment, and in the first time for more than a week, he touched the white card on his computer. Holding it in his hands, he worked up the nerve to dial the numbers listed. He had no intention to leave a voicemail or speak to someone. This was simply preparation; practice dialing the numbers; maybe even rehearse saying what he had written on his legal pad. But instead of a dress rehearsal, he ended up being center stage in front of a live audience.

"Roland Burrows," the voice came through his phone. Alex held his breath. Surely, this was just a voicemail system answering. He waited for the beep, but instead of a beep, he was met with, "Hello?"

Alex exhaled. Show time.

12

A rriving for her first day at the *Phoenix Talon* a half hour
early, Amanda hoped to make a good impression on
Frank. The front door was locked. She peered through the
front window, her hand hovering inches from the dirty glass. No
Frank. From her limited interaction, she suspected he was sleeping
one off. She plopped on the park bench and debated whether it
would be more effective to just go home and never come back or
leave a note to tell Frank she quit. Amanda jumped up from the
bench, ready for a fight when she saw him turn the corner and slink
over to the door of the *Talon* an hour-and-a-half later.

"Did you forget I was starting today?" Amanda said.

"Who the hell are you?" Frank growled, slurring the last word.
His white button-up shirt was crumpled, the right side of it barely
tucked in, and his black hair was equally pasted to his forehead and
standing up in the back.

"Mandy Jackson. You hired me yesterday morning. You told me
to start today. I've been sitting here for more than an hour. You
don't remember any of that?"

"Oh yeah, Mandy, my new ace journalist. Welcome to the

Phoenix Talon," Frank said, the sour smell of whiskey wafting from his mouth.

He fidgeted with the keys once more and the door unlocked. Without another word, Frank walked into his office and closed the door behind him. Amanda stood there, mouth agape. After waiting for him to reappear for several minutes, she collapsed into the ripped-up chair behind the front desk. A plume of dust filled the air from the beige stuffing. Amanda shot up, cringing at the thought of what could be living in the chair.

"I so don't need this job," she mumbled to herself and dusted off her bottom. She peered in the room behind her and found an old metal folding chair leaned against the wall. It wouldn't be comfortable, but at least she wouldn't have to worry about sitting on decade-old dust mites. She took a minute to explore the back work-room. A large table full of paper scraps, pica rulers and paste sat in the middle of the room. An ancient computer from the nineties took up a corner of the bench with a very non-ergonomically-correct bar stool perched in front of it. Another room jutted off the side of the workroom with tall metal racks lining the walls as well as two that stood as islands in the middle of the room. She walked down an aisle and saw they were lined with hundreds of archived newspaper issues. The first two rows were in perfect order with every issue neatly arranged. As Amanda continued to walk among the shelves, she realized that the more recent dates were in complete disarray.

While thumbing through some of the papers, she heard the door to Frank's office open and, seconds later, the bathroom door shut. Amanda sighed; there would be no *Phoenix Talon* 101 for her. Frank's office door was open and a large pot of coffee sat on a table across from his desk. She hoped he sobered up by deadline, when-ever that was. The toilet flushed and Frank emerged, shirttails untucked.

"Frank, sorry to bother you, but is there something I should be doing?" Amanda made no effort to hide her sarcasm.

Frank stopped and looked at her with his head cocked to one side. "Well, shouldn't you be putting a newspaper together? Dead-line is in...," he stopped and closed an eye to look at his watch.

"Deadline is in five hours." He walked back into his office and slammed the door shut.

Amanda shook with fury. *If Frank isn't going to tell me how to do my job, then I have no reason to work. Passive aggressive behavior is my specialty.* She propped her feet up on the flaking corner of the desk and perused the previous issue of the *Talon* in hopes of finding another job in the anemic classified section. At a quarter to noon, the door chimed and Amanda found Dugan wearing an impeccable blue and white seersucker suit with a brown lunch bag clutched in his hand.

"Good morning, my dear Mandy. How are you? Myrna worried that you didn't have anything to eat for lunch and asked me to come by with some morsels and to see how you are getting on during your first day on the job."

"Well…" Amanda didn't want to disparage her boss on the first day, but her eyes wandered over to his closed door. When she looked back at the smiling Irishman, the anger she withheld all day came rushing forth. "It would be a lot better if my boss would sober up long enough to give me some direction. I don't know the first thing about how he puts the paper together. I'm supposed to do the police blotter and obits, and forget local reporting because I don't know jack about this town. I don't want the advertisers mad because their ads aren't in the right place, or worse, there's no paper tomorrow."

"Don't worry, my dear, there will be a paper tomorrow and everything will be perfectly fine," he said, that same serene smile crossing his lips.

Dugan's Yoda-like cryptic musings only amplified her frustration. "Dugan, please don't take this personally, but how in the world can you possibly know that everything is going to be fine? My deadline is in four hours, and I don't even know where to begin. So unless you know where the owner's manual is for this place, then no, things will not be fine."

There, she did it. She had the temper tantrum that had been brewing in her all day. Her words hung in the air; Amanda had no choice but to pick some nonexistent lint off her new pants.

"I know that everything will be fine because Henry comes in at three to lay everything out and the advertisers haven't changed in years, so the paper is always the same," he said, not addressing her tantrum.

"Oh. But, Frank said that it was just the two of us working here." Who was this Henry? She didn't realize that another employee of the paper was coming to her rescue in a mere three hours.

"Well, Henry isn't an official employee. He owns the printing company in town and lays out the paper in trade for free advertising. Perhaps that computer is still functional," he said, his head nodded towards the archaic machine. "I must be on my way. Enjoy your lunch. I will stop by Henry's shop to request he come early to help acquaint you with the paper."

The old computer did work, and even more surprising was the revelation that it had a dial-up Internet connection. Fifteen minutes later, Amanda was on the Web researching content for the *Talon*. The news headlines mocked her. Everywhere she clicked, Chicago. She jammed down the scroll button every time she saw something that had to do with the financial world, Chicago or even guns. As she surfed, she bookmarked only happy stories: stories of survival, stories of reunions and stories of success. The only story that did not fall within that category was one of an automobile recall, which Amanda included out of obligation to the citizens of Phoenix. She worried if the one person in the city had that model of car and the brakes stuck, their death would be on her hands. *I can't take any more chances.*

Myrna's Buick was gone when she arrived home stressed from barely making deadline and feeling more alone than ever. She sat down in the grass and watched the river float by in the fading sunlight, wondering what to do with her evening. No cars passed over the bridge. No voices in the distance. It was just Amanda, the river and the great old oak tree.

When Amanda realized she was alone, she let her loneliness sweep over her. Like an abandoned schoolgirl on the playground, she tucked her knees to her chest and rested her head across her forearms. Her face relaxed and with it, so did the hold on her tears. The sobbing grew into hiccups as the grass below turned into a green blur through her tears. A breeze lifted the sounds of her sobs to merge with the bubbling river and the gentle whirring of the leaves. Images of her parents floated in front of her closed eyes. It had been months since she last saw her parents. Even though they lived in the same city, she'd never made the time to visit despite their pleading. She was always busy.

God, my parents. They have to be worried sick, but what can I do? The SEC is probably watching them. If I call, they would find me, or draw Mom and Dad into my mess. If I sent a letter, they could intercept it, trace the post-mark and find me. Same with email. I wasted so much time with Josh.

Josh. Her shoulders shook with anger as she pulled up handfuls of St. Augustine and threw them at the river.

"Damn you, Josh," her scream was drowned out by a passing truck.

Fresh tears came with his name. But why? Leaving her to face indictment alone was a pretty clear message that he didn't love her. But did she love him? What was their love? A mutual appreciation for success? Convenience? Empty acts and an even emptier bed?

This time last week, Amanda was a strong, confident woman. She was secure in her job and satisfied with her relationship. But both were complete fabrications, falsehoods of faith.

"I should just turn myself in," she said aloud. "How bad could it be? I didn't steal the money, Josh and Keith did."

Sure, she probably should have asked more questions about the financial statements and press releases she issued, but she trusted Josh. He was the CFO; he should have known what he was talking about. And, he did. He knew his actions were illegal, that's why he bolted out of town just before everything surfaced. *Dammit Josh.* She pulled up more of Myrna's perfect lawn. With the two primary suspects missing and the majority of her office dead, Amanda knew that the brunt of the punishment would fall on her. Liz said so, she would be made an example, she would be given jail time to show others that they can't steal other people's money, or lie about the stability of a firm. The families of those affected, both who lost their investments and lost their lives, would come after her.

Just when she thought her well of tears was dry, fresh droplets found their way out of her eyes. She couldn't go back. It was just too much; it would be better if everyone, including her parents, thought she were dead.

The sun dipped behind Myrna's house and cast a heavy shadow across the lawn. The spring air was nippy and Amanda rubbed the goose bumps on her bare arms. Lights popped on in the houses across the bank, and frogs croaked along the riverbed. Her stomach grumbled, but she wouldn't let herself move until she came up with a plan. Another day couldn't pass without some sort of idea of what the future would hold for her.

If Josh was indeed in El Paso, he had at least four days on her. There was always the possibility that it wasn't his final destination. She didn't see what information the other pieces of paper held before he came into his office, but there was a very real chance he continued on somewhere else. If he traveled with his own passport, he'd be sitting in jail right now. But he operated ten steps in front of everyone else, so in all likelihood he traveled under the guise of someone else.

Only she could find Josh. Only she knew his habits and proclivities. She owed it to so many people. El Paso sat half a state away, but sitting in a quiet backyard, Amanda's resolve to chase after her ex waned like the fading daylight. She needed money, access to documents and, most importantly, she needed to think about where he was going.

Phoenix was a good place to rest, but like a shark in the ocean, she had to keep moving or fear dying.

13

"You're late," Frank said gruffly, leaning forward on his desk so he could catch her eye when she walked in the door.

"I-I, I'm sorry," she stuttered, caught off guard.

Amanda allowed herself to sleep in a little bit the next morning. Knowing that Frank wouldn't be there on time, she felt no need to hurry through her morning ritual. She helped herself to Myrna's paper on the driveway and enjoyed her first pass at the *Talon* over cold cereal and coffee.

The day was just as pretty as the previous, and she took pleasure in her leisurely stroll through the streets of Phoenix. When she arrived at the *Talon* office at nine-fifteen, the Frank from yesterday was gone and this one was more intent on the work ahead of them. He came out of his office without acknowledging her apology.

Frank had cleaned up considerably overnight. His too-dark hair was combed back and his standard uniform of black pants and a white button-up shirt were neat and tidy. He walked into the front office with a copy of the morning's paper and tossed it on Amanda's desk.

"Not a bad first effort, but please explain to me how an automobile recall made the front page."

"This company is recalling one hundred thousand vehicles because of bad brakes. Don't you think there are some people in Phoenix who need to know that?" Amanda explained, holding her ground.

"I guess if it was an American-made car company, but that's a foreign car company and more people here drive American cars. You need to do a better job of knowing your audience."

Amanda felt her face get hot. She opened her mouth to argue further, but decided she should pick her battles with Frank, and this wasn't one worth pursuing.

"A fax came in from the funeral home this morning for an obituary. You need to take that, type it in and make sure the facts are correct. I don't want pissed-off, grieving family members calling me because you got something wrong. Also, you need to go introduce yourself over at the police station as the new contact for the crime blotter. Shouldn't be much to write on that beat, nothing happens here except for some snot-nosed brats making mischief, but we are coming to the end of the school year and the kids get bored and raise hell around here during the summer," Frank rattled off his instructions for the day before picking up the paper he tossed on Amanda's desk and heading into the bathroom.

Amanda booted up the old computer and pulled the paper off the fax machine tray, reading over what the funeral director sent while the computer clicked and wheezed itself alive. An elderly woman who once lived in Phoenix passed away in a nursing home in Abilene at the admirable age of ninety-seven. All the information was there, Amanda just needed to type it in and call the funeral home to make sure she didn't miss anything.

The old computer took longer slogging to life. Amanda set the fax next to the keyboard, grabbed a reporter's notebook and headed for the police station. She left a note on Frank's door to let him know where she was.

Amanda crossed the street to walk in front of the old courthouse. Several crepe myrtles stood around the perimeter of the courthouse grounds, small fuchsia-colored buds dotting the end of each limb. She could only imagine how beautiful this courthouse would look once those buds were in full bloom.

The police station sat directly across the street from a small volunteer fire station, most likely out of convenience rather than urban planning. A sickly clean smell hit her as she walked in the door. She stood there for a second wondering if someone would greet her. The station was quiet except for the occasional buzz of a radio. She walked down the short hall and found a woman reading a *TV Guide* while monitoring a switchboard with several phone lines and a radio.

Amanda cleared her throat to get the woman's attention, but it wasn't audible over the buzz of the radio. "Excuse me," she said, a little louder than she had planned.

The woman barely lifted her eyes from her magazine.

"Hi, I'm Mandy Jackson. I work at the paper, and Frank Diamond wanted me to come down here and introduce myself to you for the crime blotter."

The woman continued to barely register her existence.

"So, here I am," Amanda added, nervously.

"You need to speak with Captain Stephens, and he's out patrolling right now," the woman answered her while turning a page. "He'll be back after lunch, you should come back then."

Just then, one of the phone lines lit up, and the woman spoke into the microphone on her headset without putting down the magazine.

"9-1-1 what's your emergency? Oh, hi Bob, how you doing? I'm just fine, yep, pretty quiet day here as usual. The Whites' cattle are out again? Any on the highway? Okay, I'll alert the boys to slow down traffic and call the Whites to round them up. Thanks, Bob, appreciate. Alright, you tell Peggy I said hi."

Amanda realized her conversation with the woman was over and headed down the hall when she heard her on the radio.

"Hey ya'll, the Whites' cattle are out again, and this time they are headed out towards the highway. You boys need to go slow that traffic before someone gets a heifer to the windshield."

That afternoon, Frank had Amanda pull more stories than they had room for so he could review them all and determine which should be the lead story. His micromanaging was aggravating, but she decided to make an effort to learn his preferences to keep him off her back. After reviewing stories of the day, he handed her the Ag teacher's farm report and asked her to clean it up and type it into the computer. The teacher wrote in longhand and, between his horrible handwriting and even worse grammar and spelling, it took nearly an hour to decipher his one-page report.

The day stayed beautiful, and she decided to do something she hadn't done in a very long time: go for a run. In college and in her early days at JWI, she spent the whole day in anticipation of her evening runs along the lake. There was something soothing about thinking only of putting one foot in front of the other.

The sun was about an hour from setting when she took off for her jog, just long enough to hit a few streets and still make it home before the sun went down. Her first few paces resulted in a wobbly start, her ankles unused to new terrain. Then, muscle memory set in, and she quickly hit her stride. A brief encounter with side stitches forced her to walk a block, but she felt better when her legs were moving, not worse.

Listening to the sound of locusts in the treetops cleared her head, and she focused on her rhythmic breath. *Two breaths in, one breath out,* she hummed in her mind. A figure a block and a half in front of her brought her out of her reverie. Like her, he jogged in the same direction. Amanda thought she was dressed appropriately in sweatshirt and shorts with the slight chill in the air, but he was wearing shorts and a t-shirt with the sleeves cut off. She admired how the muscles in his back moved as his arms pumped, and she tried to mimic his strong arm movements. It made her move faster, but also made her tire.

The runner turned left down a street and Amanda sped up so she wouldn't lose him, again pumping her arms as he did. Turning left, she saw he was heading straight. Her eyes darted from his back, and she noticed he ran with a slight limp because of a heavy knee brace on his right leg. Even with this piece of hardware, the man continued to run with a good pace and Amanda challenged herself to keep up with him. She continued on, running behind him and turning where he turned while the sky darkened, not paying attention to where she was headed. He took another turn down a rock covered road flanked by pastures dotted with a few grazing cattle. Without thinking about anything but his back muscles, Amanda followed him.

She pulled herself out of her tunnel vision to realize that this wasn't a road, but a driveway with a house at the end and an old Ford truck parked in front. The man continued running, oblivious to his tail. Amanda stopped dead. Afraid of being discovered, she turned and sprinted as fast as she could back down the darkening road, gracefully hurdling potholes and large rocks. She turned left when she got back to the main road and stole a glimpse down the driveway. Even in the waning light, Amanda could see the man standing in front of his house with a water bottle, watching her escape.

The next day reminded Amanda of her age. Parts of her body not even used for running ached. No matter how much it hurt, she speed-walked to work. *I've got to get a car. I wonder if the classifieds have anything decent.* When she arrived, Frank was nowhere to be found. Twenty minutes later, he rounded the corner whistling a Beatles tune.

"Mandy!" he greeted her in a boisterous voice. "Have you been waiting long? I'm so sorry about that. I'll get you a key so you don't have to wait for me."

Once again, he was dressed in his usual outfit, but instead of the gruff taskmaster, he was the friendly boss. In three days of working for Frank, she had seen at least that many personalities.

Frank invited her into his office so they could strategize the remaining week's issues over coffee. The *Talon* printed Friday and Sunday editions, but no Saturday or Monday, he explained. The Sunday edition was only slightly larger than the average weekday issue, and it would be sent to press on Friday.

"I'm a fan of getting an early start to the weekend, so if we can work together on getting the Sunday paper to bed early, then we can head over to Riley's to celebrate the end of your first week. My treat," he said.

"Thanks, Frank, I appreciate that."

After spending the rest of the morning huddled up talking about the types of stories she would need to find, she excused herself to spend some time becoming familiar with Phoenix. With her reporter's notebook in hand, she scribbled businesses to feature and took down the names of people she met. On a street parallel to the square, she discovered a decrepit bookstore that she wasn't convinced was still in business. She made a note to talk to the proprietor about book reviews for the paper.

Frank was true to his promise on Friday, and after they put the Sunday paper to bed, he locked up the front doors. Riley's on the River was south of the town square and had a back deck that looked out over the Tejas River.

"I'll give you a lift over to Riley's," Frank said, motioning for Amanda to follow him around the side of the building.

"It's only two blocks, right? Wouldn't it be just as easy to walk?"

"You could say that, but I'd rather have my car at the bar than have to walk back here later." Amanda thought it would be better the other way around, but she didn't want to argue away his good mood.

Only a few tables of men dotted the bar, and the Texas Rangers game took precedence over any conversation. Frank opened the door and walked in, leaving Amanda to follow behind him. He went straight to a table and waved at a man behind the bar.

"Hey Eddie, two Miller Lites," he said, ordering for Amanda. Eddie brought over the beers and Frank offered the neck of his to toast to the end of the week.

Amanda was a little apprehensive about having drinks with Frank. She wasn't sure what they would talk about outside of work. But, her worries were pushed aside when it became obvious that Frank was more interested in the baseball game than conversing with his employee.

"You a baseball fan, Jackson?"

"Huge fan. I went to games with my dad all the time as a kid," she said, thinking that a little bit of truth couldn't hurt.

The baseball game finished up just as the after-work crowd settled its tabs to let the evening crew come in to close down the little bar. Frank had switched to something stronger than beer during the seventh-inning stretch, but Amanda stuck with beer, taking modest drinks. Nevertheless, she felt somewhat buzzed.

As the bar filled, Frank glad-handed other patrons. On the occasion he remembered his employee, he introduced Amanda. But, as the night continued and the more he drank, the introductions were fewer and far between.

Amanda enjoyed the company of others, even if they were total strangers. Without saying anything to Frank, she headed to the back patio for some fresh air. The outside deck was only half full with a few smokers fogging the air and a small cluster of guys chatting. She found an empty spot against the rail and leaned over, looking down at the inky black water swirling below her. The swift moving river and beer in her stomach gave her an odd feeling of vertigo, causing her to sway.

"Whoa, steady there," a voice spoke in her ear as a hand cupped her elbow. "Trust me; you don't want to go swimming in the Tejas. Too many water moccasins."

Amanda looked up. The last time she saw his face was in the near-dark as she escaped her accidental stalking during her run. He was taller than she realized and was even more handsome up close than from a block and a half away. She wanted to say something pithy, to call him her knight in shining cowboy boots, but before she could speak he led her away from the railing and to a table that just opened up.

"Let's sit you down before I have to jump in and save you."

I would gladly dive in if you'll be the one to give me mouth-to-mouth, she thought, but then shook her head. *What am I thinking? Chances are a guy like this in a town as small as this was already taken, ten times over.*

"I'm David Stephens, by the way," he said, extending his hand as he pulled his chair close to hers. "I heard you were looking for me the other day."

Amanda opened and closed her mouth a few times. Did he see her following him? She thought she made it out of his driveway before he got a good look at her. "Yeah?" she asked, trying to think of something with more syllables to say as she took his hand. "Mandy Jackson."

He smiled and deep dimples dotted his cheeks. "You're the new reporter. You came by the station looking for me the other day?"

Oh, David Stephens, as in Captain Stephens from the police station. He really was a knight in shining armor then. Or, maybe black polyester.

Amanda laughed. "Yes, I did, sorry. I guess I'm still a little dizzy there," she said, which was much more appropriate than saying she was dumbstruck by his dimples. "Frank wanted me to come by and introduce myself for the police blotter. So, hi."

"Hi," he said, still smiling as he took a sip of beer. Amanda knew she was staring, but the alcohol washed away her social graces. Where Josh was Armani good-looking, David was Marlboro Man hot. Not that she thought he smoked. She figured that a guy who could run the pace he ran with a knee brace probably never smoked a cigarette in his life. A metallic taste flooded her mouth at the thought of Josh, as if she were caught cheating.

"You okay? You're looking a bit green. Do you want some water?" David said. Amanda nodded and he walked back inside the bar.

She shouldn't be sitting here enjoying a beer just a week after her colleagues were killed. She should be sitting in jail or lying in a grave. Not flirting with a handsome police officer in a small town in the middle of Texas. What was she doing here? Her flesh pimpled as a sweat broke out. Her blood thumped in her eardrums. Images flooded back to her mind, and her nose filled with sulfuric smoke.

Her eyes avoided the bar as she walked out the front door of Riley's. It was only when she walked up Myrna's front lawn with her pumps in her hand that her breathing steadied and her heart quit drumming in her chest.

14

"Bloody hell that must have been one monster hangover."

Roland pulled a cigarette from a pack inside his leather jacket while seated at a table at Alex's second home, the bar. He half-offered one to Alex, but already had the pack back in his pocket before Alex finished shaking his head.

"Honestly mate, I expected your call the next morning, the way you carried on."

A waitress asked for their orders. Roland said two Scotches as Alex named his beer preference. The waitress raised an eyebrow and continued to stand by their table, as Roland clarified, "Scotch for me; beer for my friend."

Roland tapped the end of his cigarette in the ashtray and leaned back in his chair, one arm draped over the back. Alex fidgeted and tugged at the collar on his shirt. He wasn't ready for this. His finger hovered over the "end" button when he heard Roland say his name. Damn caller ID had betrayed him. He had no choice but to speak and set up a time to meet in person. It was a fleeting thought to call Roland, not a conscious decision. Cell phones should come equipped with a breathalyzer.

"You don't really want to be here, do you?" the Brit said.

Alex laughed and rubbed the five o'clock shadow on his chin. "How did you guess?" The waitress reappeared, and they each went in for a drink. Alex shifted in his chair. The waistband of his chinos cut into his expanding gut. *Back to the gym after tonight*, he promised himself. He'd skipped a week's worth of workouts to meet this man again. Here he was. *I just need to say what I came here to say, then I'll be back to hitting the gym after work instead of the bar.*

"I want all of this to be off the record."

Roland nodded as he took a long drag on his cigarette.

"Mate, I didn't come here for off the record."

Alex stared into his half empty glass of beer. The clear bubbles floating through the amber liquid offered him no advice. Alex drained the last of his beer and motioned at the waitress to order another round for both men. Two sips into his second beer, he leveled with Roland.

"The agency is washing its hands of the case," Alex said.

"What? Did I hear you correctly?"

"Yep, end of the month, it'll be suspended. Without any suspects, there's no case. We don't have the resources to search for them so we're going to wait until they just turn up." As Alex spoke, Roland lost his arrogance and leaned in, listening intently. "Williams and Cooper were gone before the indictments. They knew it was coming. Not Martin. She made no changes to her habits in the days leading up to it."

"She was as surprised as I was that she was even part of it," Roland mumbled under his breath. "I think you are on to something, Alex," he continued. "I caught her off-guard when I called her. She wasn't even in the office yet; I got her on her mobile. And she was quick to hang up; said she would have to call me back. Unusual for Amanda, she was always prepared with an answer. Are we sure that she's not dead or one of the injured? She could have been burned beyond recognition in the fire, or lying in a coma somewhere."

Alex shook his head. "All the dead and injured have been identified. We got confirmation today. She's not one of them. They all ran. Your offer to help, how does that work?"

"Fairly simple mate, we partner together and investigate. You're an analyst, you analyze. I help out with resources when you need them."

Alex thought it sounded too good to be true. "What do you want in return?"

"Exclusivity," Roland said. "Don't tell anyone what we're doing, and let me publish the story when we're done. But, Alex, you can't be off the record."

Alex didn't need time to think about it. His knee bounced under the table, eager to jump into action. This could be an opportunity to cut his investigative teeth. If he could bring just one of the three in to face justice, Harrison would have no choice but to promote him. Or, Alex could even score a job at the FBI once they realized he belonged among their ranks.

"Okay, I'm in," Alex toasted with his half-empty beer.

"Splendid, I knew you would be. First thing Monday I'll make some calls to some of my sources. I think I can get the FBI to call in a couple of favors for us."

Alex nearly choked on his beer.

"The FBI?" Alex said.

"Well yeah, I mean, who else could get us access to passenger manifests and security tapes?" Roland cocked his head slightly and knitted his brow. "Something wrong?"

"It's just, well," Alex didn't know what to say that wouldn't sound like he was whining. "I thought I was going to be the investigator on this case."

Roland exhaled a cloud of smoke over Alex's head.

"Alex, look, I realize how important this is to you, but you need to stop being selfish and understand that if you and I work together as a team, we can bring these people to justice. Now, I could have gone off by myself that night after you were bitching to me about how botched this case is, but I waited for you to call me, didn't I? Now, are you with me or not?"

Alex felt admonished, like a child who soiled his good pants.

"Okay, I'm in. What's our next move?"

15

Sunday morning greeted Amanda with a grumble. Flirting was fun, especially with someone as handsome as David, but she couldn't allow herself to feel anything other than remorse.

She slipped her feet into a pair of flip flops and padded down her wooden stairs for the Sunday edition of the *Talon*. Clouds churned over her head, deep thunder rumbled inside. It wasn't raining yet, but the darkening skies and rising winds promised it would be soon. Myrna's car was gone; already on her way to Sunday school and church. Dressed only in her camisole and pajama shorts, she moved swiftly out of modesty.

Back inside her apartment, she brewed coffee and settled back into bed with the paper. The crossword puzzle she picked for Sunday's paper looked intriguing.

Amanda's concentration broke when the impending storm moved closer. Each flash of lightning seemed brighter than the last, each grumble of thunder louder. The tiny apartment did little to shield her from the storm. She imagined the giant live oak reaching its branches further over her apartment, guarding her like a parent protects a child.

The wind picked up and whistled through microscopic gaps between the wood and windows. A shiver radiated from her core as the air in her apartment took on a breezy chill. She climbed out of the warmth of her bed and refreshed her cup. The whistling grew louder, and the branches of the tree scraped the roof above her head. She went back to her crossword puzzle, perplexed over eight across. *What's a young swan called that starts with a "c"?*

Just as her mind became lost in words, a flare lit up her apartment followed by a crack of thunder. The clashing sound reverberated in her stomach, jostling the consumed coffee and toast. The next flash of lightning found her hugging the toilet in her small bathroom, spilling her breakfast into the bowl. She closed her eyes and images flashed like lightning. A man in a windbreaker jacket with a backpack. His tennis shoes walked over Liz's body as he tossed a grenade like a ball. The gun. All she could see was the gun. More lightning followed by more thunder and it finished with complete darkness and a moment of silence. Amanda hurled again, emptying her stomach, the acidic coffee burned her throat. Lightning flickered and a shadow paced the apartment; a tall shadow. Amanda tried to make herself as small as possible, to wedge herself between the toilet and the shower, but it was too tight. The shadow was going to find her. She counted. *Ten.* Flash of lightning. *Nine.* Heated thunder. *Eight. Seven. Six.* Lightning. *Five.* The heavens cackled at her. *Four. Three.* The branches gnashed against the roof of the apartment, clawing their way in. *Two.* The shadow grew. *One.* Her throat clamped shut.

Something within Amanda sprung to life. *Move, move, he's not looking*, she told herself. Her bare feet slipped on the wet wooden steps. The ground was heavy with water and freshly cut grass clung to her legs. She felt exposed in Myrna's expansive backyard. Relentless rain pierced her skin and eyes. Another rumble boomed above her, and she instinctively knelt down in the grass and covered her head, rain splashed up at her, splattering her thin shorts. Even with her eyes closed, she could see the flickering around her. *Run*, her mind ordered, *run*.

The next boom launched her like a racer at the starting line. She ran down Myrna's driveway toward the road, hurdling some puddles and running straight through others. Her body moved on autopilot, and she took a left at the end of Myrna's street onto the main road. The rain deluged harder, her eyes stung. She ran past Edna's; the parking lot empty and water pooled in ruts from the farm trucks. The road curved to the left and led her back to the highway, forcing her to retrace the same steps that brought her into Phoenix.

Wiping the water from her face, Amanda looked up, hoping to see the skies clearing. Instead, a large gray-green cloud moved quickly from the west, lightning shooting out from it as hail fell from the sky. Amanda picked up the pace, unflinching at the pain in her bare feet.

A piece of hail pelted in the back of her head with such force that she fell, catching herself with her hands on the coarse gravel. The sudden shift in momentum made her stomach lurch again. Pain pierced the back of her skull as she vomited into the rain. Mixed in with the last bit of coffee was blood. It was over. The shadow captured her even though she tried to escape. There was no other choice but surrender. This was how it was going to end, shot by a shadow; she was getting the death she deserved. She stared at the ground, intrigued by the sudden peacefulness that consumed her. A bright light shone over her, and the gray, rain-splattered concrete. She had heard about going towards the light and thought it was only proper that she should stand. Before she could move, she looked up and a man appeared beside her with an umbrella. She didn't expect Saint Peter to carry an umbrella.

"Are you okay?" he yelled over the sound of the rain and the thunder. Her first impulse was to ask Saint Peter why he didn't wear a robe and why, if she was in Heaven, it was still raining so hard. Maybe she wasn't in Heaven.

"Are you hurt? Here, let me help you," the man said and knelt down to help Amanda stand. She looked at his feet, expecting to see sandals but found his nice leather shoes showing signs of water stains. "I'm a doctor, I can help you."

He led Amanda to his black Suburban and opened the back

driver-side door and helped her climb in. She looked at the pristine car, afraid she was going to ruin his seats with her rain-soaked clothes. The man climbed into the driver seat and put the car into gear. He cautiously glanced around before pulling the car onto the road and down the path from where Amanda came.

"I'm sorry about your shoes," she said to the back of his head.

"What's that?" he asked, looking at her from his rearview mirror. All she could see was his bright blue eyes. "I'm Dr. Brown, the doctor here in Phoenix. What's your name?"

Amanda came to her senses. She couldn't give him a fake name, the town was too small and she wagered that he was the only doctor here. Sooner or later, she was going to cross paths with him again. In this case, honesty, or at least some form of it, was going to have to be the best policy.

"Mandy Jackson," she said, shaking from the cold, damp air.

"Nice to meet you, Mandy. I wish I could say it's a nice morning for a jog."

Amanda wanted to respond with a smart comment, but her brain crept along with the conversation, unable to formulate a sentence.

"Are you the new reporter?"

She nodded and studied the back of his head. He was clean-cut, with a good thick mane of brown hair, but it looked like it had been graying for some time. She guessed him to be in his late thirties. "Mandy, was that blood back there on the road?"

"Wait, that's my turn." Amanda ignored his question.

"I'm concerned about you throwing up blood. Let me check you out, and then I'll bring you home."

The black Suburban pulled into a handicap spot outside the red brick clinic. He opened his umbrella for Amanda, not like it would do any good; she shivered from the cold and wrapped her arms protectively around her. She followed him to the front door and waited while he unlocked it. When they walked in, she was hit by both a chill from air conditioning and the sterile smell of a hospital.

"Wait here. I think I've got some scrubs you can change into."

Water pooled on the white tile floor peppered with gray flecks.

The thin pajamas, pregnant with water, clung to her body while rivers of rain slid down her bare legs, leaving goose bumps in its wake.

Dr. Brown rounded the corner back into the lobby. Amanda heard his footsteps stop, and when she looked up from the floor, his eyes floated up her body to her eyes. Acting without embarrassment, he led Amanda past a receptionist counter advertising that payment was due when services were rendered.

"Why don't you get changed before I examine you?" he said without looking at her.

"Look, I appreciate this, but it's really not necessary. I'm afraid of storms, it's that simple. I just had a momentary freak out. I'm all better now," Amanda said. She wanted nothing more than to be home standing under a hot shower.

"I'm sorry, but I'm afraid I can't do that," he said, his voice calm yet firm. "Call it an occupational hazard, but when I see someone in distress and blood on the ground, I have to help."

"Really, I'm fine. Plus, I don't have insurance."

"Never mind that."

"I don't make much money."

"Pay whatever you want."

"You are probably on your way to church. I'm going to make you late."

"Big guy upstairs will understand."

Out of arguments, she closed herself in the bathroom to change. The fluorescent light flickered on, and she saw what he saw—which was everything. The thin, light pink cotton of her camisole clung to her breasts and made no secret of how the chill affected her. The starched cotton scrubs scratched at her skin. She exited the bathroom and found Dr. Brown working the paper's crossword in an examination room.

"Alrightie, hop up on this table," he motioned at an exam table covered by a thin sheet of paper.

Amanda studied a collage picture frame on the wall featuring a pretty blond with a warm smile in the center frame flanked by towheaded twin girls. Dr. Brown caught her looking at the pictures.

"That's my wife Lisa and our two little girls, Emily and Katherine," Dr. Brown rolled his stool towards the examination table. "What were you running from?"

She hoped for the gentle, non-invasive questions that the doctors of her past always asked; the kind of questions mundane enough to not spark any serious discussions.

"I told you, I've been afraid of thunderstorms since I was a kid. This one snuck up on me and I wasn't prepared." This was mostly true, she just didn't tell him about the part where she thought the ghost of the gunman was chasing her.

"How long have you been throwing up blood?"

"That was a first."

He pulled the stethoscope from around his neck and put the earpieces into his ears.

"Just breathe normal," he commanded. "Have you been throwing up much?"

"A little bit over the past couple of weeks," she said.

He nodded.

"Where are you from?" he asked.

"Montana." Simple question, simple answer.

"Ah, big sky country. I've been fly fishing there a few times. Beautiful up there." Damn, this is what she was afraid of, someone who knew the area and would want to engage her in conversation on a place she had never been. She was literally saved by the bell when Dr. Brown's cell phone rang. He grabbed it from the clip on his belt and flipped it open.

"Hello," he said, turning his back to Amanda. "No, no everything is fine. I just had to meet a patient at the clinic. I'll be there soon." He clamped the phone shut and turned back to his patient. "My wife."

After the call, he seemed more intent on wrapping up the exam. Perhaps his wife voiced her concern over her husband skipping church to attend to a dripping wet patient alone in his office. Amanda imagined that later, over pot roast, he would tell his beautiful wife the story of the crazy woman running down a country road in a hailstorm clad only in pajamas.

"Aside from vomiting, do you have any other symptoms? Cough, fever, anything like that?"

Amanda shook her head.

"It sounds to me like you could have an ulcer. I'm going to give you something that should help," he said, softening a bit.

He opened a cabinet and took out three boxes of medicine and put them in a plastic bag. He handed her a pair of surgical slippers to wear outside and another plastic bag for her wet clothes and started turning off lights and closing up his clinic with Amanda close behind.

"Let me give you a ride home," he commanded, opening the front door. "Those slippers won't make it very far with the streets all wet."

The storm had passed, but a drizzle remained. Amanda climbed in the front seat of his Suburban this time.

"Thank you," Amanda smiled at him as he put the car into reverse.

"Mandy, why don't you come back to see me in two weeks so I can see how that ulcer is doing and if we need to try anything else?"

"Dr. Brown, you do practice doctor-patient confidentiality, right? I mean, it's a little embarrassing that an adult can be so afraid of thunderstorms," Amanda said before getting out of the Suburban.

"Of course, you have nothing to worry about. It's between us."

16

Shiloh Garcia cursed in Spanish as her unlit menthol cigarette tapped compulsively on the bar. She narrowed her eyes at the difficult crossword puzzle in the *Talon*. Perched on a barstool on a quiet afternoon at Riley's, she stressed over a clue. This was her ritual, her way to make herself feel a little bit smarter between readying the bar for happy hour and the patrons coming in. Now, instead of feeling smarter, she felt stupid.

"What is a young swan and who really cares anyway?"

Frustrated, she lit the cigarette and exhaled a quick column of smoke.

"Shi, what have I told you? Put that out," her older brother Eddie, the bar manager, ordered. "It makes you look trashy and offends the non-smokers."

"I really don't care," she said, not looking up from the crossword. Eddie walked back to the office without another word.

The bar was quiet. Cooks prepared the evening bar foods, and the busboy took the trash out from the weekend. The jukebox played a quiet theme to a muted baseball game on the television.

She took a long drag of her cigarette; the icy hot smoke of the menthol filled her lungs. Aggravated with the crossword puzzle, she started coloring in the "o's" of all the words on the page. The chime of her cell phone distracted her. Her boyfriend Rex texted to see if he could bring by a buddy from work and drink on her tab that night, which was code for free. Shiloh wasn't in the mood for babysitting Rex that evening, but she shot back a quick "*sí*" and clamped her phone shut. *Might as well add one more thing for Eddie to complain about.*

She moved on from that clue and pondered the next one. The door to the bar opened, but she didn't bother to look up. It was probably just a delivery, even the town alcoholics didn't come in this early. If someone wanted a drink, she wasn't in any hurry to serve them; they should do something other than bother her at work. She felt the newcomer stand in front of her, but she refused to look up and took another drag on her cigarette.

"Cygnet."

"We don't sell that here," she replied.

A chuckle made her look up. The sound of his voice took a moment to reach back into the deepest realm of her memory, one she locked away a decade ago. "That's what four across is, a young swan is called a cygnet," said Clint Brown. She tilted her head to one side, curious as to what would bring the doctor into her bar in the middle of a workday. It was the first time she had seen him in close proximity. *He should shave that ridiculous mustache. It makes him look like he's only pretending to be an adult.*

"Clint. Shouldn't you be wiping noses or something?" Shiloh snubbed out her spent cigarette and pulled another out of the pack. Not that she was a chain smoker; she just disliked Clint enough to want to blow smoke in his face.

"May I?" he asked, reaching for her pack. She shrugged her response. "These things will kill you," he said and released a cloud of smoke over her head. *So much for trying to get rid of him.*

"What do you want?" she asked as she stared down at the cross-word puzzle.

"Vodka tonic," he said. "You really should call me Dr. Brown."

Shiloh rolled her eyes and slammed a glass on the counter and went heavier on the tonic than the vodka. *A weak man deserves a weak drink.*

"That will be five dollars, Dr. Brown. Why don't you go sit over there so I can work on the crossword alone?"

He ignored her suggestion, sipped his drink and finished his cigarette. As much as she tried to ignore him, she could feel his eyes on her.

"What?" Clint didn't just drop by. He was here for a reason.

"What do you mean 'what'?"

"What do you want? Why are you here?"

Clint laughed into his drink. "Can't a man just come into a bar and have a drink?"

"Yes, a man can, but you don't fall into that category. So, what do you want?"

Shiloh felt her temper rise, and she really wanted to hit something. Instead, she pulled a beer out of the freshly stocked cooler and flicked off the top with the bottle opener tucked in the back pocket of her jeans. Clint generally kept his distance from her, which could be considered a small miracle in this town, and Shiloh honored his request by visiting a doctor in the next town on the rare occasion she got sick. *It's coming up on the tenth anniversary. Maybe he's feeling nostalgic, too.*

The crossword puzzle was impossible. She gave up and continued coloring in the blank squares. The three dollars she put in the jukebox was over, and the bar was silent except for the clatter in the kitchen as the cooks prepared for the evening.

"I'm going to tell Frank to quit putting the hard crossword puzzles in the paper," she said, mostly to herself because she had forgotten that Clint was still there. "This is the first time I haven't been able to solve it."

"You should tell that to the new girl," Clint said, draining the last of his vodka tonic. "Can I get another and this time, Shiloh, please put some vodka in it."

She made him another drink, this time overcompensating for the missing vodka of the first drink. The comment about the new girl stuck in her head.

"What new girl?"

Clint watched the silent baseball game. She knew he heard her even if he pretended not to.

"Clint, what new girl?" she asked again.

He turned his attention back to her. He wasn't as handsome as he used to be. She remembered that summer when she was in high school and Clint was home from his first year of medical school. He was too old to be hanging out with a couple of high school girls. Shiloh wondered if she would even recognize her sixteen-year-old self now, the girl she was before Clint entered her life and stole her best friend. Ten years felt like a lifetime to her, and even though everything changed, nothing really did. She was still stuck in Phoenix and Clint had taken over his dad's clinic just as planned. It was the past that stood between them now.

"Actually, that's why I came to see you," he said. "I was on my way to church yesterday morning during that hail storm and found some strange woman sprinting down the road."

"So what? Maybe she was out for a jog and got caught by the storm, have you thought of that?"

"It's not that. She was half naked, for one."

"Lost stripper?"

"She was in her pajamas, with no shoes. But more than that, she was somewhere else in her head. She barely registered that I was standing there when I stopped to help her."

"Okay, that's crazy. Is that what you want to hear? Look, it's going to get busy here soon and unless you want me showing up at your clinic next time I have a yeast infection, I suggest you finish your drink and leave." Shiloh congratulated herself on her bitter tone.

Clint gave a surrendering grimace, threw back the last of his drink and stood.

"Just be on the lookout for her. There's something about her that I don't trust," he said as he pulled a twenty from his wallet and tossed it on the counter.

Shiloh turned her back to ring up his tab and get his change. When she turned again, Clint was already at the door.

"Clint, so what is this mystery woman's name?"

"Mandy Jackson."

"*Dios mio,*" Shiloh mumbled. "*Yo deseo Clint se alejaría.*"

If Clint would move away, I wouldn't have to relive the last night of my best friend's life every time I saw him.

She lit a candle every day in hopes that the killer would be found, but Clint didn't even seem to realize that the tenth anniversary of Katie's murder was quickly approaching.

17

"You wouldn't believe how close I was to organizing a search and rescue for you," David's playful drawl barely registered in Amanda's ears. She was trying to read the faxed obituaries of the weekend's dearly departed when David appeared in the *Talon* office early Monday morning.

Even midway through her fourth cup of coffee, Amanda's thoughts were slow in forming. The hallucination of a gunman in her apartment unnerved her. Never in her life had she felt something that was so real, yet so implausible. Ghosts don't exist. Gunmen don't follow their prey thousands of miles. Or, do they? A thunderstorm can't hurt someone. Can it?

"Oh, um, yeah, sorry about that." That was a pretty weak thing to say to a guy who would have encountered snake-infested waters for her. Then again, Josh said swoon-worthy things to her during their flirtatious stage and look where that got her. "I wasn't feeling well and just wanted to go home."

"You should make it up to me. Maybe buy me a drink one night or something."

Would he be so willing to accept a drink from her knowing that she was crazy? Or worse, that she was a criminal? He's putting himself in harm's way just talking to her. Who knows when she may snap again and think that a ghost is chasing her?

"Look, Captain Stephens."

"David."

"I kinda find it a bit unethical to date my sources. So I appreciate it, but I have to decline."

David chuckled at her. She squeezed her eyes shut and gave her head a slight shake. Guys don't laugh when you blow them off. Did she not say what she thought she just said? Maybe she's even crazier than she thought.

"Who said anything about a date? You need to learn about what goes on around here, so you'll just have to have a drink with me to find out. See you tomorrow night at Riley's."

Before she could protest, a voice radiated from the radio on his shoulder. A woman locked herself out of her car at the grocery store and needed someone to jimmy the lock. With only a quick wave, David left her standing in the lobby wondering if she should have asked Dr. Brown to check her hearing.

While Frank read through the articles she'd compiled, she set off for the bookstore. Amanda wasn't surprised that Frank was clueless that a bookstore resided in Phoenix, and that he had no idea if it were still in business or were just a skeleton of its former self.

Foster's Bookstore occupied a small, old house that looked like it walked right out of the pages of a horror novel. A chain-link fence fortified the house and circled two large sycamore trees that loomed over the property, blocking out the midday sunlight. Grass long gave up hope of populating the front yard and only the hardiest of weeds survived. Amanda smirked as she imagined scary organ music playing in the background and a colony of bats flying out of the dormers.

With her curiosity piqued, Amanda walked up the crumbling path leading to the front door. The shoddy foundation had settled and cracked, causing the space between the porch and the top step to be wider than her pencil skirt would allow. With the help of the surprisingly sturdy railing, she made her way to the front door.

The smell of pulp mingled with cold air when she opened the

door. A gray tabby cat jumped off a stack of books in the front room and weaved through her legs; its silky fur tickled her ankles.

"Hello there. Is this your bookstore?" Amanda knelt to pet the purring cat.

"Can I help you?" a voice came from behind a stack of books.

Startled by the sudden sound of a voice, Amanda jumped up. A slight man in black oval glasses stood in the corner of the room, his brown sweater vest and brown pants camouflaging him against a wall of bookshelves. The bookstore was dark; light had to sneak in from small gaps in the heavy drapes that covered the drafty windows. Everything about this man was gray. His hair had a layer of gray covering it as if dust rained down on him and permanently settled in his hair; his skin was so ashen he seemed to glow. But somehow his eyes stood out in the darkness of this little shop.

"Hi, I'm Mandy Jackson. I'm the new reporter for the *Phoenix Talon*. It's nice to meet you." She offered her hand, but the man only stared as if this customary greeting were completely foreign. "Are you Mr. Foster?"

"I am a Mr. Foster, but not the Mr. Foster on the name of this wilting bookstore," he answered, his body tense and frozen in place. "Why are you here?"

"I wanted to talk to you about a regular book review column for the paper. If you're willing to do it, I bet it would increase your business."

"Why would I want to do that? The literary community in this godforsaken town isn't exactly booming."

That didn't come as a shock. The people in Phoenix were probably more interested in farm trucks and beer than the classics, but she told Frank she could do local reporting. *The harder I work, the less time I have to be crazy.*

"Well, there's the rub," she admitted. "Maybe the literary community isn't thriving because people here think you're closed."

Amanda crossed her arms in front of her, not to appear stubborn or unwavering, but to keep herself from fidgeting. Since she walked in the door, Mr. Foster had not moved his body once. When he did come alive his eyelids fluttered, a movement that on him seemed all-encompassing, as if he were a robot grinding to action.

"You quoted Shakespeare."

"Hamlet, to be exact," she answered, glad that subtle placement of a phrase caught his attention.

"Well, if you're looking for something to write about, you should consider the impending tenth anniversary of Katie Shelton's murder. Best I can tell, the town forgot about her while her murderer walks free."

Murder? In Phoenix? Amanda had serious doubts that this reclusive bookstore owner spoke about something that actually happened and not something he read in a mystery novel. The unexpected comment gave her no time to steady her baffled expression.

"Don't just stand there with your mouth open. It's rude."

Amanda closed her jaw and mumbled an apology.

"Let me make sure I heard you. There's a cold case murder right here in Phoenix? Who was Katie Shelton, and why hasn't her murder been solved?"

The frozen man finally moved from his mannequin state and crossed the uneven floor towards a table of boxes. When he spoke, he didn't look Amanda in the eye; instead his attention focused on emptying the contents into neat stacks.

"Katie was a teenage girl who was brutally murdered. Oh, she was such a pretty girl. An avid reader, too. She loved the classics. A huge Austen fan, and she adored the macabre in Edgar Allen Poe. Katie got literature, in ways that very few people ever do." Amanda wanted to interrupt him, to ask him what a dead girl's reading preferences had to do with her murder, but instead she made a few notes. Sherlock Holmes never dismissed the little details. He thrived on them.

"And it's unsolved because?" Amanda nudged him to get back to the story.

"Well, that's a question for the authorities. Now if you'll excuse me, I must get some books stocked."

Amanda half-heartedly nodded and turned to leave, mulling over the information she just learned. Frank would be ecstatic over the additional circulation as a result of solving this murder. But more importantly, Fate spoke to her. Maybe this was part of the plan. She was meant to get on that bus. That bus was meant to break down just a few miles down the road. She was meant to stumble on this prosaic town and miss her bus. Just as she was meant to wander into this bookstore in hopes of a book review column, only to learn of a mystery suited for one of the novels lining the shelves. Suddenly, her life didn't seem so wasted. Maybe Fate even stretched further back, putting her in Josh's line of fire to launch the chain of events that culminated with her standing in a dark bookstore in a small town discovering her purpose.

The steady porch rail assisted her as she crab-walked down the uneven porch steps. A voice stopped within the clutches of the sycamore's shade.

"Oh, Ms. Jackson," Mr. Foster called her from the barely open front door. "I'll do the book reviews. But promise me you will find out who killed Katie. That's the only way the poor girl's story could come to a close."

She nodded, stepping out from under the canopy of the trees as the sun warmed her face. Out of darkness comes light.

18

A manda didn't know what to expect while perusing the archives of the *Talon*'s library. She would have been less shocked to find something living among the stacks of faded newsprint than when she found the issues from Katie's disappearance and murder.

A pretty teenage girl smiled up at Amanda from the front page. The story was important enough for Frank to spend precious money on color ink rather than the standard black and white. The girl was tan, her hair sun-bleached blond and a faint spattering of freckles across her nose. She was as fresh-faced as any teenager in a face wash commercial.

Amanda read the story below the headline proclaiming "Local Teen Missing," and jotted in her notebook. The girl was about to start her junior year at Phoenix High School when she went missing. The details were sketchy on the first story, simply stating that she didn't come home from spending the night with a friend. A county-wide manhunt was in progress and anyone with details should call the Phoenix Police Department. Amanda picked up the second paper.

This one was in black and white, no need for color here to

capture any attention. A different picture was used for this story. Amanda guessed it was a school yearbook picture. Katie wasn't squinting into the camera but instead gently smiled with wide-open eyes. Several days had passed and still no news of Katie. Some speculated she ran away from home. Katie's parents were worried sick over their missing daughter.

God, I hope my parents aren't going through this.

Amanda went through another month's worth of issues. Each one still in black and white, each one containing less and less news about Katie Shelton. Finally, just days after learning that the Phoenix High School football team dedicated its homecoming win to Katie, another color edition of the *Phoenix Talon* rose from the stacks. This one proclaimed a body had been found in a wooded area north of town. Torrential downpours unearthed a shallow grave, stumbled upon by deer hunters. The body was badly decomposed, but dental records showed it to be Katie Shelton. Inside the grave, someone had placed a single rose in the girl's hands and sprinkled rose petals over the body. Amanda had to sit down and ponder the horror. *Jesus.*

The subsequent issues of the *Talon* that Amanda perused did nothing to shed light on Katie's murder. The whole town attended the funeral and tied red ribbons around the trees in hopes that someone would be arrested in her murder. Her best friend Shiloh Garcia, the girl she spent the night with when she went missing, was inconsolable. A heart-wrenching picture showed her crying in agony at Katie's funeral. There were no suspects in her murder and autumn rains washed away any evidence. The best estimate was that someone kidnapped Katie after she left Shiloh's house early in the morning. Amanda shivered at the thought that such a gruesome crime could take place in broad daylight, but then again, she committed her crimes under the glare of fluorescent lights.

She soon exhausted the remaining stacks with little additional information on Katie. One small article noted the anniversary of her death. There continued to be no clues and no suspects. The Phoenix police chief and authorities from the Texas Rangers all declared her murder unsolved and suspected a transient seen walking down the highway the morning she went missing must have committed the heinous act.

"Unbelievable," Amanda said to herself after re-shelving the papers. "How could this happen in a town like this?" Something like this was in the paper daily in Chicago, but it had to be a rarity in Phoenix. Maybe David could shed some light on the case. Amanda guessed he was in his mid-thirties, if so; it could be possible that he worked the case.

Amanda grimaced while she typed up the weather forecast for Phoenix. Hot, humid and a chance of afternoon thunderstorms. None of those scenarios bode well for someone whose sole means of transportation was her feet and a pair of cheap pumps. While killing time before her non-date with David, she decided to test the power of her paper's classified ads. The offerings for a used car that didn't haul cow manure were very limited. One to be exact.

"Hi, I'm calling about the '87 Bronco you have for sale," she said in response to a man who answered the phone with what sounded like "yellow." "You do still have it, right?"

"Yes 'em. The A/C doesn't work, but I fixed that problem. I cut the roof off and turned it into a convertible, even fixed it with a ragtop," the man said. Amanda had to listen carefully to catch his words beneath the thick accent. "She's got a new transmission, stereo and fresh coat of baby blue paint. I'll sell it to you for eight hundred dollars."

Amanda didn't think a convertible with no A/C would help her with her heat, humidity and rain problem, but it was better than walking. They discussed the price a little more and the man offered to bring the car to the office the following day for her to test drive. She agreed to bring cash.

"I was starting to think it was me," David said, standing when she entered the bar fifteen minutes late. Her hand jerked, wanting to shake his hand like she would any other business acquaintance, but he only moved to indicate she should sit.

"Sorry, I had to finish a few things at work," Amanda said. David didn't wear his uniform like she expected; he probably jumped at the chance to dump the bulletproof vest. Did cops in

Phoenix wear bulletproof vests? If not, they probably should, especially with a killer on the loose. "Look, I want to apologize again for my disappearing act the other night. That probably wasn't the best first impression for a source."

She added the part designating him as a source on purpose. No matter how handsome he was sitting there in a t-shirt, jeans and old cowboy boots, or how much he sounded like Matthew McConaughey, she wasn't interested.

David opened his mouth to answer her when a pretty Hispanic girl interrupted. "*Hola, Dah-veed. Quieres una cerveza?*" she said, her back arching for his benefit and her "r's" rolling more than necessary. David only gave her a quick glance, and his eyes rested back on Amanda's face.

"Hey, sure Shiloh, make that two. Have you met Mandy Jackson yet? Mandy, Shiloh Garcia."

Shiloh Garcia. Katie Shelton's best friend? Amanda could barely see the resemblance; a decade had taken its toll on her features. That, and the only picture Amanda had seen of her was the teenage version fraught with grief.

"Hi, Shiloh. Nice to meet you." This time Amanda did offer a hand, but the woman only scowled down at her.

"I need to see your ID."

"What? Why? Trust me; I'm old enough to drink."

Shiloh smiled sweetly at her. "You should take it as a compliment that I need to check. Plus, it's the law, anyone I suspect as underage; I have the right to card. Right, David?"

"She's right. Riley's could lose their liquor license if you're underage." David seemed to be enjoying this a little too much.

Amanda willed her hand to not shake. This was a simple action. Something she had done many times before. But, could David spot a fake from across the table? What if Shiloh had to confirm that it was real against a database somewhere? She hadn't even asked about Katie, and she was already going to be outed as a fraud by a two hundred dollar pawn shop fake. Shiloh pursed her lips as she read the little piece of plastic. Amanda silently counted backward. *Five. Four. Three. Two.*

"Montana, huh?" she said and thrust it back at Amanda. Before Amanda could snatch it out of her hand, David intercepted.

"Really, I've never seen a Montana license before."

Her hand moved of its own accord when it snatched the ID back from him, and she cringed when she felt particles of his skin underneath her nails. Both David and Shiloh stared at her, one with a look of surprise and the other with disgust.

"Sorry, it's just a really bad picture."

"I'll say," Shiloh agreed curtly before she walked back to the bar with an exaggerated swing of her hips. A moment later she was back and set two bottles on the table. Amanda noticed that David's beer already dripped with sweat and hers was merely room temperature.

"She has the hots for you," Amanda said after they both took a pull from their beer.

"Who? Shi? Nah."

"I can see it a mile away."

David shook his head and a small blush tinged his cheeks. "She's like a little sister. I've been friends with her older brother Eddie my whole life, and she's dating my cousin Rex. Anyway," he said, leaning close and narrowing his eyes. "She's not my type."

Amanda knew in the universal script for flirting, she was supposed to ask him, "What's your type." He would respond with something that was meant to indicate her. She would blush and act coy. He would lean in for a kiss. And, before she knew it, he would manipulate her into committing securities fraud only to leave her to clean up the mess while he partied with co-eds in Cabo. Or wherever the hell he ran off to. Amanda deviated from the script with a long drink from her warm beer.

"So," she said. "How long have you been captain here?"

David leaned back, allowing a little bit of hurt to show itself before he took a drink. "Three years. I joined the force about nine years ago."

"What goes on around here?"

"Not a whole lot," he said. "Every now and then a pretty woman shows up and becomes talk of the town."

Here he goes again. Amanda needed to nip this in the bud before she did something she'd regret.

"Look, David. You're hot, okay. No secret there, but really, I don't date sources. So, can we please keep this professional?"

"You should quit the paper then." If he hadn't laughed, Amanda would have walked out on him and let the pretty Latina waitress have him. "Don't worry, I'll play nice. I promise."

For the next hour, they passed the time talking about the types of crime typical in Phoenix. "It's really hard for me to play the bad cop here when I catch the kids playing the same pranks I did." The few town drunks knew to call David if they had too much to drink and he'd give them a ride home without any grief to keep them from getting behind the wheel. He even knew a few ladies that engaged in petty shoplifting from time to time, but he also knew they were in abusive marriages and tried to go easy on them. The more he talked, the more Amanda realized he was nothing like Josh. Except for the fact that he was male. And in that case, he was everything like Josh.

"What about murder?" she asked after he rejoined her with two fresh beers. David appeared unbothered that Shiloh avoided their table and shirked her waitress duties.

"What about it?"

"Does it ever happen here?"

"Not since—" he stopped himself and his body grew rigid, a muscle in his jaw flexed as if biting his tongue. "Not in a long time."

"Not since Katie Shelton."

"How did you know?" he tilted his head slightly.

"I saw some stories about it in the news archives and gathered it was unsolved. That's the same Shiloh, right? Katie's best friend."

He nodded, "Don't bring this up to her, okay? She was pretty messed up about that."

As if opening some imaginary floodgates, David began speaking. "I wasn't living in Phoenix when it happened. I was in Austin, getting ready to start law school." Amanda thought about asking what happened to law school, why he wasn't an attorney, but she decided to keep the conversation on Katie.

"Her murder was tough on this town," he continued. "Most thought she ran away, the rest thought she was kidnapped. Even within families people differed on what they thought happened, like her parents for example. They divorced less than a year after her funeral and both have since moved away. It took some doing to mend fences, but the town eventually moved past it, and everyone is back on friendly ground."

"What about Katie?" Amanda asked.

"What about her?"

"No one is concerned that her killer is still out there? What about justice for the victim?"

"Look, you probably saw in the papers that in all likelihood a transient did this. He's probably locked up in jail somewhere else, or dead. I hate that we never put the son-of-a-bitch on trial, but there's nothing we can do for her now."

This was just the opening she needed. "Well, maybe there is," she said. "We're coming up on the tenth anniversary. I want to re-open it for the *Talon*. Help me, and maybe we'll find something," Amanda dropped her voice. "And maybe, it will give us a chance to get to know each other better."

"Look, Mandy, just because you see a snake's nest doesn't mean it's smart to go poking it," he leaned back again in his chair, looking at some far off corner of the bar. His bouncing knee jostled the small table. "Let me sleep on it."

19

"I'm really disappointed, Alex," Roland said as he rubbed his hand over the stubble on his head. "I used my resources to get the passenger manifests for the airports here. I thought you were some hotshot analyst, and it's pretty clear you can't analyze your way out of a paper bag."

Alex threw his pen down on his legal pad and exhaled a lung full of frustration. He was done. He put aside all personal plans to pore over manifests, except for a coffee date with a young woman his mother introduced him to, which surprisingly wasn't too disastrous. But despite all his efforts, Roland seemed to do nothing other than chastise Alex and tell him where he was failing.

"What do you want me to say?" Alex shot back. "Dude, they didn't get on a plane. Do you want me to lie and say they did to make you feel like this is going somewhere? Hell, I even checked to see if there were any hits on their passports since we're so close to Canada. Nada, so don't blame me."

Quitting this project with Roland seemed like the best possible solution. Maybe Harrison was right, maybe it wasn't really worth finding them. Maybe one of the cases he half-assed at the office was really his career launcher, not this one.

Alex watched Roland stand from the table that served as their office in their favorite bar. He felt his blood pressure rise as Roland paced back and forth across the wooden floorboards.

"Okay, okay, you're right, mate. But my editor has been breathing down my neck for a big headline. You know, not a good time to be a reporter with advertisers dropping like flies."

Roland sat back down and looked more at ease. Alex exhaled. If he were to help solve this case for Roland, maybe there would be a position for him at *Financial News*. He thought he was a pretty decent writer, but maybe he and Roland could become an investigative team, like Bernstein and Woodard.

Alex picked up his abused pen, ready to brainstorm next steps.

"This just means they didn't fly out of Midway or O'Hare, or didn't cross into Canada with their passports," Alex sat up straighter, mostly because it took pressure off his growing stomach. Since he hadn't worked out, he switched to light beer or even just water during their meetings. And, he was proud of himself that he avoided cheese fries for a full week. "Should we widen our search parameters?"

"It's a bit unrealistic to study the manifests of all the major airports," Roland said.

"Well, let's consider other modes of transportation."

Roland nodded. The property of all three suspects had been seized, including their cars, but it was possible they had cars not registered in their names stashed elsewhere.

"If you're suggesting they all hopped in a car and drove off into the sunset, then there is no way we can find them. We might as well give up."

Alex didn't like Roland's mood swings. In the matter of ten minutes, he went from angry to despondent. Now it was up to Alex to bring him back to engaged and motivated.

"No man, listen, we can do this. We just need to stick with it and work really hard. Tough times don't last but tough people do. We're tough, we can do this."

That was the only pep talk Alex had ever given anyone, and he was pretty proud of himself. Roland studied him for a moment and then one of the few smiles the Brit allowed crossed his lips.

"Are you quoting motivational posters?"

Alex leaned back in his chair, his waistband cut into his stomach just as Roland's words sliced through his hope.

"But you're right, we just need to stick with it and maybe come up with another approach. Let's look back at the timelines."

Alex flipped a few pages in his legal pad to the recreated time-lines for each of the three suspects.

"The day before the attack, Keith Cooper left work early and gave no clue to where he was going, he just left," Alex read.

"He's going to be the hardest to find, right? Cooper emptied his bank accounts in the weeks prior so he's good as gone, right?"

Alex continued reading from his notes. "Williams was in the office late the night before the indictments. A trader that survived thought it sounded like he was shredding paper in his office the week before. His accounts were mostly cleaned out, as was his office."

"But Amanda," Roland said. "She was truly shocked when I called her. I know her fairly well; this girl's a pro at dealing with curveballs from the media. But she struck out with my fastball."

"Yep, a security camera in her bank showed she waited in the lobby the morning of the shooting," Alex read. "She took a phone call, from you, we assume, and then left the bank without seeing a teller. Maybe she was going to clean out her account as well."

"I don't know, mate. I'm still convinced that my call was the first she heard of the charges."

"Security cameras," Alex thumped his pen against his legal pad. "Can your guy at the Bureau get us access to more security cameras?"

"I don't know. That may require warrants, and my friend told me that his help ended at warrants. What are you thinking?"

Alex felt a thought tingle in the back of his mind. It tried to push through the mush of his brain caused by staring at line after line of data and information. But it was there, like a diver ascending for air, working its way to the surface. He hoped it wouldn't rise too quickly and die from the bends.

"What if we could trace their steps using security cameras? For example, Williams lived in a pretty swank building. Do you think there's footage of his coming and going that could help us find him?"

Roland seemed to chew on this for a few seconds. "Okay, that's a possibility. What about the other two? Do you think we could trace them through security cameras, too?"

Alex shook his head. "Cooper had a townhome so the chances of a security camera capturing him are pretty slim. Amanda's apartment building is an older, historic building. I doubt they have cameras installed there."

"Worth a shot," Roland said. "Why don't you try Josh's building and see if they have anything. Report back on what you find."

The next morning, instead of his usual commute to work, Alex made his way over to the swank new residential tower where Josh Williams owned a condo. The building was tall, sleek with a minimalist design. As he sat in the lobby, Alex noticed its contemporary style with sculptures and expensive art covering the walls. *Wonder what a place here costs. Hell, I probably couldn't afford a parking spot.*

The building security officer was more than accommodating and dropped several hints that he always wanted to work for either the police department or the FBI.

"The other guys have already cleaned out his condo, but I can let you up there if you'd like to look around."

"Sure, I'd be happy to see it."

The guard led them to a penthouse apartment with the best view of Chicago Alex had ever seen. Books from Josh's bookcase were off the shelves and stacked neatly on the floor. A quick glance in his office revealed a gaping hole where a laptop likely sat on a sleek, contemporary desk. Josh's style was stark, clean, with no personal items placed about. Like an apartment ready for a photo shoot.

Josh had a full set of luggage and no pieces were missing. His closet was full of suits, so if he packed anything he left behind his more formal clothes.

"Okay, nothing here really stands out," Alex said to the hovering security guard. "How about taking a look at that footage?"

The man eagerly agreed and closed up Josh's apartment behind them. "I've got it queued up."

They settled into an office with multiple screens. The officer turned on a small television set with a DVD built in and hit play. Alex noted on his legal pad that the time stamp showed it was after eight the evening before the indictments. Josh pulled his Porsche into a parking spot in the garage and got out of the car. The camera was grainy, the image only in black and white, but Alex saw a disheveled man in the picture. Josh had his coat off and walked in with his tie hanging loose in one hand, trailing behind him on the floor of the garage.

"Okay, so do you have any other angles?" Alex asked.

"Just this one of Williams in the garage, from there he went to the elevator up to his condo."

"Cameras on the elevators?"

"Nope, just the garage and lobby," the security officer said. "But believe you me, I wish we did. You should see some of the hotties he brought back here from time to time. If you know what I mean."

Alex let out an exasperated sigh. "Do you have anything else that would help me with my case?"

"Oh yeah, I've got this." He ejected that disc and popped in another. Time stamped at three in the morning, Josh stepped off an elevator at the lobby rather than go the extra floor down to the garage and passed a sleeping security guard at the front desk. He was dressed in jeans and a flannel shirt and carried a duffel bag. He walked coolly and confidently past the sleeping guard and out the front door. It was over in the matter of ten seconds.

"That's it?" Alex asked, trying not to get upset, but he knew Roland would say the same thing.

"Well, there is one more," the security officer smiled broadly. "I think this one will crack your case."

That disc out, another one in. The camera's view was stationed outside the building and pointed down the walkway leading up to the expensive highrise. It was also time stamped the same as the one in the lobby. A light over the front door illuminated the walkway for about five feet, but beyond that, it was a dark abyss. The back of Josh's head moved under the light, his hair radiating under the eerie glow. This recording was much shorter. In the span of four seconds, Josh was out of the frame and swallowed alive by the darkness outside of the security camera's frame. Alex leaned forward, trying to will his eyes to see something that would make sense. No headlights came through from the street, no other images appeared. There was nothing else but a moth that floated in the camera's frame.

"So, did I solve the case for you?" the security guard asked.

"Did he come back?" Alex felt his throat tighten. "Did he get any visitors? Maybe his girlfriend, Amanda Martin?"

"I know who you're talking about, but we don't see her too much. Guess she would get in the way of all his other girlfriends."

Alex could only muster a meek thanks. He left the tiny office and walked out of the fancy lobby.

He was pretty far from his office and should have splurged on a cab ride, but he wanted to walk while he digested what he saw. Roland would probably be upset when he heard that the only lead this morning produced was the fact that Josh left at three in the morning with a duffel bag.

Alex was shocked to find that Roland was instead very pleased with the news.

"This is brilliant, mate! Good work," Roland offered his Scotch to toast.

"I don't get it, I learned nothing other than he changed clothes and packed a light bag."

Roland explained the two possibilities that the video showed. One, Josh could have enlisted the help of one of the ladies that he brought home. Or, two, he could have used another mode of transportation to leave the city.

"How can we be sure he didn't just rent a cabin somewhere?" Alex said, feeling like Roland just days earlier. "He looked like he was going to chop wood or something, not meet up with some supermodel."

"Well, let's go through the process of deduction," Roland exhaled smoke. Alex really hated Roland's nicotine habit. By now, his lungs were probably as black as Roland's. "I'll call my friend at the Bureau to see if he can help with security tapes from bus and train stations. We're narrowing our window of time; if we don't see Josh there, we assume he left by car. In which case ..."

Roland let this thought trail off. The words hung over the table, like one of his clouds of smoke. Alex knew those words were as cancerous as the second-hand smoke and resisted the urge to wave them away with his hand. Roland examined the burning end of his cigarette, holding it just inches from the end of his nose, his eyes crossed as he stared at the crooked, glowing cherry. Did he look for some answer in the burning tobacco?

"In which case," Roland repeated himself. "We're royally screwed, and they made off with a few million dollars."

20

"I hate working the lunch shift," Shiloh whispered to herself. "It's such a waste of my time."

People didn't come to Riley's for their so-so burgers or greasy chicken-fried steak and lumpy gravy. They came in after a long day of working their farms, or herding cattle, to have a drink at the only bar in town and catch up on the daily gossip. A local paper was only a formality; people got the real news before supper at Riley's.

With her two tables digging into their lunches, Shiloh lit a cigarette and perched on a barstool to read the work of Mandy Jackson. Clint left out the part that she was young and pretty. Not that Shiloh wanted to admit Mandy was pretty, but the woman wasn't exactly ugly.

The ringing door chime forced Shiloh to twirl around in her seat. David shook hands with two men from one of her tables. She bounded up from the bar stool and strode back to the office where Eddie was doing the books.

"Hey Eddie, David's here."

"Oh good, see what he wants to eat, and I'll come out in a minute and join him."

"Why don't *you* see what he wants to eat?" Shiloh shot back.

Eddie's reply was a stern look and Shiloh rolled her eyes. Eddie quickly slipped into a parental role after their father died when she was a baby and he was eight. Even now, he could give her a look of admonishment to force her into submission. She liked to think this was something he inherited from their father, so she didn't mind when his parental instincts won out over brotherly love.

When she returned, David was already seated at the bar perusing the short menu.

"Eddie said he'd be right out," Shiloh said as she stubbed her dying cigarette so the secondhand smoke wouldn't bother David. He kept up his healthy eating and workout regimen despite the fact that his football days were over. "Know what you want and I'll put the order in for you?"

"Sure, a grilled chicken sandwich and iced tea."

When Shiloh returned from the kitchen, she found him reading her newspaper.

"So, where's Mindy?" she asked, knowingly getting the woman's name wrong.

"Mandy," David said, not looking at her but instead focusing on the farm report. "At work I guess."

This was not the David that Shiloh knew. Conversation was never hard to come by with them. He may have been sitting at the bar at Riley's right in front of her, but he was hundreds of miles away.

"Shi, can I ask you a question?"

Yes, I love you. Yes, I'll run away with you and forget about Rex. Yes, I will have your baby. "Sure, shoot."

"You and Rex have been together for a long time. How soon did you know he was the one? Was it something that hit you upside the head or did it come on gradually?"

What would you do if I told you the truth? What if I told you that it hit me like a lightning bolt when I was nine and you made me PB&J sandwiches and played video games with me while Mom worked double shifts? That over the past seventeen years my love for you has only grown? Even though Shiloh was happy with his cousin, Rex was a runner-up.

She couldn't say any of that to him. Not then, not ever. They were friends, nearly family between David's friendship with her brother and her relationship with his cousin. If she ever told him what she felt, she would lose him in every aspect of her life. That was harder to deal with than not having him love her back.

"Well," she began, craving another cigarette but successfully fighting the urge to light up in front of him. "A little bit of both I guess."

He nodded and went back to the paper. Shiloh knew what was eating at him. Working the bar at Riley's for as long as she had, she'd seen her fair share of couples flirting over beer and hookups ripening during last call. It didn't stand out initially, but David eagerly awaited Mandy's arrival the other night. Shiloh had tried to determine who he waited for, who it was that caused his face to brighten every time the door opened, only to freeze in hidden disappointment.

Shiloh was on her way to David's table that night when the door opened once more and this time there was nothing to hide. He was genuinely happy to see the girl that joined him. The girl was pretty in a plain way. She was tall. But, then again, at five-foot-two, everyone was tall to Shiloh. Her straight brown hair draped over one shoulder and her porcelain skin suggested she was new to the scolding Texas sun. *This must be the new girl Clint saw running down the highway during a hailstorm.* A look at her driver's license confirmed that, but it raised Shiloh's suspicions. The woman in the picture was a haggard-looking blond who looked like she hadn't slept in days, nothing like the girl across from him. Shiloh chewed on the inside of her cheek as she debated telling David what Clint shared with her.

It wasn't just a simple flirtation for him, that woman somehow got under his skin. Would Clint approve of her telling David that Mandy was possibly psychotic? Would David believe her, or Clint? The two men shared a mutual dislike of each other, so chances were David wouldn't believe what she said.

"Is this about Mandy? I saw how you looked at her," Shiloh added in response to David's raised eyebrow. "You just met her. You know nothing about her."

David's mouth opened as if he were going to argue with her, but he only nodded and looked up at the television above the bar. Before she could say something to soften the blow she just dealt, her brother came out of the office and slapped David on the back. Shiloh went back to check on her tables while the two friends caught up. Watching him from across the room, the glimpse of sadness in David softened her harshness. At an age when he should be married and teaching his son how to throw a football, he was still single. Living in a town as small as Phoenix, the choices for a spouse were slim. Shiloh should be happy that a pretty young woman showed up in their town giving David a chance at a life he obviously wanted.

Jealousy slammed into her like a bucket of ice water. No, David would come around. There was still the possibility that he would wake up one day and confront his own love for Shiloh. On that day, he would rush up to Riley's, run into the bar, grab her by the waist and kiss her like she always fantasized. If he fell in love with Mandy, that fantasy would never become a reality.

"It was like lightning," David said, causing Shiloh to jump. She was so wrapped up in her own thoughts she didn't see David approach her. For a moment, she thought she was daydreaming, that David would grab her and kiss her. Shiloh even tilted her head towards him as she had imagined time and time again in her fantasies. "The first time I saw Mandy, it was like all the light in the world shone on where she was standing. You know what I mean?"

Shiloh knew exactly what he meant. After all these years, the spotlight on him never waned in Shiloh's eyes. It only grew stronger. So strong in fact that sometimes it blinded her.

21

D avid's avoidance was all the answer she needed. It wasn't because Amanda dredged up an old, forgotten murder. It was just one sentence, but it was one she wished she had never said. All those years with Josh had warped her. She was no different than him. Like Josh, Amanda considered using David to get what she wanted.

He managed to evade her so deftly she wondered if the whole town was involved. She would see his head in the window of the Mexican restaurant at lunch, only to find the table empty when she entered. His truck would be parked outside Riley's, but there would be no sign of his mischievous smile inside. Calls to the police station for updates resulted in two minor incidents faxed to her for the crime blotter, handwritten and signed "Capt. D. Stephens." Yep, he was avoiding her.

During an evening jog to straighten out her thoughts, Amanda saw David. Just like before, he ran ahead of her. In the growing Texas heat, he jogged shirtless, which Amanda was too, suddenly feeling modest in her sports bra. He once again ran with the heavy brace on his right knee.

Would it really be awful if she just let herself go out on a date with him? He drives drunks home rather than arrest them; how bad could he be? Maybe guys in Texas were different. The closest Porsche dealership was hundreds of miles away, fine Italian suits probably wouldn't last in this heat and the fanciest restaurant in Phoenix would have two stars at best and paper placemats rather than laundered linens. He was nothing like Josh.

Josh. It had been weeks since he left, since Amanda left. Was he worried about her? Did he try to find her? Did her now-ruined phone have concerned text messages or voicemails full of anxiety over if she were dead or alive? Or, she smiled, might he be in jail?

"You're never going to catch me if you don't lengthen your stride."

Amanda screamed as she rounded the corner of the bank building on the square. Her perspiring forehead struck his sweaty chest before she could stop her momentum. Lucky for both of them, he braced for the collision, or she would have knocked him on his back and landed on top of him. *Not that he would have minded.*

"Oh geez, David," Amanda said, trying to wiggle out of his grasp but only succeeding in soaking her sports bra through with his sweat. "What the...are you going to let me go?"

"Why would I? I apprehended a stalker," he smiled down at her. Amanda could think of a hundred reasons not to reach up and kiss him; they just weren't coming to her.

"Stalker?" Now that she stopped running, the night air danced with the sweat on her arms, causing goose pimples to rise. That's what she told herself. "How long did you know I was back there?"

David finally relaxed his grip, but Amanda didn't step away. When she realized the endorphins were going to make her do something she would later regret, she shifted and leaned her back against the warm brick wall.

"Tonight? For the last mile or so. That first night, I figured out you trailed me about a quarter of a mile from my place," he leaned his back against the wall next to her. "I was curious to see if you'd make it all the way to my front porch. Disappointed you didn't."

"Well, I'm sorry I didn't properly introduce myself that night."

"Apology accepted. I also know you've been following me all week."

Amanda took a deep breath. "You've avoided me all week. I shouldn't have used your interest in me as a reason to help with the Katie Shelton case. That's not what I meant. It just came out all wrong. I'm sorry."

David looked down at his feet. After an awkward pause, he looked at her. Like two magnetic poles, their faces drew together and finally joined. His lips were soft and salty. Her heart quickened and every cell in her body wanted to lean into him. It was one of those kisses that could have meant so much more, but the headlights of an oncoming car brought them back to the present and they separated.

"You're forgiven," he said. Amanda hoped she didn't visibly shiver.

"Please don't take this the wrong way, but I could use a friend more than a boyfriend right now."

David nodded. "Then I'm your man." Amanda felt relief when his face revealed no hurt or disappointment.

He took her hand and led her to one of the park benches in front of the courthouse. The sky was ablaze with orange and pink as they talked about nothing in particular; favorite foods, favorite bands, favorite childhood memories. As the sky turned from gray to black and stars popped on like streetlights, their conversation took a bolder path; life's hopes and dreams, desires for children, politics, religion. No matter how many times Amanda wanted to bring up Katie Shelton, she swallowed back the words for fear of ruining one of the best nights of her life.

Maybe it was David no longer being upset with her, or the fact that she could now call someone her friend. It could even have been having the first real conversation with another person in weeks or the fact that everything she shared was the truth. But, it was most likely the kiss that made Amanda feel effervescent the following morning despite sitting on the square until they could no longer stand the mosquitoes. She should have been exhausted when her alarm went off, but instead she was alert and energetic.

Mr. Foster's first book review was due that day, and while Frank reviewed the wire stories, she walked over to the bookstore to pick it up. It was another hot and humid day, just the kind of day that initiated her need for a car, but rather than drive she walked. By choice. Actually, she wanted to skip, but that would look strange in her heels.

Even the gloomy front yard of Foster's Bookstore couldn't defuse her good mood. Inside, the stale, dusty air accosted her nose, making it tingle with a stubborn sneeze. She found the proprietor in a different room of the house cataloging a shelf of mystery novels.

"Mr. Foster, you should really consider opening up some windows. It's probably not good for you to breathe in all this dust." As if to prove a point, her stifled sneeze punctuated her sentence.

"Sunlight is bad for the books," he said, not looking at her but instead writing the name of a book on a legal pad. "I take it you have come to retrieve my book review, Ms. Jackson?"

"That is correct."

He abruptly put down the legal pad and walked out of the room. Without any invitation to follow, Amanda stayed put and perused the titles in front of her.

"Don't touch anything," he called out, and Amanda gasped at his psychic capabilities or the idea that security cameras were tucked between stacks of dust-covered books.

"I hope you don't mind that I took the liberty to change my book assignment," he said and handed her a two-page typed review. Mr. Foster didn't own a computer, so she would have to re-type it, but at least working off typewritten pages would be faster than deciphering handwriting. Glancing at the first few sentences, Amanda frowned and tried to hide her disappointment.

"Mr. Foster, we talked about doing a series on the latest bestsellers. This," Amanda said, quickly reading over the first paragraph. "This is a true crime book on a serial killer. Hardly a bestseller if you ask me."

The man bristled, and his gray-blue eyes narrowed, staring so intently at Amanda that a tiny amount of adrenalin rushed from her brain to her heart, causing the blood to rush through her ears in the quiet house. Every nerve ending screamed at her to get out of the house.

"You know what, it's okay," she said, no longer caring about the assignment. "Thank you for doing this. It will be in the paper tomorrow."

Her hand was on the doorknob, itching to escape, when he called out to her. "Ms. Jackson, I upset you, didn't I?"

She couldn't understand how the man managed to move so silently in the old house. Every board of the hardwood floor creaked when Amanda stepped on them. Mr. Foster must know which boards creak and which were silent.

"I'm not mad, really. I just have to explain to Frank the difference in the review."

"I apologize. Next time I will not deviate from your request."

Amanda thanked him, pulled the door open and stopped abruptly when he called to her again.

"One more thing, Ms. Jackson. Have you given any more thought to my suggestion of looking into Katie Shelton's murder?"

Amanda sighed and fought the urge to leave the front door open to allow precious fresh air in. Instead, she gently closed the door, but left her hand on the doorknob.

"Actually, yes. I did some research. What a terrible thing to have happened to that poor girl. I'm talking to the police about re-examining the case. Thank you for the lead."

"Are you sure that is the best course of action? I'm sure you saw in your research that people thought the police botched the case."

"Don't worry. I'm working with someone who wasn't even here when it happened."

"Oh, who would that be?"

"David Stephens."

Mr. Foster harrumphed at the name. Amanda looked at her watch. The errand was taking her longer than she anticipated and with having to type Mr. Foster's review into the computer, she was going to cut it close to deadline. She thanked him again and promised to keep abreast of the case."

"Well, you should know that he has a conflict of interest."

"What's that?"

"His brother was the prime suspect."

22

"Why didn't you tell me your brother was named a suspect in Katie's murder?"

David put his beer down and wrung the back of his neck. Several emotions played across his face; embarrassment, anger, denial and finally, betrayal. There was no mention of a Stephens in any of the *Talon* articles on the murder. For whatever reason, Frank censored this information to protect David's family, but someone betrayed that and told an outsider a family secret.

"I didn't see how that was really any of your business."

Ouch.

"Anyway, he was never a suspect, just a person of interest. There's a difference."

"Okay, I get that it's not something you bring up on a date, but still."

"Oh, so we were on a date when you asked me for help now? Funny, I seem to remember someone being very adamant about not dating sources and needing a friend instead of a boyfriend." David leaned across the table and lowered his voice. Lucky for them, the patio at Riley's was empty with the rest of the patrons opting for the live music and air conditioning the inside bar offered. "Make up your mind, Mandy. Are we friends or are we more? I'm having a hard time keeping up with our relationship status."

Amanda opened her mouth to apologize, but David cut her off.

"That was rude of me. I'm sorry."

"That's my line," Amanda laughed.

David shrugged. "That's why I never went to law school. My parents could barely afford to help me out, and I was going to drown in student loans for the rest of my life. When this came up, and they needed money for a defense attorney for Cody, I withdrew and entered the police academy."

"Why was he suspected?"

Even though they were alone, David spoke quietly. Amanda had to lean forward to hear him over the din of the music inside and the rushing of the river below them. "My brother went to school with Katie. They were sweethearts all through elementary school and junior high, but the summer before their sophomore year, Katie dumped him. Said she fell in love with someone else.

"Cody sort of snapped," David continued after draining his beer. "He became obsessed with trying to find out who she was seeing, but you ask me, I don't think there was anyone else. I think she just outgrew him and didn't know how to end it. Anyway, he was the only person that had any beef with Katie, and the morning she turned up missing he was late getting to work and wouldn't explain why."

"Where was he?"

David laughed as he took a drink from the fresh beer a waitress just left him. "Sleeping one off. But it took a few days to get him to admit it; he was in too much shock to think clearly. For some reason, he blamed himself for her disappearance and murder, thinking that whoever she was seeing was the killer and that he should have been able to figure it out."

"Do you regret it? Not going to law school?"

"There are moments when I wonder if I made the right decision, but for the most part, I couldn't be happier," he said, leaning back in his chair as a playful smile crossed his lips. "Actually, I could be happier, but if I bring that up my friend might hit me."

Amanda decided to let that one slide. Not that she was averse to some playful banter with David, but something he said struck her. If his brother, someone who knew Katie intimately, suspected a secret boyfriend was behind her murder, why didn't the police? Was there some truth behind the theory?

"Did your brother ever figure out who she was seeing?"

"Don't think so."

"Well, can we ask him?"

"Sure, if you can find him. He left home after he graduated from high school and is stationed somewhere in the Middle East. I've only spoken to him a few times since then. He doesn't call or come home much."

Amanda sipped her beer and studied his face. Did David's revelation of his family ties to the Katie Shelton case mean that he was going to help her? He didn't have to explain the situation. Or even take it a step further and offer his brother's whereabouts. He could have simply said that yes, his brother was once tied to the case but was since cleared.

"No, that doesn't mean I'm going to help you," David said. Amanda worried that she spoke her thoughts out loud. "I could tell what you're thinking."

What else could he see? Did he realize he sat across the table from a criminal? Did he care that she hid more secrets than he could ever imagine? She cleared her throat and tightened her face. Outside of the Darwinian landscape of Chicago she relaxed her shield. Not smart, considering she shared a drink with a cop trained to find criminals, skilled in reading a guilty face. She took a long drink of her beer, hoping it would wash away any other emotions that may be present, like worry and fear.

"Why?"

"You relax around me. Which is nice, you trust me enough to let your thoughts show."

"Why won't you help me?"

It was David's turn to put up his wall. His jaw tightened, and he looked away. She wasn't the only one that was an open book; he relaxed in her presence as well. Every time they were together he made no secret of his feelings for her, both verbally and non-verbally. Maybe Amanda had the same effect on him that he had on her, the desire to laugh, flirt and live in the moment.

"What is it with you and this case? We've been perfectly fine the last ten years without some outsider telling us we need to catch a killer that is likely in prison for another crime or dead. So, just leave it alone, Mandy."

"I take it that's a no, then." Amanda's face flushed and her neck grew warm. No matter what she felt at that instant, it was only a flash and would be gone the next time he smiled at her or the next time he kissed her. She hoped there would be a next time.

"Yeah, that's a no." David fished some bills from his pocket. Amanda finished her beer in the company of Andrew Jackson and a chorus of frogs.

23

I t's been years since Shiloh found herself on the banks of the Tejas River. She sat on the hood of her car, a forgotten cigarette between her fingers burned down to the filter. The little spot where high school kids came to drink and park hadn't changed. The dirt of the makeshift parking lot was still devoid of any vegetation and compacted from the tires of the cars and trucks that visited the area daily. Shiloh watched the last of the families and kids leaving this quiet area after an afternoon of swimming. As soon as the sun went down, it would trade its family atmosphere for one of forbiddance.

Shiloh squinted into the late afternoon sun. She had sunglasses in her car, but her eyes weren't registering the bright rays; instead she recalled sitting on the folded down tailgate of Clint's old truck passing a bottle of tequila between Katie, Clint and herself nearly a decade ago. She could taste the liquor in the back of her throat, a sensation that still ignited the gag reflex even today. A long sip of sweet tea helped extinguish that tang.

In the days after Katie's disappearance, Shiloh kept vigil here, not only hoping that her friend would emerge from the surrounding woods, but also trying to will the foggy memories of that night forward. Ten years later, the manifestation of Clint in her bar forced her back to this parking lot and back into her memories.

She'd always wondered if Clint had anything to do with Katie's murder. As smitten as Katie was with him, Shiloh never trusted the man and felt uncomfortable with his mere presence. *If you ask me, a man nearly ten years older had only an unnatural interest in a teenage girl.* But, Katie had the same feelings for Clint that Shiloh harbored for David; and Shiloh thought that if she chaperoned Katie and Clint's outings then nothing bad could happen to her friend. A lot of good that did.

Shiloh laid back on the hood of her car, the warmth from the sun relaxing her tense muscles. With her forearms shielding her eyes and her body relaxed, she went back to that night in August. It was hot and dry and everyone seemed to move a little slower that summer. Katie was going to spend the night at Shiloh's, the usual cover for her overprotective parents. Shiloh's mom worked the night shift and her brother Eddie was already working at Riley's, so the evenings belonged to Shiloh and Katie. And Clint.

That night, Clint picked them up. "Oh, great, Shiloh is joining us," she recalled Clint's sarcastic tone. The one thing that Clint and Shiloh had in common was their mutual dislike.

"Ya'll know the rules," she said. "If Katie is going to tell her parents she's with me to see you, I'm going to be there. If she ever decides to tell her parents the truth, then I would be happy to find something else to do." Shiloh remembered being especially cranky that night. No one involved liked it, but they seemed to live with it that summer.

Shiloh smiled when she reminisced on Katie's imaginary checklist. Varsity cheerleader? Check. Homecoming court? Check. Straight A student? Check. The summer before their junior year, she had a few more items to check off her list; losing her virginity and getting drunk for the first time. That night, Clint had a surprise for Katie, a bottle of tequila. Her smile vanished when she recalled Clint hoped the tequila would kill two birds with one stone.

They drove around for a little while, Katie sitting in the middle of the truck cab. Air rushed in through the open windows of Clint's truck, forming a tornado of blond and brown hair as he sped down the highway. Finally, they settled in that little spot by the Tejas River. Shiloh hoped others would be there that night, and she wouldn't have to suffer being a fifth wheel alone, but no such luck.

The bottle passed back and forth. When Clint asked Katie to go for a moonlight walk in the woods, Shiloh lost her temper.

Shiloh pounded her fist against the hood of her car. She wanted to change history. She wished her last exchange with her best friend didn't end with calling Katie names. If she'd known her outburst would upset Katie so much, resulting in her own argument with Clint, setting in motion the events ending in her friend's death, she would have left everything alone. What did it matter to her anyway? Katie was old enough to make her own decisions.

After Katie stormed off with Clint, Shiloh took longer drinks of the liquor in hopes of accelerating the numbness that started in her lips through the rest of her body. She remembered lying down in the back of Clint's truck, watching the stars pass by overhead and swearing she could feel the Earth moving.

Shiloh must have either dozed off or passed out after Clint and Katie walked away.

"Wake up, Shiloh," he said, pulling her arms to get her to sit up. "Do you want me to take you home or leave you here to wait for your bitch of a friend?"

The tequila-crafted confusion hazed her mind. Clint doted on Katie. What was he talking about? And, where was Katie?

"What?" Shiloh couldn't muster much more than that before she had the urge to throw up. Clint must have seen that coming, and he pulled her out of the back of his truck and held her up while she got sick. After her body rejected all the alcohol, she felt somewhat more lucid. "Where's Katie?"

Clint didn't answer her right away. She watched him pace the small parking lot with fast, angry steps, stumbling from time to time over a large white rock. Shiloh forced herself to sober up.

"Stop moving, you're going to make me sick again. Just tell me, where is Katie?"

Clint sat down on the tailgate of the truck, and Shiloh sat beside him. Even in the darkness, she could see how worried he looked.

"I thought I'd finally get some tonight." No matter how drunk she was at the time, Shiloh could still remember his words. "But she was pissed off at you and stopped me, said she was feeling sick from the booze. I was a jerk. I called her a tease, told her she was just a child." Ten years later, thinking back to those hurtful words he admitted saying to her best friend, she could still imagine the pain Katie felt. "She stormed off in the other direction. I thought she'd cool down and come crawling back. I got tired of waiting. The bitch is trying to teach me a lesson, I know."

"How long ago was this?" Worry washed away the alcohol haze. Sure, Katie knew how to take care of herself and nothing bad happened in Phoenix, but the river banks weren't exactly stable, and she feared that Katie may fall into the river if she were drunk.

Clint illuminated his digital watch. By his guess, she stormed off about two hours earlier. Panic gripped her chest. Shiloh took off running into the woods, only to trip and fall over the first tree root that she came too, skinning her knee. With blood running down her leg, she got up and continued at a slower pace, calling out Katie's name. Clint stayed behind, leaving the search to her. Shiloh half expected to hear his truck start up and drive off, but it didn't. Shiloh wasn't familiar with the woods, and honestly, she was a little afraid to be out there by herself. Her grandmother always told her stories of Mexican ghosts and demons that inhabited the river bed and even though she didn't believe them now, the sounds around her made her wonder if there was an ounce of truth to the Mexican mysticism.

When she came back, Clint was still sitting on the tailgate of his truck. It was nearly four in the morning, and they were both tired. They sat there in silence for another hour, the sky behind them started to lighten as the sun made its approach, but they stared west, into the darkness. Shiloh wondered what he was more concerned about, Katie or his reputation. Clint finally broke the silence.

"Let me take you home," he said. He helped Shiloh up. Her

knee ached, the stiff scab pulled as she tried to move her knee and blood pooled in her sock, making one foot colder than the other.

She expected to see Katie waiting on her front porch, but she wasn't there. Shiloh was so tired that she only took a second to wash the blood off her knee and shin rather than shower. Her head hurt; the hangover kicking in already. She didn't wake up until the next afternoon when the ringing phone invaded her sleep. The caller ID box informed her that the call was coming from the Sheltons.

"I am so going to kick your skinny blond butt," Shiloh said when she answered the phone. Instead of receiving an apology or some quip, she heard the worried voice of Katie's mom.

"Umm, Shi, it's Sandy," the woman said. She paused before saying anything else, obviously not expecting the response she received from her daughter's best friend. "I was calling to see if Katie was there, but—"

The first lie came almost too easily. Shiloh didn't lie to cover herself, she lied to cover Katie. At that moment, the thought that Katie was kidnapped or killed was the farthest thing from her mind. She imagined Katie just holed up somewhere, angry with Clint and sleeping off her first inebriation.

"Oh, hi, Mrs. Shelton. Katie was here, but I woke up this morning, and she was gone."

After Shiloh hung up with Sandy, she called Clint. His groggy voice mumbled, "She's not here." They agreed to meet back at the river, see if they could find Katie somewhere out there. It was even hotter that day, and the humidity made their hangovers worse. They walked around, swallowing their nausea and calling out Katie's name. No response and no sign of their friend. After a few hours of looking, they returned to the parking lot and sat on the back of Clint's truck in silence.

"Where do you think she went?" he said.

Shiloh had difficulty breathing and her stomach churned. "We need to call the police."

"No, it will only get Katie in trouble. Get you in trouble too for lying."

"I don't care. I don't care if both of us are grounded until college. I want my friend back."

"You can't mention my name."

"What?" Shiloh was confused. How could she only tell the police half the truth? She needed to tell them where they got the tequila, about the arguments and who brought Shiloh home that night.

"If you say that I was with you, I'll deny it. I'm going to be taking over my dad's clinic in a few years. I can't have something like this hanging over my head, scaring away patients. Okay?"

Shiloh was so numb with fear that she only fought Clint's logic half-heartedly. "You selfish son-of-a-bitch."

"You bring me into this, I'll tell the cops you were out with someone else, that you were just trying to save your own tail. Think about it Shi," he said, gentle as if coaxing a scared puppy out of a corner. "Who will the police believe? A future doctor whose father has been a pillar of the community for forty years, or some teenager who is lying not only to protect her friend, but her own reputation?"

He manipulated her so easily that she never fully realized it until several weeks later.

"It's really simple," Clint said. "I'll call in with a tip that a man was walking down the interstate near the road to Phoenix the evening before she disappeared. Katie got up early to go for a run, it is possible that this man walked into town and saw her leaving your house."

With each telling, the memory of that night out by the river washed away and was replaced with the new memory. Katie had come over to spend the night. They went riding around for a little bit, but decided to go back to Shiloh's to watch movies. They fell asleep in her room sometime after two in the morning, Shiloh woke up around noon and Katie was gone; no note, but Katie was a fitness fanatic and probably went for an early morning run.

When Katie's body was found, she wanted nothing more than to put Clint in a shallow grave. He went back to Galveston for his final year of medical school just a week after Katie's disappearance, and he never called Shiloh. Two weeks after Katie's funeral, she grew tired of waiting and called Clint from a payphone outside a convenience store. Shiloh was stunned when he said he knew Katie's body was found. And, even more shocking was his absolute lack of emotion to this news.

"Clint, I'm going to ask you this only once, and I want you to tell me the truth," she said, the tears flowing down her cheeks in their usual route. "Did you kill Katie?"

"No," his voice was flat.

With the sun now behind the trees, Shiloh crossed her forearms over her chest. They were wet, the tears once again flowing freely as they did just a decade earlier. At that time, she only believed Clint because she wanted to believe him. When he moved back to Phoenix a few years later with his medical license in hand, it shocked Shiloh to see how much he had aged. His hair had grayed, and he had grown a ridiculous mustache to make himself look older. He visited her once at Riley's on a quiet afternoon, and they made their agreement.

"My fiancée is a sweet girl from East Texas, and she doesn't know a thing about Katie. If you'll visit a doctor in Stephenville, I won't come in to Riley's. I can't have Lisa worrying over a dead girl."

They coexisted in the small town peacefully for six years, running into each other only a few times but never acknowledging each other's presence. Anytime she thought about Clint, she thought about how he forced her to lie. Every morning when she woke up, she lit a candle on her dresser and said a prayer for her friend. *Please God, forgive me for my sins*, Shiloh prayed. *Forgive me for lying. If I never lied, Katie would have been found before she died. I should be lying in that grave, not Katie. And, God, please find Katie's killer, and please let him succumb to justice.* Nearly ten years and countless spent candles later, she began to doubt that her prayers would ever be answered.

24

"I need to make this play, mate," Roland said, not elaborating when Alex pressed for an update on the security tapes. Roland brooded more than usual and hunched his back over his Scotch. "It's just taking longer than I planned. Be patient, my source will come through. It just may be a few more days."

Alex didn't mind the hiatus. He had a full-fledged date with Helena, the girl that he had coffee with previously. A sweet girl in her mid-twenties, Helena worked as a kindergarten teacher. *The perfect profession for when we have our own kids.*

During their date, he did everything perfectly. He took her to a nice steakhouse, bought a nice bottle of wine and even tipped the waiter when the night was over. They walked over to a jazz bar and listened to music. It was hard to tell if she had a good time, or if she was just there because her parents put the pressure on her to marry a nice Greek boy. He knew his own mother pressured her parents to convince their daughter to marry a nice Greek boy, just like her son. He caught her texting twice, but figured she just told her girlfriends how much fun she was having.

"Would you like to share a cab home?" Alex asked as their date wound to a close. She didn't shirk away when he walked close to her, instead her dark curly hair clung to his arm as if fusing the two together.

"That's not necessary since we're so close to your place," Helena answered, her chin tilted up and her lips parted. Alex already had a cab flagged before the words were fully out of her mouth.

"Good point," he said, holding the cab door open. "Well, it was fun. Have a good night." Alex stood in front of the open car door with his arms open and wrapped Helena in his arms in a brotherly hug, the kind he shared with his sisters and nieces and nephews. He watched the cab pull away from the curb, perplexed by the strange look she threw his way from inside the cab.

As he climbed the stairs to his apartment, he checked his cell phone, curious if Helena would call or text to say how much fun she had. He had a new text message, but it was from Roland. *Bar, tomorrow, 2 p.m., need to talk.* Alex took the rest of the stairs two at a time, one for the success of his date with Helena, whom he now considered to be his future wife, and one for the progression of his career-launching case.

When he met up with Roland the next afternoon, he knew something was up. Roland usually sported the George Michael on-purpose five o'clock shadow look both with his beard and his head, but he hadn't kept the look up, so his beard was thicker than usual and his head revealed a significantly receding hairline of stubble. "Hey man, what's shaking?" Alex's thin lips stretched into a wide smile, and his skin glowed beneath a scraggly beard. "Got some good news for me for our big case?"

Roland glanced at Alex with red eyes and sullen cheeks. This was such a strange look to Alex that he didn't know how to react. Rather than answer Alex, Roland motioned to the waitress, ordered their drinks and lit a cigarette. They sat in silence until the waitress arrived with drinks and each man took a sip.

"Roland, you're scaring me. What's wrong?" Alex's voice was soft and worried. The man sitting in front of him looked so different from the friend he had come to hate with fondness over the last few weeks.

"I've got good news and bad news. What do you want to

hear first?"

"Bad news," Alex said. He thought it would be better to face the negative first, and then finish up with the positive. At least that's the gist from a favorite motivational poster.

"I could be losing my job by the end of the month."

Alex felt like he just went over the first hill of a roller coaster. Roland couldn't lose his job.

"No!" Alex shouted. A few heads in the bar turned and looked in their direction. "What? What do you mean? You're good at what you do. This can't happen. Can I talk to someone?" Alex spoke quickly, each word picking up speed as if it were the train of the roller coaster.

Roland just shook his head.

"But, but——" Alex couldn't process his thoughts, his mind only thinking about the vertical loop coming their way; the one that would turn their investigation on its head.

Finally Roland spoke. "The publication is hemorrhaging money, mate. No one wants to read about the financial markets going to hell, so circulation is dive-bombing. And that's not the worst of it. Our advertisers are pulling out faster than we can change our budget." He took a long drag from his cigarette and reduced its length by half when he finally pulled it from his lips. "My editor gave the heads up that a significant workforce reduction is coming by the end of the month. He doesn't know if my job is safe or not, but without a company sponsoring my work visa, I may have to leave the country." Smoke floated out of his mouth as he spoke.

"No wonder you look terrible," Alex said. *And, no wonder he's chain smoking.* "Shit." They both sat there, shoulders slumped forward, drinking and silent. "What's the good news?"

"Oh, right, I do have a spot of good news," he said before he took another long drag on his cigarette. "After much begging and bargaining, my friend at the Bureau agreed to obtain the security tapes for us from the local bus and train stations, but only a twenty-four hour window. If Josh took off outside of that timeframe, we're out of luck."

Alex quickly forgot about his friend's woes and let out a whoop of excitement, causing heads to turn in their direction.

"No way, man!" That is wonderful news. Let's order a round of shots."

If there was footage of any of their suspects getting on a train or a bus, then the case would take a significant leap forward, and Alex would get the promotion he deserved.

"Pardon me if I'm not doing cartwheels, mate."

"I don't get it. Why aren't you excited? This is huge. This could be exactly the thing we're looking for."

Roland lit another cigarette. When he exhaled, he didn't observe his normal manner of blowing the smoke away from Alex. This time he blew the smoke directly in his face, causing Alex to break into a coughing fit so violent he worried his beer would come back up.

"What is the matter with you?" Alex said, scolding his friend.

"What is the matter with me? What the bloody hell is wrong with you?" Roland's eyes widened, and he pointed the lit cigarette at Alex. "Do you ever think of anyone other than yourself? Here I am, offering to help you with a case that your agency botched because I felt sorry for you. And all you do is whine about why things aren't going your way and how if this case doesn't get solved your career is in the shitter. Well, mate, *my* career is in the shitter, and you don't give a damn. This is bollocks."

All the eyes in the bar turned in their direction. Alex was afraid to break eye contact with Roland, fearing the Brit may sucker punch him.

"I-I'm sorry," Alex whispered. "Can I help? I'll write a letter to your editor or your publisher to tell them how great you are to help me."

"As if you have any pull," Roland scoffed, his sullen mood replaced by outright anger.

Alex motioned to their waitress. "Two glasses of the best Scotch you have," he said, disregarding the hefty price tag each sip would carry.

"Thank you," Roland mumbled when their drinks arrived. The men resumed their somber postures and sipped the Scotch.

Alex thought about what Roland said. As much as he hated to admit it, he was so myopic on this case that he didn't realize there was someone else involved that may have his career riding on this too. Without Roland's help, the JWI case would be truly inactive and Alex would be focusing on someone else's case, not his own.

"I am an ass," Alex said, a snorting laugh into his glass burning the inside of his nose with the smell of the liquor.

"I'll drink to that," Roland quipped, causing both men to laugh.

"Seriously, man, I want to help you. What will it take to make sure you're not on that list of job cuts?"

I need to make sure Roland keeps his job. After all, if he got axed before we make any significant findings, well, that would be a serious kink in the investigation. Alex banished those thoughts. This was the time to be selfless, to stand up for someone who had helped him and return the favor. "This is a time for you to be a man," Alex could almost hear his late father's voice.

"Well, I need big headlines. I need something that people will buy the paper to read, or something that I could sell to other publications."

The afternoon darkened and the bar emptied. Alex ordered another round of expensive Scotch, secretly hoping Roland would offer to split the tab.

"Do you think there is anything on those recordings?" Alex asked. He was eager to break the silence.

"Guess we'll find out soon enough. I'm picking up the discs tomorrow afternoon. We need to spend time going over what's on there. Can you take a day or two off from work to analyze them?"

Alex nodded. "You said you need a headline, right?"

It was Roland's turn to nod.

Since Roland's outburst, this idea floated around in the recesses of his mind, but he held back saying it. If Roland agreed, it would be career suicide for Alex, although it would be the shot of adrenalin that Roland's career needed. *I've been standing on the edge long enough. It's time to step over.*

"If there is anything on those recordings, I'll go on the record as an independent investigator. You can have your scoop."

25

A manda took care and time in dressing like she would in preparing for an expected run-in with an ex. Not that David was an ex. Yet. He would be after he got her letter.

David's abandonment of her at Riley's prompted some much needed retail therapy for Amanda at the discount retailer in town. While the equivalent of trading a world-renowned psychotherapist for a small-town shrink, it served its purpose. Her appreciation for the almost-famous designer grew with the purchase of a summer plaid shirtdress and strappy heels. She even picked up a bottle of that iconic perfume she and every other pre-teen wore to junior high. The musky fragrance rewound the years in her mind, recalling simpler days when her only concerns were boys, braces and boobs.

It took time for Amanda to become reacquainted with her reflection in the mirror, but the brown-haired girl with bangs staring back no longer shocked her, despite the many years of her unnatural blond. Now, it came as a greater shock to see the flaxen-haired woman in the driver's license picture.

David crawled out of his patrol car when her Bronco pulled into a parking spot in front of the *Talon* office. Amanda avoided looking in his direction, afraid that the anger on his face would force her onto the defensive. He waited while she pulled the ragtop in place. From the corner of her eye she could tell he avoided meeting her gaze as well.

They avoided each other's gaze for another moment as they walked towards each other. Amanda stopped inches in front of him, cornering him with his back against the brick wall of the *Talon* office. It was early, Frank wasn't at the office yet. Only a few cars dotted the town square, and the sun hadn't peaked over the eastern buildings. She had anticipated seeing David first thing in the morning, but not this early.

"Open records request, huh?" he said as he finally looked at her. He didn't yell, growl or spit it at her as she anticipated. He was soft.

Amanda nodded. She was ready for a fight, ready to scream at him for withholding the truth, for interfering with justice and stifling her First Amendment rights. She didn't have a play against defeat.

"Come by the station at the end of the day, and I'll have copies of everything you need."

The shuffle of his body indicated he was eager to be back in the safety of his patrol car, but the invisible forcefield Amanda created between him and the vehicle didn't weaken. An apology surfaced from her throat, but she swallowed it back. This had nothing to do with the letter she sent to the Chief of Police citing Texas' Open Records Act, or the fact that David would be forced to comply.

"What's so wrong with me?" he whispered. If they had been standing on a busy Chicago sidewalk, his question would have been drowned out by the hum of the city, but in the early morning hush of Phoenix, she heard him perfectly.

"What's so right with me?" She looked up at him and images of their brief kiss flashed in front of her. She'd never had a kiss with such intensity as from him. It was like the opening paragraph of a beloved book, the beginning chords of a stirring song or the first glimpse of a moving work of art.

His eyes darted down to hers. She felt the familiar flutter of a panic attack, same but different.

"I wish I knew exactly. You're smart, determined, beautiful and unlike any other girl I've met. I've spent the last decade of my life settling with what's been handed to me, but I'm not doing it anymore. Not with you. So if you tell me that you don't feel something, that you have no interest in me, then fine, I'll accept that. But, I won't settle with you hiding behind your job as an excuse."

Amanda leaned up on her tiptoes with her face less than an inch from his. If she was really going to do this, if she was going to let go of everything holding her back she had to be sure.

"Don't do this out of pity," genuine pain crossed his eyes as he whispered.

"I'm not." His lips were cool from the early morning air. Goose bumps exploded on her arms and electricity pulsed from every nerve ending. Like before, the simplicity of their kiss awakened happiness, fear, excitement and trepidation. "Saturday night?"

The playful smile she missed reappeared as he tried to catch his breath. "Saturday night." He brushed past her, pausing for a second as if he wanted to return her kiss but instead moving to the side of his car. "If I'm not there this afternoon, Darlene will get you everything you need."

Darlene who? Oh yeah, Open Records Request. The mention of the 9-1-1 operator's name jogged Amanda's memory.

"Frank, what can I do to make today's paper the best ever?" Amanda asked during their quick editorial meeting. If Frank noticed that something was up with his lone employee, he kept quiet. Amanda cranked up the volume of the old radio as soon as Frank left the office for the morning.

Country music blared from the radio at Amanda's workstation, as she sat half-focused on compiling wire stories for the paper. The other half of her focus replayed David's electric kiss. Now that the flush of serotonin died down, Amanda worried that she was too impulsive. *Am I being selfish for getting involved with David? If I get caught, would he become an accomplice for harboring a criminal? It would kill him if he ever learned the truth. I should have left Phoenix weeks ago, but I'm not ready to leave yet—not without knowing if Katie's murderer is still here.*

The next song came on the radio and Amanda sang along. Her assimilation to small-town Texas life had moved along quicker than she thought. She had always pictured the fans as mysterious men in black and big-haired women who were the devoted stand-by-your-man types.

Amanda printed a few stories and danced to the printer to retrieve them. Her hips swayed out of time with the music, and her karaoke pitch would make her the butt of a singing contest judge's joke, but it didn't matter. The infectious glee of the love song cracked through the gloom that sullied her earlier spirit.

Maybe I'm over-thinking things. SEC agents hadn't apprehended her. A SWAT team hadn't forced its way in the *Talon* office to detain her. She wasn't in FBI custody. The few times she'd read the headlines from the disaster at her office there'd been no indication any arrests had been made or the authorities were closing in on suspects.

That ember of a future in her kiss with David was Fate's way of telling her she would be fine. But, as easily as Fate giveth, it could taketh away. A second chance came with high expectations. She would have to love David more than he loved her, which was a tall order considering he had a head start. Every wrong would need to be righted. She couldn't cause pain and suffering; instead she had to inject contentment and joy. Amanda would have to be truthful and honorable in every decision she made.

She retrieved the pages from the slow, monstrosity of a printer for Frank to review. All the articles were tales of happiness and promise; a long-lost wedding band that found its way home, a doctor who performed a risky, life-saving surgery successfully on a newborn baby, and a student from a neighboring county who won a full scholarship to an Ivy League school. Once again she avoided the financial pitfalls, the real estate hazards and employment downturns.

The sound of the door chime announced what she thought was Frank's return. She gathered up the papers and hurried to the front of the lobby to turn the music down.

"Hey Frank, sorry about the music," Amanda stopped mid-sentence when she saw that instead of Frank, Dr. Brown perched on the corner of her desk. The doctor looked out of place compared to everyone else in Phoenix. Once again he wore fine leather shoes, silk-wool blended pants and a French-cuffed shirt with brilliant blue cufflinks that set off his own blue eyes. If he got rid of the lopsided mustache he would be a handsome man.

"Hi Mandy," he said, arms folded across his chest. "I hate to say that as nice as it was to see you half-dressed, you look even better clothed."

Her hand moved to secure the gap that revealed just the slightest bit of her collarbone.

"Um, Dr. Brown, what brings you here?"

"I came by to see how you were doing. You were supposed to come back and see me, remember?"

"I didn't realize some doctors still made house calls."

"I can come by your house if that's your wish." He pushed himself off her desk and took two steps towards her. Amanda's feet answered by taking three steps back into the workroom, colliding with the island workbench. "But I'm more than happy to give you a thorough examination right here."

Amanda's breath shortened as he studied her with the intensity of a starved soldier staring down a finely cooked steak.

"I'm feeling much better, thank you," her voice barely a whisper.

"Let me be the judge of that," he took another step towards her and grabbed the back of her neck, stroking the side of it with his thumb. "We shouldn't waste an opportunity when we're alone like this."

Amanda pivoted around him and hurried back into the lobby, into the safety where passersby could see in through the dirty windows.

"Dr. Brown, you need to leave. Right now. If you don't, I'll—"

"You'll what? Call your boyfriend to come arrest me? I'm sure he would love to hear how his half-witted girlfriend was rescued from a hailstorm, dripping wet in her pajamas with nothing left to the imagination."

His eyes trailed from hers, and her arms crossed her body trying to hide whatever he imagined. She wanted to avert her eyes from his face, but if she looked away she would miss any tiny flinch he made in her direction. The door chimed behind her, and Frank's heavy footsteps echoed in the silence. She closed her eyes, finally able to take a deep breath.

"Hi-ya Doc, how are you doing?" Amanda was afraid to look at Frank, worried he would see the fear and loathing in her eyes. Lucky for her, all those years of drinking seemed to wash away most of his brain cells, and he was oblivious to any tension in the room.

"Hey there, Frank," Dr. Brown said over Amanda's shoulder. "I was just in the neighborhood, and thought I'd drop off my advertising payment for the clinic. I better get going. I've got lives to save." The two men chuckled at his last comment, and Dr. Brown's hand cupped Amanda's shoulder as he walked past her. To the outside observer, it would have been an innocent gesture of farewell, but to Amanda, it was a signal that he was far from done. Once Frank was tucked away in his office to read the printouts she gave him, she quietly locked herself in the bathroom and threw up her breakfast.

26

The humidity and heat should have been the equivalent of the hot shower Amanda needed to rinse away the disgust she felt, but they weren't. Amanda read the stories in magazines of women who overcame sexual attacks to find themselves stronger, but as close as she was to becoming one of them, she didn't think there would be any way she could recover from something so brutal. Dr. Brown wasn't a large man. She was eye to eye with him in her three-inch heels, and with his slight build she could easily fight back. But, it was his eerie charm that he wore like sheep's clothing. The same type of power that she found so attractive in Josh frightened her in Dr. Brown.

If she could just talk to someone, share the experience and no longer have to bear the entire frightful situation herself, she would feel better. But whom could she tell? Frank thought he walked in on a subscriber simply dropping off a check. Myrna wouldn't care to hear she had a renter who suffered from delusions. David probably already thought she was a bit off by her single-minded desire to solve an old case. As Amanda put her Bronco in park in front of the police station, she accepted that this was something that she alone had to endure and she would have to avoid Dr. Brown with every ounce of her self-preserving instincts.

David's truck was parked in the empty lot next to the small police station, where all the police cruisers would have been parked if they weren't on duty. Though disappointed in not seeing David, she was glad she'd be able to grab the files and go home.

The cool blast of the air conditioner hit her skin inside the police station. This time she didn't have to search out Darlene; the woman was in the hallway.

"You must be the little girl making me run all these copies," the woman said with notable annoyance. "You're lucky David fancies you, or I'd be mighty teed off right now." Amanda wondered if this was her normal personality. "You stay put, I'm waiting on a few more copies to finish up."

Left alone, Amanda studied the narrow hallway. The building was stark and utilitarian, a design element carried throughout the interior as well. A corkboard on the wall displayed the latest FBI Most Wanted. She breathed easier knowing she was not pictured. A couple of picture frames held newspaper photographs of the chief and the mayor. A few steps down her eyes rested on David's official police photo. Despite the stereotypical stern and austere image of the other officers in the photos, a half-smile played on his lips and his dimple was just on the verge of emerging on his cheek. Stern and austere just wasn't him. It was staring at his picture where Darlene found her.

"You better be good to him," she said.

Amanda smiled at the woman. "I will."

The crow's feet around Darlene's eyes showed themselves for a brief moment as the woman smiled back at Amanda, but then stopped as if she remembered she was supposed to be annoyed.

"Here you go. I'm going to need you to sign for this."

Just as Darlene handed Amanda a manila folder stuffed with photocopies, a radio in the control room buzzed with a voice.

"Well shoot. You wait right here while I see what the boys need."

Amanda thumbed through the papers but became distracted

when a box on the corner of a desk came within her line of vision. It was a white banker's box with the lid askew. Nothing special about it except for the black block letters that spelled "Shelton" and the red sticker below that said "Evidence."

Darlene was still busy in the other room. From what Amanda could overhear, a case of vandalism at the high school was in process. She tiptoed to the box and peered inside, afraid to touch it in case the box was wired to an alarm. A void towards the front of the box indicated this must be where the files Darlene copied were stored. But it was the items in the back of the box that piqued Amanda's interest.

It was a framed picture of Katie Shelton wearing an oversized football mum standing next to a younger, shorter version of David. This must be Cody. Like his older brother, he was dark-haired and handsome, but his face was softer and rounder and he was probably a head shorter. The next picture frame was Katie holding a golden retriever puppy. Then a picture of her and Shiloh in cheerleading uniforms, both with their long hair pulled back in a ponytail held in place by a ribbon.

Past the picture frames Amanda saw two copies of the Phoenix High School yearbook, the only two copies that Katie would live to collect. She wondered if there were messages of hope, inside jokes and proclamations of love written inside those pages. It was the final item in the back of the box that made Amanda feel bold enough to actually bring it out of its safe haven.

Just slightly larger than the palm of her hand, the pink fabric-covered diary felt no different than her own teenage journal likely still hidden away in her childhood bedroom. The word Diary was written out in glass beads, with the last bead in the 'y' missing, and the string holding the others into place starting to unravel. The journal was once locked, but it appeared that in the course of the investigation the lock was snipped away. Amanda knew from experience those locks didn't really protect the secrets and desires of an adolescent girl from the outside world, especially when a nosy younger brother was involved. Or, in this case, the police. Amanda didn't recall seeing any photocopies from diary pages in her quick glance through the file Darlene gave her.

"Alright boys, I just called the kids' parents, and they are on their way up to the school now." Darlene's voice startled Amanda and broke her from her memories. She carefully slipped the diary into her open purse and quietly moved back into the hallway where the dispatcher left her.

"You got everything you need?" Darlene asked when she reemerged in the hallway.

"Sure do. Thank you," Amanda answered, smiling so brightly that her face hurt. She had never stolen anything before in her life. Well, not counting the money that Josh gave her, but he did the stealing in that case. "Okay, well I'll get out of your way then."

Amanda turned to leave and Darlene cleared her throat.

"Aren't you forgetting something?"

Amanda's back stiffened and her eyes froze open. Were there cameras inside the police station? Could Darlene tell that Amanda was snooping through the evidence box and stole Katie's diary?

"Umm."

"David says you're smart as a whip, but I'm not convinced. I need you to sign for this to show that I gave you the copies you requested."

Darlene thrust a clipboard her way, and Amanda steadied her hand long enough to sign her name. "Thank you again for all of your help," Amanda said, giving the brightest smile to prove Darlene otherwise.

She used every bit of her self-control to not run out of the police station.

27

"I can't believe how unfair you're being." Shiloh slammed a case of bottled beer on the counter so hard she feared, and hoped, they would break.

"Sorry, Shi. I need you here Saturday, so you'll just have to find another night to take off," Eddie cajoled his angry sister. Riley's busiest night of the week, with or without a band, usually meant all hands on deck. Shiloh made enough money on a Saturday night to pay half her rent for the month, but sacrificing a lucrative night just to avoid witnessing David and Mandy's now-infamous first date was worth it to save herself the heartache.

She couldn't avoid the quick-spreading gossip when Mandy agreed to go out with David.

"He's just so smitten with her," Darlene, the den mother of the police station, said to anyone who would listen at the bar.

"She's such a pretty girl," someone else chimed in.

"His momma will be so happy he found a sweet girl."

"Mandy has worked wonders with Frank. He's cleaned up since she started at the *Talon*, and the paper is better, too."

"What a godsend."

Shiloh slammed the cooler shut. She was tired of everyone else's excitement over a stranger dating the love of her life. For both her and David's sake, she wished Phoenix were big enough to have multiple options for a first date, but Riley's was the only place that offered such entertainment.

"Shi, shut the door behind you," Eddie said. "I know why you're asking for the night off." They argued about this for two days, but she thought she'd give it one more try when her shift started on Saturday afternoon.

"Rex and I just want to have a date night like normal people do," she said, even though Rex didn't know that yet.

Eddie shook his head and stood from behind his desk. "It's because there is a ninety-nine percent probability that David is bringing Mandy here tonight for a date. You've had a crush on him for as far back as I can remember."

Shiloh's mouth dropped open. Not once in all these years did she think her older brother realized her feelings for David.

"How? Why?" was all she managed to get out, but what she really meant was how long did he know? And, why didn't he say something in her favor to David?

"When you were a kid you weren't very good at hiding the fact that you stared at him all the time like he was some rock star. I never said anything to him because you found Rex, and I thought your feelings for David were only puppy love," he came from behind his desk and stood next to Shiloh, putting his arm around her petite shoulders. "I only just realized that you're not over it and to you, it was more than just a little crush. I'm so sorry, Shi. I wish I had known."

Shiloh's lower lip trembled no matter how hard she bit down on it. If she would have been bold enough to say something to Eddie years ago, she wouldn't be standing here having this conversation while the love of her life prepared for a date with a complete stranger.

"It's okay, really. I'm happy with Rex and despite what you think, he is good to me."

Eddie had always been hard on Rex. Not that they weren't friends, but after all these years together, he thought that Rex should have proposed to Shiloh by now. What Shiloh never told him was that every time Rex brought up marriage, she would quickly change the subject or drop hints that she was not the marrying type. In all honesty, Rex would have married her years ago if she encouraged him.

"How about this, let's just play tonight by ear. If we're not busy, I'll cut you first. If we are, I'll move you to a section where they aren't sitting. What do you think?"

Shiloh put on a big smile and hugged her brother. She was going to have to get used to the idea of David dating someone else eventually. A guy like him wasn't going to remain single for the rest of his life, so if it wasn't Mandy it would be some other woman. And, if it was some other woman she may take him from Phoenix, beg him to move to another town—some place larger like San Angelo or Abilene, or maybe even Dallas or Houston. Shiloh remembered David saying that as much fun as he had going to school in Austin, if it wasn't for his football scholarship he would have been just as happy at a community college closer to home. Mandy seemed at home in Phoenix, so with her David wouldn't leave Shiloh completely.

Unfortunately for her, it was one of the busiest nights in months. Maybe the whole town decided to come out and witness the date between the most eligible bachelor of Phoenix and the new girl in town. Or, perhaps it was that one of the most beloved country bands in a five-county area was playing. But most likely, it had to do with being one of the final pleasant spring evenings before summer's cruel grasp clamped down on Phoenix.

Shiloh started her shift out on Riley's back patio. Unless David and Mandy went outside, she would never know they were here.

A few regulars came in and tipped her well. She waited tables while another co-worker tended the small outside bar. Once the sun went down and the strung Christmas lights popped on, the murmur of voices outside competed with the music of the band. Eddie found Shiloh in the employee parking lot taking a smoke break.

"Shi, I hate to do this to you, but I'm going to need to move you inside and put Andrea on the patio," Eddie said, referring to the newest waitress he hired. "She's overwhelmed with the crowd inside and working around the dance floor. You're a much better waitress, so I could use you inside."

Shiloh sighed and exhaled a plume of smoke. "Are they in there?"

Eddie nodded. "David's got a tab at the bar, so I've been waiting on him. They're dancing, so you likely won't even see them."

"Fine," Shiloh sighed. "Let me finish this cigarette, and I'll be right in." Eddie nodded and left her alone in the parking lot. She appreciated that for once, her brother didn't chastise her for smoking.

Despite the bar's air conditioning running at full blast, it was hot inside from the sweating, dancing crowd. For the first half hour of her shift, she was so focused on her tables that she never saw David's head tower over the crowd or glimpsed Mandy's pale skin twirling around the dance floor. It was only when she was behind another waitress at the side of the bar waiting for Eddie to fill up her tray with drink orders that she spied David just a few feet away. He talked to a man next to him, waiting for his drinks to be delivered. With his back to her, Shiloh was free to observe him without fear of being caught.

He deviated from his non-law enforcement uniform of jeans and a t-shirt only slightly. Still in jeans, he wore a button up shirt untucked with the long sleeves rolled up to his elbows. Eddie brought David two beers, and he disappeared into the crowd. Shiloh moved around a few patrons to maintain her line of sight as her eyes followed David to his destination.

Against the far wall, he stopped in front of Mandy seated on a bar stool and he rested their beers on a small ledge.

"Dammit, I wanted that dress," Shiloh muttered when she realized Mandy wore the same emerald green halter dress she'd admired earlier in the week. She put it back on the rack after trying it on, the green did nothing for her dark skin and hair, and the intended above-the-knee length hung past her knees, emphasizing her short stature. But on Mandy, the dress played up her pale skin, and her brown hair shone under the dim lights.

Conversation would be hard to come by in the noisy bar, but David made an attempt by leaning in to Mandy's ear. Whatever he said produced a wide smile on the woman that lit up her whole face. Where the rest of Mandy could be considered average—normal height, regular build, a common face and standard hair—her smile could transform her entire face from ordinary to striking in one simple gesture. She could see why David thought all the light shone on her. When Mandy smiled up at him, her eyes emitted a warm glow.

David leaned in for a kiss. "No," Shiloh said in an intake of air and hurried back to the bar to find her drink order sweating profusely on her tray and empty bottles waiting at her tables. After a quick delivery and check on the rest of her section, she escaped to the bathroom.

Lucky for her she timed it so that the typically long line of women was absent and only one stall was occupied. Shiloh pulled her red lipstick out of her back pocket and reapplied her already crimson lips. Something about Mandy's smile made her feel the need to enhance her own. With her pout perfected, she lifted her long, dark hair to wipe the sweat off the back of her neck. She made more in tips with her thick hair hanging loosely, but on a night as busy as this she would probably do just fine with her hair pulled up. In the midst of transferring the ponytail holder from her wrist to her hair, the toilet flushed and a flash of a green dress caught her eye.

Shiloh tried not to stare when Mandy emerged, but the woman caught her eye in the mirror and beamed that hypnotic smile at her.

"Hey, Shiloh. How's it going?"

I'll tell you how it's going. You're on a date with my soulmate, and it's so effing obvious that he's in love with you that I want to be sick, and everyone is cheering you on because they want David to be happy, but you don't fool me. I know that something is wrong with you. You and your strange Montana driver's license picture and your hailstorm freak out. Don't think I'm not watching you.

"Good," Shiloh smiled back at her.

Mandy washed her hands and pulled her own lipstick out of her purse. Shiloh was about to escape the closet-sized bathroom when Mandy spoke again.

"Can I ask you a question? Is Dr. Brown the only doctor in Phoenix? Or, is there another doctor in the next town over?"

Shiloh hated it when people proposed asking a question with a question. To her, it was a waste of air.

"Why do you ask?"

The woman hesitated and something strange floated across her eyes before Mandy fluttered her eyelids, blinking away whatever was there. "Oh, it's just that I think I'm going to stick around for a while and, you know, I could use a doctor for girl stuff."

Was Mandy asking if there was an obstetrician in town? Were she and David already planning on having babies? Clint wouldn't let that happen.

"Dr. Brown is the best in the county," Shiloh said while straightening her ponytail, hoping that indicated their conversation was over.

Mandy didn't move. Instead that same look crossed her entire face.

"What?" Shiloh couldn't stop her curiosity from getting the best of her.

"It's just," Mandy started, but toyed with the paper towel in her hands. "It's nothing really. It's just I get a weird feeling around him."

You and me both, sister. Then she remembered she hated Mandy.

"What, you can't be satisfied with just David? You want the happily married town doctor falling for you, too? You better hope it doesn't get back to David that you're putting the moves on Dr. Brown. But if it does, you can count on me being there to pick up the pieces."

As Shiloh exited the bathroom, the mirror beside the door revealed the shocked look on Mandy's face.

28

"**M**ate, did your maid up and quit on you?" Roland asked, standing in the doorway of Alex's small apartment.

Alex didn't think he needed to tidy up before Roland's visit, but as he looked at it from Roland's point of view, it was pretty bad.

"And would it kill you to hang something on your walls?" Roland smiled.

"This was never meant to be a permanent home," Alex admitted.

"How long have you lived here?"

"Six years. We should get to work."

They were each armed with a laptop, ready to pore over surveillance video.

"Right," said Roland. "Let me take the train station. I've spent more time with Amanda and Josh and could probably pick them out of a crowd better. Is that kosher?"

"Sure, I'll get the bus station then." Alex tacked pictures of the three suspects on the wall for easy visual reference in case someone stood out.

"Did you tell your editor what we're doing?" Alex asked.

Roland nodded. "He wants a story this week if we find anything on the video."

They ordered takeout Chinese food and got to work. There would be no beer or Scotch during these work sessions. Both men needed to be sharp in order to recognize a face out of the grainy, black-and-white crowds of the bus and train stations. During the first few hours of the surveillance video, they watched the footage in fast forward since the crowds were extremely light or non-existent during the pre-dawn hours. Once the crowds thickened, each man watched the video in near slow motion, analyzing each face, even glancing up at the pictures tacked up on the wall to check features.

On their second day of watching the videos, they approached the time of the shooting at JWI and watched even more intently. The silence of Alex's apartment-turned-command center was broken only by the occasional frustrated sigh or need to stand to stretch their legs.

By Thursday night, they neared the end of the allotted twenty-four hour period and nothing had stood out.

"This is bollocks." Roland threw an empty water bottle across the room. "My editor is breathing down my neck, and all I'm looking at is a bunch of homeless people begging for money."

Past midnight on Friday morning, Alex struggled to keep his eyes open despite drinking copious amounts of coffee. The empty bus terminal and the repetitive moves of the janitor buffing the floors began to lull him to sleep. A woman came into the frame. He initially dismissed her as a homeless person coming in from the cold, but when she approached a ticket window Alex took a second look at her. The woman was dressed only in a t-shirt and jeans, no coat, nothing covering her arms. Her tangled, long hair hung down her back in loose knots. When she turned from the ticket window, the camera had a perfect view of her face, and of her tucking something into the waistband of her jeans. Alex paused the video and stared at the face on his laptop. *Man, I wish I was watching this on one of those high def screens at the Bureau.* The camera was forty feet from the woman, but he felt sure enough to rouse Roland from his own stupor.

"Hey man, come check this out," Alex said.

Roland's head snapped up, as if he'd dozed off while watching his footage.

"At first, I thought this was just a homeless woman looking for some warmth. Remember that late freeze we had?" Alex said, rewinding the footage. Roland leaned in close to the laptop.

"The homeless have better sense than to just wear a t-shirt and jeans out in this cold," he said, as he watched the woman at a ticket window. She spoke to a worker who was on a cell phone. After the transaction was over, the woman turned her back to the ticket window and faced the camera, tucking something into the waist-band of her jeans.

"Oh Amanda, you clever little minx, you," Roland purred. "Where is she heading?"

Alex found the next camera on the disk. This one pointed outside, where the buses lined up for departure. This time, Amanda was easy to pick out, even sporting a sweatshirt she must have purchased inside.

"She's not sure about getting on the bus," Roland said. "No luggage. She left in a hurry." They watched the grainy black and white bus with its door yawning open swallow Amanda into the darkness. After several minutes, the bus driver boarded, the door closed and the bus left its terminal, carrying the only lead they had to some unknown destination.

Alex's apartment remained cloaked in silence. Neither man breathed, spoke or moved after the bus left. They sat there, in utter disbelief that something useful was on the video.

"Well, my friend, there is your headline," Alex broke the silence.

"Let's meet at the bus station tomorrow night," Roland suggested as he packed up his laptop for the evening. "Maybe we can talk to that woman at the ticket counter, see if she remembers Amanda."

"I'll print out some of the frames from the video to show around."

Roland waited for Alex at the bus station the next evening. They arrived at approximately the same time that Amanda bought her ticket, guessing that the workers were on a set schedule. Like the night she left, the terminal was mostly empty and quiet. No janitor buffed the floors, but a woman with a wide broom swept long rows on the tile floor. Instead of two ticket windows open, only one was open this night. And instead of a woman working, a young man sat at the lone window with his head bowed over a book, his hands covering his forehead, blocking out the empty terminal.

"Excuse me," Alex said. "Is this woman working tonight?" Alex held a picture of the woman who sold the ticket to Amanda. The young man looked up. He took a brief look at the picture and shook his head.

"Nah, she got fired two weeks ago. Why, what did she do?"

"That's classified information that is part of an ongoing investigation," Alex always wanted to say those words. No sooner than he finished his sentence did Roland start his own.

"Listen mate, we're not really concerned about your former colleague, just the woman she's talking to in this picture. Isn't this you sitting next to her?"

The man looked at the picture again, this time more intently, leaning up on his elbows to get a better look through his thick glasses.

"Yeah, I work most evenings so that's me there. Why, what do you need?"

Alex and Roland smiled in unison.

"Do you remember the girl that she sold the ticket to?" Alex asked. He pulled out the only picture they had of Amanda's face out to show the man.

The young man pursed his lips, and his eyes went up to an imaginary spot to the right of their heads, as if looking for some lost memory in his brain.

"Yeah, I think I do remember her. She smelled like smoke, like she had been huddled around a campfire or something. I didn't think much of it at the time. I was studying for a physics mid-term and just remember her smell."

"Splendid, do you recall where she was going?" Roland's words rolled together through his accent.

The man shook his head. "Naomi, the lady that used to work here, she was on her cell phone every night, the whole night. That's why she got fired. I try to study when it's quiet, but with all her talking I had to wear headphones. So no, I didn't hear where she bought a ticket to."

Roland turned to walk away, his shoulders hunched forward.

"Wait," Alex said. He pulled out another picture. This time it was the waiting bus with Amanda climbing aboard. "I take it not many buses depart here around 12:20 a.m. Do you know where this bus was heading?"

The man straightened his back and brightened. "Yeah," he said, obviously excited. "That bus goes down to Memphis."

Alex and Roland thanked the young man profusely and left the bus station to grab a late coffee.

"I'm going to work on a story over the weekend and turn it in to my editor first thing Monday," Roland said after sipping his black coffee. "I wish we had something more than a suspect might be in Memphis, but I need to show that I'm on to something and indispensable."

"Is there a chance we could tip Amanda off if you say where we think she is?"

Roland shook his head. "I'm not going to say where she is in this piece. It's going to be short, just to say that some new information is available."

When Alex got to work Monday morning, he made more trips to the coffee pot, and thus the men's room, than usual in hopes that he'd see Harrison's office door open. It remained closed, and finally, by mid-morning Alex stopped by his boss's assistant's desk to ascertain Harrison's whereabouts.

"Hi, Allen. Can I help you?" she smiled sweetly as she tried to hide a magazine under her computer keyboard.

"Uh, I'm Alex. Is Mr. Harrison in? I really need to speak with him."

"Oh he's having a root canal and took the day off. He's available on email if you need him," she finished her much-practiced spiel.

Alex slunk to the men's room and checked to make sure he was alone. Then he dialed Roland's number.

"Hey mate, have you seen the story yet?" Roland answered; his voice livelier than usual. "My editor is thrilled with the piece, and he's even got the publisher's media relations person shopping it around to some of the networks to see if any of the cable news outlets want the broadcast story."

"Dammit." This was not going to end well for him. "Did you name me as your source?"

"Of course I did," Roland said. "Alex, are you alright? Is something wrong there?"

"No, no, I'm great," Alex hoped he sounded convincing. "Just wanted to check in with you, man. Alright, back to work."

Acid rumbled around in Alex's stomach. They agreed to meet up for celebratory drinks that night, and Alex went back to his cubicle, wondering if he should start packing up his belongings.

It would have come as no shock if Harrison called Alex from the dentist chair to fire him. What did come as a shock was when the afternoon came and went with no sign from his boss. Alex had to go online and check for himself that Roland's article was posted and actually named him as a source; otherwise, the lack of any acknowledgement from his colleagues made it seem unreal.

Alex waited until nearly six to leave the office. He felt like a prisoner waiting for his executioner, only to find that the person to deliver his sentence was otherwise occupied. He rode the elevator alone and would have walked right by Harrison in the lobby if his boss didn't reach out and grab his arm.

"Alex," Harrison said, the side of his face swollen and one corner of his mouth slower to respond than the other. "Take a walk with me."

The two men strolled in silence for a few minutes. Alex wasn't sure if Harrison had a path in mind, maybe to the guillotines for his betrayal. As they walked, Alex played an imaginary argument in his head. Harrison screamed at him, asked what he was thinking. Alex countered, he was doing his job. Harrison lashed out that Alex wasn't doing the job he gave him. Alex sulked that Harrison ignored him for weeks and only gave him busy work. Harrison's face grew red. Alex broke into a sweat.

And yet, the only conversation was between their footsteps. Alex followed Harrison's lead if the man veered to any direction.

"I let you down, I know that," Harrison was the first to speak. His voice was much softer than Alex expected.

They arrived to a park overlooking the lake. Harrison motioned to an empty park bench and they both sat. The make-believe argument in Alex's head was nothing like the actual conversation they had.

"I spent the better part of this afternoon trying to save your job," Harrison said, pulling a cigarette from a pack. "They told me no gum for a couple of days, so I figured that a smoke here and there wouldn't hurt." Harrison laughed as he said this, the right side of his mouth not moving.

"Mr. Harrison," Alex began, but his boss cut him off.

"Don't say a word, Alex?"

Alex nodded.

"I knew you weren't done with the case, son," he took a drag on his cigarette, his eyes focused straight ahead. "That's why I avoided you. If I saw what I suspected, I would have been forced to stop you." Harrison finally met Alex's gaze. "I didn't want to stop you.

"I've got to hand it to you, kid," he continued. "That was pretty damn resourceful. How in the world did you get a reporter to help you like that and not spill the beans about it until now?"

Alex shrugged. He never suspected that Roland would have betrayed him at some point for his own benefit.

"Why was the agency so eager to brush this case aside?" Alex asked. It was the question that constantly burned his throat like bad heartburn.

Harrison let out a long exhale of smoke. "Without going into details, bureaucracy, plain and simple. I fought to keep that case open, but the higher ups thought everyone involved was dead and was ready to hand it off to the police. Believe it or not, I don't have that much pull with my superiors."

Runners jogged by. Dogs enjoyed their first bit of freedom all day and pulled their owners down the trail. A herd of bicyclists rode by, soundlessly parting around someone moving slower on the path.

Alex had the urge to speak, but at Harrison's request remained silent until it seemed like his boss wasn't going to offer any more information.

"Am I fired?" Alex asked.

"Indefinitely suspended without pay," Harrison replied. "I had to negotiate that one; otherwise they were perfectly fine with canning you for breach of confidence."

Alex nodded. It was bad, but it could have been much worse. The good news was that Alex wouldn't need to take vacation time to finish the investigation.

"So, what's next?"

"I need you to lay low for several days," Harrison said. "And, I need your employee badge to show management that you are suspended."

As Harrison spoke, Alex realized that Harrison never told him to stop what he was doing, to stop the investigation. But, what Harrison told him, between the lines, was to stop using the SEC's name, and that he had to work the rest of this case as an independent investigator.

"Alright son, I've got to get home to Millie before she sends out a search party," Harrison stood. Alex rose too, but neither man made any effort to leave. Harrison laid a hand on Alex's shoulder. "Alex, look, I wish I could help you, I wish I could give you guidance, but I've got my pension to worry about. You're young, you have a future. I'm just biding time until I hit that golden age for retirement, so I can't take the chances you can. But please know that no matter what happens, I'm proud of you. And I'm proud that I had an opportunity to work with you for the last ten years. You got that?"

For the first time, the man that Alex regarded as a surrogate father spoke to him as if he was a son. Instead of becoming angry with Harrison for not offering more, Alex was pleased with what he got.

29

Amanda spent Sunday afternoon basking in the glow of her and David's perfect date. But despite its perfection, something was off. It wasn't anything notable during the date, and it wasn't anything that happened when she went home with him afterwards. Everything felt natural. This was definitely the kind of guy she could take home to her parents.

Home. Her parents. It snapped up in her face like the stubborn root of a weed she pulled from Myrna's garden. That's what was off. David was falling in love with Mandy Jackson, the brown-haired, discount-clothed, small-town reporter from Montana. *What would he think of Amanda Martin?* He would probably see her as shallow, petty, disdainful. Then he would arrest her, because that's what he does. He kept people like her off the streets and away from the innocent; he didn't fall in love with them. Dirty tears streamed down her cheeks. *I don't deserve his love, but how can I explain without breaking his heart or ending up in jail?*

By the time she pulled up to work Monday morning and saw David waiting for her, she catapulted back to the sunny side of the mood spectrum.

"Hey gorgeous," he said, opening her car door and helping her out. "I wanted to be the first person you saw today." *I can do this. Loving him would be so easy, especially when words like that come out of his mouth.* "Can I see you tonight?" They chatted for a bit longer and parted after Frank rounded the corner.

"Jackson, you're doing such a good job, I think I'm going to reward myself with a vacation in a couple of weeks. You think you can keep the paper running while I'm gone?"

I don't necessarily see how you going on vacation rewards my good work, then again... "Sure, Frank. I'm happy to hold down the fort for you. Going anywhere special?"

"One of my ex-wives is getting remarried, so I'm going to take a trip to Padre to celebrate having one less mouth to feed."

It was a quiet day at the *Talon* office, so it didn't take long for Amanda to get ahead in her work. With Frank tucked away reading the wire reports, the classifieds updated and no obituaries to write, Amanda pulled out the thick manila folder on Katie Shelton. The diary was tucked away in her one desk drawer that locked. She couldn't run the risk of Frank finding stolen property.

There wasn't much in the police files that she didn't already know. Amanda first read Shiloh's affidavit on their whereabouts the night before and day that Katie went missing. As in the newspaper stories, Shiloh's sworn statement was that the girls spent the night at her house and when she woke up the next morning, Katie was gone. After that was the 9-1-1 operator's statement that an anonymous call came in the day after her disappearance reporting a stranger was seen walking down the highway. She flipped through Cody's statement. As David told her, Cody was guilt-ridden and thought that whoever Katie was seeing was behind the murder, but he didn't have anything more than a hunch.

Amanda was grateful that David spared her any photos from the crime scene or autopsy. The medical examiner's report was pretty short and to-the-point. Cause of death was asphyxiation and the time of death was roughly a month before her body was unearthed. It was obvious this was a tough case to solve with the lack of evidence or any solid leads.

When Frank left for lunch, Amanda finally had the privacy she needed to crack open the diary. With her sandwich forgotten, she prepared to dive into the head of Katie Shelton. It was a bit daunting, like idolizing a favorite singer from a distance only to realize that he stood on the other side of the door, within reach but a world away. Would she like Katie? Were the words written on the pages of the pink fabric diary enough for the teenager's voice to come through? Was it filled with teen angst and nothing solid?

The journal struggled to remain closed, its spine not cracked for nearly a decade. The pages were stiff and brittle, and the pink ink of Katie's loopy writing faded in places. The first entry was dated almost two years before she disappeared and coincided with the start of her freshman year of high school. It was nothing of significance, the teenager went shopping with her mom for school clothes, she was upset that her mom refused to buy her a pair of pricey jeans and she longed for high school graduation and going off for college.

Other entries debated her feelings for Cody. She cared deeply for him, but wondered if there was someone else out there for her. In her musings, Katie contemplated ending things because they were so young, worrying that neither would reach their full potential because of the other. For someone so young, Katie's concerns caused her more anguish than necessary.

It wasn't until the summer after her freshman year that the journal produced something tangible for Amanda. The teenager wasn't a consistent chronicler, sometimes skipping months between passages, moments when the new wore off. But, pages were devoted to her and Cody's break up. She planned to end things after school was out for the summer so they wouldn't be forced to see each other every day. Initially, it was simply so they could grow without holding each other back. But, one entry indicated something, or someone, else may have been the necessary catalyst.

Dear Diary,

I really thought there's no way I could break up with Cody. But, I found the strength. I thought it was my imagination at first—that I was reading his being nice to me as flirting. And, when he called me to ask if I was seeing anyone I thought it had to be a joke. I told him no. What could I say? He's older, handsome and is going to be rich. I have exactly three days to break up with Cody before our date. I don't want to cheat on Cody. I can't do that after all this time. But I gave myself a deadline. It's really for the best. I hope.

As David's brother suspected, there was someone else in Katie's life. The next few entries came as no surprise. Cody didn't take the break up well, Katie worried about him and about her decision. There wasn't another mention of the other guy until a few entries later after they went on a date. Katie was smitten, but there was also a forbidden element. Whoever she was seeing was older. Katie never said exactly how much her senior, but enough that they, or, reading between the lines, *he* decided to keep their relationship a secret. It was so much a secret that she never used his name.

Amanda's grumbling stomach reminded her to eat, and she gnawed on a carrot while stealing a glance at the clock. A few more pages were all she would allow herself before she needed to lock up the journal before Frank's return. An entry written the spring before she died, that Amanda would have flipped past quickly, caught her attention, not because it held any clues to Katie's secret love, but because it contained David's name.

Dear Diary,

This is one of those days I'm wishing Cody and I were still together. Not because I miss him, but because Shi finally confessed that she's madly in love with David. I mean, what girl isn't in love with the Phoenix Football God. And, since his knee injury killed any chance of going pro, her competition field narrowed big time. If Cody and I were still together, I could suggest a double date. But, I doubt David would go for it. Anyway, looks like he won't be coming back home after all. I heard at the beauty shop that he's going to law school in the fall. Poor Shi. I can't talk about C for a while around her.

C. Amanda read that last time again. Did Katie shorthand Cody's name, or was there another C? It had to be Cody. It would be logical that if Katie spoke to her best friend about her ex-boyfriend, David's younger brother, it would be equivalent to rubbing salt in the wound. Then again, Shiloh may be the only person in Phoenix to hold the identity of the enigmatic C. While her mouth munched on another carrot, her brain chewed on the idea of confronting Shiloh.

Voices on the sidewalk drew Amanda back to the present, and

she quickly put a Post-It note between the pages of the journal as a bookmark and slid it back into the desk drawer. Frank walked through the front door moments later with sweat circles under his arms.

"Whew, it's a hot one today," he said, working a piece of food from between his teeth with a toothpick.

"Lovely," Amanda sighed. "Hey Frank, I need to head over to Foster's for his next book review. That okay?"

"See if you can get that squirrely little man to buy some ads while you're at it," Frank said, examining whatever bounty his toothpick dug out for him.

The hot air enveloped her the moment she walked out the door. She had a tough choice: bear the heat inside her non-air conditioned car for the short drive to Foster's Bookstore or walk. Either way she was going to sweat. She pulled out her cheap sunglasses and walked along the edge of the buildings, hoping to stay within the anemic shade cast by the early-afternoon sun.

When she entered the store, she jumped at seeing Mr. Foster staring at her just feet away from the door, expecting her to walk through the door at any minute.

"Good afternoon, Ms. Jackson."

"Mr. Foster, you startled me. Did you see me walk up?" She hated to think that the statue of a man stood there all day staring at the door, willing it to open.

"No, your very uncouth boss called to make sure you tried to sell me some advertising."

"Sounds like Frank. Sorry about that."

"Here is my assignment," he said, handing her two sheets of typed paper. "I think you will be very pleased with my work."

She read the opening paragraph and was pleased to see Mr. Foster himself was quite adept with a pen. "This is perfect. Thank you."

The bookstore's cool darkness chilled the sweat on her neck, and she was in no hurry to get back to the heat. She searched for something in which she could engage the man in conversation, but only one subject came to mind.

"I'm still working on the Katie Shelton case," she volunteered. His head tilted at the teenager's name, like a cat hearing the squeak of a mouse.

"Oh?"

"I haven't found anything new though. I'm just going through the police files now," she said. Could she trust Mr. Foster with her secret of stealing the diary? Would the man betray her to David? "Did you know Katie well? You said she was an avid reader. Did she shop here? Were you friends?"

The skin on his face was so taut that when a smile broke, Amanda's cheeks hurt for him. "Oh yes, not just for her school assignments, but she read frequently. She loved everything, the classics, oh we would talk for hours about the types of stories Chaucer would have told the pilgrims on their return trip if he lived long enough to complete them. And travelogues, she was destined for a much bigger life than Phoenix offered. She picked out the name for my cat, Chaucer." When he finished speaking, his face moved back to its normal state.

She decided to broach another subject, one that she couldn't get off her mind no matter how she tried. "What about Shiloh Garcia? Did she ever come in here with Katie?"

If Shiloh and Katie were really as inseparable as everyone claimed, including Katie in her diary, maybe Mr. Foster knew how to break through the girl's jealous shell.

The reaction Shiloh's name produced was markedly different than Katie's name. His head flinched, recoiling like she slapped him, and his eyes blinked so rapidly that Amanda feared he was having a seizure.

"Mr. Foster, are you okay?" Amanda reached out for him, but he took a step back from her.

"Why would you poison the air with her name?"

"I'm sorry. I didn't mean to—I was just trying to get to know Shiloh better."

"She is evil, Mandy Jackson. Pure evil. You stay far, far away from her, or else—" his monotone voice went up an octave and broke. The cat, hidden among the bookshelves, ran from the room.

"What did she do to you," Amanda whispered.

The man turned his back to her, and his shoulders hunched over, shaking as if crying. Amanda took another step towards him, her hand outstretched to comfort him, but the electricity in the air pulled her arm back. After a moment, Mr. Foster cleared his throat and turned to face her. Any sign of emotion was wiped away, and his face once again smooth as granite.

"I would like for you to leave now, Ms. Jackson," he said, barely moving his mouth.

30

S hiloh tuned out Rex's idle chatter about a new transmission he was putting in a vintage Mustang. If they had been in the bar alone, she would have told him to go back to work and quit drinking for free in the middle of a Tuesday afternoon, but by feigning interest in what he told her, she avoided the woman at the other end of the bar.

At first, when the door opened, she welcomed the distraction. But that excitement faded when she made eye contact with Mandy. She had no reason to ignore the woman, other than the fact that she hated her.

"Baby, you just can't imagine the sweetness of this Mustang," Rex proclaimed. "When I get the transmission done, want to go for a ride with me before I call the guy to pick it up?" he added, obviously looking for validation from his girlfriend.

"Sure," Shiloh said, staring out the window and away from Mandy sitting at the far end of the bar.

"Hey babe, don't you think that lady down there would like a drink?" Rex asked. Mandy had been sitting there some time, and it took him a little while to process that Shiloh hadn't even asked her what she wanted.

"She doesn't need anything."

Rex seemed to accept that response. Through her peripheral vision, Shiloh watched Mandy sit patiently. She looked thin, her arms revealing the sinewy look of someone who worked out too much and didn't eat enough. She wore conservative black pants with a beige chiffon shirt. *She must be asking for it. What is she doing here? And, what is going on with her and Clint? Honestly, wouldn't shock me if they are screwing. Poor David, does he realize what's going on?*

"Yeah, the old boy that owns the Mustang will love the six speed on the flo—" Rex's cell phone rang, leaving Shiloh with nothing to occupy her while he talked. She turned her head to look down the bar at Mandy. Mandy turned her head too, made eye contact again and smiled at Shiloh. *Dammit. I'll just see what she wants, so she can get out of here.*

"I'm sorry, I didn't see you sitting down there," Shiloh said. It made her feel better to be mean to David's girlfriend. "Can I get you something?"

"No problem, Shiloh, just an iced tea, please," Mandy said, smiling at Shiloh. "I was wondering if I could talk to you about something."

Shiloh had her back to Mandy when she spoke.

"What?" she said, as she filled a glass of lukewarm, freshly brewed tea, sans ice.

"It's about a story I'm working on for the paper."

"Oh, sure, yeah," Shiloh said. She watched Mandy take a drink of the warm tea, hoping to see the woman grimace, but she didn't seem fazed. Her mouth opened with a word perched on her tongue when Rex interrupted.

"Hey baby, I gotta run. Need to pick up a broken down car out east." For a second, Shiloh wanted to ask if it was safe for him to drive the tow truck after two beers, but no matter how dumb Rex was, he was careful to a fault on the road.

With him out of the bar, she found herself alone with Mandy. Shiloh reached into the beer cooler and pulled out a drink for herself. They eyeballed each other for a few moments, each one sizing up the other, like boxers in a ring. When the imaginary bell sounded, they spoke simultaneously.

"Why are you in Phoenix?" Shiloh asked, throwing out her first verbal punch.

"Can I ask you some questions about Katie Shelton?" Mandy asked, blocking Shiloh's shot with one of her own.

They stared at each other again. Mandy smiled.

"It's obvious you don't like me," Mandy said, quietly and in a non-threatening way. "And that's okay, I understand. But, I'll make a deal with you. I'll answer your questions if you'll answer mine."

Shiloh folded her arms across her chest. "Okay, I'll go first. Why are you in Phoenix?"

"That's an easy one," Mandy said, taking a drink of her tea before continuing. "I was on my way to El Paso when my bus broke down. I got off to stretch my legs, wandered down the road and stopped for breakfast. Dugan convinced me to stay for a bit so here I am."

"Why were you going to El Paso?" Shiloh had her next question ready before Mandy finished her answer. Mandy shook a finger at her.

"Not so fast, my turn. Was Katie secretly seeing someone when she was killed?"

I'll hand it to her, she doesn't mess around. Anyway, Mandy just said someone, she didn't ask for a name.

"Sure, I think she may have been sneaking around with someone. Why were you going to El Paso?" Shiloh hoped that her face didn't tell the truth while her words lied. Beyond Mandy, only David's brother suspected her friend had a secret boyfriend, but everyone chalked that up to Cody's jealousy. Katie was so secretive of her relationship that she forced Shiloh into some adolescent pinky-swearing ceremony that would certainly result in Shiloh's hair falling out or her face breaking out in explosive acne if she ever uttered the name of the secret lover. Shiloh wondered what the statute of limitations was for these types of promises.

"To find something. Was there really a transient in town the day she went missing?"

"I never saw one, but that didn't mean he wasn't here." There, the actual truth. "When are you leaving?"

"I don't have any plans to," Mandy said, taking another sip of tea. "Do you think Katie's murderer is still here in Phoenix?"

Shiloh took a deep breath. She was already getting bored with this game. "That would mean that whoever killed her either lived here or stayed here after he did it. What do you want with David?"

"The same thing he wants with me, love. Did Katie really spend the night with you the night before she disappeared?"

Careful new girl, you're treading in the deep end.

"Ask your boyfriend, the police found her overnight bag at my house," she said, hoping Mandy wasn't smart enough to catch on that she didn't really answer the question. "My turn. What are you running from?"

"What makes you think I'm running from something?"

Shiloh had her in a corner. Phoenix was the place one ran away from, not to. "Is that one of your questions or would you like to rephrase that?"

Mandy took another drink. Shiloh saw her cheeks flush, and she knew the woman was trying to control her anger.

"Fair enough. I'm not running from anything. Who have you been lying for all these years, and is he worth it?"

Shiloh's temper flared. Not once in the ten years since her friend disappeared did anyone question whether she lied to the police. Not her mother, brother, the chief of police or even Katie's grieving parents. They all took her concocted story as gospel. But, sitting in front of her was a complete stranger, an outsider to their tiny town, who questioned her honesty. Ever so briefly, she entertained the thought of coming clean, of telling Mandy what really happened. Then she remembered Clint's warning that something wasn't right about Mandy. If she were to tell the truth now, her reputation would be forever damaged in Phoenix, and as much as she wanted to leave this small town, it was home. She had nowhere else to go. Begrudgingly, she admitted to herself that trusting Clint got her this far.

"How dare you. You walk into my bar and question me on something that is none of your damn business. Not only that, but you waltz into town and steal the heart of," Shiloh had to swallow the real word perched on her tongue. "Of, David. I want you out of my bar. And, don't get too comfortable here either, because I want you out of this town."

Mandy fished a five out of her purse, and left it on the bar. Shiloh watched as Mandy paused at the door, her hand on the handle.

"Before you go, one last question," Shiloh said and the woman looked towards her. "What's your real name?"

For a split second, Shiloh could see the fear in her eyes and her neck flush. It was only a guess that Mandy Jackson wasn't her real name. She remembered her driver's license picture, the girl in the picture looking practically homeless, a far cry from the woman sitting at the bar. She didn't expect the question would cause such a physical reaction.

The woman looked down at her feet and then back up at Shiloh, her face soft and pleading, almost like she was going to beg for mercy. She saw Mandy swallow hard and exit the bar, slamming the door behind her.

Shiloh watched her walk out of the parking lot and head back towards the town square. She waited until she couldn't see the woman any longer and pulled her cell phone out of her back pocket, placing it on the bar. Her first instinct was to call Clint, to ask him the truth. How did Mandy seem to know so much more than anyone else? Was it possible that Mandy was someone who had lived here ten years earlier? Or, did she know Clint from school and he confessed something to her his final year of medical school? Maybe Clint lied to her a few weeks ago—maybe Mandy didn't really have the nervous breakdown that he told her about, but instead Mandy threatened him?

Shiloh's head swam with so many possibilities. Rex would be of no help. If she called David, he wouldn't believe her; she saw how smitten he was with Mandy. Like it or not, Clint was her only choice.

Deep down, she agreed with Mandy. *Why am I covering for Clint?* The answer was simple. *I can't bring Katie back, but if the case is re-opened and Clint is found guilty, I would be guilty for lying for him. I'm too tangled up in this now.* She watched enough *Law & Order* to know she would be seen as a co-conspirator and would go to jail. Katie wouldn't want that. She was back to relying on Clint.

She flipped open her cell phone and dialed a number. It rang twice and went to voicemail. She hung up and dialed it again. Same result. The third time she called, Clint answered.

"Dr. Brown," he said, quietly into his phone.

"It's Shiloh, I need to see you."

She could hear shuffling and his muted voice say that he would be right back, it was a call from a colleague in Fort Worth.

"Why are you calling me?" he hissed.

"We have a problem. You have a problem." She wanted to see him in person, to see his face when she relayed her conversation with Mandy.

"What are you talking about? You're not trying to threaten me are you?"

Clint could be so dramatic sometimes. *What did you see in him, Katie?*

"Don't be stupid. It's that woman, Mandy Jackson. She was just here." Shiloh hoped that would be enough to pique his interest. Instead it was just met by silence, which meant that he wasn't catching on. "Clint, she asked about Katie."

That did the trick. Clint cancelled the rest of his appointments for the afternoon and met Shiloh at the small parking lot at the Tejas River. She felt apprehensive about meeting Clint there alone, worrying that Mandy was right and Clint would be inclined to get rid of Shiloh the same way he did Katie. Just to make sure he wouldn't get away with two murders if something did happen, she left a note tucked away in the cash register at the bar. Eddie agreed to watch the bar while she ran an errand, so if she made it back alive and well, she could slip the note out. If not, Eddie would find it while he was closing up that night. It didn't do anything to ensure her safety, but that didn't really matter. She didn't deserve to be safe.

"I think it's quite obvious what we have to do," Clint said, leaning against his black Suburban. "We have to get rid of her."

"Oh no, I'm not killing anyone. I'll turn myself in before I do that."

"Really, Shiloh. Turn yourself in for what? What makes you think I want to kill her?"

"How do you plan on getting rid of her?"

"Well, we'll just work together from two fronts," he said, his eyes squinting in the late day sun. "I'll let you decide your strategy. You could either bully her to death in hopes that she'll get fed up and leave; or you could go to David with your suspicions about Mandy."

"And what are you going to do?"

"I'm already working on it. A med school buddy of mine works for the hospital up in Billings. He's searching some medical records for me right now for a Mandy Jackson fitting our girl's description."

"What if she never went to the hospital?"

"She had to have had a cold, or seen a gynecologist. That's a small city. If anyone knows her; he'll be able to dig that up for me."

Another question bubbled to the surface of Shiloh's mind. "She asked if there is another doctor around the other day, and she was genuinely freaked out. What did you do to her?"

A half smile curled Clint's lips. "I was just going to see where that got me. Guess we'll never know since you're hell bent on getting her out of Phoenix, will we? Pity, guess David will be the only one to know how good she is in bed."

Shiloh rolled her eyes and hoped that the face she made was an accurate account of what she felt. Why did all the men, bachelors and those taken alike, throw themselves at Mandy?

"One last thing," she said, wanting to make sure that she wasn't digging herself into a deeper hole. "Remember the question I asked you when I agreed to cover for you, to hide that you and Katie were seeing each other?" Clint winced. Shiloh knew he didn't like to be reminded. If it was up to him, he would never have moved back to Phoenix, but he promised to take over his father's practice. "I asked if you killed Katie, and you told me no. It's been ten years, if you did, congratulations, you got away with murder. But I need to know, does your answer change?"

He took a deep breath and let out a long sigh, running his fingers through his salt and pepper hair.

"This may come as a complete shock to you, but there is not a day that goes by that I don't think about Katie. Did it ever occur to you that I named one of my daughters after her, Katherine?" It was Shiloh's turn to wince. She stayed so far away from Clint that she remembered the birth of his twins, but couldn't recall their names. "I loved her, just as much as you did."

For the first time in ten years, she felt just as lost as she did that day when her friend disappeared. She couldn't hold back the tears and didn't stop Clint when he pulled her to him and hugged her while she cried. The tears that rushed forth flooded her face in the same way the flooding rains unearthed Katie's body not far from where they stood. A summer of memories and a lifetime of grief forever bonded her with Clint. He was not her enemy, but he wasn't her ally either. He was simply the man who loved her best friend.

31

"So, Sherlock, you crack the case yet?"

The only exchanges made during the last mile of their run were the harmony of their breath. She was so lost in her thoughts that David was forgotten until he spoke. There was an unsaid agreement between the two; she wouldn't bring up the Katie Shelton case if he wouldn't. But tonight he violated that silent pact.

It wasn't a competition, but Amanda couldn't help but feel that her confrontation with Shiloh earlier that day ended in a draw rather than a win. A draw was much better than a loss, but she knew she could have done a better job of blocking the sucker punch about her past. She just hoped Shiloh didn't pick up any non-verbal reactions. She hadn't prepared herself to be on the defensive; she had only prepared to be on the offensive. Both women let a sliver of a secret show.

Who was it that Shiloh protected? Was it possible that David's brother was in fact responsible for Katie's death? It was obvious to anyone with eyes that Shiloh had feelings for David, so covering for his brother could be just another way of confirming her affections for him.

Amanda recalled one entry towards the end of the diary that frustrated her the most. Whoever this mysterious C was, he liked to talk. Brag to be exact. In an attempt to impress the teenager, he explained to Katie that he knew how to make a body disappear. The girl was touched by the exaggeration of her suitor, but had Katie really listened to what he told her, she would likely be alive. There was nothing she could do with this little piece of illegal information. Asking David to investigate anyone whose name started with a C would be one hell of a hunch. And, inquiring if he was really sure his brother was innocent would be the swift and final end to their relationship.

"Earth to Mandy," David said. She really wasn't in the mood to talk about this, especially with him.

"What do you care?" Amanda said, speeding up. David's one limitation in running was his inability to sprint due to the cumbersome knee brace.

"I care because I care about you," he shouted after her. "What is your problem?"

A gun went off at the starting line of her temper. "What is my problem? Seriously? No, I haven't cracked the case, and you want to know why?" She stopped running, and they stood in the middle of a residential street. The sun rested behind distant clouds on the western horizon and cast an orange glow on the street. "Because my boyfriend abandoned me."

"What do you mean I abandoned you? I did what you asked me to. I don't know what you thought you were going to find that we didn't already know. You can waste your time chasing ghosts if you want, but I sure as hell won't."

"Oh, so I'm a waste of your time?"

"Mandy, that's not what I said, and you know it," his voice low and controlled, the opposite of her shrill shouting.

She did know that, but she itched for a fight. It didn't matter who was on the receiving end. It could have been Frank earlier in the afternoon when he caught a typo in one of her stories, or Myrna when she clucked at Amanda for ruining her white towels with a stray pair of red thongs, or the teenager at the gas station who had the gall to suggest she have a nice afternoon. David happened to have the spark to set off the explosion.

"You are just like all the others," she spat. "You're all about the chase, but the minute things go south, you're out the door and I have to clean up your mess."

"What are you talking about? I didn't ask you to clean up a mess."

"I'm your girlfriend, not your damn janitor."

A porch light popped on in the house across the street and a dog barked nearby.

"Mandy, you're not making any sense. Will you just listen to what you're saying?"

"You know what? Screw you!" she screamed. Those words lit the fuse of David's anger. His previously exasperated expression and calm voice morphed into a rigid jaw and narrowed eyes.

"Screw me? Screw me? No, screw you because all you've done since you got into town is mess with my head." A head poked out of a screen door. "I'm done. I'm sorry I asked."

"Fine." Amanda turned and ran back the direction they came.

"Where do you think you're going?"

"I'm going to finish my run. Alone."

"Fine, I would rather be alone if you are going to be a complete bitch," David yelled after her. She heard him mumble an apology to a member of their audience before she turned the corner to backtrack.

In less than two blocks the fury melted from her face and guilt stifled her endorphins. It would be easy to turn around and chase after David. If she sprinted she could catch him, grab his arm, beg him to forgive her, blame PMS for her behavior. He would even apologize himself for calling her names, although she really did deserve it. They would embrace in the middle of the street, kiss and all would be well. The sun would set behind them, the heartening music would swell, the credits would roll and they would live happily ever after.

Not really, but it was much more romantic to think that way

while she ran away from him, putting at least half the town of Phoenix between them.

Her breathing settled back into its rhythmic pace, and she let her mind roam freely, giving it absolute free reign to go where it felt the need to go. She thought about Katie, accepting the fact that she wasn't able to ride in on a white horse, or Greyhound Bus, and solve the murder. Katie settled in with the ghosts of the others she disappointed; her parents, Liz, her colleagues, her hundreds, no maybe thousands, of unknown victims. She didn't want her thoughts to go this direction, but her free-reigned brain chose otherwise.

Phoenix's telephone lines were likely blazing alive with the news of her and David's bitter argument in the middle of the street. Was Shiloh already consoling him? Did she wrap her arms around him, her thick dark hair enveloping him? Was she whispering sweet Spanish nothings?

Her anger was not just rooted in her failed attempts at redemption, but the fact that even Katie's best friend seemed to be so blasé about the girl just a mere ten years later. Was Amanda just as forgotten two months removed? Chances were, yes. Her shallow circle of friends probably paused, nattered over the fact that Amanda and Josh were involved in something so scandalous, but deep down, it didn't shock them. Amanda showed excitement over her latest wardrobe acquisition and Josh flaunted his most recent conquest when Amanda wasn't around. She was more than easily forgotten. She was never there to begin with. To David, she was more than a mere apparition. Unlike her friends in Chicago, his memory of her wouldn't lapse with her absence.

David. Countless blocks after their argument Amanda felt sheepish. The words that she screamed at him were not intended for David, they were meant for Josh. *This is really for the best. David is too good for me, it's better if he hates me.* Josh was a better match for her than David. She could even make an argument for deserving whatever perverted thoughts flowed through Dr. Brown's mind. An involuntary quake rattled her body at the memory of standing nearly naked in the doctor's office.

Streetlights popped on ahead of her, the hum from the electric currents hitting her like waves; growing louder as she approached one, softening as she ran away from it, only to have another hum wash over her.

She was so entranced with her thoughts that she didn't realize a car followed close behind. Her awareness came only after the dark road illuminated and her long shadow raced ahead of her. Amanda hugged the curb, giving the car a wide berth to pass her on the small streets, but it never did. She turned right and ran up on the sidewalk and continued her stride. Running on the sidewalk made her nervous, the streets were in much better shape than the sidewalks and she feared that an overgrown tree root would trip her. The car turned right and kept a steady pace behind her.

She wasn't afraid at first. Only when she turned to look behind her when the sedan passed under a streetlight did the fear kick in. She couldn't see the driver's face, hidden by the shadow from a baseball cap. Her brain had a brief moment when it chose fight before flight. She stopped running. The car stopped moving. She turned to face the car, to confront the driver, but the car sat in the dark in the middle of the road. The hairs on her arm stood and her fingers tingled with numbness. She narrowed her eyes to try to see inside the car better, but as she did, the image of what her eyes actually absorbed were lost in translation to what her brain manifested. Rather than see a petite figure with her hair pulled back in a baseball cap, Amanda's brain registered an elderly man in a windbreaker. Rather than see the girl inside rummage through her purse for her cell phone, her brain registered the man pulling a pistol out of his backpack. Rather than see the glow of a cell phone flipped open to make a call, she saw the gleam of a gun.

Fight was put aside in favor of flight. Amanda had always been a distance runner, but when she thought she saw a gun, she became a sprinter. She took off running down the street as fast as she could. In the moment of panic, she forgot where she was and ended up running the same block twice. The car followed her, never speeding up enough to drive alongside her or pass her, but keeping its distance behind her, making her feel like a guinea pig stuck in a wheel.

"David! David!" she screamed, but her shouts were met by silence. He probably gave up his run after he cooled down from their fight and was already home, commiserating about his crazy girlfriend over a beer and a baseball game. He wasn't going to come to her rescue.

Rather than take that block for a third time, she turned left and found the surroundings growing familiar. Her body followed the narrow walkway that led to Foster's Bookstore. She ignored the "closed" sign and ran up the front steps, mastering the extra wide top step, and twisted the front door knob. It was locked. The car pulled up in front of Foster's. The glow of the cell phone was once again mistaken for a gun. Amanda banged on the door as if her life depended on it.

"Please, Mr. Foster, let me in. It's Mandy, please if you're there," she begged. It was only when Mr. Foster opened the door did she calm down and realize she was still alive.

"Ms. Jackson? Are you alright?" he asked. There was no air of pretension about him, it was concern combined with apprehension. "You are going to wake the dead with all that noise."

"A car," she said, gasping for breath. "A car. Was chasing. Me. Man inside. Had. A. Gun." She couldn't get her breath and leaned forward, her hands on her thighs bracing her.

"Mandy, you'll never get your breath leaned over, stand up straight, your lungs need to have room to expand." Mr. Foster didn't reach out to touch her; instead he offered her assistance verbally while physically recoiling from her. "What car? I don't see a car."

"What? There was a car." Amanda spun around and the street was dark. No car. While the adrenalin washed away, her rational mind came back online. "But, I don't understand, I saw it, and the man inside."

They both stood there, Amanda sweating and panting on his front porch trying to rationalize what she saw and Mr. Foster standing in the ten-inch opening of his front door, unwilling to do any more than he had to help the woman.

"I must have imagined it," she said, logic finally winning over. "I'm so sorry to have bothered you. Goodnight."

Before she made it to the bottom step, Mr. Foster called out to her.

"Mandy, would you like to have tea with me before you go? It will help calm you."

Amanda nodded. She wasn't too eager to head back into the dark and welcomed any distraction from her delusions.

Mr. Foster led her to the back part of his bookstore home. For the first time, lamps were switched on in the bookstore, illuminating nooks and crannies that were previously only shadows. In an area marked "employees only" she found a small eat-in kitchen. He untied a cushion from a chair and indicated that she should sit there. With no words, he retrieved an extra teacup and saucer and poured some tea. She welcomed the warmth it brought at her first sip.

"Thank you," she said.

The silence continued, and Amanda could tell that Mr. Foster had a thought on the tip of his tongue.

"I apologize for my abrupt request of you to leave the other day," he said, not looking at her, but instead spooning sugar into a freshly poured cup of tea. "I was shocked to hear that woman's name. Why on Earth did you utter the name of such a foul human?"

"Well, foul is a stretch, but she's certainly not pleasant. I think she knows something about Katie's murder, I just can't figure out what," Amanda said, appreciating that someone else shared her dislike of Shiloh. "I came across Katie's journal in my investigation," she began, too tired and shell-shocked to lie, but omitting how she came across the journal. "Even with the diary, I'm no closer to solving the murder or finding something even remotely newsworthy for the tenth anniversary. Katie was sneaking around with someone. Shiloh knows who, but for some reason she keeps lying for him. And since she hates me because of David, that information is locked away." Amanda's voice broke, and her eyes batted back tears.

Frustration got the best of her, despondence won out over confidence and her heart ached over her argument with David—something she planned to apologize for the minute she could find him. The hot cup of tea wasn't working as well as she hoped.

"A journal. Really?" His head jerked to one side slightly, but the movement was enough to cause the tea to dribble down his chin when he took a sip. "I doubt you would find anything of interest there. Gossip. Nonsensical musings of a silly girl. What is so important about a journal?" As he spoke, the tea continued its trek down his chin and pooled into a heavy droplet. Something crossed his pale, smooth face, something cloudy, dark. For the second time that evening, Amanda's hands went cold.

"Mr. Foster, look at the time. I better get going. Thank you for the tea…for answering the door." Amanda stood and shivered; she hoped he would assume it was the chill of her sweaty clothes in the air conditioning.

Mr. Foster followed her out of his kitchen and to the front door. Amanda unlocked the door. He finally spoke.

"You remind me of her."

Amanda stopped mid-twist of the doorknob and turned her head.

"When the light hits the side of your face," he said, his hand tracing the side of her face from six inches away. "I'm sorry; I got carried away in my nostalgia."

"Mr. Foster, why do you hate Shiloh?"

His gray-blue eyes didn't register Amanda perspiring at his front door, but perhaps instead a pretty, teenage girl with freckles and long blond hair. After several non-blinking seconds, he finally spoke, his eyes fluttering twice and fat tears rolling down each cheek in perfect unison.

"She stole something from me. Something, very, very precious," he cleared his throat. "Now, if you'll excuse me."

32

It took Mandy so long to realize that someone was following her during her run, that Shiloh grew bored. Just before turning to go home, Mandy stopped.

Shiloh's small sedan halted in the darkness between two street-lights. She thought Mandy must have seen her, or knew that it was her car when the woman turned to face her. Even in the dark and ten feet away, Shiloh saw Mandy's jaw set and a flash of anger cross her eyes. This was not a normal reaction of someone being followed. Shiloh reached into her purse for her cell phone. She wasn't sure who she could call. After all, she was the one doing the tailing. Mandy had every right to be angry and confront her. That look and the stance that Mandy took when she turned towards Shiloh's car scared her. It was only then that Shiloh realized how stupid she was for following Mandy. She knew nothing about this woman. For all she knew, Mandy could be a serial killer.

She started scrolling through the phone for Clint's number. He was probably sitting down to have dinner with his wife, but Shiloh didn't care. This was his idea anyway. Before she found his number, she saw movement out of the corner of her eye. Mandy sprinted away.

This was a more normal reaction. Shiloh followed Mandy as she sprinted, not looking back to see if the car was following her. She did one block twice. Shiloh couldn't decide if she tried to lose her tail or if the girl was just scared witless. During her pursuit, Shiloh felt a brief pang of guilt. She remembered the days following Katie's disappearance, wandering through the woods alongside the Tejas River, looking for any sign of her friend, while feeling like someone watched and followed her.

After the second trip around the block, Mandy turned left rather than right and seemed to run on a more determined path. This street was much darker than the last. Shiloh had a hard time following her, her headlights only lighting up the reflectors on the back of Mandy's sneakers. Suddenly, Mandy turned up a walkway towards a house. Shiloh knew this wasn't where Mandy lived. She slowed, trying to determine to whom the house belonged when it suddenly hit her.

Shiloh thought about speeding away the minute he opened the front door. Shiloh hadn't seen Horace Foster since he graduated from high school. As the yearbook photographer, he often lurked in the shadows, snapping pictures of carefree teenagers at the prime of their lives. Even though he was a senior when they were sopho-mores, Shiloh wasn't aware of his existence until she wandered into the yearbook office one day. There she encountered stacks and stacks of photos, more than their meager yearbook could ever use. It wasn't the quantity that stood out, it was the subject. Katie.

When she confronted Horace with Katie and half the school as witness, her friend was mortified and vowed never to return to his grandfather's bookstore, but Shiloh wasn't convinced. Her friend's fatal flaw was her need for male attention. Adoration was her drug. If she had a bad day, she would find any man, it didn't matter who, and bask in his worship. It wouldn't have surprised her if Katie continued to visit Foster's Bookstore behind Shiloh's back just to have her admiration fix. *I'll have to drill Katie on that.*

Shiloh winced. Not long after Katie's disappearance, she found herself wanting to tell her something, only to have her breath taken away when she remembered she couldn't. She hated her mind for that faulty circuit, that glitch that allowed her to momentarily forget that her best friend was gone. Without meaning to, Shiloh let herself succumb to loneliness.

Katie had always been the social one, the one who made friends, and Shiloh would pick them up along the way. In the days after Katie's funeral, their friends and classmates babied Shiloh, constantly asking if she was okay and wanting her to hang out on the weekends. Shiloh knew that no one would admit it, but it was hard to like her. She was cynical, abrasive and prone to melancholy.

Teenagers weren't equipped to handle death. In their world, they would all live forever and only a handful had lost a grandparent by then. Not Shiloh. Loss lingered over her like fog. Her mother cried at night over the loss of Shiloh's father. Her brother lost part of his youth by starting work at an early age to help support the family. Shiloh felt loss every time she made eye contact with David only to see friendship looking back at her. After the shock of Katie's murder wore off, Shiloh's peers left her alone to find her own way. Her brother wanted to send her to therapy to talk about it, but Shiloh refused, too afraid that a therapist might realize the truth about what happened. If loneliness was her penitence, she would embrace it.

She watched Mandy double over. Horace wasn't looking at the street where Shiloh sat in her car; instead he was talking to the scared woman who appeared on his doorstep. With Mandy's breathing trouble serving as a distraction, Shiloh carefully drove forward and headed home.

Her duplex was dark when she pulled into the driveway. She could see the blue-white light of her elderly neighbor's television flickering in the other half of the building, but thankfully, her side was pitch black. Rex didn't live with her, but he was there so much that she considered asking him to help out with the bills from time to time. Or, at least pitch in with the groceries. Inside, she turned on all the lights and tossed her baseball cap on the coffee table. Even though she was the pursuer, she felt a little edgy. Mandy's fear must have rubbed off on her with the unexpected side effect of seeing

Horace and experiencing the assault of a memory of her long-dead friend.

The rough brown carpet scratched at Shiloh's now bare feet as she walked into her small bedroom. It wasn't much different from the one she had in her mother's house. She could have stayed with her mom instead of getting her own place. Her mom wouldn't mind, and she never asserted any unnecessary rules on Shiloh. She could even have moved in with her older brother, but she knew he was hoping to get married and start a family soon, and she didn't want to impose. Her duplex suited her just fine. It was small, simple and, when Rex wasn't parked in front of the television, hers.

Before sitting on the edge of her bed, she pulled a photo album off the bookshelf in her bedroom. If she was going to wallow in sadness she might as well go all the way. Looking at the album was really only a gesture. At this point, Shiloh knew all the pictures by heart; even the silly captions she and Katie wrote beneath each picture. The motion of turning the pages in the book did exactly what she hoped it would, deepening the chronic sadness in her heart.

There were the classic teenage pictures; the girls doing each other's makeovers, hanging out with friends and at school pep rallies and football games. Then there were the school pictures starting with the year they met and became best friends, second grade. Shiloh perused the pictures, noticing how they grew up together, yet how different they were. Both girls were beautiful in their own way. Katie was the All-American girl next door with strawberry blond hair and aqua blue eyes. Shiloh was the dark-haired, dark-eyed Mexican beauty.

Shiloh often wondered where they would be now if Katie hadn't died. When she couldn't sleep at night, she would let her imagination take over, sometimes playing the same scenario, oftentimes inventing a different path, much like the *Choose Your Own Adventure* books she was fond of reading as a kid. Sometimes, Katie made it to NYU for college and Shiloh went with her; Katie would become a famous fashion designer and Shiloh would be her business manager. They both would fall in love with handsome men—sometimes

David was part of this fantasy, more often than not—and they would live happily ever after. Other times, she and Katie moved to Dallas, got jobs in downtown high rises and fell in love with real estate moguls. Shiloh even imagined them moving to Los Angeles, fulfilling her own little-known dream of becoming an actress. Once, when she was having a particularly lonesome day, she even imagined that she and Katie had a big falling out and were no longer friends. Shiloh was curious to see if this made it any easier. It didn't.

During tonight's unpleasant trip through her memories, Rex sent her a text message asking her to join him for a beer at Riley's. She ignored it, not feeling like being social this evening. With the photo album exhausted, she pulled out her and Katie's sophomore yearbook. Her eyes fell to the pictures of Rex. Aside from Shiloh making him finally cut the mullet, he looked exactly the same now as he did in high school.

Shiloh started to text Rex to ask if he wanted to spend the night at her place when her home phone rang. It was nearly ten o'clock and only her mother called on her home phone. It was too late for her mom to be calling; unless there was an emergency. On the third ring, she answered, her stomach falling in fear of what she may hear next. Which, initially, was only silence.

"Hello?" Shiloh said into the phone. "Is anyone there?"

More silence. Shiloh listened, but she couldn't tell if the other end of the phone was alive or dead. She hung up, guessing it must have been a wrong number. Her heart still pounding, she picked up her cell phone and finished her text to Rex. As soon as she pressed send, her home phone rang again. She really wished she would have spent the extra few dollars each month for caller ID.

"Hello?"

Again, silence. But this time, she could hear shuffling. Her cell phone buzzed back with a message from Rex, making her jump. When she spoke again her voice was an octave higher.

"Look, I can hear you. I know you're there. Trust me, you do not want to mess with me," she felt like she didn't get her point across with her voice so high. "Hello? Why don't you quit being a chicken shit and just say something."

Finally, she heard a throat clearing.

"Well, I can't say it's a shock that you are just as classless after all these years."

The voice was flat and monotone, a man's voice, but one of those that could just as easily have been a deep female voice.

"What the—who do you think you are calling me and insulting me like that?" She felt like she knew the voice, but couldn't place it, which infuriated her even more.

"Well, who do you think you are following that poor girl and scaring her senseless? She was absolutely inconsolable when she appeared on my doorstep."

Horace Foster. Shiloh's heart sped up when she realized that he saw her in front of his house. He knew it was she who terrorized Mandy that evening, and if he told Mandy, then David would know. How could she explain herself to David without acknowledging that Clint told her to bully Mandy? And then she would have to explain why Clint was involved.

She heard a snort on the other end of the phone. "Now who's silent?"

"What? What do you mean?" Shiloh's voice was much quieter now, missing the feistiness from earlier in the conversation.

"Think I didn't see you sitting in the car, Shiloh Garcia?"

It was no use arguing.

"Did ... did you tell Mandy it was me?"

"No," he said. Shiloh tried to keep her sigh of relief from being audible. "Unlike you, I thought I would offer you the benefit of the doubt."

Shiloh closed her eyes and rewound back to that moment in high school when her unbridled temper resulted in an outburst heard by the whole school. For the rest of his senior year, the other kids tormented Horace with his infatuation of Katie. There was no way that she could tell this man her suspicions that Mandy lied about her identity. He owed her nothing.

Shiloh decided that being bitchy and shallow would be her only way out of this.

"It's really simple," Shiloh said as her voice regained some strength. "I don't like her. She's dating a friend of mine, and I think he can do better."

"Following her on her evening run would get that point across?" he asked his question so quickly that she had barely finished her sentence.

"I was driving home and saw her running. I thought about confronting her, telling her she wasn't good enough."

Shiloh felt like she could easily defend this answer should it get back to Mandy or David.

"Well, isn't that the pot calling the kettle black."

"Who do you think you are?" Her teenage tongue itched to scream obscenities, but her adult brain reminded her she already did enough damage.

"I am someone who knows that your secrets have secrets."

This time Shiloh was too stunned to hide her gasp. Did he know about Katie and Clint? Even more important, did he share that information with Mandy? Why else would the woman run to his house unless they knew each other? Maybe Horace had already confided in her that Clint was Katie's secret boyfriend.

"Listen here, you creepy little man. If you want to tell Mandy I was following her, then fine. Do it. But just know that you may find the toe of my shoe so far up your a—."

She didn't get to finish her sentence; Rex walked in the front door.

"Hey babe, who are you bitching out this time? I can hear you all the way out to the street."

Shiloh hung up the phone without another word to Horace, even though she wanted to address the irritating chuckling she heard coming out of the phone as she put it down.

"Oh, it's just another telemarketer, honey."

33

Amanda Martin's trail was almost colder than a Chicago winter once Alex and Roland got to the Memphis bus station. The bus that left Chicago in the middle of the night arrived in the city early in the morning, and all attempts at trying to place her next steps within the bus station were blocked by the simple fact that she didn't stand out to anyone.

Alex didn't tell Roland the severity of his punishment; only that it would be wise for them to cease using his agency's name. And it didn't seem as if they needed to use the SEC's name while they questioned workers at the bus station. Alex guessed they were used to having a photograph waved in front of their faces asking if they remember seeing the person pictured. At some point they might have protested, saying this was private information and a warrant would be needed to divulge of a particular loved ones' whereabouts; but that gave way to a deeper desire to just answer the question and get on with their day.

They spent a whole day at the bus station, making several rounds in hopes that a shift change would produce a worker that did see Amanda. At nearly ten o'clock that night, they called off the first day of searching and decided to get dinner.

"Tomorrow, I think we should split up," Roland said between bites of his pulled pork barbecue. "One of us should go back to the bus station and see if we get any leads there, and the other should try some of the local businesses around the bus station."

Alex nodded his agreement, his mouth full of coleslaw. He had never been to Memphis, but had always heard about the hole-in-the-wall barbecue places the city was known for. He swore as soon as they found Amanda, he would get back on his workout regimen and even diet. But, in the meantime, he embraced his expanding girth and even celebrated it with a new pair of chinos, two sizes larger.

"I'll walk the streets and talk to the businesses," Alex said, after swallowing. He examined his plate of food, the largest the restaurant served, and thought a day of walking would do him good. Roland didn't seem to notice his weight gain, or if he did, he didn't feel the need to taunt him about it.

Roland nodded his agreement, his mouth full as well, but eating a much smaller meal made up mostly of pulled pork and some steamed vegetables. Alex looked from his dinner to Roland's and lost his appetite before he could even dig into his peach cobbler.

The dinner conversation was light. He and Roland had only known each other for a short time, and their discussions revolved almost exclusively around the case. Once this case was solved, or stalled completely, would they remain friends? Alex didn't have many friends. None, actually, now that he didn't have a job either. This man sitting across the table from him was the closest thing he had to a friend. And yet, he knew nothing about him.

"So, hey, uh Roland," Alex started, unsure of how exactly to start. "So, what's your favorite color?"

Roland looked up at Alex; his fork with a broccoli floret paused halfway to his mouth. "Mate, did you just ask me my favorite color?"

Alex considered denying it, especially seeing Roland's disbelief.

Roland put his fork down. "I get it. You're trying to make small talk, especially considering that our whole relationship has been based on the JWI case and nothing else." Alex picked up on

Roland's choice of the word "relationship" rather than "friendship."

Alex nodded and took a sip of his beer. Roland didn't want to be Alex's friend. And, in some ways, Alex didn't think he really wanted to be Roland's friend either. What if he and Roland had nothing in common? What if they tried to be friends, but over time, they drifted apart and eventually they would only run into each other at the neighborhood bar?

Roland chewed on his broccoli, seeming to think the same thing.

"Don't think me goth, but my favorite color is black," Roland said, after several minutes. "I like the simplicity of it."

With that simple act, the tension in the air melted away, and the two men spent the rest of the evening talking about everything except the JWI case and what could happen if it went unsolved. Roland told Alex about growing up in the middle of London. Alex explained to Roland the complexity of his large Greek family. They talked sports; Roland explained the rules of rugby and Alex spouted statistic after statistic for the Cubs. The restaurant staff finally had to ask the men to leave when it came time to close.

The next morning, Alex was up earlier than necessary. Something about the day felt good to him, like there was positively charged electricity in the air. He went downstairs early and skipped the continental breakfast bar in favor of a simple cup of coffee. An overstuffed armchair beckoned, and he took up residency there to read *USA Today* while waiting on Roland. Even with the positive feeling, he still felt some apprehension. If they found nothing again today, they were going to check out of the hotel first thing the next morning and drive back to Chicago. There, they would re-examine the case and try to figure out the next course of action. Roland needed something concrete to stay in the game. And, Alex needed something to win back his job.

Their scheduled time to meet came and went. Alex decided to cut his friend some slack and finished his paper. A half hour later, Roland still hadn't shown and Alex grew bored. The smell of the fresh cinnamon buns wafted over and his stomach grumbled. Alex was about to help himself to one when the elevator dinged. Roland strode across the lobby, a big smile on his face. His boisterous voice echoed across the hotel lobby.

"You won't believe this mate," Roland said. He approached so quickly that Alex braced himself for a hug.

"Did we get a break in the case?" Alex figured that it had to be something really good for the normally cool Brit to get this excited.

"No, better. I just got off the phone with my editor and the head of our media relations department. One, I survived the layoffs, my job is safe. Number two, our media relations flack has booked me to go on the *Judith Nash Show*, that woman who tries to bring all these criminals to justice."

"That's awesome," Alex hoped he sounded happy. *Holy crap, what is he going to say? Could he tip Amanda off? Is he going to mention this was my case, and I brought him into it?* "Congratulations."

"Alright, you ready to get to work? We have a lot of ground to cover, especially since we probably need to head back late tonight. My editor and PR person want me in the office bright and early tomorrow morning to start working on my talking points." Roland poured himself a cup of coffee in a to-go cup. His face glowed with relief. "Oh and mate, you don't mind driving back tonight, do you? I need to be well-rested before work tomorrow."

Alex shrugged his agreement as they walked out of the hotel.

"Listen up, mate. When you visit the businesses nearby, start with those closest to the bus station as well as places that sell the basics: food, clothing, anything that you would need if you're traveling with no luggage," Roland paused to light a cigarette. "And, if you think someone is holding back, feel free to tell them this is for the *Judith Nash Show*. Maybe that will help loosen some lips."

Alex tuned Roland out at that point. He verged on asking if he should go on the show with him, since Alex broke the case and was the one who discovered, through hours and hours of poring over financial statements, that something was amiss. He was the one who gave up the last year of his life to ensure that he made no mistake; well, almost no mistake. Alex was also the only person who sacrificed his career to make sure this case didn't go unsolved. With each step he took, and each word that went from Roland's lips into Alex's right ear and out his left, he grew angrier and angrier.

Then, a sideways glimpse of their reflection in a storefront window gave him a good answer as to why Roland didn't invite him on the show. Alex was a mess. Luckily, his height helped hide the twenty or so pounds he'd put on, but he was in dire need of a haircut, his face breaking out from all the greasy food he'd consumed and the collar of his shirt straining against the fat deposits around his neck. Even if Roland hadn't consciously thought it, Alex would agree that he wouldn't want to sit next to himself on national television either. Alex needed to put aside his jealousy.

When they parted at the bus station, Alex went to a few street barbecue vendors. He showed them Amanda's pictures—the one from the bus station in Chicago and a copy of her Illinois driver's license photo. The people were nice. They all took time to look over both pictures and think through if they saw her, but he came up empty-handed every time.

By noon, his stomach grumbled for lunch, and he stopped in one of the little restaurants. He thought about calling Roland to join him, but he needed a break. Alex remembered why he had few friends; they were tiring and wore on his nerves. He flirted with the waitresses and he liked how they called him "sugar" and "hon." He handed the pictures of Amanda to the waitress to see if she recalled her. When she asked if Amanda was his girlfriend, he lied and said she was his sister. She got pregnant by the jerk of a boyfriend who dragged her off. The family thought she might be in Memphis. Alex was so proud of himself. When he stated that their dying mother just wished to see Amanda one more time, he even produced a well-timed tear. By that point, all the waitresses and even a cook were gathered around his table. A chorus of "ahhhs" fell over the little restaurant. But no one could say they had seen Amanda.

Alex dragged in the afternoon heat. He was torn between getting a beer and making a trip down one more street when he passed a little pawnshop. He looked in the dirty window at the array of lawn equipment and small kitchen appliances, wondering if there was anything in there that Amanda would deem necessary. *What if she didn't come in here to buy something, what if she came in here to sell something?*

There was only one other customer in the tiny pawn shop, an elderly man asking a short, portly man about a lawnmower in a loud voice. Alex guessed the old man didn't realize he needed to change out the batteries in his hearing aid. If Alex hadn't been there on such a serious mission, he would have found the exchange between the two comical. Finally, the old man seemed convinced that the shop owner wasn't trying to scam him, and he wheeled the lawn-mower out the door.

Alex didn't waste any time when the man was finally free of his geriatric customer.

"Excuse me, sir. Have you seen this woman in here about two months ago?" Alex laid the two pictures of Amanda on the countertop.

The man didn't even look at the pictures; instead he opened up a sports section of a newspaper flat on the counter next to them. "Never seen her."

"You didn't even look at the pictures. Come on man, that's my sister and our dying mother really wants to see her again."

"I don't care if she's goddamn Mother Teresa, I ain't seen her."

Alex winced and fought the urge to cross himself for the man's curse. Leave it to him to find the one jerk when he didn't have Roland here to smooth talk his way in. The man turned the page of the newspaper and didn't say another word to Alex or acknowledge that he was still standing there.

After a few uncomfortable minutes, Alex turned to leave.

"You're going to give up, just like that?" the man shouted out to Alex.

Alex froze and turned around.

"What do you mean? You said you never saw her."

The man harrumphed at Alex.

"You're lying about who she is. She looks nothing like you."

"We're adopted."

"Bullshit." The man never looked up from his paper. Alex considered just leaving, but something told him this guy spoke to him for a reason other than just to toy with him. "If you tell me who she is and why you're looking for her, maybe I'll look at the picture and answer your question."

Alex didn't need long to decide. He told the man a short version of who Amanda was, why he hunted for her and why he thought she may still be in Memphis. The only bit that he was untruthful about was his involvement; instead of saying that he was a suspended SEC agent he said he was a private investigator.

A wide smile crossed the man's big face. "Well then, as a private investigator, you can compensate me. For my trouble."

Compensate? For his trouble? He just made up that last bit, and he wasn't a licensed private investigator. He wondered if he would lose too much face if he backtracked. Probably. At this point, he just needed to power through the rest of this unpleasant conversation.

"How much?" Alex hoped he sounded smooth, but didn't think he did. He mentally counted the money that he had on him. He figured he had just a little over one hundred dollars in cash on him, and if he needed more he could always find an ATM.

"Depends on how much you want to know."

Alex sighed. He had no patience for cat-and-mouse games.

"You know, I'm starting to think you know nothing, and you're just jerking with me. Thank you for your time."

Alex was on the sidewalk outside the pawn shop when the man called out to him.

"Hey, hey, you, big guy. She was here, okay. Come on back, and I'll prove it."

Alex turned and followed the man back into the pawn shop, surprised the man moved as fast as he did with his short legs and wide girth.

"Consider that my donation to your cause. Anything else you want to know is going to cost you."

"Okay, look man, just tell me how much. I don't feel like playing games."

"Ask a question, and I'll tell you the price for the answer."

Alex thought about this and tried to determine questions that would maximize the money in his pocket.

"Did she tell you where she was going?"

"Question like that, twenty dollars." Alex laid a twenty on the counter. "No, but I didn't get the feeling she was sticking around here."

"What did she come in here for?"

The man raised his busy eyebrows. "Ah, good question, you're catching on quick. That one will be fifty dollars." Alex counted out fifty dollars and waited. "She needed something."

Alex thought for a second. Amanda was the kind of woman who had everything. What in the world would she come into a pawn shop to buy? He looked around. Maybe she needed a gun. Maybe she was worried about her own protection.

"You won't find it out here," the man said with a laugh that soon turned into a hacking cough.

"What did she need from you?"

"That, my friend, is the hundred-dollar question."

"What? I've already given you seventy dollars for you to tell me that she's probably not here and that she needed to buy something from you. I don't have another hundred dollars."

The man went up on his tiptoes, his large, beetle-like eyes studying Alex through thick bifocals.

"What's that around your neck?" the man asked.

Alex's hand went to his neck. Sure enough, the gold chain had caught on the corner of his collar. He normally kept this hidden away under both his undershirt and his button-ups, but in the Memphis heat he shucked the undershirt, which gave the chain more freedom than usual.

"Nothing, just some chain. Look, can I go to the ATM and get more cash. Will you agree to give me fifteen minutes to do that?"

"No, I want to see that."

Blood drained from his head as he pulled the chain over his head, the man's eyes widening as he saw the gold-and-diamond Greek Orthodox cross. This was the first time the chain and cross had been off his neck since his dad placed it there the last time Alex saw him alive, the day his parents took him to college. He hadn't expected how naked he would feel without it.

"Well, well, that is some fine workmanship. The price just went up, but I'll make you a deal. I'll throw in what I sold to this girl, the exact same thing, in exchange for this."

Alex went white. "No, no way you're getting that. It belonged to my father. I'll give you whatever you want. However much money. Just not that."

The man shook his head. "No deal, I'll get a lot more selling that cross than you could probably give me, especially if you have to visit an ATM. Those things have limits, you know. It's up to you. How bad do you want information on this girl? I'll be honest, what I have to give you may be the break your case is looking for."

Alex wished Roland were there. He wouldn't have let this man bully him. Or, maybe Roland had something they could use in exchange. As Alex brooded over his decision, the man went back to the newspaper, unfazed by the anguish he caused.

"You're an asshole," Alex said. "I want to see what you have before I hand this over."

The man shrugged and wobbled into a room behind the counter. Alex wasn't sure if he should follow or sit tight so, he chose staying put to avoid being around the pawnshop owner any more than necessary. Something mechanical clanked to life and whirred in the other room.

When he emerged, the man didn't appear to have anything in his hands. *I knew he was yanking my chain.*

"Well?" Alex said.

The man held out a small plastic card, Alex leaned forward and realized it was a driver's license. He reached for it to get a better look, but the man jerked it away.

"Not until I get the cross."

"How do I know that's her?"

"It's her. Do we have a deal or what?"

Alex needed to take this chance. From the quick glimpse he'd been able to get, the picture did look like Amanda. He said a quick prayer for guidance. No sooner than he finished, the thought was very clear in his head. He had to do this.

"Fine."

The men made the exchange. Alex looked at the license. It appeared to be Amanda Martin, except that according to this, she was Mandy Jackson from Billings, Montana.

"That's the address that was on there," the man told him. "Don't think you'll find her up there."

"Why? I thought you didn't know where she was going."

"Look kid, I've run this pawn shop since you were crapping in diapers. You get to know people in my line of business. She watched the clock, like she had a bus to catch. I know someone on the run when I see her."

Alex just turned and walked to the front of the store.

"Good luck," the man shouted to Alex's back.

He responded by flipping the man off.

34

S weat tickled Amanda's collarbone and disappeared into the V neck of her t-shirt. She envied the kids taking advantage of the Tejas River. Not just the refreshment from splashing around in the swift-moving water on a warm, muggy day, but their oblivion to the fact that they played less than a mile from where a teenage girl died at the hands of an unknown killer.

With her blue convertible SUV tucked under the shade of a tree, she set off down an overgrown gravel path. Her nerves still frayed from being followed the evening before, Amanda pushed aside her fear. She reminded herself that the driver was simply lost, and it was residual fear that caused her reaction at Foster's Bookstore. For leaving town with nothing but the clothes on her back, she carried too much baggage with her from Chicago.

Amanda closed her eyes and inhaled, forcing the smell of gunpowder and smoke from her nostrils and inviting the musky scent of the trees and earthy aroma of the ground. With each exhale, she pushed out the images of the car following her, of the strange look from Mr. Foster, and of the Chicago gunman. *I am safe here. I am safe here. Who am I kidding? A girl was killed here.* But she came looking for answers. What was more important—finding the truth about a dead teenager's murder or finding true love?

According to the police file, it was about a mile down this path and then ten feet to the right where Katie's body was uncovered a month after she disappeared. The notes alluded to an X spray-painted on a pecan tree to show where to turn off the main path. From there, she wasn't sure what she would find—a memorial with withering teddy bears and an out-of-place cluster of flowers, a marker acknowledging a life taken too soon, or maybe the grass growing back and Katie's temporary grave had been completely forgotten.

Once the shouts of the kids faded into the distance, the whooshing of the flowing Tejas was the only sound in the shallow woods, reminding her of that morning two months earlier when she stepped off the bus to stretch her legs and walked into her new life. What was she expecting to find then? *Nothing.* The smell of bacon and the lure of a small town drew her in. What did she expect to find now?

"Nothing," she spoke over the crunch of a twig beneath her. Sunlight filtered through the leaves of tall oak and sycamore trees, a stark contrast to the squat mesquite trees that dotted much of the landscape around Phoenix. More sweat drained down her legs as she stomped down the path, making as much noise as possible to scare away anything that might slither nearby. Her childhood camp counselor would admonish her for walking through a forest without long sleeves and long pants. Then again, the counselor never felt the Texas heat and would surely understand her decision to wear shorts and a t-shirt. A liberal application of bug repellent would keep away any fleas, ticks, mosquitos and serial killers in a three-mile radius.

The further she walked into the forest, the denser the trees and undergrowth. Bare branches reached out for her, trading bits of her skin for pieces of bark. Jagged limestone rose to her left as the path began a sharp descent, boxing her in between the stone wall and the river.

"God Katie, why did you let someone drag you here?"

Amanda stopped in the middle of the path and closed her eyes again, conjuring images of a teenage girl on the last day of her life. The sun was barely up, but the August heat already enveloped the sleepy town as Katie jogged through the familiar streets. By all indications in her journal, she was a clever girl and wouldn't be easily lured from the safety of her friends and neighbors to this exile, boxed in by a limestone cliff and raging river. Not without a fight. Not without the early rising ranchers and farmers of Phoenix hearing her cries for help. Unless it was someone she already knew.

She rubbed her temple and more images flashed by. A car slowed next to a jogging Katie, and she leaned into the window, maybe even giggled before pulling the door open and climbing inside. The back of a man's head taunted Amanda. The car lurched forward, and the taillights faded like an apparition.

"She came here with him," Amanda's eyes popped open and focused on a faded orange X on the crooked trunk of a pecan tree. She turned right and measured out ten paces before stopping under the canopy of four trees. Another several steps ahead, the edge of the river bank dropped sharply. Amanda looked over, half expecting it to be miles down; instead, the river flowed six inches beneath her feet without a sound.

"Why am I here?" she said, perching on an outcropping of limestone after dusting it off.

Amanda didn't expect Katie's ghost to whisper the answer on the wind. She was here because she got off the bus. She was here because an unsolved murder spoke to her need for absolution. She was here because a handsome cop made her swoon and was a really good kisser...among other things. And, she was here because he was mad at her for sticking her nose where it didn't belong.

"But that doesn't explain why I'm in Phoenix," she answered, rubbing her palms on her bare thighs. "What does this have to do with finding Josh?"

Amanda closed her eyes again, and the puzzle completed itself. Katie's strawberry blond hair and Liz's blue eyes. Katie's lean and long figure holding an ankle over her head in a cheerleader pose and Liz's supermodel physique even while nine months pregnant. Katie's smile and Liz's lips and Jackson's dimples. If Amanda hadn't read the coroner's report, that confirmed through dental records that the body found in a shallow grave near where she sat was Katie Shelton, she would have believed her friend Liz and Katie were one and the same. And now they shared another shocking similarity.

They are both dead. Amanda exhaled, the air knocked out of her lungs as if she'd fallen flat on her back.

"Okay, I get it," she said. "So who brought you here? Who, besides Shiloh, knows his name?"

Rustling leaves overhead answered her with silence.

"Exactly."

A line of ants went about their work on the next rock over, scurrying down the wall, across the flat limestone and disappeared towards the ground. What would it be like to be one of them? You simply move a few eggs for the queen or bring some food home to the colony rather than carry the weight of mistakes made and people hurt. She'd always heard that ants could carry more than ten times their body weight, but Amanda guessed that an ant lugging her baggage would be crushed easily.

"It was C, wasn't it? Who is he? And, why am I willing to ruin things with David to find out? Anyway, what am I doing with him? I need to find Josh."

A gentle, hot breeze stroked her cheek, drying the sweat that dripped from her temple. She lifted her chin to the wind and felt her hair blow back as if she were driving on the highway with the top down. It would be so easy to hop in her car and continue to El Paso. Maybe there she could figure out why Josh had a boarding pass for that border town. All she needed was ten minutes to shove her belongings in her backpack. A quick goodbye to Myrna and she'd be on her way. Eight hours later, she'd pull into the city to start scouring the streets for that blond head and cocky smile. A couple of days later, Frank would realize his only employee left town. But how long would it take David to realize she was gone? Would he feel it the minute she left the city limits, or would he interpret her silence as punishment?

The breeze died down and with it, her resolve.

Like a hand pulling her underwater, that handsome cop held on tight, even though she feared he would let go. If their argument the night before was any indication, David was close to it. Calls to his phone went unanswered and she prayed her voice didn't shake when she did leave a message to suggest they meet the next evening. Amanda pushed herself from the rocks and walked over to the river-bank. The chocolate milk-colored water flowed lazily at this part of the river, but just upstream a small rapid stirred up the water, frothing it like a child blowing bubbles through a straw.

He was right; she did mess with his head, but it was only because there were too many problems and personalities swirling inside her. If she were to jump into the Tejas River, the sins of Amanda Martin would cause her to sink to the bottom. It was Mandy Jackson who lived a carefree and effervescent life that buoyed her to the surface. A life without market pressures, a constantly chiming BlackBerry and a philandering boyfriend. Mandy's life was filled with silence, simplicity and David. The Katie Shelton case was to absolve Amanda Martin of her sins, not Mandy Jackson.

Amanda began her climb back to the car. She crossed the little clearing where Katie's body was found, saying a prayer for peace and tranquility to both a dead girl she never knew and her dead best friend. Tears wove a latticework down her face with each quiet goodbye. Katie. Liz. Josh. Her parents. With every step she took from the past, she began to realize the reason she got off that bus, and, more importantly, what made her stay in Phoenix.

Her body may have spent twenty-seven years in Chicago, but this little town in the middle of nowhere Texas was where it had finally reunited with her heart.

When Amanda returned to her apartment, the lure of a cold shower drew her in, but a shift in the air caused her to freeze in the door. Someone had been in her apartment. She looked down at the keys in her hand and recalled the soft click of her lock moving out of place. The garage below her sat empty, Myrna likely still in Stephenville at her bridge tournament.

"Hello," Amanda called out. "Is there anyone here? With a pulse?"

She held her breath and listened. A mockingbird answered over the gurgling of the river below her. Her eyes jerked around the one-room apartment, eager for any movement, and her body tensed, poised to bolt out the door and sprint down the stairs to safety. The bed was empty, the comforter pulled tight over the sheets. Dishes sat in the drainer. The love seat to her right still held her backpack. *My backpack.*

Amanda lunged to grab the ratty, second-hand bag. Her numb fingers trembled as she pulled open the zipper. *Ten. Nine. Eight.* She stopped her countdown as she unfolded her money and collapsed on the love seat when she realized it was all there.

"My imagination is going to be the death of me."

When the blood returned to her extremities, she pushed herself up and locked her door, refocusing on her shower. Electricity pulsed through her body when she walked into her bathroom. Her new lavender nightie, the one she planned to bring to David's when she apologized for picking a fight, was no longer hanging over the shower door where she left it to dry. She remembered hand-washing it the night before and seeing it hanging there that morning as she dressed.

Lavender nighties don't grow legs. Only two suspects came to mind: Shiloh or Dr. Brown. Shiloh wouldn't steal a nightgown—taken a pair of scissors to it maybe—and Dr. Brown would have stayed there waiting for her. Amanda's back slid down her bathroom door as her weak legs refused to hold her up.

Even though she called a truce with the gunman's ghost, she couldn't help but feel he wasn't done with her.

35

The thought that someone had a key to her apartment continued to consume her the next morning at work as she hunted for batteries. The dying door chime was mewing on a loop, reminding her of a hungry alley cat that wouldn't give up until someone threw out some scraps. After thirty minutes of the maddening noise, she was ready to dig into Frank's whiskey stash herself.

Over the past several weeks Frank had cleaned up his act, coming in with more vigor and less vice. But that morning, whiskey percolated from his pores, and his black pants and white shirt were rumpled beyond repair. Whiskers dotted one half of his face while one cheek was as smooth as a baby's behind, making his face look even more asymmetrical than usual.

"Can't you do something about that noise," Frank barked at her, his face turning a shade of green as he spoke. He belched into his handkerchief and Amanda blanched at the thought that Frank might get sick in the lobby, and she would have that to clean up as well.

"I'm trying, Frank. I can't find any batteries. Look, I'll just run to the store. I'll be back in a few minutes." She was gathering her purse to escape when Frank walked over to the door, reached up on his toes and pulled the beige box off the frame, the chime dying in a final heartbreaking whine.

"That would take too long." Frank tossed the chime in the wastebasket. "You keep the noise level down today, you hear me? You damn well better answer the phone before it rings. Got that Jackson? I'm in no mood to mess around."

Amanda nodded. After seeing the fate of the chime, she got it.

The rest of town seemed to have gotten word of Frank's killer hangover. The morning was quiet, even by Phoenix standards. The phone never rang, not that it did much to begin with, but with Amanda's call to David she hoped it would at least once. The fax machine stood silent. Even the ancient printer seemed to churn in a low hum for the benefit of its maniacal boss. As she worked, the silence of the office enveloped her like a warm, secure blanket.

"That fragrance you're wearing reminds me of the girl I lost my virginity to. I was a high school freshman, she was a senior, and she taught me so, so much. Would you like to see?" The blanket was yanked off by a voice in her ear.

Amanda squeezed her eyes shut, hoping she'd only imagined the warmth on her neck. The stool twirled around and her hand clung to the computer mouse as if it could anchor her in place. His body held her captive against the workbench, the wood grinding into her lower back as she pulled away.

"Come on Mandy, open your eyes. I may not be tall, dark and handsome like Stephens, but I'm not that bad."

She could see his shadow through her closed lids. If this was going to happen, she didn't want to see it, she wanted no visual memory of it. A tear slid through a microscopic crevice. The hairs of his mustache scratched her cheek as he kissed it away. A whimper escaped her throat as fresh tears found safe passage from her sealed eyes.

"Look at me," he said.

She shook her head.

"Look at me." His voice louder.

She shook her head harder.

"Look at me," he shouted. If she could hold out, maybe Frank would come to her rescue. In the space between his words, she heard her boss' rhythmic snores.

"I'm not going to hurt you. Quite the opposite, you remind me of her, that senior, whatever her name was. I think there are things you can teach me." His lips brushed the side of her neck as his hand moved up her waist and scraped the underside of her breast. Her eyes fluttered open, her brain ready to confront what was there.

"Dr. Brown, please don't." She directed all the strength in her body to her vocal chords, but her voice still came out weak, damaged.

"Oh good. I have your attention now. I'll make you a deal," he said, his hand moving from her breast to grip the side of her desk, locking her in place. She could see flecks of gold in his blue eyes and the black rim of his irises. If she weren't paralyzed with fear, she would have stabbed him in the eyes with anything she could find. "I won't tell your boyfriend what I found out about you if you will show me everything that body of yours can do." He moved closer, his full intention pressed against her shins.

"Please," the tears came freely now. *This isn't fair. I am done with Katie. I am done with the gunman. I'm ready for David.* His threat came as no shock. Anyone with enough suspicion and an Internet connection could figure her out. The past had no place in her future, but it wouldn't give up that easily.

"You'll be gentle with me, right?" he said, once again his lips moved along her neck. Amanda's ears rang, and she grew light-headed as the blood from her brain washed down to her stomach. Passing out would be the best defense. The ringing in her ears grew louder until she realized it wasn't from fear, but from the telephone just a few feet away. She prayed it was David.

"I need to answer that. It'll wake Frank," she whispered. Amanda hoped the doctor would set her free so she could make a run for it.

"Let the machine get it."

The ringing paused briefly before commencing again. His hand fumbled with the top button of her shirt. She didn't make it this far only to be blackmailed into sex. If it came down to it, she would tell David the truth herself. Dr. Brown couldn't hurt her if David was aware of her past. He might reject her—it was a chance she would have to take—but at least it would save her.

The doctor shifted, his stance widening to hover over her. When his body moved, a light draft of air danced on her knee, telling the nerves to alert the tendons that it was safe to move. Her right knee flew up, not enough to do any damage, but applying and maintaining enough pressure to get her point across. His head drew back, and his eyes locked on hers.

"Do *I* have *your* attention now? Good. I don't know who you think I am or what you think you know, but you have exactly ten seconds to get out of here or I will scream loud enough to wake Frank and the dead," her voice finding the strength it attempted to summon earlier. "And no one will be able to dispute your intentions." She upped the pressure on his erection to prove her point. "Ten, nine." She ticked off the seconds as much for his benefit as to calm her own nerves.

Dr. Brown narrowed his eyes, and the right side of his mouth pulled up. He took two steps back, and turned his back on her, confident enough that she was rendered immobile to not look behind him. *He's lucky I don't want to add manslaughter to my résumé, or I would stab scissors in his back.*

She watched him walk across the street and get into his Suburban. As the car backed out of the parking space, the phone started ringing again and Frank stormed out of his office.

"Jackson, what in the hell did I tell you about noise? Answer the damn phone."

"Sorry, Frank," her voice broke, but if Frank noticed, he ignored his crying employee.

Amanda arrived late to Riley's. She wasn't trying to make a dramatic entrance or debated which of her two pairs of jeans to wear; or prove a point by making David wait. She was late because she almost couldn't go. The encounter with Dr. Brown made her feel tainted, infected with a disease she feared would spread to David. She hurried home after work to scrub his contamination from her skin. It would be cruel to afflict David's virtue with her sin.

She parked next to David's truck, relieved he was there even if he didn't return her call. Riley's was busy, but not overly crowded. Amanda thought she caught a flow of black tresses from the corner of her eye, but if Shiloh was there she tended to her thirsty patrons and avoided Amanda like an unruly drunk. Without slowing her stride, she walked out the door to the patio bar. It might have been her imagination, but a single beam of sunlight shining through the canopy of trees landed just behind David's head. She paused, smiling at the halo effect the light created, believing it a sign from a higher power that she'd made the right decision.

Before she took a step towards him, her eyes darted to another man seated at the table, his back to the door. Both men leaned in close together in conversation. She knew the back of that head; it was the same one she'd studied from the back seat of a Suburban.

David hadn't seen her yet, and she tried to read his face. If Dr. Brown had told him about her past, her breakdown, maybe even their confrontation earlier that day, there was no look of fear, disgust or even concern from David. His face was blank except his eyebrows knitted together. He craned his head to the left, looking over his shoulder and out over the Tejas River. When he turned back, he made eye contact, but his smile was slow showing itself. She had no choice but to approach the table.

"Hey," she said, stretching her face into her most confident smile.

"Hi, you must be Mandy. Dr. Clint Brown. I've heard a lot about you," Clint offered his hand. Amanda didn't move. Blood thumped in her ear. Her gaze said everything her mouth couldn't, at least not at that moment. *How dare you pretend we have no history. You narcissistic son-of-a-bitch, does your wife know what you tried today? Am I the only one? No, I bet there are others. I'll make you a deal, you stay away from David and me, and I won't tell what happened.* His eyes blinked furiously fast; he understood.

"Well, it was good seeing you, man," Clint said to David, and slapped him on his shoulder with his ignored hand.

"An old friend?" Amanda asked, hoping that David didn't hear her voice shaking.

David didn't look at her. He craned his head again to the left and looked out over the river. Mandy followed his gaze. All she could see was a grove of cattails sticking up out of the swiftly moving water. Whatever David saw was invisible to her.

"Something like that," he muttered.

36

I f Clint told David all of her secrets, then David was a master bluffer.

"Yeah, what were you guys talking about?" she asked.

"Just catching up." David's words were terse. Amanda breathed deeply to keep from acting antsy. Lucky for her, she had an opportunity to change the subject.

"You probably think I'm crazy," she said after the waitress took her drink order. "I was frustrated and in a bad mood."

"Nah, you're actually quite sane compared to some of my exes," he quipped. "You probably think I'm an ass for getting so mad. I'm sorry, you just struck a nerve."

"I told Frank there is nothing new with the Katie Shelton case. I'm done, moving on to some fascinating topics, you know, church potlucks and award-winning tomatoes."

"Pulitzer-worthy, no doubt," he said. His smile melted the fear in Amanda's chest. "Seriously though, I owe you an apology. I probably could have been more helpful to you. The chief hired me to solve that case. He doesn't like an unsolved murder hanging over the town, but I've been nothing but stumped. Guess my dumb male pride worried my girlfriend would figure out something I couldn't."

"You know what, that's the past, and I will no longer drive forward looking in the rearview mirror." She offered her glass to him in a toast.

When they finished their drinks, David seemed to be back to his old self. "You know what's the best part about a fight? The make-up." By the time they went to bed, Amanda had forgotten that Clint and David spoke earlier in the evening at Riley's.

But she couldn't sleep. Whenever she closed her eyes, she imagined the conversation between David and Clint. Possibly, Clint asked David if he knew about her past, about who she really was. Perhaps Clint shared with him that he found her half-dressed running barefoot down the road in the middle of a hailstorm. David had tried to hold back his shock, but he'd probably been blindsided by the revelation that his seemingly put-together girlfriend was truly crazy. Maybe Clint told David she needed to be committed. Lying there in the dark, Amanda gave herself a mental check-up. It's true that she did have some vivid hallucinations. She was a rational woman, always seeing everything in either black or white. There was no reason to believe the gunman followed her to Texas. No matter how she tried to convince herself it was a harmless elderly woman, she saw someone in a baseball cap following her on her run. What if he did? What if he were so determined to make her pay for what she did to his family that he survived the blast and followed her all the way to the bus station and then on to Texas? It happened all the time in the horror movies.

That thought sent a chill through her body. Even with David sound asleep next to her, she felt the need to check all the locks in the house. She was probably safer there with David than anywhere else. He kept his gun on the bedside table. It was overkill, especially in a town as quiet as Phoenix, but she appreciated it.

His home was dark and cool, and the full moon outside cast strange shadows through the house. The front door was locked, as was the back door just off his kitchen. The windows all seemed secure as well. Still, she couldn't shake the unrest that settled over her, like something was waiting to happen. Rather than crawl back into bed, she decided to stand sentry in David's living room.

Amanda doubled her legs under her on David's sofa and pulled an afghan over her. She fought sleep and insomnia simultaneously, so when she thought she saw a shadow cross in front of the moonlight, it was hard to determine if she was asleep or awake.

She sprung up and pulled open the aluminum blinds to look out David's long front drive. From her vantage point, his front lawn was empty, and the driveway stood alone. A few cattle clung together, their bodies creating a still void in the moonlight, but another void crept among them.

Tails twitched as the shadow moved past them and grew longer, reaching its dark fingers towards the house. Reaching for her. Threatening David.

David's gun. Amanda needed David's gun. If something was coming for her, it might not stop just with Amanda. She loved David enough to protect him from whatever was out there. He didn't ask to get tangled up in her mess; he didn't even know what he was dealing with. It was Amanda's responsibility to take care of it.

When she turned to retrieve the gun from his room, more shadows moved inside the house, including one stalking silently towards her. Despite all of her precautions, he had gotten into the house. She turned back to the window; the shaking corn was quiet now. Amanda didn't really believe in ghosts, but only a ghost could move from the corn field through locked doors. He wanted her, not David; and the only way she could save David was to draw the apparition out of the house.

Once again, she sprinted away from the shadowy figure, but this time, she didn't run in total fear. The only way to be free of it was to fight it, stand up to it. But she couldn't do that in David's house. Gravel crunched behind her. She heard her name shouted. It wasn't until a sharp rock sliced into her bare heel that David caught up to her.

"Mandy," he said, while grabbing her around the waist. "Where in the hell do you think you're going?" Like her, he was in his pajamas and barefoot.

"I thought—I thought," was all she could manage before the pain in her foot registered with her brain. "Owww, my foot."

David examined it, picked her up and carried her inside. Amanda thought that was a bit heavy-handed, she could have walked with just some assistance, but maybe it was to restrain her. As he carried her, she noticed his limp on his bad knee and worried he'd aggravated his old injury in his pursuit.

With Amanda seated on the toilet, David silently cleaned the wound on her heel. Luckily, it was a shallow cut, but Amanda thought David poured more hydrogen peroxide in it than necessary, probably hoping the burn would teach her a lesson. She didn't scream out, but instead gripped the sides of the toilet seat cover and tightened her whole body. He dried the skin around it and covered the cut with a Band-Aid. The only words he spoke were to tell her she might want to take a break from running until the cut healed.

Once he was done tending to her wound, he put away the first-aid kit and limped back into his bedroom. Amanda waited a few minutes and then followed him in. The room was dark. David sat on the edge of the bed, hunched over with his forearms resting on his thighs. Amanda stood at the doorway, unsure if David wanted her to come back to bed or sleep on the couch for the rest of the night.

"Thank you." She sat on the bed next to him.

"What were you running after?" She was glad he thought she ran after something rather than ran from something.

"Something was stirring the cattle. I thought someone was out there."

"Why didn't you wake me instead? It was probably nothing more than a coyote."

Sitting there with David, she realized that it was only in her head. She hadn't given any thought on exactly how she planned on fighting whatever haunted her.

"Do you know how much you scared me? I get up for a drink of water and find you gone. I walk into the living room, and I see you bolt out the front door like the devil himself was chasing you."

He was.

"I don't even think you heard me calling your name."

All Amanda could do was nod. She looked at the clock, it was nearly four in the morning, and she felt sleepy for the first time all night. "I'm sorry; I didn't mean to scare you. It's just, I was afraid someone out there wanted to hurt you. I know it may seem silly, but I'm falling in love with you and I was just trying to protect you."

The words didn't stick in her throat like she thought they would. It was true. Against her better judgment, she was falling in love with him. She did think someone would want to hurt him, albeit someone she thought had managed to get into the house. She was trying to protect him. David looked at her, the harshness of his anger faded. He kissed her on the forehead.

"Let's get back to sleep," he said.

When Amanda woke, the sun shone through the blinds and she could smell bacon frying in the kitchen. David had the radio tuned to his favorite classic rock station, and he sang along from the kitchen. Before getting out of bed, she examined her foot. Luckily the bleeding had stopped pretty quickly, and she didn't need to change her bandage, but it was definitely tender when she tried to put any weight on it.

David laughed as she hobbled into the kitchen.

"Guess that will teach you to go chasing after boogeymen barefoot, huh?"

She watched David move around the kitchen and was relieved to see that he moved without a limp this morning. David made her sit at the kitchen table and served her coffee and breakfast.

"How's your foot feeling? You still up for the town barbecue tonight?" Amanda had nearly forgotten about Phoenix's annual Memorial Day barbecue. It was one of the most anticipated events of the year; something always happened that left the town talking for the next year. The Fourth of July was too hot for a big patriotic celebration, so the town assigned that task to the somewhat cooler weather the end of May offered.

"I'll hobble around. I wouldn't dream of missing it."

With her foot injury, Amanda had to alter her wardrobe plans slightly from a summer dress to a white eyelet tank top and baby blue shorts, something that looked much more cohesive with tennis shoes. David parked in the police station parking lot, and they held hands as they walked to the square. An outside observer would have seen them as a young couple happily in love. They would never guess that Amanda had a fit of paranoia just twelve hours earlier.

A band played country music and people cheered. In addition to beer and barbecue, the town square was littered with classic cars and arts and crafts. David snuck away to look at some of the cars while Amanda walked among the arts and crafts stalls. One stall sold pickled vegetables and jams in simple Mason jars with the names scribbled in black Sharpie across the top. Another sold an array of crocheted products and potpourri.

David caught up to her, and they stopped for a plate of barbecue and sweet tea. It was only then that Amanda realized how impractical it was for her to wear white while surrounded by people drinking beer and eating barbecue drowned in red sauce.

They made their way back to the side of the square that was home to the classic cars. David talked to a few of the people while Amanda pretended to be interested in the old cars. She perused the list of features in a '69 Mustang when the sound of her name pulled her over to David.

"Mandy, this is my cousin Rex," David nodded to Rex Travis. "Rex, this is my girlfriend Mandy Jackson. She's new to town but works over at the newspaper. I don't think you two have met yet."

Amanda gave a bright smile and hoped he wouldn't recognize her from the afternoon she was at Riley's, waiting for her confrontation with Shiloh. She offered her hand, "It's very nice to meet you, Rex."

Rex scratched the back of his head with one hand while he offered his other. "I think I've seen you before," he said, one eye closed as if the synapses would work faster with less distraction.

"Oh yeah, maybe just around?" Amanda suggested.

"No, like on TV or something," he said.

Amanda froze, her face locked in a smile. She had sequestered herself from television and any news related to Chicago, the financial markets or anything that had to do with death, but was it possible that her picture had been plastered all over the news, and she had no clue.

"I got it," he said, both eyes wide open. "You look just like one of the female wrestlers, but without all the scary muscles and stuff."

David broke into laughter and patted Rex on the shoulder.

As David and Rex talked, Amanda scanned the crowd to see if she saw anyone else. She spied Dugan seated on the steps of the courthouse with a gaggle of children at his feet. His role at this festival must be that of storyteller. Myrna was stationed behind a table marked Phoenix Garden Club with a few other ladies, selling seedlings. Everyone had a smile on their faces and seemed to be enjoying themselves. Amanda thought about the paper for the last week; every story was about happiness rather than the nose-diving stock market. If she had included any of those depressing stories about war, financial doom-and-gloom and job loss, the mood of this festival might have been much more subdued.

Amanda found herself drawn to the steps of the courthouse and to the man who first welcomed her to Phoenix. Dugan regaled his audience with the tale of the Alamo, and Amanda was so drawn into the story that she didn't realize David had joined her until Dugan ended the somber yet hopeful tale and cheers erupted with the famous phrase, "Remember the Alamo."

The afternoon turned to dusk and white Christmas lights strung around the square lit up as the headlining band got up on stage. Amanda and David's earlier attempt at country dancing was comical at best, but this band played mostly line dances. So, after downing a couple of beers and at the urging of those around them, they decided to join in. Lucky for Amanda, the lady next to her was pretty drunk and didn't seem to mind that she was several steps behind everyone else. At the end of the dance, she was sweaty and thirsty.

Amanda took his spot at the makeshift bar. Only a single wooden plank served as the uneven bar top, and she had chosen the middle line, so she stood shoulder to shoulder with many of the same people she saw earlier eating barbecue ribs with their fingers. The man to her right got his beer and walked away, only to be replaced by a slightly drunk woman who juggled a huge plate of ribs and potato salad. Her enormous plate teetered on the unsteady bar as the woman waited for her beer.

Shiloh worked ambidextrously, and as much as Amanda hated to admit it, she was impressed. Being outside, Riley's only sold beer on tap with Shiloh filling plastic cups to the rim. It came as no shock when Shiloh passed over Amanda in favor of the woman to her right. She craned her head around to see if she could ask someone else in line to buy her beer for her when something cold and slimy slid down her chest. She turned back just as people gasped.

The woman's plate of barbecue and potato salad now stuck to the front of Amanda's shirt, with red barbecue sauce splattered across her chest. Even a cup of beer somehow managed to join the party on her clothes.

Shiloh feigned shock and surprise, but Amanda saw a grin when everyone turned their focus from Shiloh to the mess created by the woman's plate. Amanda's fists rolled into balls. The astonished murmurs of the people around her faded and all she saw was Shiloh's smug smile.

"Oh my word," the woman next to her slurred. "That is all my fault, I should have made Jim hold the plate while I came for beer." The woman wiped the barbecue sauce with a cocktail napkin, but only smeared it around a larger area.

"What. Did. You. Do." Amanda said to Shiloh through clenched teeth. "Will you stop that?" Amanda snapped to the woman, who retreated with a sniffle.

"Well, like Luanne here said, it's all her fault. She shouldn't have put such a big plate of food somewhere I could knock it off. You won't do that again, will you Luanne?"

The woman, upset by her actions, broke down in tears as others consoled her.

Exhausted by the apparitions of a gunman, drained from the unwanted advances from the doctor, and furious with the jealous actions of a child in a woman's body, Amanda's temper snapped like a taut rubber band, resulting in her balled-up fist connecting squarely on Shiloh's cheek.

"You bitch," Amanda screamed. "You did this on purpose."

And before she knew it, she launched herself over the makeshift bar after Shiloh. At first, the people around them were shocked to find two grown women in a fight, but once the brain cells were rattled awake, the men tried to pull the two apart. Shiloh was also stunned by Amanda's sudden action, and although she was protected by the bar, she was hit over the head with another one of Amanda's punches.

Amanda had never been in a fight before, but she called forth everything she learned during her two-week affair with kickboxing, hitting mostly the bar and collapsing one side of it. She was so focused on pulverizing whatever her fists connected with that she didn't even realize David grabbed her around the waist and picked her up, her fists still moving but only connecting with the air around them.

"Mandy, what has gotten into you?" he pulled her out of the crowd of people.

"Shiloh started it. She ruined my clothes." Amanda's lower lip trembled as she fought off tears. The last thing she wanted to do was break down crying, but the river of tears pushed against the levee of her dignity.

"She wouldn't have done it on purpose."

"Yes she would. And, she did," Amanda countered.

"David, you better arrest that bitch for assault," Shiloh screamed. "You got that? Arrest her ass." Shiloh's brother Eddie held her back, but she broke free and grabbed a handful of Amanda's brown locks. This time Rex was close enough to grasp Shiloh by the waist to pull her back, but not before she gave Amanda's hair a good yank.

The two cousins stood there, each holding his girlfriend by the waist to keep the women from fighting. Both women stood there, at first fighting to get away from their handlers, but finally giving up and panting from the exertion.

"If you're arresting me, then I want you to arrest Shiloh, too," Amanda said.

"No one is getting arrested tonight. Not because you both don't deserve it, but because we have only one holding cell. I'm afraid to imagine what would happen if you two were locked up together."

The excitement over, the crowd dispersed.

"So, cuz, I guess this means no double dates," Rex quipped, when it was just the four of them. He alone laughed at his joke.

37

S hiloh's temper hadn't even begun to cool down when she sat in Clint's empty clinic Sunday morning. She knew she didn't need stitches for the cut on her cheek from the one good punch Mandy managed to land, but she wanted him to survey the damage as soon as possible, especially since she held him partially to blame.

"Man, the twins picked an awful time to get sick," he said as he patted the inch-long cut. "I would've paid good money to see that."

Shiloh narrowed her eyes at him. "Stop laughing, it's not funny. She could have really hurt me. Anyway, she's crazy, you're right. What person does something like this?"

In Shiloh's telling of what happened, she downplayed what actually started the fight, and when she did mention the flying plate of food, it was simply an unfortunate accident. Shiloh knew it was an impulsive decision, and one that would have consequences, but she couldn't help herself. Luanne's big plate of food beckoned for Mandy's white blouse.

"Well, the good news is she didn't break your cheekbone, and you won't need stitches; bad news is you'll have that shiner for a week or so."

Great. Shiloh didn't want to have a reminder every time she looked in the mirror.

"Tell me about your conversation with David. You had a long visit with him," Shiloh was curious. She sent Clint a text as soon as David had arrived at the bar and immediately gone to a table on the patio. It was only a guess that he was meeting Mandy, but it didn't really matter if he was or not. Clint needed David alone.

"Just as we planned," he said, pulling his latex gloves off. "I just had to ask him if it's true he's seeing Mandy, and he opened right up. Shi, it was perfect because without prompting him, he told me that he thought Mandy might be the one. He walked right into it."

Shiloh winced at the thought that David could love someone she loathed.

"So anyway, after that I asked where she was from, what she did before Phoenix and if he'd met her family yet. David explained that she was far from home, so I made the smallest joke that he should make sure she's not married or running from the law, especially since her past is pretty thin. That got to him," Clint leaned against the sink in the examination room. "You should have seen his face. It was like he was thinking it all along, but just didn't want to admit it. I successfully planted the seed of doubt, and we just need to sit back and watch it grow. The best was when Mandy arrived."

"What do you mean?" Shiloh had glimpsed Mandy coming in out of the corner of her eye, but hadn't seen the woman for the rest of the evening.

"Well, remember how I said it's a shame that only David would get to know how good Mandy was in bed? Thought I'd give it one last try."

Shiloh grew enraged. "Clint, are you stupid? What were you thinking? She could have called David, and then you'd be arrested. For once can't you just keep it in your pants?"

"Number one, she wasn't going to tell anyone. Women that damaged don't go to the police. And number two, it never left my pants; she stopped it before I could even get her top button undone."

"What if she wouldn't have stopped you? Huh? What if she

took you up on the threat? Would you be willing to cheat on your wife with her?"

With an exaggerated sigh and shrug, Clint answered her. "Guess I would just have taken one for the team."

Shiloh slammed her hand against the pad of the examination room table. This was nothing more than a game to Clint. She was trying to protect David from getting hurt. She also was trying to protect Katie's secret, and in turn, Clint's secret. But Clint was using this as an opportunity to add another notch to his belt. Regret bubbled up from the depths of her gut. Her own jealousy could have put Mandy in harm's way. Doubt, bitter with age, joined regret.

What if she helped Mandy rather than trying to stop her? Could it be that Katie's spirit stopped Mandy's bus just outside of Phoenix and lured the woman to their town? Shiloh had nothing against Katie's murderer being caught. And, at this point, she had come to terms with the fact that she'd lied to the police.

"Don't get pissy with me. You wanted her gone. I'm just doing my part to help."

"It's more than that. What if we're wrong? Maybe she was meant to be here, meant to solve this case. Maybe Katie sent her."

Clint laughed. "I never would have pegged you as someone who believed in ghosts. Really, Shiloh, how many times do we need to go over it? What good will it do? It won't bring her back. You're just being selfish. If it comes out that Katie and I were together the night she disappeared, then it will ruin my practice, my wife will leave me and I'll never see my daughters again. I'll have to move out of Phoenix to find work and that will leave this town without a doctor. Think of all the people who need to have a doctor here," Clint paused. "Don't be selfish and cause those people, the elderly and sick, to lose their one healthcare provider."

Once again, Shiloh hated Clint. Moments ago he admitted he was willing to sleep with a woman who was not his wife, only now to insinuate the possible demise of his marriage would be on her if the truth came out. But, in his own melodramatic way, he was right. No other doctor had moved to Phoenix, and before Clint agreed to take over his dad's practice, the older Dr. Brown searched for other physicians that might be interested in coming to their small corner of the world. It was no shock that he came up empty-handed time and again.

"Shiloh, will you do me a favor, once this is all over, will you finally snap out of it? You have been wallowing in grief for ten years now; you shouldn't do that to yourself. Not to mention this whole mourning thing is getting a bit tiresome. I honestly don't know how Rex puts up with it."

If Shiloh didn't have the fight beaten out of her the evening before, she would have punched Clint. Deep down, he was right. She wasn't the same person, and she knew it. Even she was growing tired of the grief. Maybe she should finally see that therapist her brother wanted to send her to years ago.

Riley's was closed on Sunday and Memorial Day, and Eddie made her take a couple of extra days off to recover from the altercation. She protested, saying that she needed the tips. But in true big brother fashion, Eddie offered to help if she needed extra money.

Laziness was never one of Shiloh's shortcomings. Even when she was sick she didn't sit still, and as long as she wasn't contagious, she would still come to work. But this forced time off gave her an opportunity to clean some clutter from her apartment, mainly items she'd held on to as a way to remember Katie. Now, thinking about Clint's advice, she wondered if these things didn't just hold on to Katie's memory, but actually held Shiloh back from moving on. She spent Sunday afternoon packing various mementos in boxes, took them to her mother's house and stored them in the closet in her old bedroom. She knew she should have just thrown them in the trash, but she opted for a trial separation first. If she didn't want them by the end of the summer, by the tenth anniversary of Katie's disappearance, she would honor her friend by moving on.

Monday, Shiloh cleaned her apartment from floor to ceiling. She even thought about going for a jog, craving some physical exertion after seeing Mandy run. But the jarring motion ached her cheek, and her cigarette habit made her short of breath. She needed to heal and quit smoking before she could try that again. Lucky for her she was still the same size as she'd been in high school, so the urge to run wasn't for vanity's sake.

On Tuesday, she drove to Stephenville to visit her elderly grandmother. Time with her *abuelita* always made her feel better. Maybe it was just from juxtaposing her life with that of an octogenarian, but she drove home with her windows down and music up high. She was glad that her grandmother's failing eyesight didn't register the caked on makeup over her right cheek. It would have been tough explaining the fight to her grandmother, especially since the woman had a way of drawing information out of Shiloh.

By Wednesday, her final day off, she fought boredom and spent the day camped out on the couch watching television. Her only source of entertainment was the talk shows with their unoriginal content of women who rose above adversity, or brothers who were sleeping with the same woman. On her second cycle through the channels, she became enamored with a woman who was nothing like the other female talk show hosts. Where they were caring and kind, gently probing their guests, this woman was tough and didn't shirk from the hard questions. By the end of the show, Shiloh was forever a Judith Nash fan.

38

"You are bloody brilliant," Roland said as Alex drove them back to Chicago. He turned the plastic card over and over in his hands, holding it up to get a look when passing headlights lit up the dark car. Alex wouldn't let him turn the dome light on anymore; not only did it make it hard to see the road, it prevented his chatty friend from going to sleep. He really wanted to be alone with his thoughts so he could beg forgiveness for what he considered a blasphemous act.

"I can't believe our good fortune," Roland continued. "I'll ask my editor and our flack if they'll spring for you to fly over to New York with me. You know, you should really be there next to me. I don't know why I didn't think of that before."

Alex smiled. Maybe good things do come to those who sacrifice.

"Sure, man. My schedule is clear, I would really like that."

The next afternoon, they waited to board their flight to New York. Alex could barely eat, his stomach flip-flopped, and he broke out in cold chills. His mother was so excited that he was going to be on national TV that she called all the ladies from church to watch his big debut. Alex didn't have the heart to tell her that when they flashed his name up, it wouldn't say SEC analyst, it would say private investigator.

Later, they met in the hotel lobby and slowly walked the half block to the studio. Roland's hand shook as he lit a cigarette, forcing the ember to burn unevenly. The receptionist smiled when they arrived and asked them to be seated until one of the producers came to get them. The television showed a promo for the *Judith Nash Show*. She looked like an average soccer mom, someone who would have been more at home driving carpools and arranging snack duty. But, when she got someone in the hot seat, she turned into a bull-dog. Lucky for them, they were on the right side of the law. Alex shuddered to think what it would be like for those few criminals who unknowingly showed up on her set only to be skewered on live TV.

They didn't have to wait long. A young man with a headset and radio clipped to his belt came for them and led them to the green room.

"You gentlemen don't mind if I send one of our makeup girls in. High-definition leaves nothing to the imagination. She'll just dust a little powder on you so you don't shine." He didn't wait for them to answer; he just hit a button on his radio and asked Naomi to come in when she had a minute.

Seconds later, Naomi showed up carrying a small toolkit of makeup. She blotted each man and dusted powder across his face, asked if they would like something to drink. She too didn't wait for an answer; she pressed the button on her radio and asked Julian to bring them some ginger ale. Alex felt green; he must have looked a little green as well.

Naomi waltzed out and Julian breezed in, carrying two bottles of ginger ale.

"Can we get you anything else?" Julian asked. Like the others, he wore a headset and radio.

"Will we get a chance to meet Ms. Nash before the show?" Alex asked. *She's not going to eat me. She's not going to eat me. She's going to chew me up and spit me out.*

"Probably not, but one of the producers will be back before we go on to talk through everything with you."

Julian put his finger to his headset, pressed a button to answer a question and was out the door. Alex and Roland had over an hour to wait. Like the lobby, the green room was playing a highlight reel of Judith Nash. Alex wanted to go over their strategy for the show, but he was afraid to open his mouth. His stomach roiled with apprehension. There would be no way Harrison could save his job once this was over.

Finally, twenty minutes to show time, another producer came in to outfit them with microphones. She led them to the studio. Alex had never been in a television studio before, and he was surprised by how small and dark it was. Seated behind the desk, Alex could barely make out what was beyond the massive cameras.

"Now, just follow Judith's lead," the girl said as she put the microphones on the backs of their pants and wove the wire behind their jackets. "She'll lead the discussion, direct her questions to each of you. This is live, so if one of you freezes up, the other will have to jump in and help, okay? And, don't look at the cameras. Look directly at Judith. Act natural, breathe. You are only having a conversation with her." Luckily, Roland was seated closer to Judith and Alex on the other side of him. Maybe the camera would forget he was there.

Ten minutes to show time, Judith arrived. She wore a bright red suit, and even in her high heels, she was nearly a foot shorter than the two men. Alex had no clue she was such a small woman. Watching her show he would have guessed that she was a giant.

"Hey ya'll," she said with a surprising Southern twang in her voice. "I'm so glad ya'll could be on my show. I'm Judith." She reached a well-manicured hand to Alex and then to Roland. "Did Anna talk through everything with ya'll?"

They just nodded, both a little star-struck.

"Good," she said, taking her seat. Alex realized that she sat on a much taller chair; this must be why he never realized she was so small before. "Now you boys just sit back and relax. I don't bite. Hard." She started laughing. "That's just a little joke there."

A producer started counting down until they were live. "Ten. Nine. Eight." Alex froze, he could feel sweat starting to form on his brow. *Dammit*, he thought. *I can't do this.* "Seven. Six. Five. Four. Three. Two. And, we're live."

"Good afternoon. Imagine waking up one morning to find out that your entire life savings is gone. Well, that's nothing new for those that suffered the misfortunes of a plummeting stock market. But, imagine if it wasn't the stock market that robbed you, it was the people that you trusted to invest your money, to guard it as if it was their own. That's what happened to the customers of Jefferson Williams Investments, and today we're going to talk to the two men who are working to bring justice to those who lost their whole life savings. I'm Judith Nash, and thank you for joining me."

Gone was the friendly, Southern drawl and in its place was a crisp, clear voice barren of any emotion. His jaw muscles lost their grip and saliva dammed in his throat.

"Here with me is Alex Kostas, a private investigator. Now Alex, correct me, but weren't you with the Securities Exchange Commission when you uncovered the fraud taking place at JWI?"

Crap. Alex hoped to fly under the radar with this.

"Yes, Judith, you're correct," he tried to say that to Judith, but his head swiveled in the direction of the large cameras.

"And, Roland Burrows, senior reporter at the *Financial News*. Roland, you were the one who broke the story, correct?"

It must have been all the tension that led up to this moment, but sitting there in the bright lights of the studio, Roland's body relaxed, and his British charm worked on the cool host. Judith angled her body towards Roland, her elbows rested on the desk and her smile brightened.

During the first commercial break, one of the producers reminded Alex not to look at the cameras while reapplying the powder. When they came back, Judith asked Alex to explain the crimes. He shocked himself at the ease at which he was able to speak.

"Let me get this straight," Judith said, the red tip of a fingernail punctuated her point. "Not one of the three people indicted have been arrested, correct?"

"That is correct, Judith," Alex said, feeling bolder.

"Unbelievable," Judith said. "What can you say on behalf of your former agency as to why this was botched?"

Botched? What do I say? That I was too busy setting up news alerts and looking online for motivational wall art to realize that Williams and Cooper were cashing out their stock options? I can't say that. Not on national TV. I didn't even want to go on this damn show. Can I ask for a commercial break? I need my ginger ale. For once, Alex was afraid to look at the camera.

"Actually, Judith," Roland said. "I would be remiss if I didn't answer that one for my mate. You see, I got a tip that these indictments were coming. If you are looking for someone to blame for botching this, then you could probably blame me. That's why I joined forces with Alex. To right my wrong."

Is that really why Roland is working with Alex? Does that mean that Roland searched out Alex that night at the bar? Or, did he say that to get his friend out of the hot seat? Whatever the reason, Judith seemed satisfied and moved on.

Until the next commercial break, she focused her questions to Roland.

"Tell me about the three people from JWI involved."

"Well, you've got Josh Williams, the suave, Ivy League-educated, only son of founder Jefferson Williams. As CFO, Josh had access to all the accounts. He was a playboy, as well, living large and spending money faster than he could make it," Roland said. "To get away with his fraud, Josh needed help from two people in the firm, the chief legal counsel, Keith Cooper and the vice president of communications, Amanda Martin."

"When we come back from the break, we're going to find out where these three people are now."

"Alex, buddy, you've got to loosen up," Judith said. She kept her game voice on, but Alex would have felt much more comfortable if she had her sweet Southern voice back. He nodded and mumbled that he would do better.

Back on the air, Judith directed her question to Alex. "Alex, where are Williams, Cooper and Martin?"

"Well, Judith," he swallowed back acid in his stomach. He

hoped Harrison wasn't watching. "Williams and Cooper vanished; they must have been planning for this. But, as Roland said, Amanda Martin most likely wasn't aware what she was doing was illegal. She only got tipped off when Roland called her for comment. We do believe that Amanda is still in the country, though."

Judith turned back to the camera.

"There was another tragedy that took place that day. This one with a much darker and violent twist. Samuel Whitfield was a retired soldier and factory worker and a devoted husband to his wife Betty. Betty has been battling cancer, and her insurance wouldn't cover experimental treatment. Sam contacted JWI about cashing out his pension, which he invested entirely with the firm, in hopes of saving his wife. Suspecting something was amiss, he was on his way to meet with Williams that fateful morning, only to learn that his pension was gone, worth nothing, and with that the hope of Betty's recovery."

Judith paused here, as if giving everyone time to digest what she just said.

"Next up, we'll play the video we shot of Betty late last week. She lost her battle with cancer this morning."

When the producer announced they were clear, Alex bolted from his seat. The man who wreaked violent havoc at JWI had previously been nothing more than an obstacle to Alex's case, someone who was selfish and ruined the investigation simply for his own gain. In Alex's mind, this man had been the one who botched everything and was just as guilty and greedy as Williams, Cooper and Martin. Faced with the realization that the gunman was a living, breathing man who cared so much for his wife he went to such extreme, Alex's stomach lurched. A producer followed him into the bathroom, trying hopelessly to get him to turn off his mic before he was going to be sick. No such luck.

Back in the studio, everyone seemed to share in his nausea.

"Alex, maybe you should watch the rest of the show from the green room," Judith said, her sweet Southern drawl back.

A producer whisked him away and a ginger ale awaited him in

the green room. There he watched the recorded video of a painfully thin woman. Her skin was gray and hung on her face, her eyes sunk so far back into her skull that Alex couldn't tell if they were open or closed. And her head was wrapped in a scarf. She spoke quietly, in short sentences as if that was all that her breath could carry. The woman was both proud of her husband for fighting for her, but ashamed that so many people had to die with him. He just wanted to take care of his wife, the only family he had left. Now, the woman said breathlessly, she was going to have to die alone.

When the video was over, Judith announced that they would be right back. Alex hoped the woman really didn't die alone, that a kind doctor or nurse was there to hold her hand. And, he prayed her husband had been granted forgiveness so they could at least be reunited in death.

"Thank you again for joining us," Judith said and then launched into a quick update on the show's topic. "Roland, this case isn't dead, right? Some new information came into your hands earlier this week that may give some peace to the souls of Betty and Samuel Whitfield, those killed in the massacre and all the other thousands of people who lost their life savings because of Josh Williams' and Keith Cooper's greed. Tell us about that."

"Right. As you said, I hold new information literally in my hands," Roland held up the driver's license of Mandy Jackson. The camera zoomed in on the tiny plastic card. "We tracked Amanda to Memphis, where my partner Alex found that she obtained a fake ID and is possibly going by the alias Mandy Jackson."

Judith spoke to the camera operator. "Let's get a real tight shot on this license so our viewing audience can see what Amanda Martin may look like now. Where do you think she's hiding?"

"Well, that's the million-dollar question. She could be anywhere."

"Billings, Montana is the address on the license, could she be there?"

"Doubt it," Roland said. "Most likely she was heading for the border. Maybe to meet up with Williams. You know, they were lovers. It's a possibility that they arranged a rendezvous somewhere."

"Like a modern-day Bonnie and Clyde," Judith said.

"Well, except they didn't kill anyone," Roland replied.

"They may not have pulled the trigger, but people died because of them."

39

M

emorial Day couldn't have been more appropriately named. While the citizens of Phoenix hung flags, grilled burgers or splashed in pools, Amanda spent the day holed up in her apartment replaying the fight with Shiloh in her head. The buzz from the beer reduced her self-control to non-existent. It would have been so much easier if she would have just let herself be the victim, but she was tired of that role. Standing up for herself was the only way she could turn the tables on whatever Shiloh or Dr. Brown planned for her next, two people with nothing in common except for their constant terrorizing of her. When she said she was done with Katie Shelton, she was also done with the abuse, and if that meant that David would never speak to her again, well that was just a tragic casualty of her strength.

After the fight, he drove her home in silence. No words were spoken as she exited his truck. The sound of gravel crunching under his tires filled the air as he backed out of Myrna's driveway before she made it to the steps leading up to her apartment. Sunday was filled with silence. Monday was a void. By the time she awoke Tuesday morning, she thought her ears would bleed from the quiet.

With Frank out of town, she parked in his covered spot in the back of the building. She was so accustomed to a soundless world that she nearly missed Dugan sitting on the bench outside her closed office until she unlocked the front door.

"Mandy, may I have a moment of your time," Dugan said softly. The sly smile and twinkle in his eye that she was so fond of was gone and replaced with sadness and concern. "And Frank, if he's available."

"Of course, anything for you, Dugan. But, I'm afraid Frank is on vacation," she said. Something about his demeanor caused her breathing to become shallow. He carried a briefcase in one hand and his cane in the other. "Would you like me to try to get him on the phone?" Amanda added, but Dugan waved off her question.

"I live a simple existence," he started. "One of my many careers was that of a stockbroker, so I've always managed my own retirement fund."

Amanda knew what was coming. She could almost finish his speech for him. He didn't have the luxury of a portfolio manager to keep track of the changing stock markets. When his statement came in the mail the previous week, he was shocked to find that he lost so much money. At that point, he began looking at some past copies of the *Phoenix Talon*, the only newspaper he took, to try to figure out how he missed such a major financial event. He didn't miss it, it wasn't there. Not knowing what happened cost him most of his savings.

"Thankfully I am not completely ruined," he said. "But I daresay that it kept me up last night worrying about my future. I've seen other cycles like this and have always survived, but I am into my eighties. I fear that I may not fully recover financially from this loss."

Amanda's face flushed, and her eyes filled with tears. It was only then that she realized that she wasn't saving her fellow citizens from worry; she marched them blindly into a battle. How many other people in Phoenix were like Dugan? How many others managed their own money in the stock market and received statements informing them that they were broke? Did Myrna lose her and her late husband's life savings? Would she lose her beautiful Victorian home?

"I'm so sorry, Dugan," Amanda whispered. "I thought I was helping. I saw all that awful news and." She stopped.

Dugan nodded. She would have felt much better if he screamed at her, but instead he was ever the gentleman, and his voice remained quiet. Without another word, he turned and left the *Talon* office.

That day, she didn't hide from the despair in the financial markets and the corporate world. Instead, she bitterly embraced it. It didn't take her long to pull the news she would need for the paper. She vowed that, until Frank's return, she would not shirk from anything that made her uncomfortable. And she would confess her wrongdoing to Frank. He might choose to fire her, and in reality, she had that coming. But, while he was out of town, she would do her best to keep her neighbors fully informed.

While she picked at her lunch, she tried to work up the motivation to go by Foster's Bookstore for the next book review. What did it matter? A book wasn't going to save anyone. Because of her, the people of Phoenix were all going to be on food stamps and live in cardboard boxes. And what about David? Was he now at risk of losing his home? The ringing phone broke her wallowing. It was David.

"Hey, I was just thinking about you," she forced her voice to sound bright and chipper. At some point she needed to share her most recent lapse of judgment with him, but it would just have to get in line with all the others.

"Can we talk after work?" he asked quietly, drained and flat. "I'll come by your office around five-thirty."

"Okay, sure—"

"Alright, I need to go." He cut her off before she could say anything else.

This didn't sound good. But, she couldn't think about it now. There was a wrong that needed to be righted, the financial ruin she caused Dugan and maybe countless other people. Again. *If financial destruction were a super power, I would be the Bankrupter.*

But rather than filling herself with motivation and purpose, she filled herself with loathing and dread. She hated Shiloh, for many reasons but mainly for being the catalyst to her and David's silent screaming match. She hated Frank for hiring her. She hated David, because he loved her. She hated Dugan for talking her into staying in this town. She hated the weather; it was hot and humid again today and large thunderheads loomed in the distance, teasing with the threat of rain. But most of all she hate Josh. For everything.

Five o'clock came and went. The paper was off to press and Amanda got a head start on the next day while waiting for David. That earlier feeling of dread washed over her again. It was nearly six when she decided to lock up the office and wait for him on the bench outside, the same one where Dugan sat earlier in the day waiting for her.

The town square emptied as the workday ended. The sun sank just below the tops of the trees and cast a gray glow on the square. Crickets hummed somewhere down the street. The wooden planter to her right was ablaze with pink and purple petunias and buzzed with bees weaving in and out of the flowers.

Finally, David pulled up in his truck. He wore his police uniform and Amanda guessed he had a long day at work. Without looking at her, he sat next to her on the bench.

"Hi," he said, staring down at his balled up hands, his shoulders hunched over.

"Hi," Amanda answered, suddenly feeling the urge to cry.

Neither spoke for several minutes.

"I'm trying to figure out where to begin," he said. Amanda didn't think that statement was directed at her, but that he was instead talking to himself.

"I'm sorry about Saturday night," she said, believing he sought an apology. "I was a little bit drunk, and I thought she did it on purpose. I know that had to be really embarrassing for you. I'll make it up, I'll apologize to Shiloh. Starting today, no matter what she does to me, I'll just take it."

Three pre-teen boys rode by on their bicycles, laughing and

making their bikes jump the curb. Amanda wanted to chase after them, begging to be let in on their joke.

"That's not what I'm here to talk about," he said quietly. "I need you to be honest with me." David rubbed his open palms across his cheekbones; his hands covered his mouth, holding back whatever words were perched on the other side of his closed lips. "Who are you?"

For the first time that evening, he turned to look at her. Gravity pulled the blood from her head. She felt dizzy, and her vision field narrowed to seeing only a single crepe myrtle on the courthouse lawn. Amanda was afraid to look at him, fearful that if she did, she would start telling him everything she'd wanted to tell him. Here was the perfect opportunity; he initiated the conversation. But she wasn't ready yet. She found she had no response to the question, and now, she truly pondered the question herself. *Who am I?*

"What do you mean?"

"I ran your driver's license number, it's fake," he said. Out of the corner of her eye, she could see that he wasn't looking at her. "I copied it down the other morning, while you were still asleep."

She felt the urge to get angry with him for going through her purse, for running her license number, but really, he had every right to do that. Anyway, it was done. She couldn't change that.

"Oh," she said, exhaling to hold back the tears. She heard David take a deep breath himself. Finally feeling strong enough to look at him, she turned her head. In the twilight of the day, she could tell that he was crying. She waited to see what else he would say.

"I can help you, I want to help you. I just need you to be honest with me," his voice broke at the end. Amanda wanted to reach out to him, but she was afraid he would recoil from her. He cleared his throat and started again. "Hell, I don't even know if your name is really Mandy."

"It is."

"This is really my own damn fault," he continued, not acknowledging her answer. His Adam's apple moved as he swallowed. "I pushed you into this. Now I know why you were so hesitant. I brought this on both of us."

"I—," Amanda started.

"Let me finish, okay? Did someone hurt you? Are you running from an abusive boyfriend or husband? I can protect you if that's it. Or, God I hate to think this, but did you do something, is that why you have a fake ID? Look, I can help you with that, too."

David looked at Amanda, signaling that it was her turn to speak. She stared straight ahead, trying to compose her thoughts into words. Yes, she hesitated, but that was for his benefit, not hers. No, she did not have an abusive boyfriend; although that was the answer David wanted to hear, as well as the answer that would bring him back to her. But she couldn't stack another lie on top of all the ones she'd already told him. She wanted to come clean, to explain herself. But she wasn't ready to lose his love. If she told him all the horrible things Amanda Martin did, he would not only handcuff her and take her to jail; he would banish her, refuse to speak with her.

"David, I," she started. She wanted to start with her name, maybe to soften the blow she would introduce herself as Mandy Martin, but the words stuck in her throat. "I'm sorry."

That was all she could say before the tears started. She knew if she said anything else, he would hate her. She couldn't do that yet.

"Ten, nine, eight, seven, six, five," she took a deep breath. "Four, three, two, one." She finished her countdown but the truth still begged for a confrontation. David listened patiently as she counted, no one else knew this little quirk, not her parents or Josh. As he watched her, his face softened. He must have read fear in her face, deciding on his own that she ran from an abuser.

"Look, I know you're hurting. I wish we weren't having this conversation, trust me. But, before we can move on, I need you to be honest with me. You have to tell me everything. Don't worry about me, I can handle it."

David turned her face to his with the tip of his finger. She fought the urge to close her eyes when he looked at her, but she knew he needed to see her, to look at her. Amanda hoped that she had enough love in her eyes to keep him from hurting. David brushed a tear away from her cheek, but it unleashed a second torrent of tears. She leaned in to David's chest, resting her head against his badge, the raised parts of the star pressing into her forehead. He sniffled above her.

"I can't do that. Not yet," she said, after the tears ran out. She felt like a fish out of water, reaching for big gulps of air as she leaned up. "I want nothing more than to be with you. Can you just give me more time?"

David leaned back against the bench. The square was now completely quiet. Amanda imagined what her neighbors were doing. Dugan worrying over his finances. Eddie serving drinks for the regulars at Riley's. Myrna sitting down to a quiet dinner, shared only with the ghost of her dead husband Edward. Mr. Foster at home in the solitude and sanctity of his bookstore. Shiloh plotting her next move to rid herself and Phoenix of Amanda.

Amanda wanted to call out to these people. How could they go on with their lives when it felt like hers was crashing to an end? How could she live in this small town without David loving her, and with Dugan and God knows how many other people broke because of her?

"I need you to be honest with me before we can go any further. How can I trust you if I know you aren't telling me the truth about your past?"

Amanda nodded. If she lied about her identity, what stopped her from lying about her feelings? That was a perfect argument, and one she couldn't fight.

"So, is this the end?" she asked. The tears dried up, and her voice sounded stronger.

"It doesn't have to be though," he said after a second. "It's your choice. But yeah, for now, it's the end. If you think you can be honest with me, you know where to find me."

Amanda went back to thinking what others were doing. Frank enjoying a drink at a bar on Padre Island.

David stood up and walked over to the truck. He opened the door, but waited before climbing in. "Mandy, don't wait forever to decide, okay. I love you and want to be with you, but if someone else comes along, I may fall in love with her." He didn't look at her as he said this; instead he looked up at the stars.

After he drove away from the square, the clock at the courthouse chimed eight. Amanda was surprised at how late it was, but felt no obligation to go home.

40

A manda let herself be late to work the next morning. Her shoulders were heavy and her eyes burned, not from crying herself to sleep. She didn't really sleep, she really just cried herself to wake.

Amanda worried about David. Did he spend the night lying awake in his bed, or roaming around his house? Did he ask himself why he even bothered looking at her license? Did he wish he could take it all back? He opened the door for her to tell the truth. The real truth. Maybe he would agree to live with her secret.

She pulled her knees up to her chest and hugged them close. Her apartment felt unfamiliar as if it weren't her own but more like a hotel room, housing her while she passed through but vanilla enough to satisfy the next tenant. It would be simple enough to pack up the items she wanted in her backpack and move on to El Paso. Nothing good awaited her here. The likelihood that another irate reader of the *Phoenix Talon* stood ready to lynch her for neglecting to report the whole financial system's demise was high. The phone lines were probably alive with the gossip that she broke poor David Stephens' heart. Nothing anchored her. She owed no one the gift of her presence. A greater gift, instead, would be her absence. But she needed to be there. Frank depended on her to keep the paper running while he was out of town.

A sigh escaped her lungs when the dingy storefront for the *Talon* stood alone. No one waited to ambush her, and no messages leered at her from the answering machine either. She was safe, at least for another day.

Amanda had no motivation for her work. All she could do was rerun David's break-up in her mind. He knew her secret, at least part of it. What he didn't know was why she lied about her identity. He defaulted to what was safe, that she was a battered woman running from an abusive relationship. But, he wasn't going to believe that until she validated it for him, or told him something worse. Like the truth.

When the phone rang, she didn't mask her melancholy for the benefit of the caller. "*Phoenix Talon*. What?"

"Ms. Jackson?" the monotone voice flowed through the earpiece. "I am sorry to bother you, but you always pick up my book reviews on Tuesdays. Yesterday was Tuesday, and you did not come by. I almost didn't call you because I realize that Monday was a holiday and thus you might be working an altered schedule, but then I heard that you were battered by that awful woman, I thought I should check on your well-being."

Amanda was shocked that the cloistered bookstore owner even knew of her and Shiloh's fight, but she smiled at his reversal of the facts.

"You're right. I'm sorry Mr. Foster. I completely forgot about it yesterday. I'll come by this afternoon."

"Why don't you come at lunch time, allow me to serve you tomato soup and grilled cheese sandwiches." His voice was shockingly lively. "I'm sure you could use a friend right now."

Goosebumps broke out on her arms at the memory of his face. It was like a cloud passed over a gray statue, darkening its already eerie hue. "I appreciate the invitation, but Frank left me in charge so I really should be here."

"I understand, Ms. Jackson," the man paused. "It's just, I, too, have been on the receiving end of Shiloh's rage and, where no one was there for me, I want to be there for you."

"Well," Amanda started. "Okay," she agreed when her rumbling stomach chimed in.

When she arrived at Foster's, she was shocked to find the man had taken her suggestion to let light in seriously. With the blinds open, the bookstore didn't look gloomy at all, but instead welcoming and cozy. What a difference a little natural light made.

"Ms. Jackson, is that you?" Mr. Foster called out when the bell tinkled above the door. He emerged from the small kitchen in a plum colored, frilly apron with a large oven mitt on one hand. "Oh good, right on time." He walked past her and locked the front door. Amanda's eyebrow arched at the man's action. "You deserve an hour to yourself. This way no one will disturb us."

He ushered her back to the kitchen and directed her to a seat, this time fitted with a cushion. When he placed a glass of sweet tea in front of her, Amanda really did feel herself begin to relax. A sigh escaped her lips after a sip of the sweet concoction.

"Now that's a sound I like to hear," he said, stirring a pot of the soup.

"Mr. Foster, that smells divine. Can I help with anything?"

"Oh no, dear. You just sit right there and relax. It's the least I can do for you after having to endure that woman's violence."

Amanda considered correcting the man, but instead decided to allow the charade to continue a bit longer. She deserved it after Shiloh essentially ruined her life. It wouldn't hurt for her to pretend for just a little bit that everything was going to be fine.

They made polite conversation while they ate, discussing favorite books and authors. Despite all of her shallowness, Amanda was always well-read and held her own in conversation with a bookstore owner; she even impressed him by challenging his opinion once they reached a level of mutual comfort.

"I've been meaning to ask, Mandy," he said, dropping the formality over bread pudding. "Was there anything of interest in young Katie's diary?"

"There was a secret crush, but I'm sure the police already went down that path," Amanda said while lightly blowing on a piping-hot spoonful. "To answer your question, no, the case is cold. Her killer will continue to go free."

Mr. Foster regarded her news with his spoon suspended midair, and his tight lips pursed in a straight line. Abruptly, he sat his untouched spoon down and left the kitchen. Amanda worried she'd offended him, that her answer was too matter-of-fact and that she should have spoken with more respect and reverence for the dead. Remembering her manners, she sat her spoon down and waited for the man's return. After several long minutes, he finally rejoined her.

"Here," he handed her a photograph. The picture was in black and white, the best choice for something taken at 1:06 a.m. according to the time stamp on the picture. She recognized the subjects immediately; it was a teenage Shiloh and the forever young Katie. Their body language suggested they were in the middle of an argument. Shiloh's fists were balled and her elbows at ninety degrees, as if she was ready for a fight. Katie towered over Shiloh, her body leaned forward and one arm raised, pointing at something outside the camera frame. "I'm sure you're aware that the date below the time stamp coincides with the date that Katie went missing. And, I assure you that the calibrations on my camera were correct."

"Where did you take this?" Amanda was flabbergasted. "Why did you take this?"

"I was really hoping it wouldn't come to this. I truly thought you were special and could solve this."

"Why are you giving me this now? Why didn't you share this with me when you told me about the murder? Do the police know about this?" The questions raced through her mind in non-sequential order.

He handed her another photo from the same sequence. This one was a close up of Katie, her arms crossed in front of her body and her chin tucked.

"As I said earlier, like you, I've been on receiving end of Shiloh's vengeful actions. The girl terrorized me when we were teenagers. She even went so far as to try to turn my only friend, Katie, against me. I feared for Katie's safety, so I took to following them from a safe distance. I swore that if Shiloh's explosive anger was ever directed towards Katie I could intervene," his voice broke. After a pause he cleared his throat and continued. "They argued and Katie ran off into the woods. Shiloh chased after her. I pursued, but I tripped over a root and injured myself. They were lost to me. Katie was lost to me. It wasn't until Katie had been missing for several days that I realized I held the key to her fate. By then, I was too ashamed of my own cowardice to come forward." He sniffled as Amanda looked around the kitchen for a tissue and instead handed the man her napkin.

"What do you want me to do about this?"

"You have the power of the pen. You are a gifted writer, run a story in the paper."

"People are going to wonder why you didn't come forward sooner."

"They won't know it's me. You are going to say an anonymous source delivered the pictures to the office with an account of the evening in question."

Amanda shook her head. Doing that would destroy any hopes of her and David's reconciliation. Then again, at this point, there was no hope for them. Still, she couldn't go forward with Mr. Foster's plan without giving David a chance to investigate first, even just as a professional courtesy. "Let me take these to the police. I'll say what you want about the anonymous source, but I owe that to David."

"No," he shouted and snatched the pictures from her hands. Amanda was unprepared for his sudden movement and jumped back, the chair screeching on the linoleum floor. "I can't let you do that. You need the element of surprise. Without it, they will simply question Shiloh and she will deny that anything happened. She will be released, and I fear that even your boyfriend will be unable to save you."

Ex.

"Do you really believe Shiloh killed Katie? Maybe it was an accident."

"Bashing Katie's skull was no accident."

Amanda took a deep breath. The clock ticked and tocked.

"How does publishing a story protect me?"

"The public outcry will force the police to detain her. You will be safer that way."

She collected the pictures and the typed account he provided her, promising to sleep on it before making her final decision.

Amanda found it hard to finish her afternoon tasks. The pictures and his testimony hidden away in her purse beckoned, but she couldn't stop the feeling that she needed to take her new information to David. Would calling Shiloh a murderer in the paper even be believable? It was no secret that she and Shiloh hated each other, and everyone would chalk this up to Amanda trying to ruin the life of one of their own. After all, she was an outsider.

41

Shiloh made her twentieth trip to the ladies' room on her first day back to work to make sure her bruised and cut cheekbone was still hidden away beneath her makeup. It was unnecessary—she hadn't worked hard enough at the bar yet to break a sweat—but it was precautionary. So far, none of the three usual mid-afternoon patrons said anything to her about the fight. Chances are, the few brain cells they had left had already forgotten about it.

Her cell phone buzzed. It was the reminder she set for herself to turn it to her new favorite show. A baseball game started, so she saw no problem with flipping to the cable news channels for an hour.

"Hey, Shiloh, what gives?" shouted one of the patrons when she switched the channel. "We're watching that."

"Willy, if you want to get off your lazy butt and come work this bar, you can watch the game. Until then, just shut up for an hour, okay."

Unfortunately, Shiloh missed the first part of the show when the beer delivery guy arrived, and she had to unlock the back door for him. With her work duties finally done, she perched herself on a bar stool to get a better view of the overhead TV. Judith wore a red blazer. *Red looks good on her. I want a red blazer like that. Maybe I can be a news anchor, it doesn't seem that hard.*

The man seated closest to Judith was a forty-something British guy, his face and head shaven, wearing a nice sport jacket over a blue button-up shirt with no tie. The combination of his accent and his gravelly voice made her swoon. The man to his right was younger, probably early thirties, and he looked like he would rather have a root canal than be on the show. He wasn't a bad-looking guy himself with dark curly hair and a boyish face. Shiloh thought it was almost comical how uncomfortable he looked.

Judith talked about a video coming up of a woman who just died. Shiloh hated coming into things when they were halfway over and thought about asking Eddie if they could get a DVR for the bar.

When the show was back, Judith played the video. The woman looked awful. Shiloh fought revulsion and pity at the same time. Rex called midway through the video, and she welcomed the distraction.

"Shi, guess what, the Mustang is ready. Can you cut loose from the bar for me to take you for a spin?" he said.

Geesh, not the Mustang again. "I'll call you in thirty minutes, okay?" The video was ending and she really wanted to catch up on the topic. That, and she really didn't want to hear any more about Rex's latest automotive project.

When Judith came back from commercial, Shiloh turned up the volume to drown out the growing din of her customers.

"Thank you again for joining us," Judith said to Shiloh. "Today, we're talking about the heinous crime committed by three individuals at Jefferson Williams Investments. Josh Williams, Keith Cooper and Amanda Martin are all on the run and all wanted for securities fraud." While she spoke, three pictures flashed up on the screen. The first one, labeled Williams, was the smiling picture of a good-looking blond man. The second one, labeled Cooper, was another headshot, but this man was heavier, older and looked almost afraid of the camera. The third picture, labeled Martin, was a pretty blond in her twenties. Her hair was perfectly coifed, her makeup was expertly done and she wore a nice suit. Shiloh wouldn't have given her a second glance if it had not been for her mesmerizing smile. She'd seen a smile like that before.

Judith turned to the man seated next to her. It looked like the other man was no longer at the desk with them. Shiloh wondered if he finally got his wish and was having a root canal.

"Roland, this case isn't dead, right?"

Roland. A very British name, and it seems to fit this hot guy with the sexy voice perfectly. She wrote the name on a cocktail napkin a few times while Judith finished speaking. When she heard Roland's voice again, she looked back up at him. Instead of seeing Roland, she saw his hands. And then, more specifically, what was in his hands. As the camera tightened its focus, she nearly swallowed her piece of nicotine gum.

"Holy," she broke into a hacking cough before she could finish the thought. She grabbed her cell phone and dialed Clint's number. For once, he answered on the first ring.

"Hey Shi," he said. "You're lucky you caught me, I was just about to see another patient."

"Clint," she screamed. "You have to turn it on Judith Nash right now."

"What? Why? I can't stand that woman. All she does is stir up trouble."

"Clint, don't argue, just do it. Mandy, Mandy is on the show." Shiloh could barely get anything else out. She was in complete disbelief. Clint didn't hang up. Together, they silently watched the final moments of the show. Shiloh knew there was something off about the woman, but she never would have guessed she was the type of criminal that Judith claimed she was. But if Judith said so, she knew.

Her name wasn't even really Mandy Jackson. Amanda Martin. She was from Chicago, not Billings, Montana. "She lied about everything," Shiloh said, both to Clint and herself. *And that bitch was sleeping with her boss. David is really lucky I was so worried about him.* Bits of Amanda Martin shone through in Mandy Jackson, the straight hair, the polished makeup and the smile. But Amanda Martin could have been any businesswoman in any metropolitan city. In all honesty, if Roland didn't have the same driver's license that Shiloh had seen, it might have taken her longer to realize the two women were the same. Looking at the two pictures side by side, she couldn't figure out what a guy as good-looking at Josh Williams saw in someone as cookie cutter as Amanda Martin. *Maybe guys like boring.*

Before the show was over, they flashed Roland's full name. Shiloh jotted it down on the cocktail napkin. Roland Burrows, *Financial News.* As the credits rolled, she heard Clint exhale on the other end of the phone for the first time since they started watching.

"Shiloh, how quickly can you make it to my office?" Clint asked.

"I need to wait for Eddie to get back from the bank. I can be there in fifteen minutes."

"Perfect. I've got one more patient to see, and then I'll close up early."

Thirty minutes later, Shiloh sat alone in Clint's waiting room. The receptionist went through her closing duties and a nurse left, having finished her tasks early. After the lone patient paid, Clint told the receptionist she could leave. The receptionist frowned at Shiloh. Rumors were going to fly.

He locked his front door and led Shiloh back to his office. She took a seat in the chair across the desk from him and they sat in silence.

"Wow," he said. "I knew it was something, but not that. I did a bit of research," he motioned to his computer. "Mandy's boyfriend stole a lot of money. And this whole thing about that man shooting up their office and all those people dying," his voice trailed off. "I read about that, but didn't think it was more than a vigilante going off the deep end."

Shiloh shook her head. Mandy sounded dangerous, she *was* dangerous, and Shiloh had the bruise to prove it. Would Mandy hurt David?

"Should we call David? Tell him?" she asked.

Clint shook his head. "He won't believe us." He turned back to his computer and pulled up another screen. There was a picture of Roland Burrows, except in this picture he had stubble on his head and a five o'clock shadow on his face. Shiloh thought that made him look much more handsome. She swooned again.

"I think we need to call this guy," Clint said, tapping his computer monitor. "Now, rather than run Mandy out of town, we need to keep her here and get the proper authorities to arrest her."

"Can't David do that? Maybe he will hold her on suspicion until this guy comes down with the Chicago police?"

"We can't chance David tipping her off. I told you, he's smitten with her. He'll give her a chance to explain, and she could probably convince him it's a mistake. She's obviously smarter than we give her credit."

"Okay, so let's call him."

Clint hit the speaker button on his office phone and dialed the number underneath Roland's profile picture on the website. The other line rang three times before voicemail picked it up.

"Roland Burrows here with the *Financial News*. I'm away from my desk, but if you've got an urgent call, ring me on my mobile," his voice said before giving a number. Shiloh wrote down the number, saying the word "mobile" under her breath. She liked how that sounded, she was going to have to use it sometime. Clint looked at her, asked if she got his number and then disconnected the line rather than leave a voicemail.

"Shall we call his cell?" he asked. Shiloh nodded, thinking if Clint said "mobile" it would only sound silly.

With his phone on speaker again, Clint dialed the new number. This time it rang only twice.

"Roland Burrows here," the voice said. They could hear cars honking in the background, and Shiloh thought it must have been another voicemail message. "Hello, can you hear me?"

Shiloh and Clint looked at each other, their eyes wide.

"Uh, hello," Clint said. "Roland, my name is Dr. Clint Brown."

"Hello, hello? I'm sorry, I can't hear you. Can you ring me back in say twenty minutes? I'm in the middle of Times Square. Thank you. Ciao."

The line went dead. Twenty minutes was going to be a long time. Shiloh looked at the time on her phone. It was nearly five-thirty. If she didn't get back to the bar soon, Eddie would track her down.

"Want a drink?" Clint asked. He produced two shot glasses and a bottle of bourbon from his desk drawer. Shiloh shrugged.

They sipped their drinks in silence, waiting for twenty minutes to tick by. Shiloh's phone buzzed alive. Rex again. Shiloh let out a frustrated sigh and sent the call to voicemail.

"Why do you do that?" Clint asked her.

"Do what?"

"Why are you so awful to him? That poor boy loves you, and all you do is kick him around."

Shiloh shrugged again.

"My unsolicited advice since you didn't ask," Clint continued. "Stop doing that, because outside of your family, he's the only one you have, and one day, he'll wise up and be gone. Then, you'll truly be alone. And I don't think you can handle true loneliness."

Well, I don't think a man willing to cheat on his wife just to run someone out of town should dish out relationship advice. But he was right. She did treat Rex badly sometimes. But Rex didn't seem to mind, or at least he never stood up to Shiloh.

After they finished their drinks and twenty minutes passed, they tried their call again.

"Hello, Roland Burrows," the voice said again. This time, there was no ambient noise behind him.

"Hi Roland, this is Dr. Clint Brown, can you hear me okay, chap?"

Chap? Who did Clint think he was talking to, Sherlock Holmes?

"Oh yes, much better. Was it you that called me earlier?"

"Yes, that was me. Look, I'm the doctor in a small town in Texas—Phoenix, Texas to be exact. My friend Shiloh Garcia and I just watched you on the *Judith Nash Show*, and we believe we know where Mandy, er Amanda as you know her, is hiding. She's here."

The line was quiet, and Clint looked to Shiloh for approval.

"Right. This is the fourth call I've gotten since the show wrapped saying that they've seen Amanda Martin, and somehow she's simultaneously in Rhode Island, Nevada, Florida and now Texas. How do you explain that?"

Clint and Shiloh looked at each other, both sets of eyes wide and mouths open. They didn't expect anyone else to claim Amanda Martin's whereabouts. Clint gave Shiloh a look that she read as doubt.

"Roland," she rolled the 'r' in hopes that he would find it sexy. "This is Shiloh Garcia, and that driver's license you have, I've seen it. I work at a bar here, and she comes in for drinks and I carded her. Billings, Montana, that's where's it says she's from, right?"

Roland took a moment before answering them, as if considering the information. Clint couldn't handle the silence, so he continued arguing their case.

"And, I've seen her as a physician. Look, I think she's suffered a recent traumatic event, like an office shooting, and has PTSD."

"Okay, listen here mate," he said after a few seconds. "I'm going to need some proof before my editor lets me go on some wild goose chase down to Texas. If you can send me something, a copy of the ID she carries, or even just a picture to prove to me you aren't like the other three loonies that called in, then Alex and I will be happy to come down there."

"Fair enough," Clint said. "We'll work on the proof, but in the meantime, here are our numbers. You call if you have any questions."

When the line was dead, Clint refilled their drinks.

"Alright, so proof," Shiloh said. Her phone buzzed again, and she ignored another call from Rex. "How do we get a copy of her license?"

"I could get my receptionist to call her, ask her to come by to make a copy of her license for our records," he paused. "Then again, Mandy is deathly afraid of me and wouldn't come within a hundred yards of my clinic."

"Maybe I could just stalk her again during one of her runs, get a picture of her that way?" Shiloh suggested. Clint nodded.

"Whatever it is, we need to think of it fast before someone tips her off and she's gone."

42

Loneliness encased Amanda like a shroud. Frank had been gone for three days, David broke up with her two days ago, and Myrna avoided her like the plague, probably at Dugan's suggestion. Mr. Foster was the only person who didn't seem to think that she was a leper.

With her work for the day done, Amanda opened the envelope and read Mr. Foster's account of what happened that night. The girls were at a parking lot by the Tejas River, he saw a bottle pass back and forth between them. An argument broke out, solidified by the pictures he took. Katie ran from her friend, Shiloh pursued. Somewhere in the woods, Shiloh caught the girl and bashed her skull in with a rock. To conceal her crime, the teenager buried her friend in a shallow grave. Amanda had to hand it to Shiloh, she was worthy of an Academy Award considering the look of anguish and despair on her face on the front page of the *Talon* so many years ago.

Tears flowed consistently, and she kept a box of tissue next to the computer to keep them wiped away. Once the stream ran dry, she got up to wash her face in the small bathroom. Her pants wiggled on her hips while she walked. She hadn't felt like eating.

When she exited the bathroom, she came face to face with Shiloh. Amanda looked at the door, to see if Shiloh had turned the lock to seal her in. Not only did it appear to be open, but the door stood slightly ajar, caught by a slight wind. Standing in the lobby with the girl that might have killed Katie just a decade earlier, Amanda surprised herself by how calm she felt. It must be the lack of sleep slowing her reflexes. Or, maybe it was because Shiloh herself looked a little apprehensive and scared.

"Shiloh," Amanda greeted quietly and folded her arms across her chest.

Shiloh pursed her lips and returned Amanda's stare. If she was there to gloat over Amanda and David's break-up, she didn't seem to be in a hurry.

"Can I help you with something?" Amanda continued.

"I, uh, well," Shiloh took a deep breath. "I came to apologize for ruining your clothes. You were right, I did it on purpose."

Amanda's arms dropped to her side, the muscles lost their grasp at the unexpected apology. What shocked her even more was Shiloh lost her acerbic, biting tone. She almost seemed genuine.

"Why are you here?" Amanda asked, unsure what prompted Shiloh's apology. Did she want to survey the damage like rubber-neckers at a car crash?

"Are you deaf?" she asked, the old Shiloh returned. "I'm here to apologize. I don't do this often, so don't just stand there and give me crap, okay?"

Amanda nodded. Maybe Shiloh was tipped off that she had evidence implicating her in Katie's murder and wanted to sweet talk Amanda out of it, or bully her, as Mr. Foster claimed she was so apt at doing.

"I'll be honest, I'm shocked." Amanda perched herself on the side of her desk. "I never expected to hear those words from you. I guess if we're handing out apologies, I should apologize for the, um, black eye."

Shiloh nodded and then smiled. "Yeah, that hurt. You've got a mean right hook."

Amanda laughed. Not once in a million years did she think she would sit in the same room with Shiloh, not only apologizing to each other, but actually sharing a laugh. Shiloh paused and pulled her cell phone out of her back pocket.

"Oops, excuse me, text message," she said, holding her phone up vertically as she read her text. Amanda thought that was a strange position to view her phone, one that her mom would have taken while trying to read something without her bifocals. "Sorry, the screen is going out, so I need to hold it up to the light to see what it says. Okay, all done." Shiloh snapped the phone closed and stuck it back into her pocket.

They stared at each other. Even with the apologies out in the open, the air was still tense. Amanda watched a small smirk flash on Shiloh's face. Maybe that was just her smile. Amanda tried to recall if she had ever seen Shiloh actually smile. Yes she had—in a picture with Katie that was locked up in police evidence. Then again, that was before Shiloh killed her best friend. Something violent snapped inside of Shiloh that night at the river. The innocent Shiloh, the teenager who still had a best friend, was gone and replaced by this more sinister woman. Suddenly, Amanda felt uncomfortable being alone with Shiloh.

"Well, I better get to work," Amanda said.

"Eddie texted me. He needs me to come in early," Shiloh said simultaneously. "So, come by Riley's one night this week, I owe you a drink or two for the ruined shirt."

Amanda nodded, relief flowing over her when Shiloh left. She watched the woman from the dirty office window. Shiloh paused at the street corner, her head hunched over her cell phone. Then she looked up, crossed the street and never looked back. The strange encounter did nothing to curb Amanda's mission to expose Shiloh as Katie's murderer.

When it seemed that Shiloh wasn't going to barge back into the office and drag Amanda from her seat at the computer, she felt secure enough to begin work. Mr. Foster didn't designate where in the paper the story needed to run, so instead of the front page, Amanda thought it safest to bury the story and the picture some-where inside. She was a coward for doing that, but she was still apprehensive about the man's insistence that she not alert the police ahead of time.

Nearly a decade ago, 16-year-old Katie Shelton disappeared early one summer morning, thought to have been snatched away during her morning jog. Instead, a month later, her body was discovered in a shallow grave a mile from the busy parking lot along the banks of the Tejas River. She was put there by someone who hated her enough to beat her skull in with a rock.

The police investigated and followed up on leads, but after a while, the trail grew cold. People went back to their lives—went back to their Sunday dinners, their evening walks and their trips to the grocery store. And, among the people who carried on their lives was Katie's killer.

Police determined the killer was a transient, that Katie's awful murder was an isolated incident and the people of Phoenix were safe. And for ten years, they were safe, but not because this person moved on; but because the killer wanted only Katie gone.

Recently, anonymous information sent to the editorial staff of the Talon *suggested the killer was someone close to Katie, someone she trusted. This information points to 26-year-old Shiloh Garcia.*

Garcia, like Katie, was only sixteen when Katie died and admitted to police that she was the last person to see her alive. But, she didn't tell police the truth of where she last saw Katie alive. According to Garcia's statements, Katie spent the night at her house and was gone when she awoke in the morning. Newly uncovered photographic evidence and an eyewitness account now indicate Katie and Garcia were on the banks of the Tejas River, arguing. The argument escalated and Garcia allegedly killed Katie with a large stone before burying her in a shallow grave.

In all fairness to the Phoenix Police, they never suspected a teenage girl would have the strength to commit such a crime. However, according to this witness' account, Garcia was enraged and capable of anything.

You may wonder why this anonymous person came forward now, after ten years of silence. It wasn't easy, but this witness found the strength to speak out and hopes to see justice for Katie Shelton. While it won't bring her back, her spirit will be able to rest knowing that her killer no longer walks the streets. The editorial staff of the Phoenix Talon *urges the Phoenix Police Department to re-open the case and to investigate Shiloh Garcia for Katie Shelton's murder.*

Amanda ran spell check and hit save. She was proud of herself.

It was short and to the point, complete with a picture featuring the time stamp. As soon as the paper went to print, Amanda grabbed her purse and looked around the empty office of her employment for the past two months. She didn't know what to expect, but she knew it would be a while before she saw the office as it was then.

Quiet. Peaceful. Home.

43

When she arrived at work the next morning, it was like any other day. Once again, she pulled into the covered parking spot at the back of the building. Even though the Bronco was old enough to buy alcohol, she worried a blossoming severe thunderstorm might harm it. The sky was an ugly shade of gray-green, and the air was so thick it was almost visible.

Okay, that's weird. I expected Shiloh to be waiting for me. Maybe she's already in jail. If not, I wonder if David would provide any protection for me. Amanda grimaced. *Probably not.*

She turned the key in the lock slowly, halfway expecting it to be rigged to explode. Click. Nothing. Just the key in the lock. At least the answering machine didn't disappoint. The red light flashed; a rare occurrence in the small office.

"Are you satisfied with your long distance service," the voice started soon after Amanda press the button.

"Damn telemarketers," she said.

"Yeah, I, uh, saw your story and wanted to say that I agree with you. That girl probably did kill that other girl. Also, I saw something flying up above the trees the other night, I was wondering if you would write something to get the police to open an investigation into that," a male voice next in line said.

"Damn UFO sightings."

"Where do you get off saying that stuff about Shiloh? I'm canceling my subscription," a female voice said.

"Now we're talking," Amanda said, erasing that message before the woman was done.

"Frank, this is Ben Riley. I'm appalled at what you wrote about Shiloh. She and Eddie are like family to me, and there is no way she could do what you said. Shiloh has mourned Katie for years, just like the rest of us. Because of your little stunt, I'm pulling my advertising. I don't need it for my business, but you sure as hell need it for yours."

Uh oh. Amanda didn't think about the advertising repercussions. She hoped this was the only one, but the machine showed another four messages. Rather than listen to what waited for her, she pulled the tape out of the machine and flushed it down the toilet.

The phone rang while she worked, but Amanda refused to answer it. She tried to focus but her mind wandered, asking her if she did the right thing. People walked by the newspaper office and some even stopped and peered in through the dingy windows. At one point, Dugan stared in at her, but when she raised a hand to wave, he had already turned to walk away.

With the office tasks completed, she retreated into the safety and privacy of the workroom and away from the fishbowl of the front office. But, she couldn't concentrate there either. The ringing phone wouldn't stop. When it paused between ringing episodes, she took it off the hook, only to be assaulted by the phone's angry buzz. Amanda found some bubble wrap in a drawer and mindlessly popped the air pockets. On her fifth pop, the front door burst open. David marched back to the workroom, crossing the entire office in seconds. His uniform was covered in sweat, like he ran there from the other side of town. Amanda stopped, mid-pop, surprised to see him so anxious. She was about to ask if he had arrested Shiloh yet, but David spoke before he even made it to her.

"Who is your source?" he asked, breathlessly.

"Who's my what?"

David walked around the large table towards Amanda. He was so close that she could smell the sweat on him. It reminded her of their evening runs together. She closed her eyes and breathed in. She missed him.

"Mandy, I'm not playing around. Who left that information? Who left the pictures? Think, baby, think. It had to be someone you know."

Amanda stared at him, her eyes wide with fear and suspicion.

"You don't believe me. You think I made it up," she whispered. She tried to stand to get away from him, but he moved closer, capturing her between the computer and himself. Her mind flashed back to the day that Dr. Brown laid claim to her secret. Her lungs tightened, and she felt as if she were being squeezed into a box.

"No, actually, I believe you. That's why I need to know who told you all that," David sounded softer this time, and his body shifted from a menacing stance to a protective posture. She thought about kissing him. Would he push her away if she did, or would he kiss her back? "Mandy, please tell me."

Amanda shifted again, this time he relented. She moved around the room, putting the long table between them.

"I see what you're doing. You didn't break up with me because you think I'm hiding something, you broke up with me because you finally realized that you have feelings for Shiloh. You're trying to protect her."

"That's ridiculous. I've never felt anything for her. Not like what I feel for you. This isn't about you and me, or even Shiloh and me. This is about that information in that article. Where did you get it?" This time his voice was louder, the softness was gone but his face was pleading. Where his voice was angry, his face was worried.

"Why are you here wasting your time with me? Why aren't you arresting Shiloh? Have you even looked for her yet?"

David took several deep breaths and ran his hand through his hair.

"I just came from Shiloh's house, she's not there."

"See, she ran, she's guilty. That proves it," Amanda screamed at him. "Instead of looking for her, you're wasting your time with me. She's going to get away with Katie's murder again."

"Mandy, listen to me, baby. Okay? Calm down and just listen," he walked around the table. Amanda backed away from him with each step he took towards her. Mr. Foster was right; David would try to hide the fact that he couldn't solve the case himself. He put his life on the line by confiding in her. Amanda deserved to die, but not Mr. Foster. "Listen to me. I don't believe it was Shiloh that killed Katie, but listen," he cut her off when she opened her mouth to argue. "I do believe that you know who killed Katie, I just don't think you realize it."

Amanda jumped when thunder rumbled in the distance. More people stopped to look in the windows of the office. She wondered if all those people could hear their argument.

"What are you talking about? Of course I realize who killed Katie. Shiloh."

A crack of thunder scattered the people looking in the window, distracting Amanda briefly from their argument.

"Someone played you, someone who knows your history with Shiloh."

David didn't make sense. He talked in circles, like he knew the answer but tried to get her to say it.

They faced each other, the long work table between them. Neither took their eyes off the other.

Amanda shook her head. "I don't know. I came to work one day and found an envelope at the door."

David's jaw set, and his face reddened. She had never seen him this angry before. His chest puffed out from another deep breath.

"You're lying. You do know, and you're not telling me," his tone was pleading, past anger and now on the verge of begging.

She folded her arms in defiance. "You should know from your pre-law classes that the First Amendment protects me, and confidential informants are considered solid. Look at Deep Throat. I can give you the photos and the typed statement this person gave me, but that's all."

David turned slightly and wrung the back of his neck with his hand.

"Are you punishing me? Is that what this is about?" his voice rose over the imposing thunder.

"This is about me protecting my source and my First Amendment rights. As a journalist, I have an ethical obligation to protect my source when they request anonymity."

"Then, you are aware it is within my jurisdiction to detain you for your own protection. Don't think I won't be back here with a warrant if you don't tell me right now who your source was." He yelled again. For the first time, fear crept up Amanda's stomach. Something he said reverberated within her head. Her own protection. Why would she need to be protected if Shiloh was arrested? Why did he seem so worried about her? Was this to take her back?

"In case you forgot, I can handle Shiloh," Amanda snorted.

David moved around the table slowly. Amanda flinched, as if to move away from him, but he held his hands up. He touched her arm tenderly, as if checking to make sure she wouldn't recoil. When she didn't, he wrapped his arms around her and kissed the top of her head.

"Baby, whoever gave you that stuff, whoever said that Shiloh killed Katie lied to you."

"What? How do you know?" Amanda broke out of David's embrace and took a step back. More fear bubbled up from her stomach.

David sighed, "Something you wrote struck me, and I looked it up in the case file. We released strangulation as cause of death so that if we ever caught a break, if ever someone decided to come forward, we would know if they told the truth or if they were just a nut job trying to take credit for someone else's crime. Look it up yourself. You have a copy in the file I gave you."

He stared at her, waiting for her to catch on, but her mind was numb. Lack of sleep and an overabundance of emotion caught up with her.

"Don't you see? Whoever told you her skull was crushed by a

rock knew too much about the case. That's why I need to know who told you."

Amanda stopped breathing. *Did I make that up for rhetoric? Maybe I got caught up in moment of writing it.* She took a step back and knocked over a trashcan.

"You're trying to scare me," she whispered, shaking her head and blinking back tears. "You said you'll get a warrant, go for it. I still won't tell you, even if that means I spend the rest of my life in jail."

Amanda ran out of the workroom and into Frank's vacant office and slammed the door shut. She held her breath. The trashcan she knocked over crashed across the room, and the front door slammed shut. The old aluminum blinds crinkled up on one end; just enough for her to see David get in his patrol car and head back towards the station.

Her hands shook so badly that she could barely work the lock on her desk drawer. She flipped through the pages and found the medical examiner's report. As David said, it listed strangulation as cause of death. The pages in the file scattered across the floor as she pulled the typewritten page from Mr. Foster from a stack on the corner. Amanda locked the front door, grabbed her purse and an ancient tape recorder and ran out the back to her waiting Bronco parked outside. Her hatred of Shiloh had stood in the way of reason. A ninety-pound teenager couldn't have done the things Amanda accused her of, but a man could. Even if he was only a teenager himself.

She struggled to find the windshield wiper switch as the first fat raindrops fell. Lightning spears etched in her mind every time she blinked. She had barely put the Bronco in park before she ran up the sidewalk to the front of the bookstore, sprinting over the tricky top step.

The cat meowed his usual greeting as Amanda flew past him. "Where is he," she growled at the cat.

The acrid smell of smoke drew her to the kitchen. Mr. Foster stood at his stove, burning a photograph over an open flame on the old gas burner. Stacks and stacks of photographs of Katie covered the kitchen table. Katie in her cheerleading uniform. Katie in street clothes. Katie running. Katie driving. Even a few of Katie perusing the shelves of the very bookstore she stood in. He made no acknowledgment of her when she walked in; instead he hummed a lullaby.

"What did you do?"

He continued to burn the pictures. One caught fire on the corner, and he dropped it into the sink. Amanda peered over his small shoulder and saw that the bottom of the sink was littered with black, flaky burnt photographs. Mr. Foster picked up another picture, studied it for a minute and then held the corner to the flame. The combined smell of the gas and scorched paper burned her nose and made her wretch. If she had been able to eat breakfast, she would have been sick.

"Mr. Foster, listen to me," she shouted over the cacophony of thunder. "Mr. Foster," she grabbed him by his shoulders, hoping to shake him into the present. Instead, he pushed back with more force than she expected, causing Amanda to stumble into the table and collapse the towers of photos. A lavender string stuck out of the debris of pictures. Amanda pulled on it, and her nightie surfaced and with it pictures of her. She and David running. Her at work at the *Talon* seen through the dingy window. A third picture was her and David kissing. She remembered that kiss. It was their first, shared while standing on the street.

"You were in my apartment that day." She balled up the nightgown and threw it at his back. "Why were you in my apartment? And why did you take pictures of me?"

"I was looking for the lies she wrote," his voice cut through the silence. "I wouldn't have guessed you to be so careless as to keep Katie's diary at the *Talon* office, then again, if self-preservation were your strong suit you wouldn't be standing here now, would you?"

He turned back to his stack of pictures, studying each picture before burning it. Seeing her stolen nightgown and the illicit pictures was tantamount to when Dr. Brown assaulted her. Without ever touching her, Mr. Foster was no different than the predatory doctor.

"Anyway," he continued. "If there were anything particularly libelous against me in her journal, then I doubt even you would have allowed yourself to be locked in here alone with me for an hour."

He picked up another picture, this one a close-up of Katie smiling. He stroked the side of the picture, the side of her face softly, before holding it over the flame. Amanda coughed as fumes choked her lungs. The house lit up in a flash of lightning with thunder booming simultaneously. The lights flickered off, and the house was quiet, except for the hiss of the gas stove burner and the crackle of burning photographs.

Fear crept up her spine in the darkness of the house. The wind howled outside. Gray shadows danced with the thrashing tree branches. Something moved along a wall. Amanda shivered uncontrollably. She swallowed at the acid rising in her throat, silently counting down from ten.

"Did Katie fall and hit her head? Was it an accident?"

"What happened to her was no accident." His voice was high-pitched, more childlike than the usual monotone. She hoped the tape recorder tucked in her purse captured his voice.

"You buried her. You put rose petals on her." Another picture emerged from the stack: her and Dr. Brown during his first visit to the *Talon* office. Amanda's back was to the window. She was spared the sight of fear in her eyes. "You must have loved her."

"I beat her skull in. Does that sound like love to you?"

Amanda flinched. Every cell in her body tugged at her to leave, but she needed a clear confession first. She owed it to Shiloh. He continued to hum and study the pictures in the darkness of the kitchen and set them aflame. When each picture sparked up, it sent an eerie glow over his calm and smooth face.

"Why point the blame at Shiloh? She did nothing wrong. Why do you hate her so much?"

"She tore Katie away from me. For what?" He reached out and stroked the side of Amanda's cheek in the same way he had stroked the pictures of Katie. Goose pimples flushed under the touch of his cold hand, so different from David's warm touch. Amanda closed her eyes to prevent herself from shuddering, only to have a stinging slap jolt them open.

"To let him have her. And, you are just like Katie, letting that doctor touch you like she did."

Amanda's hand covered her cheek, protecting it from another assault. He averted his eyes, not looking at her again. A lit picture fluttered from his hand, missed the sink and landed on an errant book.

"Be careful, you're going to burn the house down," Amanda said between coughs. The smell of gas was so strong that she wondered if he had the gas on in the oven as well. Amanda took a deep, toxic breath. "Why me?"

This time, when he lit a picture, he held on to it a little too long and the flame burned close to his fingers. Amanda watched as the skin reddened, but he gave no clue that he felt any pain. Lightning continued to flicker, momentarily illuminating the kitchen, only to wipe away the light and leave them in darkness. She looked out the small window above the sink; it would be impossible to wriggle out that window to escape.

"Because nobody would miss you when you're gone," Mr. Foster's response was so matter-of-fact. He turned his head and punctuated it with a cold stare. Amanda locked her knees, forbidding them to give up on her. "You're an outsider."

"They already know it was you," she whispered, taking a slow step towards the door.

He moved his body closer to the door and blocked her escape.

"No they don't," he cooed. "If that was the truth, your boyfriend would be here by now. As I said, you won't be missed."

The noxious fumes in the kitchen blocked the sob in her throat and tears already ran out of her burning eyes. She didn't want to die, not today. Not with David mad at her. She wanted to apologize to Shiloh; she couldn't die before doing that. And all the people she hurt at JWI, she had to make things right for them. And Josh, she couldn't die before finding him, before making him pay for everything he stole, including her life. But the list of those she wronged was too long for her to handle. Maybe it was better for her to die.

Maybe all she'd been doing was delaying the unavoidable. The only way to set things right was for her to die. The sob broke free and with it a prayer bubbled to the surface.

"Shut up. Shut up. Shut up," he screamed at her and slammed his open palm on the red-hot burner. As he recoiled in pain, a stack of pictures fell over the burner, quickly igniting. "Crying and praying didn't save Katie, and it won't save you."

The smell of burnt skin filled Amanda's nostrils. She sprinted for the door, but Mr. Foster moved quickly to block her, his right hand curled up towards his shoulder. Smoke filled the kitchen. With his good hand, he grabbed Amanda's arm and pulled her back into the middle of the kitchen.

He tried to grip the oven door with his burned hand, but a faint grunt of pain broke in his throat. His hold on Amanda's arm loosened, and he yanked the oven open with his good hand. The smell of gas accosted her. With his burned hand, he reached for a lighter from the kitchen table but fumbled it.

Amanda grabbed it and threw it into a corner next to the refrigerator. He seemed to have forgotten he was restraining her and reached for the lighter. Amanda quickly pushed him aside, knocking him to the floor while she grabbed her purse and ran.

The cat waited by the front door. Amanda scooped him up and turned the doorknob in a single move. Just before she made it to her beloved Bronco, an explosion knocked the ground out from under her and the cat loose from her grip.

44

T he day moved much too slowly for Shiloh. She and Clint were on the road before dawn to meet Roland and Alex's plane at the airport. At the end of their drive, they had to wait another hour for the weather-delayed flight to land. Shiloh recognized Roland as soon as he walked into baggage claim. He had even more stubble on his face and head than the picture on the website and wore black jeans, a black leather jacket and black boots.

"Roland?" Clint stepped forward and offered his hand. "I'm Dr. Clint Brown, we spoke on the phone. This is Shiloh Garcia." Shiloh beamed at him as she shook his hand.

"Pleasure's all mine. This is Alex Kostas," Roland said, introducing the tall man next to him. He too sported growth on his face. "Very clever there, Shiloh. That was a perfect picture of Amanda you texted me. Brown hair though? I have to say Amanda looked a bit drab."

Shiloh smiled at his compliment, and at the critique of Mandy. The two men had carried on their luggage, so they were in Clint's black Suburban for the drive back to Phoenix shortly after their arrival.

"So, tell me exactly what Mandy did," Clint said, looking up in his rearview mirror.

Alex explained how he discovered what was going on, the amount of research he did to ensure that he was right and how they got away.

"Was Mandy really as bad as that woman made her sound, you know calling her a modern-day Bonnie?" Clint asked.

"Nah, man," Alex answered. "Her charges are much lighter than the other two guys, but she misrepresented financial information to the press which impacted trading. Honestly, I don't think she knew what she was doing. We really just wanted to get her to testify against her boyfriend. She would have likely gotten a fine and probation."

Shiloh was disappointed. It sounded like Mandy was just going to get a slap on the wrist. "But she ran, doesn't that mean she has to go to jail?"

Alex shrugged as he looked at the window. "That's up to the lawyers."

The surrounding storms slowed their journey, making Shiloh even more anxious for action. She was outnumbered, as the three men agreed earlier they had the element of surprise on their side, and if they alerted David, there was a good chance that Mandy could find out. Shiloh would have to wait until they confronted Mandy first.

With the conversation about the case exhausted, they continued in silence for several miles before impatience got the best of Shiloh. "Clint, can't you go faster?"

"Settle down, Shiloh," Clint scolded her in a voice he probably used on his toddler daughters. "If we died in a car accident, Mandy would certainly get away with it. You don't want that, do you?" Shiloh sighed her response.

"So, Roland," Shiloh turned in her seat to face the man. "You got a girlfriend?"

He looked out the window and laughed. "Me? No, no girls for me." Shiloh pouted. Why would a good-looking guy like him lead a celibate life?

"So, what happened to your face?" Alex asked.

"What?" In her morning haste, Shiloh forgot to cake make-up over the yellow bruise on her right cheek.

"Oh that's a great story. Shiloh here threw some barbecue on Mandy, and Mandy clocked her. Shiloh never got a punch in, so it was pretty one-sided," Clint answered.

"Really, Amanda did that," Roland chuckled. "I always sensed there was some feistiness in her." Shiloh made a face. Did Roland also have some sort of feelings for Mandy? What was up with all these men finding her attractive?

"Amanda lives here?" Roland asked when they rolled into Phoenix. "Amazing, the girl I knew would have gone batty in a town this small. Wonder where she got her Prada fix?"

Shiloh tried to see her hometown as these two strangers saw it. Small, quaint and boring. They came from Chicago, an exciting city bustling with life. Phoenix was on the brink of death in comparison. Minutes later, Clint pulled his Suburban into a parking spot next to a patrol car in front of the *Talon* office. David banged on the door and shouted at Mandy to open it.

Shiloh bounded out the passenger door before Clint put the car in park.

"Is your girlfriend here?" she sang out. "We've got a surprise for her. You'll want to stick around for this too."

David looked awful. His face was white, his eyes were red and his shoulders hunched.

"Shiloh? Why aren't you screaming at me?"

She knitted her eyebrows and cocked her head to the side. Why would she yell at him? It was David; she would never raise her voice at him. Her confused look was met by one of equal bewilderment from David.

"You don't know, do you?" David asked. Shiloh shook her head. "There's a story in today's paper. Mandy was given information stating that you killed Katie."

She pulled her phone out of her never-carried purse, only to realize it was still on silent from when she snuck a picture of Mandy, so she'd missed half a day's worth of text messages and phone calls.

To protect the surprise, she didn't tell anyone where she was going that day or who with who, so no one thought to reach her through Clint. Shiloh's lower lip trembled. How could anyone say something so terrible? How could anyone think she did something like that?

"Don't worry, we know you didn't do it, we just need to figure out who did. Whoever killed Katie told Mandy it was you. Shiloh, do you have any idea who could have been out at the Tejas with you and Katie that night?" His voice quivered as he spoke.

Of course she had an idea. Shiloh's wide eyes focused on Clint as he exited his Suburban. *Did he set me up? Did he really do it and tell Mandy it was me? What if he and Mandy were sleeping together?* Clint wore a smug, self-satisfied smile, but Shiloh didn't read it as the smile of someone who set up a friend to take the fall for murder; instead it was the look of victory.

A call came over the radio clipped on David's uniform. "Boys, there's an explosion reported at Foster's Bookstore. I repeat an explosion at Foster's Bookstore."

At that point, the two men joined them on the sidewalk. Lightning flashed overhead, and the men cowered. Shiloh made quick introductions. "These two men are looking for Mandy or Amanda Martin as they know her."

David didn't seem surprised. "What did she do?" Alex explained for the second time that day. "Do you have a warrant?" Alex and Roland looked at each other.

"No, mate, we're hoping we can convince her to come back to Chicago with us."

"I can't let you take her without a warrant. You got that," he said slowly.

"You can't or you won't?" Shiloh challenged him.

Before David could say anything else, a second call came over as the whine of the fire truck started nearby. The chief wanted all hands on deck; the fire was spreading quickly because of the amount of paper.

David started to get back into his car, but Shiloh stopped him. "David, where is she?"

"I don't know. I got here, and the place was all locked up. I have to deal with this fire." He got into the car and sped off with his lights flashing.

"I don't care what he says. I want you two to drag that woman back to Chicago if you have to. She doesn't belong in Phoenix."

She beat on the door and screamed curses at Mandy. But the office was dark inside with paper scattered across the floor.

"I don't think she's there, doll," Roland said over her shoulder. "Could she have called it a day?"

They all piled back into Clint's Suburban and headed for Myrna's house.

"That's Amanda's home?" Roland asked, pointing at Myrna's large Victorian house. "That's more like the girl I knew."

"No, she lives back here," Clint said, pulling the Suburban into the driveway behind a late model Buick. Myrna unloaded groceries from her trunk and turned to eye the Suburban.

"Myrna, is Mandy here?" Shiloh once again jumped out of the car before Clint put it into park.

"Child, I don't know, I just got here. You okay? I read what she wrote, but I don't believe a word. I've known you since you were a baby."

Shiloh smiled at the woman and ran past her to climb the wooden staircase. She slipped on the slick steps and held tight to the banister to keep from falling. The door of the apartment was unlocked, and she ran right in.

The little apartment stood vacant. The closet on the opposite wall sat open, some hangers hung empty, and others dangled their load. A few books sat on the nightstand. An unmade bed was the only sign that anyone had been there.

"Wow, my apartment is actually bigger than this one," Alex followed behind her.

Roland and Clint joined them in the small apartment. Clint walked over to the closet, opened the door further. "She cleared out," he announced. "You hear that? Someone's coming."

David walked in the front door. He looked as confused as Shiloh felt.

"Why are you here?" she asked.

"Where is she?" He ignored her question.

"You tell me. You coming here to warn her?" Clint asked. He gathered himself up, trying to match David's height. "It would be inconvenient if your girlfriend got hauled off to Chicago, don't you think?"

"What are you saying?" David stormed across the apartment.

Shiloh looked around while the guys ruffled each other's feathers. Clint and David were never friends, an unspoken rivalry always stood between them. For the first time since she ran into the apartment, Shiloh noticed a nearly forgotten pink diary that she had not seen in almost ten years. Her hand caressed it as images of her and Katie lying by the river swam in her memory, each writing their secrets but then reading them aloud, giggling.

A letter sat folded under a handheld tape recorder. Shiloh unfolded it.

Dear David,

I'm so sorry about everything. I'm sorry that you think I don't love you enough to trust you with my secret. I didn't want it to become your burden. That's how much I love you. It wasn't a lie. When I was with you, I could be myself, the real me, the girl I forgot existed.

I'm sorry I couldn't tell you earlier who my source was. Play the tape. If Mr. Foster survives, please don't put him in prison; put him in a hospital where he can get help. Tell Shiloh I'm sorry I accused her. I was misled. Again.

You're right, I was running from something, but I'm ready to stand up to it now and face what I've done. I've paid the price for someone else's crime for too long. I have to find him before I can move forward in my life. I hope you'll understand.

I love you,

Mandy

Shiloh's finger shook as it pressed down on the play button. She knew what was on the tape before the muffled sound of Mandy's voice filled the apartment, silencing the men. He was here all along. All those years, all those candles and the man who killed her best friend lived just blocks away.

Shiloh gripped the edge of the small dining table, hoping it would anchor her in the spinning room. David, Alex and Roland joined her, staring down at the recorder as Horace's eerie words floated up. She lost her grip on the table at the sound of her name and Mandy's letter to David floated to the floor. Roland steadied her and retrieved the paper in a single gesture.

"David, this has your name on it, mate." Roland offered the letter to David who reached for the paper when the distinctive pop of a slap filled the air.

"You are just like Katie, letting that doctor touch you like she did." Horace's voice followed the slap.

David flew across the room at Clint.

"What did you do to her?" He said through clenched teeth. The entire apartment shook when he threw the doctor's back against the wall. He had Clint by the shirt with Mandy's letter balled up in one fist. "So help me God if you touched a hair on her head I will resign from the force just so I can kick your ass."

For once, Clint was speechless.

Afraid of hearing more about Katie's last night, Shiloh switched off the recorder. Her heart thumped when she realized another woman was close to losing her life at Horace's hand. Katie's death was her fault. If she hadn't called Horace out as a stalker, if she hadn't thrown a drunken fit at the river, essentially running Katie into his arms, she would still be here. And Mandy. Did Shiloh run Mandy straight into Horace's waiting arms?

Bile churned in her stomach and shot up her throat. She ran into Mandy's bathroom to get sick, but before she reached the toilet, she saw red streaks on the side of the sink and stumbled back into the room, her hand covering her mouth.

"What is it?" Alex asked.

"Blood," Shiloh fought the gag reflex. "There's blood in the sink."

David relaxed his grip on Clint and both men fought to fit in the bathroom. David won out. He leaned down close to the sink and wiped a droplet from the white porcelain with his finger.

"She's right, it's blood. Mandy's hurt," he said, his voice flat with worry. Clint muscled his way in after David to examine the sink.

"It doesn't look like much. She's probably alright."

His jaw rigid and the letter from Mandy still in his hand, David made his way towards the door. Shiloh lowered her gaze as he passed her. He hadn't read Mandy's goodbye note, but she knew that in private he would read it repeatedly.

Shiloh swallowed her vomit and followed him out the front door. "David, wait. Where are you going?" She ran down the stairs after him, losing her footing on the final slick step and landing on her back.

"To find her," he said over his shoulder.

"*Dah-veed*," she said softly, switching to Spanish.

He slowed, but he wouldn't turn around to face her.

Shiloh wasn't sure if he would believe what she was about to say, or if she was even right in her guess. But if she didn't say it; she would face a lifetime of guilt for breaking David's heart. If she would have just left everything alone, if she would have ignored Clint's invitation to stir up trouble, if she hadn't bullied Mandy, David wouldn't be hurting right now. She knew David would understand her and hoped that saying it in her mother tongue would convince him to believe her. *Please God, I hope Mandy told me the truth about where she was headed.*

"*Ella va a El Paso.*"

45

When the storms passed, she pulled over to remove the convertible top. As she drove west, the late afternoon sun looked softer, almost forgiving. Her gas guzzler needed fuel, and she wanted a map and coffee. Rather than flirt with empty for too long, she decided to stop at the first gas station in sight.

Truckers passed her by, giving her long stares. The warm air dried any beads of sweat that dared roll down her temple. Her long hair flipped around the bottom of a Texas Longhorns baseball cap.

Just before the sun dipped below the bruise-colored horizon, she saw the welcoming sign of a gas station. She pulled in and filled up the Bronco. With her chariot satiated, she went inside for some food of her own.

"Evening," the man behind the counter sang out to her over the sound of Tejano music.

"Hello," she answered back. She kept her chin tucked, hoping that the large scrape from landing face first wouldn't be noticeable.

The man went back to his magazine, and she perused the snack food aisle.

She opened her arms onto the counter for the man to ring her up. "I've got gas for the Bronco," she said. "Do you have any road maps?"

"Sure, where you headed?"

"El Paso."

He nodded and pulled a couple from a rack behind him. She followed his movement.

"Hey, are those prepaid cell phones?" she asked. "How do they work?" she added when he nodded.

After his explanation, she added one to her purchase.

Back in the Bronco, she waited to wake the sleeping beast. With her new cell phone out of the package, she plugged it into the cigarette lighter and pulled her reporter's notebook out of her purse. Her hands trembled while she dialed.

"Directory assistance. What city and state please."

"Do you have any listings for private investigators in El Paso, Texas?"

"There are multiple listings."

"The first one would be fine. And, just the number, please. No need to connect me."

Amanda jotted down the number as the operator dictated it. She thanked the woman and ended the call. The only way to satisfy the ghost of the gunman was to give him Josh, but she couldn't do it alone. *You stole my life, Josh, but I'm taking it back.*

Looking in the rearview mirror, she started her car. Her finger traced a line, and she tucked the map into the glove box.

The sun was out of the sky, and the strongest stars were starting to break through the dusk.

She thought about dialing another number. Her hand inched towards the cell phone nestled in the seat next to her, but it changed its mind and went back to the steering wheel.

Maybe later she'd call David, to just hear his voice. But for now, she just wanted to drive.

The End

SNEAK PEEK OF PARDON FALLS
CHAPTER 1

PHOENIX BOOK 2

Even though she'd been paddling across this calm part of the Rio Grande to Mexico for the past several weeks, Amanda Martin waited, holding her breath, listening for sounds other than the tinkling of the river.

The nose of the canoe collided with the shore, and she checked the depth of the river with her paddle, convincing herself the murky water wouldn't fill her rain boots.

She pulled the boat into tall, bamboo-like weeds to camouflage it, the blades of leaves grasping her bare shoulders like the fingers of the dead. Despite the triple digit heat, goosebumps erupted on her arms.

Amanda emerged and waded through sandy gravel lining the floor of the small canyon. The permanent shadow of the walls made her feel like she was ensconced in a womb, birthing her from the relative safety of far south Texas to the cartel-ruled northern Mexico. Unlike her actual birth and childhood, she was *not* the dutiful daughter who followed her parents' rules without question.

In this life, she was an orphan.

Forced on her journey alone.

Sunlight and heat welcomed her into Mexico. A man stood next to an old pickup, puffing on a cigarette. They exchanged no words; she pulled a faded, worn map from the back pocket of her shorts, pointed at a lone town sitting south of a field of black *X's* and handed him several crumpled *pesos*.

He nodded and tossed the stub of his cigarette.

She hopped in the back of his truck, the sun-scorched metal scalding the back of her legs as she settled between an old woman with cataract-glazed eyes and a young couple, the girl clutching her pregnant belly and breathing through her mouth. Her eyes darted around the packed truck bed, looking to make contact with anyone who seemed perplexed by an American woman sneaking into an area where most people fled, but the lack of acknowledgment made her feel like a ghost.

"The haystack is getting smaller, Josh," Amanda murmured to the rumpled map in her hands before tilting her face to the sun.

The gentle rocking of the old junker relaxed her as the tires dipped and rose on the rutted out dirt road like a ship meeting the waves at sea. Down, left, up. Right, up, down.

Sleep was a luxury she could no longer afford, but with the heat, the rocking, the exhaustion, her eyelids made the impulse buy.

The pickup lurched to a stop, jolting her awake. The young couple climbed over her. Everyone scooted around, spreading out and claiming more space before the driver shot forward again.

They went further south. Away from the river, the landscape quickly dried out under the harsh sun. Meager farms fought the encroaching desert. A snaggletoothed windmill stood sentry over an abandoned farmhouse. Buzzards circled off in the desert and a few on the ground fought over a lump of clothes. Amanda tried to rip her gaze away from the savage scenery, but they were frozen, watching as scavengers devoured the last of someone's brother, sister, father, child.

Would my family find me in a similar state?

She shuddered.

The truck rumbled by a grove of graves. Crude crosses constructed with sticks and string, the last testaments of someone's demise at the hand of the man who was the unofficial ruler of this part of Mexico.

She'd slipped in and out of this territory many times. Each successful trip home was one step closer to getting caught. It was a risk worth taking to clear her name, and make Josh face the consequences for the crimes he'd framed her for.

A knock on the back glass of the truck jolted her upright.

"*Gringa*, I pick you up. One hour, okay?" The driver leaned out his open window.

She didn't know his name and he didn't know hers. In an area ruled by drug cartels, anonymity sheltered everyone.

"*Muchas gracias.*" Amanda hopped down, her sweaty feet sliding inside her rubber boots. Tennis shoes would've been so much more practical.

With my luck I'd pick up one of those flesh-eating bacteria and waste away before finding Josh's sorry ass.

The town was small. Population seemed to be even smaller.

Three young boys ran past her, a soccer ball bouncing between them and a skinny dog yelping in delight. It was easy to find her first stop. The gray-green bricks of the town's Catholic Church stood out against the rust-brown landscape.

Outside in the town, she was vulnerable, but crossing the threshold of the church she felt the safety of a lost child found by another mother. The panic was still there, but at a lower volume that allowed her to think.

The air inside was markedly cooler, but a warm embrace wrapped around her as soon as she crossed herself. Incense tickled her nose. A soft rustling echoed through the cathedral.

The priest must be preparing for Mass.

She dropped *pesos* in the offering box, the clanging ricocheting off the walls. Kneeling in front of the candles, Amanda cleared her mind of all thoughts except the memory.

Josh had been avoiding her, and this time she'd catch him cheating. His office was empty. The heavy wooden desk sat devoid of its usual stacks of files and papers, except for a lone manila folder.

She flipped it open and her eyes grazed the boarding pass to El

Paso. She squinted, wishing she had a few moments to flip through the rest of the folder before her boyfriend appeared in his doorway, and began his escape from the SEC.

Her memory skipped ahead, to the image of Liz lying dead on the floor. But, her eyes never escaped that visual, as if it were a mental flogging for her part in Josh's crimes, assaulting her.

A year after parking outside a private investigator's office in El Paso, Amanda returned to that night so often, scanning her brain for another detail from her last night in Chicago that would lead her to her ex.

She hadn't expected it to take so long to find him. Hadn't expected to use the last of her stolen money to sneak *into* Mexico. Hadn't expected thorns to pierce her heart every time she thought of David, the man she'd fallen in love with during a two-month stop in the small town of Phoenix, Texas.

Like the Biblical Jonah, she could only run from the whale for so long. David had thrown her overboard so it was time to face her true purpose.

Turning both Josh and herself in.

Amanda brushed the tears from her cheeks before bowing her head, her lips moved along with her silent prayer.

Please God, forgive me of my sins. Grant me strength to continue this mission. Give me wisdom and guidance to find him. Show me patience as I try to right all of my wrongs. I don't deserve your protection, but please watch over me. And, David ...

She gnawed on her lower lip. There was so much more she wanted to say, but words would weaken what was in her heart. She mumbled through her prayer a second time, but the feeling of someone staring at her pierced her shoulder blades and her eyes flew open.

"Amen," she gasped, crossing herself and hurrying down the aisle and out of the church. Amanda headed for her second stop; the town bar.

The few Spanish phrases she'd learned proved useful, but it was difficult to pick up more than a couple of words in each conversation. For all she knew, Josh could've been found weeks ago, if her language skills were stronger.

"*Hola, como esta?*" she called to a man wiping down the bar. "*Habla Ingles?*"

The man glared his answer.

Damn, why can't this just be easy?

She pulled the picture of Josh from her pocket. It was getting soft around the edges and the paper was wavy from near-constant sweat. She cleared her throat, going over the words in her head before embarrassing herself. "*Estoy buscando a este hombre.*" Amanda slid the picture across the bar, but the man turned his back on her and busied himself with something that didn't involve talking to an American woman with bad pronunciation.

She tapped her finger on the bar, loud enough to remind him she was there but also to tick off a minute. "*Señor, por favor, él es mi novio,*" she said, picking her way through the words. She didn't know how to say 'scum-sucking ex-boyfriend' in Spanish, so she just settled on his previous title.

The bartender walked away and didn't return.

Amanda fumbled through the same exchange with a group of men clustered around a mechanic's shop.

These men actually took the time to listen to her and look at the picture, but their shaking heads indicated that she'd likely put another black *X* over this town.

A blast of cool air from a rotating fan greeted her when she entered the *supermercado*. She paused at the open door of a cooler, holding her long hair off her neck, letting the sweat dry in chilling relief. A welcomed shiver rocked her body and she grabbed a bottle of mineral water and stood in line with a few *pesos* in hand.

A pretty young woman smiled shyly at her under long dark lashes when it was her turn to check out.

"*Hola, como esta?*" Amanda asked.

"*Bien,*" the girl answered. "*Y tu?*"

Hot, thirsty, frustrated, exhausted. Lonely.

She unveiled one of her well-practiced-win-them-over smiles normally saved for grouchy investors or cynical media. "*Bien.*" She pulled the picture of Josh out and held it out to her. *"Mi novio. ¿Él está aquí?"*

The young woman froze and sucked in a sharp breath before her gaze began flitting around the small market.

"You know him. *Por favor.*" Her voice fell to a whisper. *"Ayuadame."*

The woman dropped change in Amanda's hands and leaned forward. "You must not ask about him. Not here, not anywhere." Her English was heavily accented.

She grabbed the girl's wrist, refusing to let go of the only lead for Josh. "Is he here? Have you seen him? Where can I find him?"

"He works for *Señor* Vargas. You will not find."

Her heart sped up. Josh was real, alive, close.

Mine.

"No, please you don't understand. I *have* to find him," Amanda's throat burned with desperate sobs. "Where can I find Vargas? Please anything."

The girl's skin went cold in her grasp. "Go. Now." She jerked her wrist back and her eyes darted toward a woman approaching the checkout.

The cashier ended the conversation, but Amanda refused to move.

An older woman nudged her out of the way and carried on her transaction.

More questions stacked up on her tongue, waiting for a weak spot in the wall the girl constructed between them, but a tap on her shoulder made her jump.

"You were not waiting." Her driver stood before her, puffing on a fresh cigarette. "You do not want to be here after dark, *gringa.*"

The back of the truck was empty during her early evening ride back. Amanda stretched her legs; her feet grew cold in the boots even though the heat of the day lingered.

The name Vargas wasn't new to Amanda, and it was the only lead that connected Josh with El Paso. As one of her ex's private clients, she knew nothing about him other than he was a VIP investor. Fear and elation curled around each other and settled in her stomach. The cashier's reaction should steer her away, but *finally*, after weeks of marking *X*'s over Mexican villages, she circled the town she just visited with weary satisfaction.

Here. He's here.

She relished her victory with two stabs and a slash of her pen, adding a smiley face in the circle.

The sun hung low by the time her ride bumped along the dirt road back at the river. Her chauffeur leaned out of the window when she jumped out.

"I'll be back in two days," he called.

"I'll be here. *Muchas gracias*." Amanda couldn't hide her excitement, as much as she tried to lower her voice and slow her words, her body betrayed her. It was high on hope, a drug she hadn't had a hit of in a very long time.

The girl might not have wanted to talk to her today, but she knew the power of pleasant persistence. She hadn't traveled this far and lose everything—including David—to let Josh slip through her fingers again.

He was hers.

It didn't matter who stood between them. They'd either get out of her way or get knocked down.

She jogged back through the dark canyon, shadows so thick that she reached out in front of her to avoid running head first into a rock.

On the other side, the gray twilight of evening settled over the calm river like a cool blanket. Her canoe waited where she'd left it. A quick check to make sure nothing with fangs, pinchers or poison stowed away, and Amanda pushed off the bank to paddle the fifteen strokes directly across the river.

Eager to be back on U.S. soil with enough light to secure the boat in her Bronco, she hopped out a moment too soon and water rushed into her boots. Her shoulders tensed, she could feel tiny bacteria invading her pores. "Crap," she mumbled, inhaling deeply to calm her nerves.

With a hold on the canoe, she tugged it up the shore. At the sound of a click, she held her breath and paused, squinting into the near darkness.

The only sound she heard was the lapping of the river. She took two more steps.

Three other clicks assaulted the air and bright lights battered her eyes.

"U.S. Border Patrol. Put your hands up."

The bow landed on her foot, causing a tidal wave of river water to splash her leg. Amanda shielded her eyes to try to see beyond the blinding light, but the command echoed.

"Both hands up. Now."

"Shit."

ACKNOWLEDGMENTS

Every writer begins as a reader, and I will be forever indebted to my parents, Ronnie and Frances Packard, for never refusing to take me to the library or buy me a book as a child. Much love and appreciation to my husband, Colby Walton, for allowing me to lock myself away for hours at a time to write and for his fierce editing. I am the luckiest girl in the world to have Robyn Short, of GoodMedia Press standing by my side − not only is she an excellent publisher, but a fun person to kill a bottle of wine with. I couldn't have done it without Carol Barreyre and Jayna Wallach; you challenged me and cheered me on, and I am a better writer because of you both. Thank you to the Greater Fort Worth Writers Group, especially those who read *Phoenix* in its early drafts − Jeff Bacot, C.A. Szarek, Susie Sheehey, George Talbot, and Bryan Grubbs − I really like it when you kick my butt. No really, I do. My heartfelt gratitude to my early readers; Karen Spencer, Sarahbeth Holman, Chris Blain and Gail Cooksey, thank you for spending your precious reading time on my work. To Rita Dear, you are a true author's advocate and inspiration. Thank you for leading by example. And, to my dog Katie, you were patient when I wrote hours on end, and you took me for walks when I needed to get out of my head. You were the best writing partner and I miss you every day.

ABOUT THE AUTHOR

Kimberly Packard is an award-winning author of women's fiction. She began visiting her spot on the shelves at libraries and bookstores at a young age, gazing between the Os and the Qs.

When she isn't writing, she can be found running, doing a poor imitation of yoga or curled up with a book. She resides in Texas with her husband Colby, a clever cat named Oliver and a yellow lab named Charlie.

Her debut novel, *Phoenix*, was awarded as Best General Fiction of 2013 by the Texas Association of Authors.

For more information:
www.kimberlypackard.com
kimberly@kimberlypackard.com

ALSO BY KIMBERLY PACKARD

Pardon Falls | Phoenix Book 2

Prospera Pass | Phoenix Book 3

The Crazy Yates | A Christmas Novella

CPSIA information can be obtained
at www.ICGtesting.com
Printed in the USA
FFHW02n0405130818
47667084-51283FF